Rub
Rubio, Gwyn Hyman
The woodsman's daughter /

34028057710676
KT $24.95 ocm57406170

WITHDRAWN

The Woodsman's Daughter

ALSO BY GWYN HYMAN RUBIO

Icy Sparks

The Woodsman's Daughter

GWYN HYMAN RUBIO

VIKING

VIKING
Published by the Penguin Group
Penguin Group (USA) Inc., 375 Hudson Street,
New York, New York 10014, U.S.A.
Penguin Group (Canada), 10 Alcorn Avenue,
Toronto, Ontario, Canada M4V 3B2
(a division of Pearson Penguin Canada Inc.)
Penguin Books Ltd, 80 Strand, London WC2R 0RL, England
Penguin Ireland, 25 St. Stephen's Green, Dublin 2, Ireland
(a division of Penguin Books Ltd)
Penguin Books Australia Ltd, 250 Camberwell Road, Camberwell,
Victoria 3124, Australia
(a division of Pearson Australia Group Pty Ltd)
Penguin Books India Pvt Ltd, 11 Community Centre, Panchsheel Park,
New Delhi – 110 017, India
Penguin Group (NZ), Cnr Airborne and Rosedale Roads, Albany,
Auckland 1310, New Zealand
(a division of Pearson New Zealand Ltd)
Penguin Books (South Africa) (Pty) Ltd, 24 Sturdee Avenue,
Rosebank, Johannesburg 2196, South Africa

Penguin Books Ltd, Registered Offices:
80 Strand, London WC2R 0RL, England

First published in 2005 by Viking Penguin,
a member of Penguin Group (USA) Inc.

10 9 8 7 6 5 4 3 2 1

Copyright © Gwyn Hyman Rubio, 2005
All rights reserved

PUBLISHER'S NOTE
This is a work of fiction. Names, characters, places, and incidents either are the product of the author's imagination or are used fictitiously, and any resemblance to actual persons, living or dead, business establishments, events, or locales is entirely coincidental.

LIBRARY OF CONGRESS CATALOGING IN PUBLICATION DATA
Rubio, Gwyn Hyman.
The woodsman's daughter / Gwyn Hyman Rubio.
p. cm.
ISBN 0-670-03321-9
1. Fathers and daughters—Fiction. I. Title.
PS3568.U295W66 2005
813'.54—dc22 2004065104

Printed in the United States of America
Set in Berkeley Medium
Designed by Daniel Lagin

Without limiting the rights under copyright reserved above, no part of this publication may be reproduced, stored in or introduced into a retrieval system, or transmitted, in any form or by any means (electronic, mechanical, photocopying, recording or otherwise), without the prior written permission of both the copyright owner and the above publisher of this book.

The scanning, uploading, and distribution of this book via the Internet or via any other means without the permission of the publisher is illegal and punishable by law. Please purchase only authorized electronic editions and do not participate in or encourage electronic piracy of copyrightable materials. Your support of the author's rights is appreciated.

In memory of my parents, Gwendolyn Holt Hyman
and Mac Hooks Hyman.

With gratitude to Dr. Christine Cox.

With love to Angel.

As the turpentine tree I stretched out my branches, and my branches are the branches of honour and grace.

—Wisdom of Jesus Son of Sirach, from the Apocrypha (King James Version)

ACKNOWLEDGMENTS

My heartfelt thanks to Ms. Oprah Winfrey, whose love of books helped transform my writing life. Thanks also to her book club staff, a considerate team of consummate professionals.

Again, my thanks to Dr. Michael Roy Lyles, who saved my life.

Jane von Mehren is a terrific editor, and it is my good fortune to have her. My gratitude to the following people at Viking for their hard work: Jennifer Ehmann, associate editor; Maggie Payette and Beth Middleworth, jacket designers; and to freelancer Dave Cole, copy editor.

I am also lucky to have Susan Golomb as my agent because she refuses to let me sabotage myself. My thanks to Robert Bell, who along with Susan, offered wonderful feedback during the writing of *The Woodsman's Daughter.*

My immense gratitude to Peggy Fuller, who dared to dream while I simply slept; to Eric Durbin, the computer whiz who rescued *The Woodsman's Daughter* when my computer crashed; to Brent Michael, who nagged relentless encouragement into my ear; to Dr. Christine Cox, who suggested I use the longleaf pine and turpentining as background for this novel.

Thanks to Fred Chappell, a wonderful writer and loyal friend.

Thanks to the graduates of the New Opportunity School for Women in Berea, Kentucky. Your support buoyed me during those rough times when self-doubt threatened to bring me down.

I want to say thank you to everyone in the United States and Canada who encouraged me with their e-mails, letters, phone calls, and their support at readings. Your kind words about *Icy Sparks* gave me the confidence to finish this second novel.

I am grateful to the talented authors of the following books: Janisse Ray, *Ecology of a Cracker Childhood;* Carroll B. Butler, *Treasures of the Longleaf Pine;* Pete Gerrell, *The Illustrated History of the Naval Stores (Turpentine) Industry;* Sidney Saylor Farr, *More Than Moonshine.*

Finally, I am thankful for Angel. Thank you, *mi compañero,* for being there—for being my first reader, my constant support, my love, and my friend.

CONTENTS

Monroe

CHAPTER 1

"Vampires," Dalia hissed as she perched on the edge of her bed, waving her arms in the hot July air, the buzzing orbiting her head. A mosquito lit on her forearm. She felt the sharp sting and slapped the insect with the flat of her hand. "I got it," Dalia said triumphantly to her sister. "I don't know how it slipped in." With the tip of her tongue, she licked the warm, slick blood off her palm.

"They know better than to sip mine," Nellie Ann said in the next bed over.

From outside the long window came the sound of hooves clomping in the dust. Dalia squeezed the cotton-stuffed tick, releasing the tension that had lodged in her fingers. Pushing the mosquito netting back, she slipped off the edge of the bed, her feet thumping against the floor.

"What are you doing?" Nellie Ann asked as Dalia headed over to the window and peered out.

"Shush," Dalia scolded her. Beneath the canopy of hundred-year-old oaks, the moss trailing from their gnarled limbs like long, gray gloves, their papa was coming back after weeks of being gone. He jerked at the reins and brought his horse, Tarkel, to a halt. Rising up in his saddle, he squared his wide shoulders, pushed his black hat back on his head, and stared straight ahead. He was preparing himself to face them, Dalia knew. Suddenly he teetered to the left. Drunk as always, she thought as he threw out his right arm to regain his balance. Then, digging his boot heels into his stirrups, he jolted himself upright again, his head thrown back in laughter. He flicked the reins against the horse's neck, and once more hooves clopped along the dusty road that led to Miller's Mansion. "It's Papa," Dalia said, her voice anxious and weary. "He's back, two days early."

"That's old news to us blind folk," Nellie Ann said, dramatically rolling her white, unseeing eyes. "I heard him ten minutes ago."

"He's getting off his horse now," Dalia said, watching their father dismount and hitch Tarkel to the horsehead post (the groom would stable him later). "He's coming up the walkway," she added as he strode over the flagstones toward the veranda. At the bottom of the convex steps, he pulled out a flask from his shirt pocket, unscrewed the silver cap, and upended the container. Tarkel whinnied just as he took another long, deep swallow of bourbon, his drink of choice. Wiping his mouth with the back of his hand, he twisted the silver cap back on and shoved the flask into his pocket. Reverently, he placed his hand over the container as though it held some vital organ, Dalia thought. As he trudged up the steps, she lost sight of him beneath the porch roof, but she could still hear his heavy boots, ascending slowly, coming to a standstill when he topped the last riser.

"Did you hear what I said?" Nellie Ann asked with irritation.

"I heard you," Dalia snapped. "You knew he was coming ten minutes ago. So why didn't you say something?"

"You know I don't like to seem superior." Nellie Ann giggled. "Not only did I hear him, but I could smell him on the breeze coming through the window."

"I'll be back in a minute," Dalia said, ignoring her sister, rushing from the bedroom without a backward glance, making a beeline for the staircase. She crept down three steps and sat—staring through the delicate banisters in the direction of the foyer. She could see her mother unexpectedly bending over as if in pain, her thin arms twined around her waist, righting herself back up when the small, spare form of Katie Mae, their cook, appeared. At once the two women began speaking softly, rapidly—Katie Mae's dark hands swooping in front of her as though trying to catch the words that flew between them, their voices growing louder as they spoke.

"Yessam, Miz Violet. I wasn't expectin' him back so soon," Katie Mae was saying.

Her mother flicked a gray strand of hair off her forehead, a habit of hers for as long as Dalia could remember, and adamantly pressed her palm against her chest. "Still, there's plenty of food in the pantry. You must fix him something good to eat," she stated. "He'll be hungry."

"Yessam . . . fix Mr. Monroe some food."

"Some country ham," her mother said mechanically, "with redeye gravy. Three eggs, fried soft the way he likes them. Biscuits and butter."

"Yessam, I'll fix him a good breakfast."

"And don't forget . . ." her mother said, lowering her voice, the words slurring together, so much so that Dalia couldn't make out what she said. But then her mother's voice swelled again, the words distinct and whole. "Yes, a big bowl of those fresh peaches we got yesterday—sliced thin, with lots of cream and sugar."

"Yessam." Katie Mae's voice was polite but not obsequious. She never toadied.

"Well," her mother said. "You've got a meal to prepare . . . you better get started."

Dalia looked on as Katie Mae straightened her shoulders—her spine erect as a cornstalk—and walked away. Her mother kept talking, muttering to herself now. Then, shutting her eyelids, she closed her hand over her groin, repeating, "Whore, whore, whore," in a low, angry voice, over and over, until the front door swung open and sent her fleeing for the staircase, her dark skirt polishing the floorboards.

Shaken by her mother's words, Dalia leapt up, took the steps quickly, and hid behind a gold-cushioned love seat on the landing.

"Violet," her father called out, clunking through the foyer while her mother pattered up the stairs.

The instant Dalia heard the crude sound of her father's voice, her heart stopped. For a second, it stopped. Conflicted, it simply quit beating—like a pendulum no longer swinging inside a grandfather clock. Just as she began to panic, it started to beat once more. One beat for affection. The next for disdain. The rhythmic ticking of emotions to keep itself going.

"Violet," he called again at the bottom of the staircase, but before he could mount the first step, her mother's footfalls abruptly stopped.

"There's some breakfast for you in the kitchen," she said, her tone empty. Her dark eyes opaque as pitch. "And wash up outside before you eat."

"Won't ya join me?" he asked, his voice pleading but eliciting only her mother's icy silence. Next came her father's retreat, his dejected shuffle down the hall toward the back door.

Though her mother had convinced her that he was coarse and common, no one deserved to be treated like a stranger in his own home, Dalia thought as a wave of pity washed through her. When her mother's bedroom door clicked shut, Dalia stole out from behind the love seat and hurried back to her sister.

"What took you so long?" Nellie Ann asked as Dalia crossed the threshold.

"I was spying on them," Dalia confided, walking over to the bed where her sister lay waiting. "Papa's probably in the backyard now, washing up at the pump. You know how upset Mama gets when he dirties the house."

"Mama has every right to make him clean up outside," her sister said. "He's filthy when he comes back from that camp of his. I smelled the turpentine stink on his clothes before he even set foot inside."

"Poor Papa, he can't seem to do anything right," Dalia said, unwilling to take her mama's side this time. "Anyway, we'd better quit talking and get dressed. Papa will be expecting us to welcome him home. Now sit up," she said, rolling up the mosquito netting and offering her hand.

"Don't need your help," Nellie Ann said, grabbing hold of the tick and drawing herself up.

Nellie Ann had confessed to Dalia that she saw more than people thought. She saw the outlines of shapes, blotches of light and dark. A man, she said, was a thin dark line; a woman, a fuzzy ball of gray.

"Lift your arms," Dalia said. Gently, she coaxed the white cotton gown over her sister's head.

Nellie Ann wiggled across the tick to the side of the bed. "You can pull these off now," she said, raising her spindly legs.

Dalia tugged and the bloomers slipped down, exposing her sister's yellow-tinged skin, stretched tighter than usual over her distended stomach. Fearful that Nellie Ann might be feeling worse, Dalia stood there nervously gripping the fabric. Again she pulled at the bloomers, snapping off a button near the waistband, sending it pinging against the plastered pink wall.

"What was that?" her sister asked, her skinny legs dangling, her stomach rising and falling.

At once Dalia regained her composure. "A button popped off. That's all," she said, dropping the bloomers to the floor, forcing herself to breathe evenly, making herself do what was necessary to keep both herself and her sister calm.

"A button popped off?" Nellie Ann questioned.

"Yes," Dalia replied. "Do you know your skin is as soft as a baby's behind?" she said, trailing her fingers down the front of her sister's thigh. "When you were little, Mama and I rubbed baby oil all over your body."

"Are you jealous of my silky skin?"

"Most certainly," Dalia said, moving away from the bed, facing the floor-length mirror. "You're thirteen and still look like a child. No breasts. No hair down there, either."

"I told you I'd never grow up," Nellie Ann gloated, her voice victorious.

"You're lucky." Dalia sighed. "At your age, I was already blossoming. Now that I'm fifteen, I'm . . ." She paused, not knowing how to finish.

"You're a woman," Nellie Ann said. "You've got curves. I know 'cause I can feel them."

"And when a woman gets curves, it's time for her to get married. And you know what that means?"

"What?"

"It means cooking and housekeeping and babies."

"You better start looking for a man, then."

Dalia groaned. "Maybe I can make them flat." She pressed her palms against her breasts. "I could rip up some old bed linen and bind my chest with the strips." When she removed her hands, her bosom popped up again. Through the lightweight cotton nightdress, breasts plump as peaches and hips round as cantaloupe halves shone back at her in the mirror. Disgusted, she made a face. "I could even shave down there," she said, hiding her crotch with her hands.

"Shave?"

"With Papa's razor."

"Don't you want to grow up?"

"No!" Dalia said vehemently. "I want to have fun." She arched her back and thrust her rib cage forward. "I want to be strong and free," she declared. "But with these," she complained, positioning her fingertips below her breasts and pushing them up, "I won't get to do anything."

Nellie Ann eased off the bed. Her bare feet sank into the thick Aubusson carpet. "I'd like Papa to be free of his drinking," she whispered.

"But you know he isn't," Dalia told her, "and never will be." Moving over to the green-tiled washstand, she poured water from the porcelain pitcher into a deep, wide bowl. "We'd better get dressed," she said, grabbing the washrag looped through the pitcher's handle. After she dunked the rag into the tepid water, she wrung it out and washed off her sister's thin arms and legs, next her swollen stomach. Gently, she toweled her skin, dressed her, then brushed her fine, oily hair. The lank strands hugged her scalp and made her plain round face even plainer. In a moment of pity, Dalia said, "Nellie Ann, you look beautiful."

"Really?" her sister said, fingering her pale pink dress.

"Oh yes," Dalia lied, and she knew Nellie Ann knew it.

"Why, Papa, you've made a mess," Dalia scolded, advancing toward him.

He was sitting at a blue-draped table dotted with brown biscuit crumbs, drinking coffee. "So my girls have finally decided to greet me?" he said as Nellie Ann rounded the doorway behind her. "I've been gone for days and days," he said glumly. "At least your mama made me an offering of peaches. Don't I deserve something more than a scolding from you? How about a little kiss?" He shifted in his chair and glanced up at Dalia, who, pursing her lips, took a tentative step toward him but then changed her mind. Picking up his plate, she dutifully started toward the drainboard, awash in sunlight that bled through the white-lace curtains. "Nellie Ann?" he tried, twisting toward her sister.

"What is it, Papa?" she asked, flirtatiously batting her eyelashes.

"Don't I deserve a little kiss?"

"Not until you bathe," she chided him. Scrunching up her nose, she pinched her nostrils.

"Bathe?" their father said, lifting up his elbows and sniffing beneath his armpits. "Why, I bathe twice a day!"

"You call riding Tarkel through a creek or two bathing?" Nellie Ann bantered, rolling her white eyes at him. "You stink of turpentine."

"Turpentine," their father mumbled. He held up his hands and examined his palms. "So that's my problem. I thought it was the bourbon and the tobacco you smelled." He leaned over and tugged at Nellie Ann's fingers.

She snatched them away. "You need some of Mama's perfume. It's upstairs on her dresser."

"No, what I need is a 'welcome home, Papa,' kiss from you."

Nellie Ann opened wide her milky eyes in mock horror. "Get your *sugar* from Dalia," she said, grinning, her top lip rising above a bracelet of small, sharp teeth. "Her sense of smell is not as refined as mine."

"I'll put my nose up against yours any ole time," Dalia shot back, coming to a halt beside the washbasin.

"Are we wagering one of Papa's stinky kisses?" Nellie Ann said, giggling as Dalia turned toward her.

"My *sugar* is sweet, if you'll just give it a chance," their father persevered. "Nellie Ann, why won't ya trust me?" he asked, slipping his big hand into his pants pocket, pulling up a waxy brown wrapper.

"Trust Papa?" Dalia scoffed, once more moving toward the basin. She snapped the plate on the drainboard, clamped her fingers around the water pump's handle, and in rapid succession pushed it down, then jerked it back up. "I'd rather kiss a mule."

"A sweet kiss," Monroe insisted, rocking forward in his chair. "Please, Nellie Ann. Give me some *sugar,*" he said. With closed eyelids and puckered lips, Nellie Ann listed toward him. "My kisses are so sweet," he said. From the wrapper he brought forth a small square of fudge, and before she could change her mind popped the candy between her lips.

With the fudge wedged like a cigar in her wide mouth, Nellie Ann looked foolish. Suddenly her face crinkled into a smile, making Dalia realize that despite her hard talk, her sister's heart was still pliable to him. "Oh, Papa," she said, as she slurped up the brown-colored saliva dribbling from the corners of her lips.

"A candy from my store," their father stated. "Sweets for my sweet."

With a boisterous smack, Nellie Ann swallowed what was left of the fudge. "Papa kissed me with candy," she called out to Dalia, but Dalia stubbornly pressed her lips together and refused to speak. "Sister, did you hear me?"

Dalia seized a dish towel folded neatly on the counter and with brusque circular movements dried the plate off. "I heard you," she said, thumping the plate down.

"Dalia, don't you want a kiss, too?" their father asked, but Dalia, skulking, kept her back to them. "How about a sweet kiss from your old papa?"

With slow deliberation, Dalia pressed down on the pump handle. "Nellie Ann is the only one sweet enough for your candy," she spat. "A mouthful of turpentine would be all I'd get."

Their father stood so quickly he knocked the silverware to the floor. "Where's your mother?" he asked, his demeanor instantly changing.

"Upstairs," Dalia replied.

"I come home after working hard for my family," he said, his voice stretched thin, "and what do I get?" Dalia felt his hot gaze on the back of her neck. "What do I get?" he repeated.

Slowly, Dalia pivoted around. Her eyes fell lovingly on Nellie Ann before shifting coolly to him. "Why don't you kiss Nellie Ann again?" she said, unable to cap off the jealousy that was bubbling up inside her.

"Whatever you wish, my beauty." Their father inched his fingers into the wrapper, brought up another square of fudge, and, staring intently at her, popped the candy into Nellie Ann's mouth. "My Darling Doll," he said, his tone softening. "Please, what do I get?"

Dalia threw back her shoulders and walked regally toward him. "A kiss," she said, the coldness in her voice giving way to the tenderness she once showed him. Then, lifting up on her toes, she brushed his cheek with her lips.

As they left the kitchen, Monroe wondered why he tried so hard to win them over each time he returned. Why did he work his fingers to the bone to buy them pretty things when, like their mother, they seemed so ungrateful? Why? he thought, but he already knew the answer. He pulled himself up each morning and worked as hard as his workers because this was who he was. Not a good man. Not a thoughtful man, but a man of work. A man of extremes who liked to feel the ache of his body after a long day's toil, who liked cutting boxes in the trunks of pines, cornering these boxes, chipping the bark off, applying streaks down the tree faces, dipping the gum, scraping off the dried sap, burning the tar kiln, drinking hard on Saturday nights. This was who he was. A workingman. Which was why he thrived now when others had failed to rebound after the Civil War, almost thirty years ago.

Of course, his family had prospered, but then he had known it would all along, as Violet Finster also must have known when he first laid eyes on her in 1870, five years after the war. Eleven years old, she was a skinny child with a mass of black hair and eyes as dark as watermelon seeds. He had come up to her in front of the country store and said, "One day, little girl, I'll marry you."

His first wife and infant son had died of yellow fever in the pine forests of coastal Mississippi in 1874. The baby died first; then Mary Lou also succumbed. Years later, he returned to south Georgia and rediscovered

Violet Finster. At nineteen, she became his second wife; he was twenty-three. She told him later she fell in love with him because he had resembled a hero right out of a romantic novel. Almost six feet tall, he was an impressive man. Dangerous, he seemed, in his dark large-rimmed hat with a red bandanna around his neck and a pistol in a shoulder holster beneath his coat. *One day, little girl, I'll marry you,* he said. Those words had stuck in her mind and resurfaced years later like a fate she couldn't avoid.

But though she couldn't admit it, he knew the real truth. She had fallen in love not with a dangerous man but with a hard worker, dressed in rough dungarees and sturdy, coarse brogans, the clothes of a woodsman destined to prosper. *One day, little girl, I'll marry you.* He had put into that statement the same fierce determination that he had always put into his work. A livelihood she now detested. A livelihood she wanted *her* children, *his* children to detest, too, but try as she might, she couldn't make him hate what he did for a living.

He strode over to the washbasin and pumped the handle. Filling up his palms with the cold water, he splashed it against his face, then wiped his skin off on a white towel embroidered with tiny blue flowers, leaving a stain, but he didn't care. Violet was right. He was coarse. *Your work makes you coarse. Let your turpentiners do it,* she said, often aggrieved when he left to tend his trees. *You don't have to slave alongside them anymore.* He scratched the bristles on his cheeks, glanced down to see the red smears of clay his boots had left on the floor cloth. *Go, then. Make love to your pines,* she'd sneered when he'd left this last time, but he hadn't let her sarcasm deter him, for he had to go. He longed to feel the humidity on his skin. He was addicted to the murmur of mosquitoes in his ears, the haze of gnats in front of his eyes. He relished the taste of tar in the air. He took refuge in Millertown, his town, where the woodsmen and their families lived, worked, and died. He delighted in the looks on their faces when he rode through his camp, as though he were not a man, not a mere mortal, but instead a god, their creator. *Common and coarse,* she said, as though the repetition of it would make him believe it was true. "Coarse, maybe," he whispered as he stared out the window at the fields of cotton like whitecaps on Snake River during a summer storm. "Common, never," he said aloud, the sour feeling he always felt when coming home rising in his stomach. He swallowed, sucked in his aching belly, and began walking toward the back door. He would go outside, sit beneath the double-fisted magnolia, and drink down the humid air. He had bought this grand white-columned mansion for them—to make them, not him, respectable. A shanty in the woods suited his soul better.

Breakfast over, Dalia plucked a blossom from a tangled thicket of roses bordering the flagstone walkway in the terraced garden, and positioned the yellow center beneath her sister's nostrils. "All right, Miss Sensitive Nose, what kind of rose is this?" she teased, wanting to make amends for the jealousy she'd felt this morning. "Silly goose," Nellie Ann said, "the camellias are blooming. They're so strong I can't smell anything else."

"How shall I describe it, then?" said Dalia thoughtfully. "Let's see. Each blossom has five petals. Pink, broad, and flat." She held the rose up to her own nose and inhaled deeply. "I can't smell it, either," she confessed, "but I can remember how it smells. It smells"—her voice became soft and dreamy—"like sugar tastes when you swallow a tablespoon of it, all at once, because you're hiccuping and want it to stop."

"Katie Mae made me do that once," Nellie Ann said. "It didn't help."

"That's not the point," Dalia said impatiently. "The point is, this flower smells sweet, but not too sweet, not cloying like the camellia. It doesn't bully, doesn't demand your full attention. You get a transitory whiff of sugar, tickling your nose for a second, and then—"

"Do you like sugarcane?" Nellie Ann interrupted.

"Do I like sugarcane?"

"Yesterday Katie Mae gave me a taste. She brought me some from the patch that Papa lets her tend on our land at the river. She cut off a chunk. Stripped away the thick hull, she told me, and said, *Suck on it—hard.* I did, but I didn't like it." Nellie Ann scrunched up her face and poked out her tongue. "After I sucked the sugar out, it was too stringy."

For several seconds, Dalia was silent. This morning her sister had gotten a second piece of fudge from Papa. Yesterday a bite of Katie Mae's sugarcane. All the sweetness in Nellie Ann's mouth, only a taste of bitterness in hers. "Lest we stray too far from the matter at hand," she began primly in an effort to disguise her jealousy, "I shall go on with my description. Such a modest little flower," she continued, "with a dab of yellow right smack in the center. The stem is slender—very, very fragile." Her thumb skimmed over a thorn. "But don't let yourself be fooled."

"Never," Nellie Ann asserted, stomping her foot against the flagstone walkway, crushing a yellow flower that had sprouted up through a crack.

"For below this blossom lies a prickly stem."

Nellie Ann tossed back her head. Her bangs, trimmed just above her eyebrows, parted, sweeping to each side of her puffy face. "Georgia has only one rose, sister dear, and it is the Cherokee."

"You're wrong," Dalia teased, dancing on tiptoes. "So very wrong. Your nose has led you astray, down the primrose path." She moved the blossom back and forth beneath her sister's nose. "Under hypnosis, you'll speak the truth," she said, mimicking a foreign accent. "Now guess again. What kind of rose is it?"

"Stop it!" Nellie Ann fumed, swinging at the blossom with her tiny clenched fist.

"I-I'm sorry," Dalia stammered.

"I'm not a fool, Dalia. I know it's the Cherokee."

Stilled by her sister's fury, Dalia clutched the rose between her paralyzed fingers while a queen bee in all its gold and black glory lit on the blossom. Nearby, a Bachman's sparrow, his yellowish gray feathers blending into branches of the longleaf pines, whistled before beginning his beautiful aria. The scuppernong arbor glittered in the sun. The slick, copper-colored skin of the grapes peeked out from among the leaves like a blanket of cat's-eye marbles. A soft-spoken breeze tickled the moss in the grand oak trees. Yet this abundance of natural beauty couldn't compete with the sting of Nellie Ann's fury, and Dalia stood in stony fear for a full half minute before finding the courage to reach for her sister's hand.

"No!" Nellie Ann spat, whipping her palm behind her back. "I might be blind and plain," she stated. "I might not have your pretty lilac eyes or your dark, thick ringlets, but the one thing I'm not is stupid."

"My dearest Nellie Ann," Dalia said, pressing her hand against her breast, "please forgive me. I've never thought you stupid."

Nellie Ann rocked back on her heels and blinked wide her white eyes. "You're not being honest." Dalia swallowed hard, tried to slow her racing heartbeat. "Tell me the truth," she demanded, banging the tip of her cane against the flagstone path.

"The truth is," Dalia said, staring at the cane, "you're one of the smartest people I know. I've never . . ." She kept her eyes on Nellie Ann's fingers, clutching the cane so tightly that Dalia feared the skin, stretched over her knobby knuckles, might crack. "Never," she stressed again, "thought you stupid. You have so many wonderful qualities."

"Like what?" asked Nellie Ann, her grip on the cane relaxing.

"Traits like . . . like . . ." Dalia thought. "Like adorable, loving, thoughtful, funny, talented, but most of all smart."

"Really?"

"Cross my heart and hope to die."

Nellie Ann placed her free hand on top of the hand that wielded the cane and smiled, her top lip disappearing as it rose upward. "Adorable?"

"Absolutely."

"Talented?"

"A brilliant pianist."

"Funny?"

"When you're not being so serious."

"I forgive you," Nellie Ann said, reaching out for Dalia, her cane drifting upward.

Dalia thumped her palm against her bosom. "Right here," she said. "Come to my heart." She whipped open her arms and folded them around her sister. The cane slipped from Nellie Ann's fingers and clattered against the walkway. A crow cawed raucously above their heads and swooped down to pluck a grape from the arbor. "The crows are eating Mama's scuppernongs," Dalia said.

"Then I wish I were a crow."

"So, let's be birds," Dalia said, breaking away from her sister. She bent over to pick up the cane, grabbed Nellie Ann's dress, and tugged. "Flap your arms and fly with me, little crow," she said, flapping her free arm.

"Mama will kill us." Nellie Ann giggled, waving her twig-thin arms. "Her grapes are for wine-making only."

"What Mama doesn't know won't hurt her," Dalia said, their legs zigzagging through the grass, their arms flying. "Wait here," she said when they came to the trellis. "I'm gonna climb the arbor." She pressed the cane into her sister's palm, dropping the rose to the ground.

"But you can't," Nellie Ann squealed. "It's dangerous."

"I want to, and I will," Dalia proclaimed, racing toward the mountain of dense green leaves. "Just you wait." Anchoring her hands on the trellis, she positioned the toe of her shoe on a latticed rung and carefully, inch by inch, one rung after another, hoisted herself up, her skirt snaring in the tangled vines, her white cotton bloomers showing. Upon reaching the top, she rested and caught her breath, draping her body over the carpet of vines, the skins of the grapes bursting like torn eyelids, staining her bodice with their viscous juice, the sweetly tart smell assaulting her nostrils. Dalia rose up on her elbows. "Open wide!" she yelled down to her sister, who shrieked with excitement, flung back her head, and opened her mouth. "Get ready!" she said, snapping off a grape, taking aim, and hurling it toward Nellie Ann's outspread lips. Dalia missed, and the scuppernong pinged against her sister's forehead.

"Do it again," Nellie Ann cried. She laughed and opened her mouth even wider.

Dalia plucked another grape from off the bed of vines and, narrowing her eyes as though peering through the scope of a rifle, reared back on one arm, then, lunging forward, pitched with all of her might. The grape curved upward and dropped, bull's-eye, into her sister's mouth.

Nellie Ann wrenched her lips together, sucked greedily, and spit out the skin. "I want more!" she yelled, as a scuppernong ricocheted off her arm. "More," she spluttered. "More. More. More."

Dalia kept it up, hurling a volley of champagne bullets at her sister's lips, wounding her face and splattering her shirtwaist while she hopped up and down, swatting the air with her cane.

"Not so fast!" Nellie Ann shouted. "Throw them slower."

Dalia snipped off a scuppernong that was near to popping. "Be still," she said. Nellie Ann thrust her neck out and upward, keeping her mouth open like a hungry baby bird. "Here it goes," Dalia said, heaving the grape over the trellis. It shone golden in the sunlight before hitting the dark crater of Nellie Ann's mouth.

Pleasure softened her features. With puckered lips, she whooshed out the skin. "Thank you," she said.

"It was my pleasure," Dalia answered, plucking a grape, popping it between her lips. She slurped, smacked, and spit the tough peel out—those little stabs of jealousy completely forgotten when she caught sight of Nellie Ann, squatting, her hands dipping down like fruit bats, her fingers finding a scuppernong in the grass, shoving it into her mouth as though it might be her last.

"Yes, we'll gather at the river. The beautiful, the beautiful river."

At the sound of Katie Mae's voice, Dalia quit eating and drew herself up. The trellis quivered beneath her. "Katie Mae! Katie Mae!" she cried, looking toward the vegetable garden.

"Miss Dalia!" Katie Mae hollered back, releasing her hoe, which shuddered to the ground. Making a megaphone of her hands, she yelled, "Wait there. I'm coming."

"Katie Mae's back from her cane patch?" asked Nellie Ann, craning toward the black woman's voice, grape juice shining like snail slime down her chin.

"I reckon so," Dalia said, snaking backward over the ladder-top trellis.

"She won't be happy when she sees us," Nellie Ann said, fluttering her fingertips over her shirtwaist. "I must look a sight," she whined, finding a grape skin, flinging it off.

"No more than I do," Dalia countered, positioning her foot on the top rung, weaving down.

"But you don't have them smashed—"

Dalia cut her off. "I've been lying in them, silly. It looks like I slept in them."

"You gals have been up to something bad," Katie Mae snorted. Her unbuckled shoes flopped toward them. The red rag tied around her forehead was moist with perspiration. Gray dust pockmarked her dark skin.

"Not really," Nellie Ann retorted, her demeanor instantly childlike, her voice babyish and plump.

"Why, just look at you." Katie Mae headed straight for Nellie Ann. "What has you been up to?"

"I thought you were still at the river," Nellie Ann said accusingly, her attitude now different, as if their feast of scuppernongs were somehow the black woman's fault.

"I gone and come," Katie Mae told her. "What's this?" she asked, flicking a grape peel off Nellie Ann's sleeve.

"A scuppernong," Dalia said, sauntering over, picking up the rose she'd dropped on the ground.

Katie Mae situated her hands beneath Nellie Ann's armpits and heaved her up. "You, too," she fussed, looking over her shoulder at Dalia's stained skirt. "Both of you, messes. You're way too old for this foolishness, Miss Dalia. You're supposed to set an example for your sister, not be the one to lead her to trouble."

"You want some?" Dalia asked her, extending a grape-filled palm.

"Do I want some?" Katie Mae said, tenting her eyebrows. "Get that nasty hand away from me." She swatted at Dalia's palm. "Your mama uses them grapes for her sweet wine and jelly. Ya know you ain't supposed to be eatin' them."

"We were just tasting them," Dalia said, licking off a bead of juice that was dribbling down her wrist.

"From the looks of you," Katie Mae said, eyeing her up and down, "you was bathing in them." Returning her attention to Nellie Ann, she began plucking the yellow skins off her shirtwaist. "You two ought to be 'shamed."

"I got nothing to be sorry about," Dalia sassed. "If Mama doesn't want me tasting her grapes, she should tell me so."

"I don't want to bother your sick mama about this, but if ya insists."

"If she's too sick to scold me," Dalia said, shooting purple anger into Katie Mae's eyes, "then I reckon she's too sick to make grape jelly."

Nellie Ann reached out for the black woman's hand. "Don't talk to Katie Mae that way," she said angrily. "With all she does for us, she deserves some respect."

"Why don't ya come with me, Miss Nellie Ann?" Katie Mae said, squeezing her hand. "Miss Dalia needs to spend some time by herself, needs to think on her actions. Let's you and me walk over to my herb garden. They're the strongest-smellingest things this time of year. Does that suit ya, Miss Dalia?"

Before Dalia could say a word, Katie Mae was leading Nellie Ann down the flagstone path. Together, they were walking away, their skirts dancing, their voices blending. She's just a servant, Dalia thought, choking on her approval. "A cook," she said spitefully, glaring down at the rose choked between her fingers. No, she thought stubbornly, as tears welled in her eyes and the rose plummeted to the ground. I won't cry. I won't give them the satisfaction.

Abandoning the pathway, she scurried over the well-kept grounds toward the house. She had gotten as far as the double-fisted magnolia when she heard him. "Papa!" she shouted, wheeling around. He was hiking up the carriage house door. Angling its loose frame into place, he threw the weight of his body against it and slammed it shut. "Papa!" She heard the urgency in her voice. He glanced up. The sadness in his eyes was transparent. It tempered her anger, filled her with pity, and sent her running to him, but when she got there, tilting up her face, her skin flushed from the heat, he didn't wrap his arm around her the way he usually did, but instead timidly touched her shoulder, like a distant cousin asking her to fetch him a cup of tea.

His restraint disturbed her, and they walked toward the house together, not speaking, she inching toward him, he pulling away. When he loved her too much, she pushed him from her. When he kept his distance, she wanted him back. It was this tug-of-war that made for her confusion.

They took the back porch steps and entered through the kitchen. From the front of the house came her mother's voice, issuing orders to Lucinda, the housemaid. "Did you beat the rug like I told you? Look up there," her mother said sternly. She was pointing at the chandelier in the parlor when Dalia and her father rounded the corner. "Lucinda, can't you see that dust?" Dalia had to squint hard before she detected the dull residue on the bronze fixture. "Did you polish my table?" her mother asked, walking across the room, stopping in front of the table, trailing her index finger over its rosewood top.

"Yessam," Lucinda was saying, rapidly nodding her head, which was much too large for her small body.

Her mother rubbed her index finger and thumb together. "Polish it again," she snapped. Then, breathing in deeply, she began to weave from side to side as though she might tip over.

"Mama, are you all right?" Dalia asked, rushing toward her.

"I'm fine," her mother whispered, gripping the edge of the table to steady herself. "Just fine." Wearily, she added, "Lucinda, never mind the polishing. The dust will creep back in. Filth, like illness, has a way of returning." When at last her mother looked up and saw him, the tendons in her throat tightened. "Monroe," she said in a pinched voice.

"Violet," her father responded.

For several seconds, an unbearable silence weighed down upon them. But then her mother came back to herself and with a flick of her head said, "Lucinda, why don't you go outside and beat that rug again?" When Lucinda left, she turned toward Dalia, studied her, as though she'd just become aware of her daughter's presence. "What's that on your skirt?" she said at last, her tone accusatory. Stretching out her arm, she fingered the slimy stain that ran the full length of Dalia's garment.

"Nellie Ann and I tasted a few of your scuppernongs," Dalia told her.

"A few?"

"Yes, ma'am."

"From the looks of it, you ate more than a few." Her features hard and sharp, her mother stared at her in judgment.

"The crows were eating them . . . we wanted to be crows," Dalia said.

Her father laughed. "You could do worse . . . my Darling Doll."

"So it's funny now?" her mother said, her dark eyes huffy. "My children acting like those filthy scavengers, and you're laughing."

"Violet," her father said. "The girls ate some of your grapes. Ain't that what they're for?"

"*Isn't,* not *ain't.* . . . Isn't that what they're for?" her mother corrected him, her gaze haughty as it traveled down his body and focused on the red clay on the floor. "We've been cleaning this house for days, and in the space of a few minutes you've made it dirty. Brought that dirty camp back home with you. Brought that filth into my clean house. You might be coarse and common," she hissed, "but I'll not let you turn my girls into crows . . . into you."

"I'm not like Papa," Dalia said defensively.

"Coarse, common," her father echoed as her mother whipped by him. "I may be coarse," he yelled after her, "but I sure as hell ain't common. And ya'll sure as hell ain't my family. A family is a man's own thing, but ya'll don't even want to claim me. Well, then," he said, shooting Dalia a wounded look, "if that's what you and your mama think of me, I reckon I'll ride back to my filthy camp, where my woodsmen respect me."

"Papa—" Dalia started to speak.

"Crows treat their own better than this," her father said indignantly. "You're no crow, missy." Spinning around, he stomped off toward the foyer, making Dalia flinch with guilt as he slammed through the front door.

CHAPTER 2

In every direction, Monroe saw longleaf pines. Miles upon miles, acres upon acres of the gray-limbed trees. Straight and erect like soldiers on a battlefield, like Confederate soldiers, standing tall and proud. "And undefeated," he said aloud, breathing in, drawing the acrid smell of pine gum deep into his lungs. He stared at the white notches cut near the ground, gaping wounds in the trunks of the trees. He marveled at the white streaks, flaring upward a head high, marring the bark like abscesses oozing. His eyes traveled over the scaly branches, their clusters of pine needles spiking upward. The sap stung his nose, and he pinched his nostrils hard, delighting in the strong odor. Over ten thousand acres, he thought. "All of it mine," he said, throwing back his wide shoulders, glancing around him. On a few of the trees nearby, the sap, unable to make it to the boxes below, had hardened into flakes of white, and in the dusk they looked like streams of tears. "Cry, you poor bastards! Shed some tears for your old friend," Monroe Miller shouted, pulling out his flask, upending the bourbon in a long, noisy swill, tucking the flask back into his shirt pocket. "The more ya weep, the richer ya make me."

He felt a branch of pine needles raking against his skin, but he paid it no mind. Beads of sweat dribbled down the sides of his scraggy face. Mosquitoes buzzed around him, and he slapped his thick-skinned palms against his ears, at first softly, then harshly, but still the insects droned. Above, the violet sky was turning deep purple. He heard the muffled sounds of men's voices swimming through the humidity from the side camp, a quarter of a mile away. He listened to someone singing, a dog howling, squirrels bickering while they foraged for pine cone nuts in the trees. He smelled the pungent smoke from the campfire and knew that this was where he was meant to be. Clucking, he snapped the reins. The night slyly descended as he headed his horse back along the sandy trail. Lightning bugs punctuated the darkness. The sliver of moon winked through the well-spaced pines. To his right, a great horned owl let out a cry, and, startled, Monroe tensed in his saddle. He was tired, his pride battered at the hands of his family, but riding his horse among his pines made him feel better.

"Mr. Monroe! Mr. Monroe!" In the darkness he saw Johnny Cake running toward him with his mop of yellow hair shooting out wildly like lopside Indian grass, his skinny arms flying above his head. "Daddy done kilt us some rabbits, Mr. Monroe. He's cookin' 'em now."

Monroe inhaled deeply and caught a whiff of meat roasting on an open fire. "It smells good, don't it?" he said to the boy. He got off his horse, scooped Johnny Cake up, and put him in the saddle. "How many rabbits?" he asked, walking alongside the horse, leading him by the reins.

"Three, sir," the boy said.

"Three," Monroe said thoughtfully. "We'll be eating like kings tonight."

"Cornbread and beans, too," Johnny Cake said, his voice climbing with excitement.

"Ya sound hungry, boy." Johnny Cake was ten and always hungry.

"Yessir, I could eat me a horse," Johnny Cake said. Then, suddenly becoming quiet, he leaned over, patted the horse's neck, and said, "But not you, Tarkel. I'd never eat you."

Monroe laughed. "I ate mule once," he said, coming to a halt, turning around to look at Johnny Cake. The boy stared back. "For twelve years that old mule worked hard for me. When that mule died, I asked myself, *Are ya gonna bury John Henry beneath the sandy soil and put an end to his working days, or are ya gonna let him work some more?* It was a practical question," Monroe explained, "born of respect for the beast, for all that he done for me." He hawked up some phlegm, spit it fiercely on the ground, and went on, "The more I thought about it, the more right the notion became. At first it was just a flicker in my mind, but the harder I thought on it, the bigger it grew, till I knew what I had to do. Right then and there, I skinned John Henry and gutted him. I dried the meat. Made jerky out of it and let that old mule of mine work some more."

Johnny Cake swallowed hard. Monroe could hear him, uneasy, fidgeting in the saddle. Finally, after a huge gulping sound, he said, "Well, sir, I best be watching how much work I do for ya."

Upon hearing the boy's words, Monroe Miller began to laugh. It was a great big guffaw, starting deep inside his stomach and rising upward, erupting through his broad mouth, leaving droplets of saliva in his black mustache. "I reckon you had better," he said, hooting all over again, wiping his lips with the palm of his hand, wiping his palm on his dungarees.

"But no one could ever get me to eat Tarkel," the boy added, his voice solemn. "I would never eat ya, Tarkel." He brought his hand along the horse's mane, then, in an effusive show of devotion, lunged over and threw his skinny arms around the horse's neck. Seconds later, he rose back up in the saddle and said, "We won't cook Tarkel, will we, Mr. Monroe?"

"Don't worry about Tarkel," Monroe Miller replied. "He ain't much of a worker. Too much fat on ole Tarkel. When the time comes, we'll just bury him proper."

Johnny Cake heaved a sigh of relief, which gurgled, then drowned in the wet, syrupy air. Monroe jiggled the reins, and Tarkel quickened his pace down the white trail, which looked to Monroe not so much like a trail as like a long spillage of sap, dried flake white on the soft Georgia ground.

The rabbit was juicy and sweet. Every so often, a breeze found its way through the piney woods, cooling the warm night air. Mosquitoes hummed. Tree frogs sang. The whippoorwills began repeating their name. Darnell, slow-moving but exact, sliced the rabbit on top of a skillet of fried cornbread while Sam, fast but sloppy, sloshed kidney beans into tin cups for the remaining woodsmen, who would join the other black hands at the opposite end of the camp.

Monroe cracked a leg and thigh apart. Turning toward his foreman, he asked, "Can I give this leg to your boy?"

Tick Jones nodded, and Monroe offered the meat to Johnny Cake, who sat Indian-style next to his father. "You know how much he eats,"

Tick bragged, watching his son bite into the leg. "Slow down," he told the boy. Immediately Johnny Cake began to chew slowly, his chin dimpling as his teeth crunched down. There was a loud pop, and a log, glowing bright red, split in half and sent sparks flying. Tick hit at the sparks with his broad, callused hands. "Look at him. Two gulps and that rabbit's almost gone," he said. The grin on his lips settled into his green eyes, lighting them up like stars.

"He's a fine boy," Monroe declared, meaning it. He'd always felt a fondness for Johnny Cake, always thought that if his own infant son hadn't died all those years ago, he'd have wanted him to be like this yellow-haired boy.

"The gum's flowin' pretty good," Tick said, clearing his throat, spitting.

"How many barrels?" asked Monroe, breaking off a hunk of cornbread, popping it into his mouth, chewing hard.

"Twenty-four," Tick said. "Darnell dipped seven of them. He's slow but careful. Don't go spillin' it the way the others do."

"Best damned dipper in the state of Georgia, ain't ya, Darnell?" Monroe said. Darnell quit slicing rabbit long enough to look up at Monroe and smile.

"I filled my syrup bucket up," Johnny Cake boasted, his mouth plump with beans.

"I wouldn't expect no less of ya," Monroe said, winking at the boy.

"One day, Daddy and me gonna be operators, too. We're gonna save up our money and buy us some piney woods and become rich like you, Mr. Monroe," Johnny Cake said, his tone as certain as a chuck-will's-widow's call.

"I reckon ten at the other camp," Monroe said, nodding at Johnny Cake but shifting toward Tick.

"Most likely," Tick agreed. "They only got two dippers. Ain't neither of 'em good as Darnell."

"I might ask the chippers to do some dippin', too," Monroe said. "It won't hurt 'em to double up sometimes. Hard work never hurt nobody. How's Sugar Cane doing?" Monroe asked with a smile. Sighing, he rose and grabbed the coffeepot resting near the hot coals of the fire.

"Better," Tick said. "All day long I seen Columbus babyin' that mule. Washin' off his leg, smearin' on ointment, wrappin' up the gash. That animal smells so strong of medicine he takes your breath away."

"Smartest turpentine mule I've ever known," Monroe said, pouring himself a cup of coffee, offering some to Tick.

Tick shook his head. "Come nighttime, this here squeezle is all I want or need," he said, gulping from a cup of syrup-sweetened water.

"Columbus tells Sugar Cane what to do, and that mule does it." Monroe took a swallow of the hot black coffee. Then, puffing out his cheeks, he blew the hot air through his lips to cool his mouth off. "I ain't never seen nothing like it. Columbus not even in the wagon, off somewhere in the pines, orderin' Sugar Cane around, and him doin' his biddin'. A genius mule, that's what he is. A heck of a lot smarter than us humans."

"Ya wouldn't eat Sugar Cane, would ya, Mr. Monroe?" asked Johnny Cake, downing some squeezle.

"Son," Tick said, his voice brusque, "don't go askin' Mr. Miller questions like that."

"It's all right," Monroe said, pulling out his pipe, packing it with Prince Albert. "I told your boy about John Henry, and now he's afraid I'm gonna eat all the camp animals when they die."

"John Henry was special," Tick explained to his son. "The heart of that mule weren't meant to be worm food. Not every mule deserves the respect John Henry got."

"Certainly not the likes of Sugar Cane," Monroe said, flicking a match tip against his thumbnail, lighting up. "He's smart," he said, sucking in the smoke. "Gets away with murder, that mule does." He clamped his teeth against the pipe stem. Smoke oozed from the corners of his mouth. "But a smart mule ain't necessarily a hardworkin' one." Thoughtfully, he pulled the pipe out from between his teeth. "Anyway, I don't think Columbus would let me cook Sugar Cane, even if I wanted to."

"That's good," Johnny Cake said, appeased, " 'cause I like Sugar Cane almost as much as Tarkel, and I wouldn't wanna eat neither of 'em."

"I promise ya," Monroe said, punctuating each word with a flick of his pipe, "I won't go eatin' Tarkel, Sugar Cane, or any other camp animal when it dies."

"On second thought," Tick added, grinning, "Sugar Cane might be tasty." His eyes glinting with mischief, he glanced over at Monroe. "Real savory 'cause he's so fat."

"Daddy," Johnny Cake groaned.

"Wouldn't be tough like that scrawny mule Willie," Tick said.

"Daddy."

"Stewed up with some onions and new potatoes, he might go down pretty good."

"And a fine wine," Monroe added. "Now, Tick, don't ya go forgettin' the wine. Red, ain't it? Ain't that the one that goes with mule?"

"Daddy," Johnny Cake begged, his eyes welling up. "Please don't say that."

"Dammit, boy," Tick said, throwing his ropy arm around his son's shoulders. "Can't ya see I'm funnin' ya?"

Johnny Cake shrugged off his father's hug. Sniffling, he squared his small shoulders. "I knowed it," he said, breaking into a smile. "I was just playin' ya, that's all."

That night, Monroe Miller made a pillow out of his saddle and bedded down under an old tall longleaf. He liked to breathe in the fragrance of pine gum. Sharp and clean, it cut through him like a swallow of hard whiskey and made him feel alive. He liked to look way up into the pine boughs. He liked to see the needles move in the night breeze against the star-speckled sky. In a few minutes, he was asleep.

"Go away," Monroe groaned into the night air as his family rose up behind his closed eyelids. Stronger than pine trees, their three disapproving faces pushed up through the soil of his troubled mind. His eyelids flashed open. His heart was hitting hard against his chest, as if it wanted to leap out of him, as if it were a separate creature desiring freedom from them, too. Swallowing the scent of pine, breathing in deeply, he sighed, consoled by the sweet darkness around him. Would he ever breathe easily again? he wondered. Would he never be free of their judgment?

Five-thirty and already muggy, Monroe thought, swabbing his forehead with a handkerchief the next morning. He tied Tarkel to a black pine and watched as Columbus maneuvered the heavy steel-tired dip wagon into the clearing. Four dippers climbed out. Darnell, big and cumbersome, was last, his syrup bucket dangling from his fingers. Moseying over to a hickory tree, he hung his lunch bucket—packed with chunks of dooby, a blend of cured meat, onions, and cornbread; a jar of cane syrup; and a jug of squeezle—at the end of the branch, down from the others. Next, he went back to the wagon for his dip iron and dip bucket. Casually, he loped toward the crop of longleafs. With each step he took, the dip bucket thumped against his leg, but it didn't seem to bother him like it did the others. Too often, Monroe had to get turpentine balm from the commissary to heal the raw skin on his dippers' legs. He was about to call out to Darnell but was distracted when he heard his foreman's voice.

"Sam, ya missed some yesterday," Tick said from astride Robey. Trailing behind, Johnny Cake playfully erased the hoofprints with a sweep of his brogan.

The mosquitoes buzzed, and Monroe wondered if the damn things ever slept. When the sun rose higher in the sky, the gnats would come out to replace them. Something broke through the wire grass, and Monroe spun around. The sight of the diamond-clad skin froze him to the spot, but when he detected the round head, he uncoiled his muscles and relaxed. Six feet long and as thick as a man's upper arm, it was a king snake, often mistaken for a diamondback rattler, but Monroe had made it his duty to know the difference. After all, snakes lived and flourished in these piney woods.

Monroe listened to the sound of chipping as he walked. The sting of sap burned his nostrils. A palmetto fan, which Tick had slipped beneath the bark of a longleaf, a signal to chippers that the tree had been overlooked, glimmered emerald in the sunlight. Its fronds, sharp as sword tips, snagged on Monroe's pants as he passed by. In front of him, Darnell lifted up his dip bucket and swung it back and forth. "I don't understand why ya wanna make more work for yourself," Monroe said, catching up with him.

"If I git tired of carryin' this bucket," Darnell said, his long, strong fingers wrapped tightly around the handle, "I go back and git the dip cart. I ain't goin' deep into the woods today."

"Well, don't that seem ass-backward?" Monroe said as they trudged along. "Why didn't ya just put your bucket in your dip cart and roll 'em both here?"

At first Darnell was wordless. Only his stout brogans, clumping through a patch of jimson weed, made any noise. Minutes later, he came to an abrupt stop and turned around. "Mr. Monroe, I been doin' this work since I was a youngin', and ya know I ain't never needed no dip cart. Seeing how just last night ya called me the best damn dipper in the state of Georgia, don't reckon I'm gonna change my ways now." Sweat glistened on the black man's forehead. His flour-sack shirt was sinkholed with perspiration; his dungarees stuck to his skin. At most, he would make two dollars and ten cents today. Seven barrels of gum at thirty cents a barrel. It was hot, hard work, and Darnell was good at it. Monroe kept his mouth shut.

His mind wandered back to the pine forests of Mississippi. When he told his friends that he was leaving Georgia, they had warned him, *Mississippi ain't no place to raise a family. Too many outbreaks of yellow fever.* But he had shrugged off their fears. To him, a family was a man's own thing. A family was meant to be loyal. It was meant to keep a man working hard, thinking sane, and from sinking deep into the gutter of his compulsions, the way pitch sealed a ship's seams and kept it from sinking into the sea. That was what a family was meant to be. So when Monroe lost his wife and son to yellow fever, he had grieved, drowned his guilt in whiskey, and for that next year almost drunk his life away.

Chastened, he had come back home and bought himself some Georgia pine trees. He worked, scraped, saved, purchased more land cheap, studied the ways of the longleafs. He branched out, learned everything he could about the turpentine business, and did it all—installed still buildings and equipment, a glue pot and shed, a cooper shed and wheel, and a shop for a blacksmith—because he was savvy enough to know that was where the real money would come from. Within three years he was rich enough to ask for Violet Finster's hand in marriage.

Monroe watched Darnell bend forward, the long wooden handle of the dip iron gripped in his large hands. Next, with an outward flick of his wrists, as graceful as a cook flipping a pancake, he gathered up the gum from the box and emptied it into his dip bucket on the ground. When the bucket was filled with gum, he would pour it out into one of the large wooden barrels placed throughout the crop of longleafs. "You're a beautiful sight," Monroe told Darnell, who drifted from tree to tree, dipping the gum effortlessly.

"Not as beautiful as this place," Darnell said, plucking a dirty rag from the pocket of his dungarees. He wiped off his brow, then knotted it around his high forehead.

"Ain't no other place for a woodsman to be," Monroe added, quickly turning around when he heard a crunching sound behind him.

It was Johnny Cake, sidestepping a gallberry bush, smiling like a jack-o'-lantern. "Daddy's fussin'," he panted, " 'cause the chippers are missin' trees. He says they're forgetful."

"What would I do without your daddy?"

"I wanna be a woodsrider just like him," Johnny Cake said proudly.

Monroe nodded and placed his palm on top of the boy's hot head. "Where's your syrup bucket and dip paddle?" he asked. "I thought ya was dippin' today."

"Daddy told me to git back to the side camp. Said I was gettin' too red-faced," Johnny Cake explained.

Monroe pinched the boy's chin and tilted his head back. "Your daddy's right," he said, running his index finger over Johnny Cake's forehead. "Ya look like a Creek Injun, you're so red. Ya need a big hat like mine." Monroe touched the brim of his large black hat. "Been thinkin' about gettin' ya one."

"Would ya?" Johnny Cake asked, straining forward.

"I think I just might," Monroe said, grinning.

"I don't wanna go back to the camp," Johnny Cake whined. "Can I stay here? I wouldn't be no bother. I could talk to Tarkel. That way he wouldn't get so lonesome by hisself under that tree."

"Boss, this here barrel's almost full," Darnell boasted, his head held high. "If I keep this up, I might be dippin' eight barrels today."

"The best damn dipper in the state of Georgia," Monroe declared. He grabbed the boy's grimy hand and led him over to the black pine where Tarkel was tethered. An oddity this black pine was among a longleaf forest, but beautiful, Monroe thought, his gaze falling on Tarkel, black as the pitch that would come from the pine's thick, gnarled branches, reaching upward like arms in prayer.

That afternoon, their work complete for the week, he and Tick rode west into Valdosta, forty miles away. Their horses clip-clopped along the brick-paved Ashley Street toward the town square, with its white-columned brick courthouse and its statue of the Confederate soldier out front, red petunias blooming profusely around the marble base. They rode past Harriet's Millinery, her peacock-feathered hats on a display shelf behind the wide-paned window; past the tobacco shop, in need of a fresh coat of white paint; past Citizen's Bank, with its dark granite entrance; and past Eliot's Butchery, its green shades drawn tight. They smelled the dung of horses hitched to ornate posts along the sidewalk, and marveled at the street lamps glowing like flaming lollipops on each corner. Riding through the respectable part of town, with its green-and-white-striped awnings and clean sidewalks, they took in the hustle and bustle of families climbing into their wagons and heading home after a long day of shopping, and laughed out loud at Jason's Saloon, lit up like a birthday cake studded with candles. They aimed themselves toward the red-light district, an area composed of one city block near the colored part of town. Their destination was the Hensley Hotel, sagging from old age and misuse. When they got there, they dismounted in front of its warped veranda, their boots stirring up little swirls of dust in the unpaved street, then creaked up the wooden steps toward the stained-glass entrance, broken and boarded over, looking like a face with an eye patch.

Inside, the smell of turnip greens wafted toward them from the kitchen. Monroe and Tick trudged through the entry over loose oily floorboards, climbed the rickety stairs until they reached the second floor, where a section of the banister railing was missing, and turned left down a dark, rank hallway. When they came to room twenty-three, they entered without knocking.

The room was dingy and ugly. Its rose-patterned wallpaper buckled over the door and was ripped above the bed's iron headboard. An overhead gas lamp flickered dully, then brightly, ebbing and flowing with the odor of the simmering greens. As daylight faded, Monroe Miller swigged bourbon from a silver flask along with Willard Croton, Lollie Morris, and Roscoe McKinney, all three turpentine farmers like himself. Meanwhile, Tick nursed a quart jar of coondick, a blend of grapefruit juice and cornmeal mash, as yellow as a raccoon's urine.

Squatting in the middle of the room with his right arm outstretched, Monroe pressed a stick of chalk against the dark linoleum, pivoting slowly as he drew a circle with a radius of three feet. When he finished, he lifted his head, winked at his friends, then drew a much smaller circle—about a foot across—within it. "I've got me a feeling 'bout tonight. Ole Bojangles is gonna win it all." Monroe laughed as he grabbed the silver flask from Roscoe's hand, tossed back his head, and gulped.

"Don't be so cocksure," Willard Croton said, tugging on the tip ends of his handlebar mustache. "My Pappy's got the legs of a jackrabbit." He held up a matchbox with *Pappy,* written in blue ink on its cover.

"Twenty dollars a game," Roscoe McKinney chimed in, tossing his stake into the circle.

Lollie Morris said nothing, shook his head as though dismissing the lot of them, but threw in two tens, anyway—his diamond ring shining in the descending dusk, the expression on his face smug as always.

Willard Croton anted up. Monroe followed, peeling off a twenty from his tightly coiled bills.

Tick sat on the floor with his back pressed against the iron leg of the bed, downing his coondick, just watching.

"Let's drink on it," Monroe said, bringing the flask to his lips and gulping. His Adam's apple slid up and down. "Ain't much left. Why don't ya finish it off?" he said, handing the flask to Willard.

"Naw," Willard said. "I wouldn't do that to a friend."

"Don't matter," Monroe said, standing. "I've got more where that come from." He walked over to the bed, bent down, and with a moan dragged out a crate filled with eight fifths of Kentucky bourbon.

Each of the four men dug a hand into his coat pocket, retrieved a matchbox, opened it, and placed his cockroach—palms cupped over it—inside the small circle. Monroe offered them shot glasses. Which they plunked, upside down, over their insects. The cockroaches, with antennae bending, bumped against the glasses as they tried to scurry toward the dark corners of the room.

Willard's albino roach, with its long legs, transparent wings, and skeletal body, was longer and thinner than the others. It kept jumping and hitting its head against the top of the jigger. "What did I tell ya?" Willard said. "He thinks he's a jackrabbit. Why, look at them long legs. Pappy's got the body of a high jumper."

"So?" Monroe said, eyeing Willard. "Bojangles here can dance. It takes more than jumpin' to win a roach race. My boy's rhythm will carry him through." Bojangles, obese with short, hairy legs, wobbled to and fro, buffing the floor with his torso.

"All he's gonna do is shine the linoleum." Willard laughed as he bolted down another mouthful of liquor.

Lollie and Roscoe grabbed their own fifths from the crate, unscrewed the caps, and took several swigs. Roscoe's roach was missing two legs. Lollie's insect was ordinary. "Mine's the only normal one," Lollie said, arching his eyebrows at Monroe, who flinched, recalling his white-eyed daughter.

Lollie had a way of disguising his nastiness, insulting a man without his knowing it, but Monroe knew better. He glanced over at Tick to catch his reaction to the insult, but Tick, deep in drink, was stone-faced and quiet.

"Don't think my Rebel's crippled," Roscoe said. "The blind make up for their loss by hearing better. What I'm sayin' is, Rebel uses four legs the way most roaches use six."

"Roscoe, you're speaking to an expert on imperfection," Monroe said, boisterously spanking his hand against his thigh before tuning his gaze on Lollie. "It ain't no blessing," he went on, "but it has its compensations. Blind as my Nellie Ann is, she's brilliant when she plays the piano. Your girls don't play that well, do they, Lollie?" This time, Lollie Morris winced—the muscles just beneath his skin tightening, his customary air of disdain vanishing; but then, just as quickly, he regained his composure and replanted a sneer on his lips. Monroe was disappointed. He flicked a trickle of sweat off his brow. The others, he noticed, were sweating also, worms of perspiration inching from their sideburns. Even the unruffled Lollie Morris was sweating. Excitement twitched in the men's eyes and tugged at their wilted mustaches. "Let's get this show on the road," Monroe said. "I wanna see who's gonna be the big loser tonight."

"Well, not me," Willard said. "I ain't got that much to lose. I'm a small-time operator. Never pretended to be more."

"But you've got much to win," Monroe said, slapping Willard's back. "In one night, ya could become a big man." He cocked his finger at Lollie Morris. "Ya could end up like Lollie, here—a rich man, with plenty of time on his hands, doing nothing but sitting behind a mahogany desk counting his money. Willard, have ya had any time to count your money?" Monroe asked him with a wide grin.

Lollie raised his fifth in a mock toast, removed the cap, and cleaned off the bottle's rim with his pinkie. He took a dainty sip.

"Naw, sir, I've pretty much gotta work all the time," Willard said. "I don't reckon I'm like Mr. Morris at all."

Monroe charged. "Dammit, man, don't you wanna be feared? Don't ya wanna act like a king, treat your woodsmen like slaves, make 'em live in shanties, deprive their kids of any schooling, so that they'll keep working the trees like their papas?"

"Business is business," Lollie interrupted, his manner cool. "I've built a smooth-running operation, kept my men working, put food on their tables. I'm a good businessman," he stated firmly. "Unlike you, I don't waste my talents on the betterment of mankind. I keep my workers happy. Plenty of coondick and plenty of credit. And I get something back for my efforts. I make no apologies."

"Your workers ain't no better off than they were before the war," Monroe accused him.

"And you think that's bad?" Lollie Morris said. "I bet Willard and that white roach of his agree with me."

Willard smiled and nodded at Lollie.

"Fine," Monroe conceded. "Just fine." All this bickering was beginning to weary him. "Why don't we quit wasting time and win us some money? Get ready."

The men leaned over, their heads almost touching.

"Get set."

They extended their arms, curled their fingers over the tops of their jiggers.

"Go!"

Wrists jerked back, and shot glasses rose upward. Three of the roaches scampered in different directions away from the small circle's center.

"Come on, Pappy! Run like there's no tomorrow!" Willard exclaimed.

"Look at my baby," Roscoe boasted. "Rebel's a miracle on four legs."

But then Pappy and Rebel froze, while Bojangles kept moving steadily toward the perimeter. "Dance, Bo! Dance!" Monroe demanded.

Lollie lowered his head. His roach hadn't strayed from inside the small circle. Instead, it spun around and around in an orbit of its own. "I guess cripples and albinos got the advantage today," he said, chuckling.

"Bojangles, win for your papa." Monroe jumped up and down, the floorboards creaking beneath him like old mattress springs, as Rebel and Pappy began scuttling forward.

Roscoe hovered over the race like a referee. "To hell with that fat ass of yours!" he shouted.

"To hell with your cripple," Willard said, just as Pappy, in a final burst of energy, scrambled over the finish line first.

"My fatty's faster than your cripple," Monroe quipped when Bojangles came in second, beating Rebel by a hairline.

"I'll be damned," Roscoe said.

"Double damn," Lollie said with a sneer.

The men rose tipsily and staggered after their cockroaches.

"I can't believe he won," Willard said, kissing his cupped hand.

Monroe laughed, placed Bojangles under his jigger, and picked up his bottle of bourbon. "We're all damned," he said, upending his fifth, guzzling.

"See, Willard, you proved me right," Lollie said. "The white roach is smarter and quicker than the black."

"Yessir, Pappy is a purebred champ," Willard said. "Roscoe, give us that ole Rebel yell." Roscoe cupped a hand on either side of his mouth and let out a high-pitched whoop. "I won!" Willard boomed. "Sixty dollars richer because of this roach of mine."

The evening had just begun. Willard was smiling deliriously. Monroe was laughing at the foolishness of it all. Roscoe looked disappointed, frowning as he knelt on the floor. Lollie appeared indifferent, but Monroe didn't let this bother him. The man didn't know how to have fun. Old money had a way of exacting reserve. Meanwhile, Tick was getting drunker and drunker, his lanky body slipping downward, his legs sliding over the linoleum rug.

Occasional low moans rolled through the heat. In other rooms, women were pumping against partners, releasing tension as they cast acrobatic shadows against the walls. In this room, though, gambling was the release of choice, and Monroe felt the anxiety inside him dissolving. He noticed that Willard's palms were rough, covered with yellow calluses, Roscoe's cuticles were torn and red, but Lollie's hands were soft and clean. No gum on his skin. No black beneath his fingernails. With his middle finger, Monroe started digging dirt from under his thumbnail. "I'm having me a fine ole time," he announced. "More fun than I've had in months," he said, holding his fingers up to his lips. "Shush," he whispered, his eyes scanning the cluster of faces. "Please don't tell my wife." He bent over laughing and tossed another twenty dollars on the floor. Willard followed. Then the others. Slivers of lamplight shone through the half-open blinds and fell like stripes across the backs of the four operators.

Two hours later, Willard was proving to be the lucky one, winning almost every race. Monroe had won only two, losing almost six hundred dollars in the pursuit of recouping his losses. Roscoe had won three, his bleeding cuticles betraying his nerves, while Lollie, now leaning against a chair, his upside-down jigger beside him, his roach dizzily circling inside it, had lost every one. "Boys, tell ya what I'm gonna do," Monroe slurred. "I'm gonna make this last race real exciting. I've got eight hundred acres of longleafs on the outskirts of Cross City, just over the state line, and I plan to wager it all."

"No, boss," Tick objected, suddenly sitting up, the half-empty jar of coondick cradled in the crook of his arm.

"Now, Tick, don't ya go worryin'," Monroe reassured him. "I got more pines in Florida than Okefenokee's got cypress trees."

"No way," said Roscoe, thumping his matchbox on the floor. "I ain't drunk enough or rich enough to match ya."

"Coward," Monroe snapped.

"No, sir," Roscoe vowed solemnly. "I'm out."

"Monroe, ya know I can't match that," Willard said.

Monroe caught the whine in Willard's voice. He nibbled at his mustache as he thought. "Willard, you're a lucky man," he said seconds later. "And why?" He didn't wait for Willard's reply. "Because I'm feeling generous tonight," he answered. "Stake the money you've won and the deed to your place. Show me some grit."

"Only the money," Willard haggled. "I ain't willin' to risk my livelihood. That five hundred acres is all I got."

"Ain't no one got balls in here?" Monroe asked.

"Naw, I ain't gonna do it," Willard said.

"And you call me ruthless," Lollie said with a bored yawn.

"I'm givin' the man a chance to better himself," Monroe countered. "It's a chance of a lifetime. Willard, ya could be a big man at last."

"Ya think so?" Willard said.

"What do you think?" Monroe asked.

"Don't know." Willard scratched his head with a stubby finger.

"Who's been winning so far?"

"Me, I reckon."

"Ya reckon?" Monroe said, guffawing. "Come on, man. Don't throw away a sure win." Impatiently, he strummed his fingernails against the bottle. "For once in your life, take a chance."

"All right, ya bastard," relented Willard, punching the air with his fist.

"That man's got balls as big as watermelons," Monroe said, cutting his eyes to Tick, who stared back at him with disapproval, then crawled over to a get a closer look at the race.

Willard took one last gulp of bourbon, then breathed in deeply five times. Although Monroe knew him to be a Southern Baptist, he made the sign of the Cross upon his chest.

Monroe grinned and blew Bojangles a kiss. "The Lord can't help ya now," he said. "Get ready. Get set. Go!"

Both men snapped their shot glasses upward. Both cockroaches darted ahead.

"Go, Pappy, go!" Willard yelled as his white cockroach zigzagged through the small circle, Bojangles inches behind him.

"Dance, Bo, dance!" Monroe shouted.

Suddenly Pappy slowed. Bojangles bumped into him, jolting them both to a stop.

"Leave my Pappy be," Willard warned, turning his hand into a fist.

"Go, Bojangles. Run right over him," Monroe said.

Pappy skittered forward. Bojangles, dazed, stood still.

"Move, ya idiot," Monroe hissed, kneeling over his insect, his knees grinding into the linoleum.

"Leave that no-'count in the dust," Willard begged, crawling alongside his cockroach as it scuttled forward.

"That's it, Pappy," Roscoe joined in. "Use those long legs of yours."

"Jesus," Monroe growled, glaring at Bojangles, still tarred to the floor. "Dance for me, you goddamned cockroach." Suddenly Bojangles began to scurry.

"Dance," Tick echoed when Bojangles caught up with Pappy.

Their bodies were so close together that they looked like one insect with black and white stripes. A zebra cockroach, Monroe thought, following the twelve legs moving briskly toward the edge of the circle, their antennae stretched out—quivering.

"Oh, sweet Jesus, what have I done?" Willard groaned, just as Monroe jumped to his feet and brought his brogan down, smashing both insects, smearing white residue and black specks across the floor.

"What the hell?" said Tick.

"Who won?" asked Roscoe.

"Looks like Pappy to me on that finish line," Monroe stated, going over to Willard. "Congratulations, you just won eight hundred acres of prime pines," he said, lifting Willard off the floor, giving him a bear hug.

"Congratulations," Tick said.

"Ya showed guts and grit tonight. Now nothing can hold ya back," Monroe declared.

"Guts and grit," Roscoe repeated, shaking Willard's hand.

"God bless you all," Willard said, his eyes bleary from too much drink and too much emotion.

Monroe strode over to the mangled remains of Bojangles and plucked him up. "Next time we start fresh." He looked over at Lollie

Morris, his head lolling back against the chair leg, sound asleep, then returned his gaze to Willard. Winking, he paused for a moment, then in a wistful voice said, "Life's good, ain't it?" And it was. He still had ten thousand acres of piney woods in Georgia, another five thousand in Florida. He had his workers and his trees. He had his camps and Millertown, the jewel in his crown. To hell with his family, he thought, opening his hand, letting the sticky white gunk fall to the floor.

CHAPTER 3

"This stink on my clothes is pine gum," Nellie Ann was saying, deepening her voice to mimic their father's. She stood next to the wall cut with bookshelves, in front of their father's desk, with an old ratty bandanna around her neck, a black hat like a lampshade on her head, and a pair of cast-off brogans big as paddles on her feet. "This here is a puller," she went on, raising her cane up high. "For scraping the bark off my pines." Then, as if she could see, she took a sidestep toward Dalia and knighted her with the tip end of her cane. "I now pronounce you a woodsman," she said, unwittingly tousling her sister's curls. "Are you a puller like me?"

"No, sir, I'm a dipper," Dalia said, her face and tone still as glass. "In the piney woods, I dip gum. Here at home, I dip bourbon." As soon as she said this, her face broke apart and she doubled over with laughter.

"What kind of bourbon do you dip?" Nellie Ann asked.

"Only the best," Dalia said, swallowing a mouthful of giggles. "The kind from Kentucky," she said, bringing a solemnity to her voice. "Yessir, I like to dip it in the morning, in the afternoon, and all night long."

Nellie Ann let out a guffaw. "Poor ole Papa," she said, shaking her head, giggling. "More than anything, he wants to be king of this castle, but his only kingdom is the piney woods."

"The Dipper King of the Longleaf Pines," Dalia said.

"And his subjects are the squirrels," Nellie Ann added, laughing so hard that the black hat slipped over the side of her head.

It was then the study door flew open, slamming against the plastered wall. Dalia flinched and turned toward the doorway. Nellie Ann jerked, thumping her cane against the desk.

"Goddammit," their father said, reeking of pine gum and liquor as he stormed into the room. "I could hear ya'll down the hall. Is this what ya do while I'm gone? Make fun of me in my study? I leave to get away from your ridicule, only to be greeted by it as soon as I step through the door. Who said ya could come in here, anyway?" Dalia parted her lips to speak, but he immediately cut her off. "I don't want to listen to your lies," he told her. "Katie Mae and your mama know you're not allowed in here, where I do my business. The only sanctuary I have in this hellhole you call home." He took a big step toward them. "Nellie Ann," he said, turning to her sister, "who gave ya permission to wear my old clothes?" He reached out and snatched the black hat off her sister's head—pulling her sideways, making her lose her balance—but Nellie Ann caught herself with a stab of her cane into the soft pine floor. "Where did you get these things?" He didn't give her a chance to answer. "Those brogans? That hat?" he demanded, glaring at Dalia while interrogating Nellie Ann.

"From Zara," Nellie Ann replied, her voice steady.

"Since when do you have field hands for friends?"

"Since Katie Mae introduced him to me."

"Servants and field hands. Those are your friends?" Monroe said, measuring out each syllable, sneering. "Are ya colored, child?"

"My eyes see black," she said.

"Your eyes see more than that, my daughter." He snapped the hat on top of the desk, leaned over, and untied the bandanna around her neck. "You're not strong enough to be a puller," he said, snapping the kerchief in Nellie Ann's direction. Her cane clattered to the floor. "Your shoulders are too narrow. Your arms, too weak and thin." He was quiet for a moment, his blue eyes still on her body. "If ya wanna be a woodsman, my dear, ya need to toughen up." He flexed his arm, grabbed Nellie Ann's fingers, and pressed them against the muscle. "What do ya feel?"

"Your muscle," Nellie Ann told him.

"Is it big?" he asked her. She nodded. "Now, Dalia, you touch it."

"I don't need to. I can see how big it is," Dalia said, keeping her tone even.

"I said, *touch it*," her father barked. As though rapping a watermelon to determine its ripeness, Dalia tapped her father's arm. "How does it feel, my Darling Doll?"

"Ripe," she said flatly, withdrawing her fingers.

"Ripe," he spat.

She heard the tight fury in his voice. "I—I meant strong," she stammered.

"Strong," he echoed, the muscles in his neck taut. "Yes, I'm strong, but that's not all I am. I didn't get rich through strength alone. So what else am I?" he asked Dalia. She fixed her face into a mask, said nothing. "What else am I, Nellie Ann?" he said, shifting toward her sister.

"I don't know," Nellie Ann said.

Dalia perceived the slight quiver in her sister's voice. Regaining her composure, she bit her bottom lip and eyed her father coldly. He jutted his jaw forward, the familiar little movement that meant he was gritting his teeth, then strode toward the bookshelves, his brogans scuffling over the floorboards. Scanning the rows of leather-bound volumes, he seized one off the shelf. "*Little Women* by Louisa May Alcott," he said, holding it up for Dalia to see. "This is one of your mama's. She's read it to you, hasn't she, girls?"

Nellie Ann murmured, "Yessir," while Dalia studied the gold lettering on the book's brown leather cover.

"Yes, your mama is well read," he said, slamming the book shut and shoving it back on the shelf. "She went to finishing school, knows her Shakespeare, recites her po-e-try," he said, ridiculing the word. "Your mama thinks she married beneath her." He kicked a small stool beside him and sent it sliding over the floor. It thudded against the far end of the bookshelves. He walked over to the stool, stepped up, and—without any hesitation—grabbed a thick, heavy volume with a frayed green cover and tiny tags of yellow paper sticking out like teeth from the inside pages. "Now, this one's mine," he announced, his voice grinding upward. "*The Coastal Plains of the South: The Glorious Elixir of the Longleaf Pines*." He reined in his voice and spoke slowly. "I know this book. I've read it more than once from cover to cover." He flipped the book over. "Dalia, tell your sister how long it is," he said, pointing at the page number with his finger.

"Seven hundred and sixty-two pages," she replied.

"Describe the print," he ordered her.

"Very small," Dalia said.

"This book here was my education. It helped me to become a self-made man, taught me all there was to know about pine trees and turpentining," her father said, pushing the book in Dalia's direction. "And I have read it many times over, and why did I do that?" he asked. Both Dalia and her sister were quiet. "I'll tell you," he said seconds later. "I did it because I'm smart, because I work hard—both my mind and my body." He caught Dalia with his eyes. "And that's fortunate for you, my daughters, because for all your mother's fine upbringing, for all her high-class ways, she was penniless when I married her. Penniless, I tell you. Dalia, did ya hear me?"

"Yes, Papa," she said obediently, her haughtiness leaving her like sand passing through an hourglass.

He took a long stride forward and set his book on the desk. "When the slaves were freed," he enlarged, returning his attention to them, "I was a happy man." Knitting his fingers together, he smiled knowingly. "Happy," he repeated, " 'cause it meant those highfalutin cotton planters would flounder." He released his fingers and bent over to caress the book's green cover. "Men like your mama's father had manners. Not a coarse or common bone in their bodies, I'd say, but the one thing they didn't have was a taste for hard work. The slaves did all the hard work for them. Poor souls didn't know how to get their clean hands dirty." He flicked the pages of his book with a stained thumbnail, then thrust his palms at Dalia. "But I did, my beauty. Yessir, when those big cotton planters were moaning and groaning and going under, I was being smart, makin' the most of their hard times." Pursing his lips, he said in a mocking falsetto, "*How can we grow our cotton without our slaves?* they whined. But a real man doesn't complain, my children. No, a real man shuns self-pity. He doesn't have time for such nonsense. A real man goes out into the real world and does what needs to be done. He seizes the opportunity in front of him. He opens his eyes and sees the pines, right there for the takin', just beggin' to be used. And if he has to, he'll do the work himself, with his own bare hands, and that's exactly what I did, my darlings. In the piney woods, alongside the black man, I worked. Worked long enough and hard enough to give you the gifts of time and money. *And why did I do that?* I ask myself. So that I can come home and catch you wearin' my clothes and makin' a joke of me right here in my study? You two, with nothing to show except a galling disrespect for your father."

"Papa," Dalia said, her voice now apologetic, but Monroe pushed her regret aside.

"Too little, too late," he told her. "And you, Nellie Ann." He glared at the brogans she was wearing. "You could never be a woodsman because a woodsman is tough. He doesn't sit around all day feeling sorry for himself, asking, *Why me?*"

"I don't feel sorry for myself," Nellie Ann countered. "A person doesn't miss sight if she's never seen. Regardless, my mind makes up for my blindness." Extending her arms, with fingers splayed, she sucked in her stomach, the big heavy brogans almost falling off her feet as she floundered forward.

"Dalia, take your sister upstairs," their father said stiffly. "I can't stand to look at either of you a second longer. I want you both away."

Dalia leaned over and retrieved her sister's cane. Then, taking hold of Nellie Ann's hand, she led her toward the doorway—watching her weave easily and gracefully around the furniture like a fishing line around cattails in the river, her sister's mind making up for her blindness, just like she said.

Her father had sent both of them to bed without their supper, and now Dalia was famished. Her sister was fast asleep, but she wanted something sweet, one of Katie Mae's sugar cookies in the kitchen. As she tiptoed toward the staircase, lightning flashed through the landing window and lit up the darkness. No need for this, she thought, puffing out the flickering candle, setting the holder on the floor beside the banister. She was about to descend when she heard him—his brogans thunking loudly upon the floor. Startled, she came to a standstill. Even as the rain splattered against the window, she could hear them. Her father saying, "Violet, I love you." Her mother repeating his name, "Monroe, Monroe, Monroe," in a voice that was tender, filled with yearning, as though she didn't hate him at all. It was then the wind began to blow fiercely, making the pecan trees throw tantrums against the glass.

Dalia hurried down the hallway, back to her bedroom. Quietly, she slipped under the covers. Outside her window, the shower turned into a storm. Beneath a volley of thunderclaps, she lay still as stone. Her thoughts raced with sad confusion as she listened to the jewelry box that rattled on her dresser bureau, to the strange sounds that emanated from her parents' bedroom.

At three in the morning, a bang jolted Dalia up. Half asleep, she didn't know if she was awake or dreaming. Then the door shook again, followed by the bellow of her father's voice, "Time to get up. Rise and shine."

"What?" Dalia murmured, settling back on her elbows.

Her father stuck his head through the door. Light danced over the floor as he thumped a lamp on a low stool adjacent to the wall. "Both of you, get up. Right now. We're taking a little trip."

"But Papa," Dalia grumbled, squeezing her eyelids shut, blinking them back open. Through the slit door, her papa's face protruded like a gargoyle. "It's night out."

"No, it's not. It's early morning," her father said, his voice firm and resolute. "Now both of you get up. It's time you visit my camp, see first-hand how I make my living." Before Dalia could object, his footsteps were clumping down the hallway, next padding along the plush Persian runner that ran the length of the stairs.

"*Psssss. Psssss.* Nellie Ann," Dalia whispered. "Nellie Ann."

"What?" her sister moaned. "What is it?"

"We must get up," Dalia told her. "Papa's taking us to his camp."

"But why?"

"Wants us to see how he makes a living."

"I'm sleepy," Nellie Ann said, pulling the sheet up over her head.

"You can sleep tonight."

"I want to sleep now," her sister whined.

"You can sleep in the back of the wagon on the way there."

"The wagon's hard," Nellie Ann griped, her head and shoulders sliding groggily up the headboard. "I don't want to go to Papa's silly ole town." Rankled, she banged the back of her skull against the wooden slats.

"Stop that," Dalia scolded. "Your caterwauling's gonna wake Mama up." Dalia hurled herself off the bed, stumping her toe on the pine-planked floor. "Ouch," she grumbled, limping over to her sister's bed. After whipping back the mosquito net, she roped the ends around the bedposts and, clamping her fingers around Nellie Ann's forearm, gave her a hearty tug.

"I don't want to get up," her sister said, swatting at Dalia's fingers.

"But you must," Dalia insisted, guiding her over to the edge of the bed, positioning her feet upon the bed steps.

She helped her sister dress, then quickly dressed herself, buttoning her shirtwaist by rote, the familiarity of the process unnerving, as though somehow disconnected from her fingers.

"Breakfast is ready!" boomed his disembodied voice from the bottom of the stairs.

Dalia put her arm around Nellie Ann's waist, led her out the bedroom door and toward the landing, their dark skirts dragging down the steps. On a pink marble table at the bottom of the staircase, a candle moth slammed against a brightly lit lamp, its wings depositing bruises on the globe of glass. Raindrops from last night's storm hopscotched through the oak leaves outside the drawing room window and landed on the flagstone drive. As soon as they headed down the hallway, the odor of sausage and fried eggs grabbed Dalia by the throat, and pressing her hand against her mouth, she gagged.

"What's wrong?" her sister asked. "Are you feeling bad?"

"Just nervous," Dalia replied, the nausea making her breathless.

When they crossed the threshold into the kitchen, Katie Mae looked up from the pot of grits she was stirring. The grits bubbled up and splattered white dots on her dark hands, but her eyes registered no sign of the scalding, only concern for Nellie Ann, whose cane tapped over the floor toward her.

A mild breeze rustled the pine boughs that shadowed the rutted road. The white tree faces shone in the sudsy moonlight. The sharp smell from the sap stung Dalia's nose and kept her from sleeping, even though Nellie Ann dozed peacefully beside her. They were in the back of the wagon—their heads propped up on pillows, their bodies covered by a threadbare quilt. Dalia heard their papa, briskly flicking the reins against the old mule's back. The wagon lurched forward, the front right wheel bottoming into a puddle, sending forth a spray of muddy water. Dalia tilted her face up and caught her father looking over his shoulder.

"Did Slash get ya?" he asked.

"A little," she replied, wiping the droplets off her neck, staring at Tarkel, hitched to the back of the wagon.

Her father returned his gaze to the road. "All those white blazes on the pines put me in mind of tombstones," he said, laughing. "Like those cemeteries in New Orleans, where they bury their folk aboveground."

He kept on talking, but Dalia, lulled by the rocking of the wagon and the clip-clopping of Tarkel's hooves, was drifting off. She was dreaming of sugar cookies when, through the fog of her sleep, a voice said, "Wake up, girls." Startled, Dalia jerked her eyelids open. For a moment, she was confused as to where she was, but then it came to her. She and her sister were still lying in the back of their father's wagon. Daylight bullied its way through the overcast sky. The dew-covered pine needles sparkled like prisms in the shafts of light. The plank seat creaked. There was a loud puff, followed by a plume of smoke as her father blew out the flame in the lamp beside him.

"Do ya'll see it, girls?" he said. "Do ya'll see my town?"

Dalia yawned and cast her eyes over lines of slab shanties resembling boxcars on both sides of the road. "Yessir," she said.

"Those are the homes of my black woodsmen," her father said.

Glancing around, Dalia took in cradles on cypress-covered porches, women scattering corn to chickens in bald front yards. She caught a whiff of the strong, heavy odor of mustard greens coming from a kettle over a cone-shaped pit.

"Look at those big fireplaces," her father told her. "They throw out plenty of heat when winter comes. And those thick shutters to keep the cold wind out. No pole shanties with dirt floors for my woodsmen," he said proudly. "I made a vow to treat my workers good."

Beside her, Nellie Ann was beginning to fidget, fluttering her eyelids as she awoke. "Rise and shine, sleepyhead," Dalia said.

Her father stretched out his long arm and pointed. "See the gardens out back?" Dalia sat upright, swiveled around on her knees to face the front. "The women sell their vegetables to the commissary. This way, they have more money in their pockets." A man with hair the color of forsythia rattled by in a large supply wagon. "Howdy, Jude," her father said, tipping his hat. "That's Mr. Taylor, my blacksmith. Ain't his hair yellow, though?"

"Yessir," Dalia said, spotting a two-story structure on the right side of the road. "What's that tall building for?"

"That's where the fire still is housed," her father said. "Dalia, was that your sister I heard moving around?"

"I'm up," Nellie Ann said drowsily.

"It's about time," their father said. "We've almost run out of town."

"It must not be very big, then," Nellie Ann said.

"Naw, it ain't big, but it sure is fine," their father told her.

They passed a ramshackle, gray-planked structure, which according to their father was the blacksmith's shop, where the horses were shod and the woodsmen's tools were repaired.

"What kinds of tools, Papa?" Nellie Ann asked.

"The tools of my trade, sugar—the hack, bush axe, caliper, dip iron," he listed. "Each one of them does something different." Dalia breathed in the warm, wet air, felt her clothes sticking to her skin. "The small building beside it is the cooper shed. My barrels are made out of those wooden staves stacked right there on the ground, and that whitewashed building over there with the picket fence is the schoolhouse," their father said. "I hired a teacher to come with it. He rides out twice a week. Teaches the white kids one day, the black kids the next."

"If it's a schoolhouse, why is there a cross on top?" Dalia asked.

" 'Cause it doubles as a church on Sundays," her father explained, shifting on the plank seat until she could see his full profile. "No other camp in these parts has houses as fine as mine," he boasted as they drove by a string of neat whitewashed dwellings. "My white families live in those." Dalia noted that, unlike the homes for the black woodsmen and their families, these had two large fireplaces, one on each end, and glass panes in the windows. "I reckon it was foolish of me to build them, 'cause when the trees are all worked out, they'll have to be taken down, built back on new ground. Still . . ." He quit talking, was quiet for a moment, nibbling on his mustache, the way he always did when he was thinking. "But you see, girls, most of my people have been with me for a long time," he said, breathing in deeply, wiping off a bead of sweat dribbling from his sideburn. "I don't wanna be like other turpentiners, having to recruit new workers all the time. No, I wanna be remembered. I want my name to live on, like the names of writers of famous books. I want my woodsmen to call me a good man, long after I'm gone."

Dalia wanted to say something to him but couldn't find the words.

"Mr. Monroe! Mr. Monroe!" a boy shouted as Slash drew up to a lot and barn. Dalia turned toward the voice and saw a small yellow-haired boy racing toward them. "Mama's got breakfast ready," he said breathlessly, "if ya wanna eat something." The boy hitched Slash up to a lightwood post, glistening from last night's rain. "Tarkel, ole boy," he gushed, making a dash for the back of the wagon. "I've been missing ya." He grabbed a fistful of the horse's mane and washed his face in it. "Ole Tarkel," he said, his eyes closing, air wheezing through his nose.

"Johnny Cake," her father said, his tone impatient.

The boy released Tarkel's mane and looked up. Dalia looked back at him. "Who are them girls?" he asked, blinking nervously.

"My children," their father said.

"I'm Dalia," she said, thrusting out her hand as the boy rushed over and scrabbled up the side of the wagon, his elbows braced on the wooden ledge. "And this is Nellie Ann," she added, her arm growing heavy as she waited for him to shake her hand.

"I can't. They're dirty," the boy said, jumping down, holding up his palms for her to see.

"It's all right, son," their father said, straddling over the wheel, easing himself onto the ground. "A little bit of dirt won't hurt my girls none, will it?"

"No, sir," Dalia said.

"Ya sure?" the boy asked.

Monroe Miller tugged on his black mustache and dipped his head. Whereupon the boy climbed back up the side of the wagon and squeezed Dalia's hand. "I'm Johnny Cake Jones," he said.

"Nellie Ann, shake hands with Johnny Cake, too," Dalia said, pulling her sister over with a tug on her skirt.

Her wet bangs plastered against her forehead, Nellie Ann leaned forward, sideswiping Dalia with her elbow. "Pleased to meet you, Mr. Johnny Cake Jones," she said, reaching out for his hand, which Johnny Cake promptly withdrew.

"Ain't nothing to be scared of," their father said when Johnny Cake glanced over his shoulder at him. "My girl's blind, that's all. Blindness ain't catching." Johnny Cake came back to Nellie Ann. "Shake her hand, son, like a gentleman."

Drawing himself up, Johnny Cake took hold of her fingers and joggled them. "Does it hurt?" he asked, quickly letting them go as if they were hot embers, then scrambling down.

"Not at all," Nellie Ann replied, slyly smiling, rubbing the corners of her eyes with her knobby fists. "I'm perfectly fine. No different than you are, really. Isn't that so, Papa?"

Dalia knew what her sister was doing—pretending not to be bothered by her blindness while making others feel sorry for her.

"Oh, don't worry about her, son. Her eyes don't hurt her none." Same as Dalia, their father saw through these performances of Nellie Ann. Grinning at Johnny Cake, he added, "Anyhow, she sees more than she lets on."

Johnny Cake smiled back at their father. "Mama's got a pot of coffee brewin' and biscuits in the warming oven, if ya'll are hungry," he reminded them, shaking his mop of yellow hair.

"Tell your mama thank ya," their father said, "but we ate at the house. Right now I wanna show the girls around. When they was little, I showed 'em how to box a longleaf behind Miller's Mansion, but they ain't never been to my town."

"Why don't you take 'em to the store?" Johnny Cake said, pointing at a large white structure nestled among a cluster of pine trees. "Give 'em a taste of candy."

"Candy?" Nellie Ann echoed, raising her eyebrows. "Papa, can I have another one of your kisses?"

"Not now," their father said, turning his back to the boy. "Not till we return from the drifts," he told her. "Not till you and Dalia understand what hard work is like. When you learn the value of a dollar, maybe then I'll take you."

Everywhere Dalia saw children playing. They were rolling hoops with sticks. Skipping rope. Running and laughing. Anchoring her hand above her eyebrows, she looked in the direction of the store, which had a wide front porch with a sign saying MILLER'S COMMISSARY hanging by chains from the porch roof. Suddenly the store door flew open, and a short, squat man came speeding through. He took the porch steps quickly and walked jauntily toward them.

"Mornin', Snead," her father said as the man approached.

"Mornin', Mr. Miller," the man chirped, clamping a pudgy hand on her father's shoulder. "When you get a chance, I'd like you to come see what I've done." He removed his hand and began to pinch his shirt, as though the feel of the fabric against his abdomen bothered him. "I reordered the shelves and took another look at the books, and Theodosha . . . well, you should see how she's prettied up the place." His pebble-gray eyes strayed over to the wagon. "Mr. Miller, are those two lovely girls your daughters?" he asked, his thin lips wrenching upward into a smile.

"Yessir," their father said, reaching into his shirt pocket, pulling out his pipe and a tin of tobacco. "Dalia, Nellie Ann, this here is Mr. Parrish. He runs my store." Dalia dipped her head. Nellie Ann batted her eyelashes. "My girls ain't never been to Millertown before, and I wanted 'em to see it." He tapped some tobacco into the pipe bowl and tamped it down with his thumb. Drawing a box of matches from his pants pocket, he lit up, sucked in, and blew out the rich, sugary smell.

Dalia twisted around when she heard footsteps behind her. A red-headed man was coming from the cooper shed on the other side of the road. "Howdy, Mr. Miller," he said as he strode over. Dalia had never seen such carrot-red hair before. Puckering his lips around the pipe stem, her father acknowledged the man with a nod. "We been dippin' so much gum I can hardly keep up with the barrels." The man snorted loudly, scratched the side of his nose. Dalia saw that his thumb was swollen and bruised, that there were half-moons of dirt under his nails. Tugging at his red beard, the man opened his mouth and a spate of tobacco juice hit the ground beside his boots.

"Well, then, Tysoe, if we're so busy, why aren't you working?" her father said, his tone joking. He winked at Johnny Cake. "Go on, boy, and tell your mama what I told ya." Johnny Cake sped off, his boot heels cutting little horseshoes in the damp sand. "Later, gentlemen," her father said, tipping the brim of his hat, his voice warm and friendly. "Right now I best get goin'. Gotta show my girls a stand of cat-face pines."

"Good day," the two men said, taking the pathway to the commissary.

Her father retrieved Tarkel from the back of the wagon and led him over to a lightwood post, where he tied him. Slipping his pipe from his mouth, he knocked it against the rain-splattered post and inserted the stem into his shirt pocket. Unhitching the mule, he climbed up on the plank seat. "Are ya'll ready?" he asked, glancing back at them.

"Yessir," Dalia replied.

"Nellie Ann?"

"Yessir," her sister mumbled, "I can't wait to see *your* tall pines."

Their father made a clucking sound, and Slash began kerplunking over the narrow sandy road, the wagon groaning whenever they hit a pothole. The sun had grown bright in the sky. The air heavy, like a soggy overcoat. Dalia spotted a covey of quail in a clump of wiregrass, their white, brown, and gold feathers an Indian headdress in the gleaming sun. From up high in the trees came birdsong. The wagon rolled into a small clearing. "Girls, we're here. You've got some work to see," their father said, crunching hickory nuts when he jumped down from the plank seat. After hitching Slash to the hickory tree, he helped Nellie Ann out of the wagon. Motioning for them to follow, he loped over to a black man beside a longleaf covered with white streaks. "Morning, Jigsaw. These are my girls. Show them how we cut those streaks." The black man pulled a tattered piece of cloth from a shirt pocket and wiped off his brow. Nodding at their father, he breathed in deeply. Leaning back, he threw his weight forward. The long handle of the puller sliced through the air. The blade bit the bark, and the pine shuddered, raining driblets of water from last night's storm. "What do ya think of that, Dalia?"

"Looks hard to me," she said, staring at the clean white streak.

"Nellie Ann, can you smell the sap?" their father asked.

"Yessir," her sister said, her nostrils flaring.

"Come over here to me," he told Nellie Ann. "Since ya can't see it, I want ya to touch the cut with your fingers."

Her sister shuffled over the straw-strewn ground, weaving around tufts of wiregrass, batting at pine cones with her cane.

"It does look like a cat's face," Dalia said, trailing behind her.

"That's why they call it a cat-face tree," Jigsaw said, his eyes glued on the streak he'd made. Then suddenly he pivoted, holding the puller like a shotgun against his shoulder. "Mr. Monroe, do ya see 'em? Them bobcats up there. Lookin' down on us, jist ready to pounce."

"Where?" Nellie Ann said, squealing.

"Ain't no cats up there, miss," Jigsaw told her.

"No bobcats?" her sister said, her voice falling.

"Nellie Ann, ya knew he was teasing," their father said, maneuvering the cane out of her sister's hand, giving it to Dalia. Coiling his fingers around Nellie Ann's forearm, he led her over to the longleaf. "I want ya to feel the streaks." He weighted his fingers on her shoulders. "Now squat down," he said, pushing until she was sitting on her calves. Raising her arms up high, he placed her palms against the white blaze.

"It's sticky," she said, scowling, jerking her hands away.

"That's the gum," their father explained. "It oozes out of the streaks and trickles down into the cavity below. Ya can wash it off later. Now put your hands back," he said. Tilting forward, frowning, Nellie Ann ran her fingers slowly down the tree trunk. "Can you feel the streaks coming to a point?" he asked her. She gave her head a nod. "Right below that point is the top of the box," he said. "Go ahead and feel it," he told her. Nellie Ann explored the sides of the box with the tips of her fingers. "The way it's cut shows the gum which way to flow," their father said. "Move on down a little more, and you'll come to the bottom. Reach in and touch it, Nellie Ann." She stalled, twisted her head over her shoulder, and rolled her milky eyes at him. "Don't worry, sugar. It was dipped this morning," their father said as her fingers inched over the edge and into the cavity. She brought her hand up to her nose, her features contorting as she inhaled the acrid scent.

"The sweetest smell on earth," their father said. "Ain't it, Jigsaw?"

"Yessir. Sweet as molasses."

Positioning his large hands beneath her armpits, their father helped

Nellie Ann up. "Yes, missy, the blaze on this longleaf is a big one," he said. "Lean forward and put your palms flat against it. You'll see just how big it is."

Nellie Ann did as she was told.

"Do ya feel the cat-face, sugar, that glorious elixir against your skin?"

She didn't answer, only fluttered her fingertips against the blaze of gum.

"Well, do ya?"

"Yessir," Nellie Ann mumbled.

"Tar, pitch, rosin, and turpentine are made from this gum. It puts the clothes on your back and the food in your belly, my daughter. Without these beautiful trees and the hard work of my woodsmen, where would our family be?"

With her head flung back, Nellie Ann began to sway rapturously.

"Nellie Ann? I'm talking to you. Didn't you hear me?" their father said.

"Our family would be in the poorhouse, Papa," Nellie Ann replied.

"That's right," he said. "I've worked hard to give you nice things."

Her swaying became rhythmical.

"You see, my child, I've made a huge difference in your life."

"That's right, Papa. You have," she said, still undulating. "I'm different all right, so different that the townsfolk have brushed me aside." She coiled toward their father's voice, making slits of her albino eyes. "I'm friendless, laughed at behind my back, but still tall and proud as this fine old pine." Leaning forward, she ran the tip of her tongue over the blaze. Then, planting her lips against the tree face, she kissed it.

For a full minute, their father stared at Nellie Ann, her mouth flush against the gash. Dalia saw the bewildered look on her father's face, recognized the sting of shame in his ice-blue eyes. His chin shook. His lips parted, and Dalia feared he was about to scream or, worse, break down and cry, when God delivered them all with a gentle mist of rain.

"Why did you do that?" Dalia asked Nellie Ann as they sat on a damp bench under a spindly pine. Their father was inside the commissary, talking business with Snead Parrish. The town, having surrendered to the heat, had grown quiet. Only the periodic howl of a hound broke the silence. "Why did you embarrass Papa and me that way?" Dalia swallowed a mouthful of the muggy air and waited for her sister to speak.

"I don't know what you're talking about," she muttered.

"You false, girl," Dalia snapped. "Don't pretend with me. You kissed that pine tree because you wanted to make him feel foolish. Well, I hope you're satisfied."

Nellie Ann tweezed a damp strand of hair between her lips and sucked on it. Spitting it out, she said, "If I was mad at him, I didn't know it."

"You didn't know it?" Dalia said, her tone incredulous.

"No, I didn't," Nellie Ann insisted. "It just happened."

"Listen to me," Dalia said. "Regardless of what you think, our papa loves you." She took hold of her sister's chin and turned her face toward her. "After all, you're his daughter, too."

"No, you're his daughter," Nellie Ann said, with no trace of anger in her voice. "You're the pretty one, with your thick dark ringlets and your beautiful lilac eyes. He's not ashamed of you."

"He's proud of you, too. You're the smart one," Dalia countered. "The talented one. His face lights up whenever you play the piano. You've earned his approval the hard way."

Nellie Ann blinked her eyelids uneasily, her pale lashes invisible against her skin. "Papa doesn't know anything about music."

"His face—" Dalia began.

"His face lights up," Nellie Ann restated, in a voice growing sharper by the second, "the instant he sees your beautiful face."

"I was born pretty. No effort, no talent in that."

"You've always been his favorite," Nellie Ann said. "And you know it. Your beauty is what he admires, not my talent."

"Oh, do be quiet!" Dalia exploded, jumping up. "Must I always be the one who pays? You're only thirteen, but already so bitter."

Nellie Ann reached for her cane, propped on the bench beside her. "Dalia, please . . . Dalia," she stammered.

"What?" Dalia said, spinning on her heel. "What do you want now? Are you going to apologize? Are you going to tell me you're sorry?"

The blood drained from Nellie Ann's cheeks. "I didn't mean—"

"You meant it," Dalia spat. "I can still see the jealousy in your face. There's not a trace of sorrow."

Nellie Ann stuck her cane into the soft sand and on rubbery legs wobbled upward. "But Dalia," she moaned, "I promise, I didn't mean . . ."

"Yes, I know. I know," Dalia said, her voice now resigned and weary. "It just happened. I've heard that excuse so many times before. It's always like that with Mama, Papa, and me, but never with Katie Mae, is it? Just don't bother," she said, when Nellie Ann started to speak. "The only person you admire around here is Katie Mae. You treat her with more respect than you do your own family."

"Please, Dalia, you know that . . ." her sister was saying.

But Dalia turned off the flow of her sister's words. She was tired of Nellie Ann's jealousy. Her sister wasn't really asking for forgiveness. Forgiveness was nothing more than a weapon in her hands, a way of wielding power. Dalia uttered a throaty sigh and pivoted.

"Don't go," Nellie Ann pleaded.

This time, Dalia refused to play the role of a martyr. Her shoes squelched over the damp ground as she left, ignoring her sister's cries. A squirrel was chattering somewhere in a longleaf above her. A feisty dog was barking in a yard nearby. In the distance, a hog let out a squeal. Retracing her steps through a scattering of sumac, she kept going until she came to the main road through town. Her long legs veered to the right as she loped toward the schoolhouse, the cooper shed, the blacksmith's shop. All of a sudden the hog squealed again, but this time its cry was different—high, shrill, and frightened. Dalia began to move faster, swinging her arms to propel herself forward as she followed the strange sound. She scurried through a front yard studded with dying azalea bushes, and rounded the corner of a tidy white house. Not thirty feet away, two boys, with long sticks in their hands, were chasing a large sow, her swollen tits brushing against the ground as she ran frantically from them. "Stop, Billy. Go the other way," the older boy yelled, swinging his stick like a lariat above his head. "We'll trap her."

The younger one dug in his heels, lost his balance, and reeled forward, skidding through the damp sand. "I done had me a spill," he said, leaping up, laughing.

"Shoot," the older boy said, coming to a standstill, disgustedly throwing his stick down.

"Hey, there!" Dalia called out. She waved her arms above her head and continued waving until she caught their attention. With a wrench of his thumb, the older one signaled her over. Hiking up her skirt, she ran to him. "If ya want," she said, panting,"I'll help."

"Why?" he asked, eyeing her suspiciously.

"It looks fun," she said.

"We don't need no silly girl to help us," the younger boy said.

"Hush up, Billy," the older one warned.

"But Thomas?"

"No, we gotta get Princess back into her pen," he said, turning his gaze on Dalia. "All right, then," he told her. "But if ya fall down like my brother, ya better not start bawling."

"I won't," Dalia promised, flapping her skirt like a matador's cape as she strode toward the sow.

Afterward, she meandered to the cooper shed and watched as Mr. Tysoe Austen cut staves for rosin barrels. When he showed her his bruised thumb with its blue-black nail, she winced, and they talked for a while, but then, feeling mindful of her sister, she decided to go back to the bench where she'd left her.

Near the pathway to the commissary, a flock of worrisome crows were cawing, their screeches frenzied and querulous, their wings whirring as they settled into a locust tree. She fixed her eyes on their tar-black feathers, glinting purple and blue through the leaves, her gaze jumping from one limb to another, piggybacking from crow to crow all the way down. Her mama called them nasty scavengers. *They feed on the dead,* she said. *Let fate do the hard work for them,* but Dalia, like her father, had always loved them.

As she oscillated through the sumac trees toward the pines and the commissary, she heard her sister yelling, "Give me back my cane!"

A voice taunted, "Can't ya see it, white eyes?"

What had she done? she thought, running as alarm spread like a stain through her and her heart slammed against her chest.

Another voice floated toward her. "Give her back her cane, Thomas."

"No, let her come and get it," he shot back.

Yanking up her skirt, she ran even faster, the bottoms of her shoes smacking into mud puddles, sliding over the slick wet ground. What have I done? What have I done? her mind kept repeating as she sprinted, her breathing hard and heavy. "Nellie Ann. Nellie Ann," she said, panting. Nearing the cluster of pines, she bent over, her hands on her knees, inhaling deeply. She scanned the clearing, her stomach knotting when she saw the empty bench. Her eyes flitted anxiously to the shallow puddles of gray water, to the patches of sunlight on the pine-needled ground, to the hedge of sumac just beyond her. "Nellie Ann," she gasped, panicking. It was then, through a break in the sumac, she saw Thomas, whipping the cane through the air, smacking the ground beside her sister's fingers. She was about to scream when she saw her father stomping toward them.

"You little bastard, give me that," her father said, his face twisted as his brogans splattered through a puddle. Lunging, he clamped his fingers on top of the boy's hand. Thomas jerked back. Her father's hand flew up. There was a loud, crackling sound. "Ya piece of white trash," he snarled as the boy was sent sprawling backward.

At that moment, the air seemed to crystallize in the space around them, encasing every sound—the plunk of a pine cone, the caw of a crow, the sobs of her sister as she crawled toward their father over the hot, wet ground.

"Ya hurt my brother," Billy said, coming out from behind a pine.

"My Nellie Ann," their father said, emitting a sad, disheartened cry.

"Papa," she wailed, her shoulders heaving. "Dalia left me out here all alone."

Wrapping his arms around her, he held her close. "If he hurts you again, I'll kill him," he promised, oblivious to the sound of their footsteps as the boys fled. "How could you?" he said, knifing Dalia with his eyes when she approached. "You left her alone, and those boys hurt her." Nellie Ann choked back a sob. "I didn't think you could be so heartless. I was right inside that door. Why didn't you tell me you were leaving?"

Dalia stared at the anguish in his face, at his strong arms around her sister's body. "Papa," she muttered, tears pricking her eyes. There was nothing to say, no words to defend her. Groaning, she turned away from them. She felt the guilty swish of her blood pulsing in her arteries, her heart aching with the shame it carried. She tore through the sumac and staggered back through the pines, her eyes blinded by tears, her fingers touching the scaly bark, her nose burning from the strong smell of the gum. Fool, she admonished herself, as her feet took her forward as if they held some secret and would in time tell her where she was going. She lurched over the bald earth in front of the boys' house, skimming past the dying azalea bushes. When she reached the gate, she released the latch, as though all along she were destined to do it, and kicked the gate open, but the sow, grubbing for scraps, took no notice. She kicked the gate again, so forcefully that she splintered a slat, then watched with steely calm as the animal, snorting with anger, trod through.

Papa flicked the reins to make Slash move faster down the road. He and Nellie Ann giggled on the seat up front, while Dalia sat alone in the back of the wagon, their laughter falling over her. Dalia tried to lose herself in the clomping of Tarkel's hooves, in his large dark eyes staring at her, but try as she might she couldn't block out their affection. Last week, her sister had chosen Katie Mae. Today, she rightfully chose their papa, for this was how it was and would always be with her sister. If Nellie Ann varied the orbits of those around her, they could never be sure of her love and would work even harder to win her over. This was how her sister made up for her blindness, how she wielded power.

A sparrow chirped, splashing in a puddle by the road. A white heron curled up his leg as though it were in a sling beneath him. Now Papa and Nellie Ann were whispering, chuckling softly at some shared joke. Closing her eyes, Dalia leaned back against the wagon, ruminating, when out of nowhere a scream jerked her out of her thoughts and plinked her eyelids open.

"Stop! Stop!" the woman was yelling as she chased them.

"Papa!" Dalia shouted, catching sight of the bloody blanket pressed against the woman's shoulder. "Stop!"

With a quick snatch of the reins, her father brought the wagon to a halt. In one fluid movement, he leapt over the wagon wheel to the ground. "Mrs. Taylor, what is it?" he asked as soon as he turned around.

"My baby," she cried, running over. "Look at her." She thrust the baby at him, the crimson edges of the blanket parting. "Sow done gone and bit her leg," she groaned.

Oh, my God, thought Dalia, putting her hands over her eyes.

"Dalia, come here. I need you," her father said, his voice calm and steady.

Dalia removed her trembling hands. Taking a deep breath, she flattened her fingers against the wooden slats and pushed her body up. Then, clamping her hands on the wagon side, she flung a leg over and was straddling it precariously when her father reached up beneath her skirt and tore off a piece of her petticoat. Immediately she jumped down. "Take hold of her leg," her father said as she came toward him.

"Please, don't hurt my baby," the woman begged when Dalia curled her fingers around the infant's thigh.

"Tighter," Monroe ordered, while the baby thrashed and cried. "We gotta stop this bleeding." Rapidly, he tied the strip of petticoat around the gaping wound. From his shirt pocket he retrieved the silver flask of bourbon, unscrewed the top, and stuck in his forefinger. Next, he eased his finger into the baby's mouth, repeating the process until the child grew still and quiet. "Dalia, get your sister and go to the store," he told her. "Tell Mr. Parrish what happened. Ask him to drive you to Doc Green's in town. Remember to take Tarkel with you."

Nellie Ann was cowering on the plank seat, her white eyes wide and fearful. "Will the baby be all right?" she asked as Dalia helped her down.

Like dandelion fluff in a strong wind, Dalia felt her ambivalence toward her sister disappearing, and as she was about to reassure her, she overheard their father saying—in a voice so peaceful, so calming he could have been giving grace—"Mrs. Taylor, don't ya worry, now. The good Lord will take care of your little girl."

When they left Doc Green's office, darkness had already fallen. The thin blade of moon glinted weakly through the pines, as erect as sentries. Only the lantern on the front seat and a smattering of stars in the milky sky lit up the night. Bumping along in the wagon, Dalia tried not to ponder the day. How could she have known? How could she have known the child was in a cradle on the front porch while its mother attended to the injury Papa had inflicted upon her son's face? Dalia didn't want to think about letting the sow out, but her guilty conscience, breathing down her neck, made her. Were it not for her petty emotions and impulsive actions, she never would have abandoned Nellie Ann, and the baby would have slept unscathed.

Dalia listened to her father filling the bowl of his pipe with Prince Albert, scratching the match against his thumbnail. The phosphorous burn tingled her nostrils, then came the familiar, soothing smell of the tobacco, sweet as burnt sugar. Closing her eyes, she inhaled the odor and tried to think about less troublesome things. Beside her, Nellie Ann dozed, her breathing soft and rhythmic, guiltless and free. Dalia nestled down under the thin quilt, nudging herself against her sister's body. As mesmerizing as a metronome, the wagon rocked over the rough road. Dalia yawned and begged sleep to take over. Yet in the darkness behind her eyelids, the baby's grisly leg appeared. She choked, lurched upward, grappling with the bloody image. Beside her, Nellie Ann continued to rest soundly. Twisting around, Dalia saw tobacco smoke twining upward. A breeze hit it, broke it apart, and sent it toward the longleafs, their blazes ghostly in the vaporous night air. Staring into those white cat faces, Dalia—for the first time in her life—felt her father's pain. Spanning the gulf that lay between them, she understood at last how the pines had come to save him. Like the bread crumbs of Hansel and Gretel, they had illuminated his way, replacing the white eyes of her sister with their white blazes.

While Monroe drove the wagon, his mind kept repeating, Me and Nellie Ann. When a beetle sizzled in the lantern's flame, the phrase smoked inside him. Me and Nellie Ann, the ashes said to him seconds later. In the back of the wagon, the girls were asleep, although once he heard Dalia coughing. "Me and Nellie Ann," he whispered, imagining that his hand was the hand of God, smiting the boy's face. He recalled Dalia's eyes, filled with guilt and shame when he'd confronted her, but then his thoughts returned to the hand. It was his hand that did it, his will that ruled the hand, his love for Nellie Ann that had fueled his movement. In that slap, he had resurrected the love deep inside him, transformed it into action, and proven to himself and his daughter that his affection for her was and had always been.

Me and Nellie Ann, he thought, knocking the ashes out of his pipe. He tamped the last of his tobacco into the bowl, struck another match, and sucked in as he held the flame to the soft, cured leaves. The smoke warmed the inside of his mouth, and he kept it there. Blowing it back out, he wondered why the slap had taken so long to happen. Me and Nellie Ann, he thought, smiling wistfully, recalling his arms around his daughter, his hands rubbing love into her skin. Spinning high with hope, falling low into sorrow, the day had risen again with hope as the hours passed away. The boy's nose would mend. The baby's leg would heal. In the end, no one had fallen from grace.

Her father and Nellie Ann mounted the steps together. His arm was around her sister's waist. Her head against him. Timidly, Dalia followed, wrapping herself in the old quilt to cover her bloodstained frock and her shame. She noticed the flick of drapery and knew that her mother was waiting in the drawing room for them. "We're hungry," her father said as they crossed into the foyer.

"Hungry as woodsmen," Nellie Ann said, tilting her face upward, smiling at him.

Except for the rasp of her breath, Dalia was silent. Her father wiggled his fingers behind his back, an offering of peace, but she didn't deserve his hand.

"So how was your day at Millertown?" their mother asked.

"Oh, Mama, you should have been there," Nellie Ann said, pitching forward. "It was scary but also exciting, ever so exciting," she said with a dramatic shudder.

"Dalia?" their mother asked, rising on her toes to see over their father's shoulder. "Was your day as exciting as your sister's?"

Dalia shrugged, stared down at the floorboards.

"Well, let's roust up some food in the kitchen," their mother said, teetering slightly to the left. Then, regaining her balance, she turned around. "We can talk about your outing over supper," she said as she led them through the wide-arched doorway and down the hall to the kitchen.

Katie Mae was already laying out supper when they came in. "Miss Nellie Ann, did ya cut a streak in one of your papa's longleafs?" she asked.

"I touched a cat face," Nellie Ann said.

"And you, Miss Dalia?"

Dalia lowered her head, walked over to the long, rickety table, and sat down.

Katie Mae nodded, her black eyes narrow with judgment as she stared in their father's direction. "Let's see," she said, her hands flitting over the table as she returned to the task at hand. "There's ham, corn pudding, fried okra, shelly peas, biscuits, and redeye gravy. A mess of food left 'cause Miz Violet wasn't hungry at dinner."

"On account of my medicine," her mother said.

"Yessam," Katie Mae said, wiping her hands on a red-checked apron tied snugly around her waist. "Are ya tired, honey?" she asked, eyeing Nellie Ann.

"Not in the least," she said, as their father led her over to the table and pulled out a chair.

"But ya'll left so early," their mother said.

"I slept in the back of the wagon all the way there," Nellie Ann told them.

"Sometimes, your father doesn't think," their mother said.

"Just last week, I saw him fishin' in the goldfish pond out back in the middle of the night," Katie Mae said, seizing the gravy boat and stirring the redeye gravy.

"And did you catch anything, Papa?" Nellie Ann asked.

"I was aimin' to catch Moby Dick."

"Isn't that the big orange one with the black head?" her sister said.

"Yes, it is."

"And did you catch it?" their mother said.

"I forgot to bait my hook," their father said with a laugh.

"Forgot to bait it," their mother said, holding her blue-veined hand up to her mouth, giggling.

"Must've lost my senses," their father said. "Sitting there fishing, dead drunk."

Abruptly, Violet stopped giggling. "The girls hate it when you drink." She paused, then spoke brusquely. "On second thought, I'm still not hungry. I think I'll go upstairs and rest."

"But Mama," Nellie Ann pleaded. "We haven't told you about our trip."

"Another time," she said, flinging the words over her shoulder, shattering their father's smile, adding to Dalia's despair as she left.

"He stood up for me today, and that proves he loves me," Nellie Ann said that night as they lay waiting for sleep in their canopied beds. "So his love is stronger than his shame, isn't it?" She didn't wait for Dalia to answer, but rushed head-on into what she had to say. "I've always wanted him to love me, and I've always wanted to love him back, but it's been hard with his drinking." She was silent for a moment, then added dreamily, "You say his face lights up whenever he hears me play. I'd like to tell him how it feels when I touch the piano keys. I'd like to describe how the notes come together to make a painting of sounds. All these years, I've wanted to tell him this, but I've been scared to." She hesitated, clicking her tongue before she explained, "I was afraid he'd laugh at me. Laugh at me because he's ashamed, but his love is stronger than his shame. He hit that boy to protect me," she said proudly. "He hit that boy because he loves me."

"And do you still love me?" Dalia asked.

"You left me," Nellie Ann said accusingly.

"Can you find it in your heart to forgive me like you've forgiven him?"

"If the roles were reversed, would you?" her sister said.

A nightingale's song drifted through the trees and slipped through the mouth of the window. Dalia sunk her head into the down pillow. "Of course I would," she said easily, and yet fearful of giving Nellie Ann this extra power. Loving someone was confusing, she thought. Like the beauty of the nightingale's aria. Was it singing or crying? she wondered as she listened to its song.

CHAPTER 4

Dalia watched as Katie Mae prepared food for the piano recital. They both had been looking forward to this day. Katie Mae hummed as she placed the sugar, ginger, and chocolate cookies she had baked that morning on two large serving plates. The tea was steeping, the coffee brewing. The silver sugar bowl had been filled. The dining room table had already been set.

Katie Mae checked her hair, tucked the stray strands beneath the rim of her white cap. "I want to look good and presentable for my baby," she told Dalia. "Always felt like she was my own," she said, her voice distant as memory.

But Dalia heard her. She knew the whole story by heart: how Katie Mae had been in love once, how her man had died before she could have a child of her own, how Nellie Ann was fated to save her, how the two of them had saved each other.

"Soon as that poor blind babe was weaned off your mama's teat . . ." Katie Mae was saying.

Dalia felt a bite of envy. She wanted to be the one to save Nellie Ann.

"I remember back when she was little and couldn't sleep," Katie Mae went on. "I'd get the stove kindling burnin', warm up some milk, and pour it into her favorite cup—the one with the little roses around the top. She'd drink her milk, and we'd talk. My child tellin' me how her fingers tingle when she plays the piano, how the notes come together to make a picture of sounds. I know she sees more than she makes out. I know everything they is to know about her. Ya think ya do, but ya don't, Miss Dalia. A person has to know different—taste it, feel it, hear it, be it—have different marking on her skin—before she can really know the difference in Nellie Ann." Katie Mae stopped talking, clapped her eyes on Dalia, waiting, like she always did, for the rise she usually got, but today was Nellie Ann's day, and Dalia didn't want to stain it with bickering, with their tug-of-war over whom Nellie Ann loved best. "Yessam, this is my baby's day," Katie Mae said seconds later. She held out her hands and examined them. "Ain't no dough beneath my nails." After tightening her apron, she ironed it down over her stomach. "That girl has been practicing for weeks now. Five hours a day, her fingers dipping down, kissing the keys of that piano, and me back here in the kitchen, cooking, listening to the music, feeling the beautiful sounds."

It was the truth. Dalia had watched Katie Mae move from the summer kitchen out back to the one inside the house, so as to be near the piano. She had seen Katie Mae bake more in these past few weeks than in all the years before. Thick-fisted biscuits for breakfast, thin half-dollar ones for the noonday meal, buttermilk and baking-powder biscuits for supper. For hours, Katie Mae stood over the worktable, sifting flour and salt together, cutting in the shortening, slowly adding cream and a cup of cold springwater, then kneading, kneading, kneading, making pans and pans of beaten biscuits, all the while giving an ear to Nellie Ann's playing. She fixed cream, soda, stir-and-drop biscuits. She baked cornpone, cornmeal muffins, and corn sticks, and tossed in hoecakes and cracklin' bread for their father. She whipped together desserts, too—platters of sugar and molasses cookies, tins of gingerbread, a three-tiered jam cake, and several peach cobblers drenched in fresh thick cream. It was too early for the blackberries, she told Dalia, or else she would have cooked pots of blackberry dumplings and dishes of blackberry cobbler. Over time, Dalia had learned to respect Katie Mae's prowess at concocting excuses to stay put in the roomy kitchen, within shouting distance of Nellie Ann and her piano.

"Come with me," Katie Mae said, enlisting Dalia with an upward curl of her fingers. "Let's make sure the house looks clean and good." She pointed at the chandelier above the table in the dining room. "Do ya see any cobwebs?"

"It sparkles," Dalia told her.

Katie Mae went straightway to the music room. "What about this carpet?" she asked, tapping her shoe against the plush Persian rug. "I told Lucinda to beat it. Said I'd have her hide if she put it back on my clean floor dirty."

"Looks fine to me," Dalia said.

"And these floors?"

"Shiny as mirrors."

Spotting a bit of lint on the floor, Katie Mae leaned over and plucked it up, then cast her dark eyes up to the ceiling. "I made Lucinda take every prism off that chandelier and soak it in warm, soapy water. How does it look?" she asked, but before Dalia could answer, she was mumbling to herself, counting the number of straight-backed chairs fanning out in rows from the piano. "Do ya think we set out enough chairs?"

"I think so," Dalia told her. Earlier, she and Katie Mae had toted the settee and love seat and several small end tables to the downstairs bedchamber to make room for the seating.

"I polished the piano myself," Katie Mae said, going over to it, running her fingertips across the lid.

Behind the piano was a cypress mantel, painted reddish brown to resemble mahogany. The wood of respectable families, her mother always said. In the center of the mantel stood a vase of freshly cut yellow roses, delicate in the sunlight that spilled through the long ceiling-to-floor windows.

Katie Mae meandered to the French doors separating the music room from the drawing room. "They was swabbed with vinegar and water," she said, nodding at the small panes of glass. Opening the doors, she passed from the dark sage walls of the music room into the pale green drawing room. "Looks fine. Real fine," she whispered, looking around, her gaze settling on the gold silk curtains rippling in the breeze. "I best lower the windows a little," she said, going directly to them, her hands freezing in midair when voices came wafting through. She waved Dalia over, and they peeked out.

Drinking wine on the veranda in front of them were her father and a gentleman. Dalia remembered the man clearly—his thin brown pouf of hair, his flour-white skin, the expensive diamond-studded band on his right ring finger. He had visited their house several times before. Same as then, his nostrils were drawn upward, as if he smelled a skunk.

"Well, Lollie, the other day I was privy to something interesting," her father was saying. Pressing a crystal goblet against his lips, he took a swallow. "And what I heard was troubling."

"Oh?" the man said nonchalantly, his diamond ring flashing in the sun.

"Yessir," her father drawled, and stepped toward him. "I didn't peg ya as that sort of man."

"I'm a businessman, Monroe, just like you," the man said flatly, lifting up his glass, sipping. He smiled, his top lip riding upward, disappearing into his gums.

"Yessir," her father said, gulping from his goblet. "That's what ya are. A businessman, all right." He grinned broadly. "I ain't never seen a speck of dirt beneath your nails. Not a drop of gum on your clothes. Ya sit behind a desk marking papers. That's what ya do."

"Monroe, you've told me all this before. Anyway, you'd do well to follow my example," the man said, abruptly drawing himself up in his wicker chair.

"What?" Her father's eyebrows vaulted upward. "Cheat a poor ole fool like Willard Croton? Not me. I heard what ya done, Lollie Morris. Ya talked him into it. I know ya did. I worked hard for that land, years of backbreaking work, and that fool friend of mine practically gave it to you."

"Your land?" the man quipped, a half-mocking smile on his lips. "I thought the land belonged to Willard now. He told me you let him win it. You and your swollen sense of honor made it happen. Willard can do with that land as he pleases. It isn't yours anymore."

"My Lord, Lollie, ya cheated the man." Her father's voice was indignant. "A team of mules, some turpentine tools, and a little bit of money for eight hundred acres of prime virgin pines. You ain't a poor man, Lollie. You had the money to pay him fair for it. My whole life, I ain't never cheated a man."

Lollie Morris tossed back his head and swallowed the last of his wine as though it were a shot of whiskey. Then, with an ostentatious wave of his arm, he set the goblet on the wicker table beside him. "I'm a smart businessman," he said, tapping the side of his head with his diamond-ringed finger. "You'd have done the same," he said, sharpening his tone. "Anyhow, it doesn't matter. Willard told me he wanted to stay right here. Didn't want to leave his family for any piney woods in Florida."

"But it ain't—"

Lollie Morris cut him off. "Tell me, Monroe, what would've happened if you'd let that race run its course and your roach had won? Your dear friend would be broke now, wouldn't he?"

"But I didn't let that happen," her father said, standing.

"Well, trust me," Lollie countered. "Nothing wrong with puttin' family before land. As far as I'm concerned, everyone came out ahead, except you."

"Have it your way," her father said, downing another mouthful of wine as he started toward the door. "I've got more high-minded things to attend to. This recital will be starting soon."

"Yes, we should go. I believe my daughters are playing first," the man said, rising.

"Miss Gamble likes to save the best for last," Monroe told him. "That's when you'll hear my Nellie Ann perform."

"They're coming. Let's git," Katie Mae said, grabbing Dalia's hand, whisking her across the polished floor and dust-free rugs into the dining room, where she snatched a water-stained glass from off the table and replaced it with a clean one from the china cabinet. Peeking through the royal blue fringe draped over the archway, Dalia watched as the footman moved toward the front door.

"Katie Mae? Katie Mae?" came Nellie Ann's voice from behind her. Sly girl, Dalia thought, pivoting. She had stolen down the back stairs and come in through the kitchen. "How do I look? I know you'll be truthful with me." Katie Mae propped her hands on Nellie Ann's shoulders and eyed her up and down.

To Dalia, she looked awful. The peach taffeta dress failed to bring any color to her skin. Her cheeks were puffy, her posture stooped, her hands clutched stiffly by her sides.

"Well, Miss Nellie . . ." Dalia could almost hear Katie Mae's brain clicking, searching for the words. "Ya need to stand up straight and proud."

"Better?" Nellie Ann asked, throwing back her narrow shoulders.

"Uh-huh," Katie Mae mumbled, clasping the girl's hands, tenderly massaging her knuckles.

"I don't want people to think me foolish and ugly."

"Let's give ya some color. Now lift up your chin."

"That hurts," Nellie Ann whined, flinching as Katie Mae pinched the skin below her cheekbones.

"Healthy pink cheeks," Katie Mae said, taking a step back, surveying her charge. "Why, child, ya look just fine!"

"Yes, you do," Dalia added, coming over.

"Dalia, I didn't know you were here," her sister said.

"Katie Mae and I have been inspecting the place, making sure everything's in order."

"Have you seen Papa?" Nellie Ann asked. "How is he today?"

"Papa will be fine. He's very proud of you," Dalia answered.

"Has he been drinking?"

"He'll be fine," Dalia insisted, avoiding the question. "This is your special day, and he can't wait to hear you play."

"Wish me luck, then, you two."

"Give me your hand," Katie Mae said, turning it over. "I'm crossing my fingers." She placed her fingers against Nellie Ann's palm. "Do you feel 'em?"

"Yes, ma'am."

Dalia crossed her fingers also. "Do you feel mine?" she asked, as she pressed them against her sister's skin.

"Yes, I do," Nellie Ann said, standing there motionless, her palm up, her face relaxing as though their fingers were poultices drawing the tension out of her body.

"Feel the music, like ya always do," Katie Mae told her.

"Make us proud," Dalia said.

Grinning, Nellie Ann held her head up high, moving across the room, her cane confidently silent.

Dalia swiveled around, discerned the thin shape of Katie Mae, camouflaged behind the blue-draped archway. She spotted the toe of her dark shoe, the puckered tuck of the panel as her fingers pulled it to one side. Dalia heeded her father, perched drunkenly on the edge of his seat in the back row. So as not to draw too much attention to himself, Dalia thought, feeling grateful to him. A strange look, which she'd seen before, passed over his features and settled in his eyes. The crystal goblet quivered in his hand. All day long he'd been drinking. This morning she caught him at breakfast swigging down bourbon from his silver flask. Later on, she'd spotted him leaning against the huge magnolia tree, drinking, then thirty minutes ago drinking wine on the veranda. He teetered upward and leaned forward, his goblet lifted in a toast to Lollie Morris, seated three chairs over. The man smirked, miming a toast back. Her father acknowledged it with an eerie smile. Dalia shuddered. Meanwhile, Nellie Ann fidgeted beside her, the spindly legs of her chair surreptitiously pockmarking the carpet as she rocked this way and that. Her sister's chest was heaving, her flared nostrils sucking down the damp air. At the opposite end of the row came the rustling sound of paper. Dalia tilted forward, looked to the right, and spotted her mother, the program shaking in her hands. "Sweet Jesus," Dalia whispered, returning her attention to the piano.

She listened as little girls with ribbons in their hair played first. With postures straight as pokers, they mechanically touched the keys, then curtsied like princesses when they were finished. Yet none of them were as talented as her sister. After each rendition, Miss Gamble, the spinster piano teacher, enthusiastically applauded. The roomful of parents vigorously joined her. Then Miss Gamble lithely stood up. "Ladies and gentlemen," she said, facing the audience. "Now you'll have the extreme pleasure of hearing Miss Nellie Ann Miller play Opus 15, number 3, in G Minor from Chopin's nocturnes," she announced, saying each word distinctly as though she were a teacher of elocution, not music. "This is a musical event you'll never forget—my prize pupil, Miss Nellie Ann Miller." Gracefully, she opened her arms.

From the corner of her eye, Dalia saw her father's face, filled with pride, but then his eyes once more shifted toward Lollie Morris. With cane in hand, Nellie Ann rose and inched toward the piano. Miss Gamble pulled out the piano bench for her, and Nellie Ann sat. Then, easing the cane from her pupil's fingers, she propped it against the wooden seat. Breathing in deeply, sitting up very straight, Nellie Ann arched her wrists and began to play, the music flowing easily from her fingers.

So often had her sister described the wonderment of playing that Dalia understood exactly what was happening—the way each note formed a sensation in Nellie Ann's head and each chord corresponded to an imagined color. One note would be the warm flush of a kitten's belly. Another, the nostalgic hue of honeysuckle or the soft, luxurious tint of hands engulfed in silk. In the sound of each chord, Nellie Ann would envision a pigment, sense its brightness or dullness. She would smell, taste, feel, and hear each color until it took shape inside her head, her world becoming a spectrum of colors, of images never seen, but, at this moment, retrieved, resurrected, and reinterpreted through her hands. The applause began as soon as she quit playing, followed by skirts swishing, chairs sighing as the listeners stood to clap.

"Lordy be!" Katie Mae exclaimed, clapping so fervently she lost her balance and fell into the blue velvet curtain.

Dalia turned to see her father smiling, staring at Lollie Morris. Her papa seemed more consumed with the man's reaction than with his own daughter's triumph.

Her face aglow, Nellie Ann came to her feet too quickly. Her cane clattered to the floor. When she leaned over to retrieve it, she banged her head against the piano keys, producing a clanging, discordant noise. At once Miss Gamble was at her side. Bending down, she retrieved the cane and inserted it into Nellie Ann's fingers. "That was wonderful, Nellie Ann. Absolutely inspired," she said loudly, prompting another round of applause.

Apprehensive, Dalia glanced back at her father. His shoulders were slumped, his spirit deflated. She turned around to see Lollie Morris shaking his head, smirking. "Your hard work has paid off, my dear," her father suddenly blurted out. Jumping up, he staggered through the rows of chairs toward Nellie Ann, holding the goblet out and away from his body. "I drink to the artist in the family," he announced, red wine sloshing over the rim of his glass as he swallowed. "You are perfect, perfect," he slurred. "Now you drink some, too." Lunging, he shoved the wine at Nellie Ann's hand. Her fingers grazed the glass. She reached for the goblet again, but it slipped against her skin, plummeted to the floor, and shattered.

"Papa," Nellie Ann moaned when he took a step back, stumbled against an empty chair, and toppled it over.

"Papa," Dalia said, her voice sharp as a needle.

At once the room was silent. Parents lowered their heads, squeezing rolled-up programs. Miss Gamble closed the piano lid. A little girl began to hiccup uncontrollably. Another started to cry. "Ladies and gentlemen," Katie Mae said, stepping out from behind the blue-fringed archway, "refreshments will be served in the dining room." Striding over the carpet toward them, she ordered the footman to pick up the glass.

While Nellie Ann cried into the starched pillowcase, Dalia massaged her back. "You're an artist," she consoled her sister. "People will remember that, not the other."

"My shoulder blades ache." Nellie Ann sniffled.

Dalia shifted positions, straddling her sister's thighs. "Am I pushing the anger out?" she asked, pressing down with the full weight of her body.

"I don't know," Nellie Ann whimpered. "Do you think it's possible?"

"Maybe not," Dalia replied, pushing down even harder. "You've got a lot of it inside."

"It hurts so bad."

"I know."

"Why did he do it?"

"No one knows why he drinks so much," Dalia said as she rocked back on her haunches.

"When he hit that boy at the camp, I thought he loved me," Nellie Ann said, choking back a sob, "but now I'm not so sure."

"He loves you," Dalia objected. "When he's drunk, he's coarse and common, that's all."

"Selfish and vain," Nellie Ann added. "Wants everyone to be looking at him."

"It's not so black and white," Dalia said. "He wanted you to play well, and he was nervous." In spite of her anger, she was defending him again. "He thinks the liquor calms him."

"You always make excuses for him," Nellie Ann shot back.

"That's because I know he loves you."

"He loves his bottle more," Nellie Ann countered. "As soon as I heard him coming toward me, banging against the chairs, I tried to think about safe things. I tried to breathe evenly and deeply, the way Katie Mae taught me. *Picking cotton shows you the way,* she said, so I tried to do what she did when she was a girl working in the fields, pretending the hot sun was a warm vat of honey; the scratches on her skin, streaks of red clay; the cotton bolls, whitecaps on Snake River. I tried to turn a deaf ear to him, to replace the scary things I was feeling with beautiful sounds and colors, but I failed. He frightened me anyway," she said sadly. "Tell me, Dalia," she said, her tone earnest. "What am I going to do with all the hurt that is inside me?"

"Let it work for you. That's what I do. Put your feelings into your music," Dalia insisted, leaning forward, gently rubbing her sister's back.

Dalia knelt beneath the magnolia, fury at her father seeping from her legs into the fuzz of moss that covered the ground beneath her. Through the kitchen window drifted the clinking of dishes, and Dalia shifted toward it, her eyes alighting on her mother, rooted to the back porch, gripping the railing as though it alone kept her buoyed up, kept her from falling through the cracks between the floorboards into the dusty, roach-infested space below. She should be upstairs with her daughter, Dalia thought, but as always she would let others do the comforting for her. Papa loved his liquor; Mama, the relief that came from her purple-tinged bottles. Dalia knew too well. The medicine transformed her mother's spirit. It enabled her to rationalize her passivity and call it kindness, to transform fear and avoidance—those seasoned pacifists that promoted pleasantries and circumvented confrontation—into good manners. Framed by the plum, vermilion sunset, her head bowed and her hands clasped, her mother looked like a penitent praying in a church of stained glass, but Dalia knew otherwise. Every day, her mother drank down laudanum, afterward breathing in driblets, her sunken cheeks too cowardly to suck life in. Her mother's head shot up abruptly. "No more lies," she vowed. "No more hypocrisy," she promised, spinning on her heel, disappearing into the house.

Bewildered, Dalia sat very still. The field hands had gone home for their evening supper, leaving Miller's Mansion and its environs mostly quiet. Lightning bugs sparked around her. Frogs croaked from the goldfish pond nearby. Dalia drew in a deep breath, just as the back door slammed. It was her mother returning, with a small sewing basket in her hands, tapping over the porch, quickly descending the steps, marching with purpose—resolute and steady—down the flagstone path. Quickly, Dalia hid behind the magnolia's thick trunk and peered around it. "It's all a lie," her mother said to herself as she passed. At the edge of the goldfish pond, across from the bronze maiden sculpture, her mother came to a sudden halt. "My life is a lie!" she shouted, as she hurled the purple bottles, one right after another, into the placid water.

Monroe Miller sat in his office sucking on the stem of his pipe, sipping at an expensive brandy. The only light came from a candle flickering on his desk. He longed to drown his shame in liquor. Yet try as he might, he couldn't. The hidden energy of these early morning hours summoned Nellie Ann's indignant scowl, Violet's pinched smile, Dalia's scornful gaze. Even Katie Mae's glance, cloaked in disdain, had condemned him.

How could I have done it? he asked himself, raising the glass to the candlelight, rocking it back and forth, studying the tobacco-colored brandy. He tossed off the last of it, craving the taste, both smooth and sharp like a liquid arrowhead in his mouth. Seizing the decanter, he couldn't help it and poured himself some more. Nellie Ann's recital had gone well, he reasoned. She'd made him proud, so why had he spoiled her moment of glory? He dug his fingernails into the desk, longing to remedy this heartache he felt. He took another big swallow of the brandy, set the snifter on the desk, and rose clumsily from his chair. Taking the candle holder with him, he headed out the door.

Dalia was awake, staring at the shadows on the ceiling, ruminating. She hated both of her parents. Her father's behavior when he was drinking, the never-ending luxury of her mother's suffering and the drug-induced passivity of her days. She hated the rumors, the flurry of the field hands' voices as they worked, creating rhythm from the language of gossip.

"Have ya heard about Miz Violet?"

"Shush. Shush."

"Takes the dope for her sickness."

"Shush. Shush."

"Kills the pain in her heart."

"Shush. Shush."

"Makes her so dead, she can't see."

Groaning, Dalia turned over, the tick rolling beneath her. She closed her eyes against the pillow and was comforted by the downy softness, rising up around her face like a cloud of cotton. A coyote howled in the distance, its cry riding the foggy mist off the river, carrying over the scalelike leaves of the cypress trees. Sweet sleep, she thought, mesmerized by the tree frogs singing, the night breeze teasing the foliage of the pecan trees. Her mind invoked the beauty of the Chopin nocturne, the way her sister had played it, and before she knew it, the bad thoughts about her parents began to fade.

"I love you, Nellie Ann. Please forgive me," he said, practicing courage down the hallway and up the winding stairs. "I love you, Nellie Ann. Please forgive me," he repeated when he got to the landing. "Forgive me," he murmured, standing outside his daughters' bedroom. Gently, he eased the door open. White frilled curtains trembled in the moonlight and cast hummingbird shadows over the walls. A cool breeze came through the window, and, feeling it, he was emboldened.

Stepping inside, he walked lightly across the carpet, careful not to wake them. To his right, he heard Dalia moaning, but when he glanced over at her, she was asleep. He crossed over to Nellie Ann, her face peaceful behind the white gauze. Parting the mosquito net, he examined her more closely. On the brink of apologizing, he faltered, but then he saw himself at the recital, crashing drunkenly against the chairs, and, ashamed, he bent over. "I love you, Nellie Ann," he whispered. "Please forgive me." He ran his eyes over her face, but she gave no sign she'd heard him.

His courage spent, Monroe blew out the candle, then found his way in the darkness down the stairs to his study, where the grandfather clock ticked relentlessly, reminding him the recital was over, the promise of grace passed.

CHAPTER 5

Monroe Miller sat down on a bench beneath a hickory tree, watching the children as they zigzagged through the pines with flaming cups in their hands. Pinpricks of fire shot up from the tin containers like crazed lightning bugs in the descending dusk. Johnny Cake whizzed by him, his face illuminated by the tiny blaze. The two Taylor boys, Nellie Ann's tormentors, trailed not far behind, their cups of rosin flickering. Monroe needed the noise of Millertown. Back home, it had become too quiet, and the silent recrimination drove him mad.

"Mr. Monroe," Johnny Cake said, running over. "Ain't it pretty, though?" he asked, holding up his cup.

"It's gonna burn ya if ya ain't careful," Monroe cautioned him. "Ya best go put it out."

"The woodsman's way?" Johnny Cake said, grinning.

Monroe Miller nodded and Johnny Cake, his yellow hair as coarse as a cornhusk, took off and joined the other boys, who were forming a circle. They put their rosin cups on the ground. After opening their flies, they took aim, shooting streams of urine into the orange flames. "Geez," Johnny Cake squealed as the fire in his rosin cup popped out.

"Look at mine," Thomas Taylor shouted, the flames crackling and fizzling. While little Billy Taylor continued to struggle with his pants, his rosin cup burning on the ground, the rest of the boys kicked theirs over, effectively smothering the smoldering remains in the sandy soil. "Billy, you done waited too long," Thomas said, rocking his brother's cup over with a sideways nudge of his brogan.

"It don't matter nohow," chided Jody Austen, the cooper's son. "His tallywhacker is too little to put anything out." Snickering, he wiggled his baby finger.

"Ain't big as a worm," the Parrish boys teased.

"Little hose," laughed Johnny Cake, snorting loudly through his nose.

"That ain't true," Billy said defiantly.

In unison, the boys began taunting, "Little hose, little hose." Whereupon Billy Taylor wheeled around and stomped off, his hands balled into small, tight fists. Breaking from the circle, the boys scattered in all directions, chasing each other through the copse of pecan trees.

"Mr. Mil-ler." Monroe looked up. It was Thomas Taylor. "Mr. Miller," the boy tried again.

"Yes, son," Monroe Miller said, cringing as he stared into the boy's bruised eye, his swollen nose. He'd slapped him too hard. "What do ya want?"

"To apologize, sir," the boy replied. "My mama told me to."

"Do ya do everything your mama tells ya?" Monroe Miller swatted at a blue and green horsefly on his arm.

"Yessir."

"Are ya apologizing just 'cause she told ya to?"

"Oh, no, sir," Thomas said, his face and tone sincere, his chin trembling. "I done wrong. Picking on a girl ain't right, but picking on a blind one is pure meanness. That's what my mama said. I'm sorry about how I acted."

"Well, ya should be," Monroe Miller said, bringing a stern edge to his voice. He rose. "You terrified my daughter."

Thomas Taylor stepped back. "But sir, I didn't know who she was."

"That don't make it right," Monroe told him. The boy's brogans were inching through the sandy soil away from him, throwing up little whirlwinds of dust that hung in the air for a second, then floated downward, misting the leather gray. "Who she is don't matter. You don't treat a girl that way, 'specially one who's blind."

"Yessir, I know that," he said. "I didn't act right. I know it now, and I'm sorry."

Monroe Miller didn't say anything, just moved his eyes upward, over his patched dungarees and flour sack shirt, along the dirt-creased neck and the dimpled knob of chin to the slash of mouth, the swollen nose, round as a quarter, and finally to the eyes, too close together, of no pure color, grayish brown like the bark of one of his trees. The ordinariness of the boy made him feel ashamed.

"Daddy done beat the heck out of me."

Monroe's eyes fixed on the orange-gray bruise. "Your eye . . . I'm . . ." he stammered, and quickly looked away.

"I deserved it," Thomas said gravely, clenching his jaw. "What I done was doubly wrong 'cause ya saved my baby sister's leg."

"Your dad says she's doing just fine," Monroe Miller said. "I reckon that leg of hers wasn't as bad as it seemed. So our quarrel is over with," he said, extending his hand. The boy stood rigid, his palms in his pants pockets. "I ain't gonna hit ya," Monroe said with an amused grin.

"I know ya ain't," the boy responded.

"Well, then?"

Thomas pulled out his hand, wincing when Monroe took hold of his fingers. As soon as the handshake was over, he pried his hand loose and sprinted off into the fading daylight.

There was a loud thwacking sound, and Monroe turned to see Jody Austen flying from the tip end of a pine sapling through the air like a gray squirrel onto the soft pine-straw ground. Then little Billy Taylor began his climb, the young, limber tree buckling under his weight before swinging up, tossing him head over heels. A group of black boys were hooting and pushing each other while taking turns walking inside an old steel tire from a log cart. Nearby, in a sweet, high voice, a little girl was singing, "Oh, my darling Clementine."

Suddenly weary, Monroe sat back down on the bench. Many of the older boys, he knew, were cooling off in Gopher Creek, not far down the road. They were washing the dirt from their bodies after dipping gum all day. From the woods behind the commissary came the voices of black woodsmen joking and laughing in the jook, a gray shanty where they gathered after work. Someone was strumming a guitar. Another singing, *"Payday's comin' while de pine trees grow, / Hits de surest thing dat a man can know."*

Monroe smelled the comforting odor of wood smoke rising like swamp snakes from brick chimneys and from cooking pits in backyards where wives were doing magic with gumbos, tossing in catfish and alligator turtle. If you got too close to one of those turtles, it would bite you. *Won't let go till it thunders,* so the saying went. Woodsmen's wives did their own cooking. Unlike Violet, they didn't have time to hole up in some dark bedroom, making love to their woes.

Monroe stretched out his long, lanky legs, the heels of his boots digging in the sand, exposing the red clay packed beneath. He pulled his hat down low over his forehead and listened to the buzz of his camp, a balm to his lagging spirit. A man needed this kind of energy to evolve, to survive. He needed laughter and pats on the back, a wink and a nod from foolhardy people. He felt a familiar tap—solid and firm—on his shoulder. Nudging his black hat back, he glanced up and smiled.

"Mind if I join ya?" Tick asked. Monroe pushed himself upright and patted the space beside him. "I didn't expect you back here so soon," his foreman said, slumping down, his trousered leg brushing against Monroe's.

"Can't stay away from Millertown," Monroe confessed. "It's my real home. The other one's too fancy for me."

"I wish I had that problem," Tick said, pressing his palms against his knees, leaning over, chortling.

Immediately Monroe turned serious. He took hold of Tick's shoulder and pulled him back. "Oh, no, ya don't," he said, his expression strained as he peered into his foreman's eyes. "Be glad for what you've got."

For several seconds, Tick was wordless, his eyes trapped in Monroe's bald stare. Then, swallowing hard, he said, "You don't have to remind me of my luck, Mr. Miller. I know how much the good Lord has blessed me, and 'afore too long Mary's gonna bless me with another baby."

"Another child?"

"Yessir."

"Well, ain't that fine news!" Monroe congratulated his foreman with slap on the back. "Johnny Cake'll finally have himself a little brother."

Tick bobbed his head, a wide grin spilling over his face. "That boy ain't even contemplating a sister."

"I don't reckon he is," Monroe said, shaking his head, pulling on the tip end of his black brush mustache. "Tell me. When's the blessed event?"

"April, sometime."

"Mighty fine month to be born."

"Yessir." Tick hesitated. "But . . ."

"But with another mouth to feed, you'll be needing a little more money."

"Yessir," Tick said.

"Don't worry none," Monroe Miller reassured him. "I'll take care of that newborn. More dollars in your pocket, more jugaloo for the commissary."

"Thank you, sir," Tick said, letting out a relieved sigh.

Extending his arms high above his head, Monroe laced his fingers together, turned them over, palms up, and stretched. Then growling deep in his throat, he came to his feet, unlocking his fingers. "I got a question for you."

"What is it, boss?" Tick reached inside his shirt pocket, pulled out a plug of chewing tobacco, and wedged it between his cheek and gum.

"How do you like them metal cups we're using on those pines by the river?"

"To tell the truth, a whole bunch of 'em ain't hung right," his foreman said, shifting away from Monroe, spitting. "The gum's leaking out behind the tins."

"Well, that's to be expected," Monroe said, scratching at the corner of his eye. "It takes time to learn how to hang 'em."

"The way I see it," Tick said, rounding up another mouthful of saliva, spitting, "they's a problem. When they get too gummy, you gotta take 'em down, wash 'em, then hang 'em back up again. Just more work for the men."

"No reason to worry over it," Monroe told him. "I ain't got the money for the metal cups anyhow, but common sense tells me I'd better switch over. The longer my trees live, the longer we'll be in business."

"Turpentine and black pitch," Tick said, hastily rising. "Why, just look at all them pines," he went on, pointing at the drifts of longleafs. "Gonna feed my family forever. Mary's fryin' up a batch of catfish," he said. "Why don't ya have some supper with us?"

"Don't mind if I do," Monroe said, patting his stomach. "Don't she put a little cayenne in her batter?"

"A little?" Tick responded, spittle browning his lips. "Why, it's enough to set your mouth on fire."

"Let's go to the commissary first," Monroe told him. "I wanna get your wife something. A woman in her condition gets cravings. What's she hankering for lately?"

"She's got a sweet tooth these days. Some of that toffee ought to make her happy."

The two men headed down a worn pathway, which cut through a patch of wax myrtle. Through the pines came the urgent voices of women, calling their children to supper. Monroe became aware of a woodpecker thumping at a pecan tree, working as hard as Jigsaw when he cut his puller blade into a pine. Like harps, the longleafs hummed in the breeze. Out of nowhere, Johnny Cake came racing toward them, wildly waving the black hat Monroe had given him. "Daddy!" he cried, coming to a standstill. His skin glistened with water. Shaking his head, he sent droplets flying from his thick yellow hair.

"Quit that," Tick warned, wiping off his face with his shirtsleeve.

"Been skinny-dippin' at the creek, ain't ya?" Monroe asked.

"Yessir," Johnny Cake admitted proudly. "I know a shortcut and can get there lickety-split, if I wanna."

"I done warned ya about dashin' off to that watering hole so late in the evening," Tick scolded. "You're gonna catch your death of cold."

"Aw, Daddy," Johnny Cake whined. "All the big boys do it."

"Now is the time to be lightin' up a rosin cup," Monroe teased him. "After a cold dip in the creek, it'll take off the chill."

"I like doing things my own way," Johnny Cake said, shivering beneath the damp splotches on his shirt.

"You best get on home," Tick said, grabbing Johnny Cake by the arm. "Your mama's got supper waitin'. Mr. Miller wants to buy her some candy, so we're gonna stop off at the store."

"Can I have some, too?"

"Greedy boy," Tick admonished him. "You know how poorly your mama's been of late. Candy's the only thing that sets easy in her belly." Johnny Cake hung his head, poked out his bottom lip, and pouted. "Cut it out and go," Tick said over his shoulder as he and Monroe started off down the pathway. "Mary'll give most of it to him anyway," he said. "That woman spoils him rotten."

The commissary porch was empty of people. "Snead!" Monroe called out as they crossed the threshold into the store, but there was no answer. "I'll be right back," he told Tick as he walked toward the office, which was tacked on at the rear. He noticed the red-check curtains draped like eyebrows over the windows, and the two round tables with rattan chairs up front. Commissaries weren't meant to look prissy. Still, though, he liked what Theodosha had done. His eyes lit on the large barrels of dried beans and black-eyed peas, the wooden bins of rice and beans, and the drums of flour, grits, and cornmeal lined up against the left wall. On the wall opposite were baskets brimming with shelly peas, squash, and tomatoes, fresh from the woodsmen's gardens. He passed by a long wooden shelf piled high with overalls, cotton shirts, and brogans. His eyes filled with merriment as he thumped his forefinger against a stack of black hats on a battered hunt table. Cloth bolts were arranged neatly on the table beside it, along with a box of cotton stockings and a stack of gingham sun bonnets, precariously teetering on the edge. "Snead," Monroe said, knocking forcefully on the office door.

"Mr. Miller," Snead said, opening the door, poking his bald head out. "I thought I heard somebody. Good to see ya," he bubbled, coming toward Monroe. "I'll have one of the workers stable your horse."

"Ain't necessary," Monroe said. "I already got him hitched. Seeing as Mary's gonna feed me supper, I decided to get her a bag of toffee. Just wanted to let ya know it was me and not some burglar."

"Everyone's at home eating supper or else at the jook," Tick said, sauntering over to join them.

"Yes, and if we don't hurry up, we'll be eating our catfish cold. Now, Snead, exactly where is that toffee?"

"I'll spoon ya up a bag, Mr. Miller," Snead said, scurrying toward the long wooden counter at the front of the store.

Monroe scanned the shelves on the back wall behind the counter. They were crammed with Prince Albert and Brown Mule tobacco, Three Thistle snuff, kerosene lamps, large box matches, castor oil, ointments, and lard. Tins of sugar and coffee and round wood kegs of cheese were stacked at the opposite end of the counter. Slabs of streak-o-lean and streak-o-fat were behind the sliding glass doors on racks beneath it. Hanging from the ceiling were several cured hams, dotted with so many flies that they could have been mistaken for cloves if not for the buzzing. The canister of toffee was sitting beside the cash register, along with little apothecary jars filled with herbs.

"I like this," Monroe said. "All these herbs." His eyes drifted over the glass canisters of jelly beans, fudge, rock candy, and toffee. "And the sweets, right here, just begging to be bought. Smart, real smart, Snead."

"I can't take the credit. All this is the wife's doing," Snead said. With a snap of his wrist, he unscrewed the lid on the toffee jar. "The missus wanted a pleasant place for the women to shop in. Says the longer a woman lingers, the more she buys." He was excavating a scoopful of toffee when Willena Clark, her black face twisted in anger, banged through the door.

"Mr. Monroe," she said, striding right up to him, "you is the man I been looking for. I don't want Darnell at the jook tonight," she said, her voice deep and raspy. "There ain't supposed to be no partying, no buck-guzzling, till Saturday."

"Ain't good to drink on Friday," Snead Parrish said, snapping a brown bag open. "Saturday's a workday, and work don't go well if a man's hung over."

"And a family can't eat good if all the wages is spent on folly," Willena Clark added.

"Darnell's drinkin' up his wages?" Monroe said.

"Yessir, and if ya don't do something, he's gonna drink up every red cent we have."

Tick looked up from his spot by the counter. "Mr. Miller," he said, "don't ya worry about this, now. I'll tend to this foolishness later, after we've finished our supper."

"A man can't work hard if—" Snead began, his small gray eyes even smaller.

"I'll tear that place down with my own bare hands if it messes with my profits," Monroe said.

"They know Saturday's a workday," Snead said.

Monroe held up his hand like a warning. "Snead, don't say it again."

"Yessir," he murmured, pouring the toffee into the bag.

"And put that candy back," Monroe barked, his hands shaking.

Snead dumped the toffee into the canister and quietly screwed on the lid.

"Let's go," said Monroe, fixing his eyes on his foreman, striding over the lye-scrubbed floor.

"Don't be too hard on him," Willena said before the two men passed through the door.

As they descended the porch steps, Monroe pulled the silver flask from his shirt pocket. "Want some?" he asked his foreman.

"I best practice what I preach," Tick told him. "No whiskey till after work on Saturday."

Monroe cleared his throat and took a deep swallow. He wiped his mouth on his shirtsleeve and upended the flask again. "I need to calm down when I'm about to deal with trouble," he said, gulping again. He rubbed his nose with his finger, took another deep swallow from the flask, and trudged down the path toward a cluster of slash pines among which the jook was hidden. Tick walked close beside him.

"What's going on here?" Monroe bellowed as he threw open the heavy door. At once the banjo picker stopped playing, and a fat black man kicked a crate beneath a table. "Hey, mister!" Monroe called out. "What you been selling my men?" The fat man said nothing, just shrugged and shook his head. The man with the banjo left his spot near the counter and hastened to the door, a fistful of men following him. Monroe strode over to where Darnell and Jigsaw were sitting, curling their hands around tin cups. "Darnell, what are ya drinking?" Monroe asked, leaning over, sniffing. Darnell bent his head down, didn't answer. Monroe yanked at the lip of his cup, but Darnell wouldn't let loose. "What's in that crate?" he demanded, cutting his eyes to the fat man. "If ya won't tell me, I'll see for myself," he said. Squatting down, Monroe tugged at the side of the wooden-slatted box, its corner poking out from beneath the table. "Goddamn buck," he muttered, lifting up a brown clay jug. From the corner of his eye he spotted the fat man stealing toward the back entry. "You move again, and I'll break your head open with this jug," Monroe threatened, leaping up. The fat man stood dead still. "Is this your buck?" he asked. The man didn't answer.

"I'll get him to talk," Tick said, moving toward the table.

"Stay where you are, Tick," Monroe warned, his voice harsh and low. He returned his attention to the fat man, quiet as a possum. "Turn around and face me," he said. The man turned slowly. "Open that mouth of yours and speak," Monroe demanded, the jug clutched tightly in his hand. "Did you hear me?" he asked, his breath hot and heavy on the black man's face. "Now, why are ya sellin' buck to my men on Friday?"

"I ain't sellin' it, sir. I'm givin' it away."

"Well, that's awful generous of ya. Givin' goddamn buck away," Monroe said, rapping his brogan against the pine plank floor. "Ya must be a rich man."

"It ain't my liquor, sir."

"If it ain't yours, whose is it?" Monroe demanded.

"It's the 'cruiter's."

"A recruiter?"

"Said to give the men a taste, tell 'em if they wanted more, they was to meet him at dusk by Gopher Creek."

"What else did he tell ya to do?"

"Said to tell 'em to come work for his boss man. His boss man will pay off their store debt and give 'em higher wages."

"Well, I'll be damned," Monroe Miller said, shaking his head thoughtfully. "Who is this kindhearted boss man?"

"Mr. Lollie Morris, he's sayin'."

"Mr. Lollie Morris," Monroe repeated, mulling the name over for several seconds. "Mr. Lollie Morris," he said again, the vileness of the name coating his tongue. "That goddamn bastard," he spat. Violently, he kicked the chair in front of him and knocked it over. "Treats his own workers so bad, he can't keep 'em. Decides to steal mine, same as he stole my land from Willard Croton. Ain't got an ounce of respect for me or my family. What's this 'cruiter's name?" he asked, rocking forward, his nose almost touching the fat man's.

"Don't know, sir. He's a tall, wiry white man riding a pinto horse. I swear to God, I ain't never laid eyes on him before."

"Then I reckon I better go introduce myself."

"I'll come with ya," Tick said.

"No," Monroe told him. "My business with Lollie Morris is a private matter. Go tell Mary what happened, give her my apologies, and eat your supper. And you, mister, if ya know what's good for ya—take your buck and don't show your face around my town again."

Without another word, Monroe slammed out the door, retracing his steps to the lightwood post where he'd tied Tarkel. Mounting his black stallion, he took another gulp of bourbon from his flask and slipped it back into his shirt pocket. He patted the rifle in its scabbard, then headed down the main road toward the creek. As he rode, he listened to the horse's hooves pattering in the sand, and to the stallion's breath coming hard and heavy. He pressed his hand against Tarkel's neck and rubbed the sweat between his fingers. Soon the sun would redden the dusky sky. Stretching as far as the eyes could see were pines saluting him with their long, upright needles. All around him was beauty—the grandness of the natural world, the longleafs there for the taking. Since the beginning of time, men had been using these pines, boiling the gum down, making pitch to caulk their ships' seams. A noble way to make a living, except for the likes of Lollie Morris. Monroe snatched the flask from his pocket. His fingers quivered against the silver container, his thoughts flashing fury. Goddamn Lollie Morris. Thief. Liar. He guzzled down a mouthful of bourbon. He should kill him. He drank again, the metal rim hot against his lips.

In front of him was a frazzled field of corn, the stalks stripped and dying. To his left was Gopher Creek, gurgling loudly. He heard a horse galloping. Returning the flask to his pocket, he rode swiftly toward the noise, but then the galloping stopped. Monroe came to a halt, sitting his horse in a field of yellow grass, listening. A hoot owl whooed. Looking over his shoulder, he spotted two round yellow eyes staring at him in the dusk. A mosquito bit his neck, and cursing under his breath, he swatted it, then wiped the smidgen of blood on his pants, anger oozing through him like sap leaking through a blaze into the box of a longleaf. From a nearby yellow hedge of honeysuckle, something rustled. Monroe held his breath, craned toward the sound, tried to pay attention. Gritting his teeth, he wrapped his fingers around the butt of his rifle. The yellow flowers parted, and he caught sight of the man, walking ahead of the pinto, leading him through the thicket, sneaking away like a coward.

Coward, Monroe thought, sliding from his saddle. With the reins in his teeth, he pulled the rifle from the scabbard, then tethered his horse to a solitary locust tree. Cautiously, Monroe approached the barricade of honeysuckle. "Come on out, mister," he demanded, hitting the yellow flowers with the barrel. "I said, come on out!"

"Git!" came the man's voice. There was a loud slap, and the horse skittered through the honeysuckle hedge.

Monroe cocked his rifle, his finger nervous against the trigger. Rolling its eyes, the horse neighed and stood stock-still. All was tranquil in the twilight. A slice of moon broke through the darkness, glowing like the blade of a puller. Beneath the soft gray sky, Tarkel nickered. Night birds began their mournful cry. A rabbit darted through the yellow grass. Monroe imagined Lollie Morris laughing at him, laughing at his family. White rage burned through him. He pulled the trigger, and a shot as sharp as a pine limb cracking cut through the silence. The horse with the rolling eye fell dead. From behind the hedge came the sound of twigs snapping as the man fled through the thicket.

It was then Monroe heard someone whimpering. Wheeling around, he saw Johnny Cake at the edge of the clearing, covering his face as he cried.

Monroe had to do something. Lollie Morris's double-dealing and Willard Croton's foolishness were making him crazy. Doubling the reins over, he slashed them against Tarkel's flanks, urging the poor beast to go faster, wondering if God in His wrath was conspiring against him, if God had led Johnny Cake to him so that another child would look at him with judgment in his eyes.

Monroe inhaled the loamy, fishy odor, coming off the river. The night was as black as the pitch he made. No stars. Only a splinter of moon shone through the spiny clusters of pine needles. His gut ached as though it were about to split and gush forth all the misdeeds in his life, all those careless moments when he had acted before thinking, all those times when he'd been rash and let his anger do his talking for him. A dagger of lightning ripped through the sky, followed by a clamorous roll of thunder. Monroe prayed for a summer storm to burn up his darkness, for a white bolt of lightning to scorch his heart and deliver him with a fiery blaze.

Letting out a cry of anguish, he dug his spurs into Tarkel's flesh, lashing him with the tough leather, feeling the quiver of his massive body, coveting the animal's pain. He prayed for Tarkel to throw him from his saddle, headlong into the white face of a longleaf. "Goddammit," he moaned, releasing the reins, lunging forward, collapsing against the stallion's mane, desiring the end of all things.

Yet life was all around him, pine trees extending across the coastal plain, clumps of wiregrass beneath their drooping branches. Sadly, the promise of a storm was fading, as little streaks of lightning and grumbles of thunder moved in to take its place. Heaving himself up, Monroe took control of the reins. Blowing smoke rings of fog through his nostrils, Tarkel trotted through the countryside, which was more alive now than it had ever been.

"Willard Croton!" Monroe yelled when he spotted the white picket fence rising up in the misty darkness. He brought Tarkel to a stop. Dismounting, he tethered him to the fence, unlatched the gate, and strode through. "Willard Croton!" he called out again at the bottom of the porch steps.

The front door flew open. "Who's there?" The glow of a lantern floated in the darkness above the floorboards.

"Monroe Miller."

"Monroe," Willard Croton said, his cautious voice warming, the light from the lantern illuminating his face. "What brings ya out here this time of night? Come on in, and have a cup of coffee with me and the missus."

"No, thank you," Monroe stated, his tone serious. "I ain't here to chitchat."

Reaching up, Willard hung the lantern from a hook in the porch ceiling. "So why did ya come?" he asked, craning forward.

"To get a glimpse of you," Monroe told him. "I asked myself, what sort of man trades away eight hundred acres of pines for nothing? So I came out here to see."

Willard took a step back. The muscles in his face tightened. Hinges creaked, and Sarah Croton, her belly round with child, stepped out on the porch to stand beside her husband. "The kind of man who loves his family," Willard Croton declared. His wife placed her hand on his shoulder. "I wanna work my land here, improve it, not waste my time on some godforsaken swampland in Florida."

"Oh, so you're a family man?" Monroe said, trying to control the anger in his voice. "A family man," he boomed, slapping his hand against his thigh, laughing wildly. "One of the gentle folk. Is that it?" Willard nodded. "Fornication and adultery, incest and murder, ain't this our thriving township of loving families? I ain't afraid to admit what goes on behind closed doors."

"Not behind mine," Willard said, advancing.

"Willard," his wife said, pulling back on his shirtsleeve.

"I won that land, fair and square," Willard insisted, raring back. "It's mine to do with as I please."

"Lawn tennis," Monroe Miller roared, guffawing. "Croquet. A man supports his family with his hands." Monroe thrust out his hands, vehemently curled up his fingers. "With his vision," he shouted. "With grit and guts. I gave ya the chance of a lifetime. An opportunity to become a big man. And what did you do with it? Ya just threw it away," he finished, flinging his arms down.

Again, the front door swung open. This time, a little girl with dark curls and big black eyes scurried out. "Don't you scream at my daddy that way," she warned, shaking a tiny fist at him.

His eyes stinging, Monroe glared at the three of them, all lined up for battle. Sarah on one side; the little girl on the other; Willard in the center of his family. A strangled cry slipped from his throat. Then, drawing himself up proudly, Monroe turned around, mounted his horse, and rode away.

CHAPTER 6

"Devil man," Katie Mae said under her breath as she shaved the white kernels off the last cob of corn.

"You're talking about Papa, aren't you?" Dalia asked, bounding through the back door into the kitchen.

"Ain't no other devil man around here, except maybe for the likes of Lollie Morris," Katie Mae said.

"Lollie Morris? What are you talking about?"

"Both of 'em will do anything to get their way," Katie Mae said, scooping up a spoonful of butter and plopping it into the iron skillet. "Lollie Morris, always tryin' to get richer. Your papa, always breakin' his family's heart."

"What's Papa done now?"

"Enough of this talk, I'm cookin'," Katie Mae said, pouring the corn into the melted butter, then adding several tablespoons of sugar, a dash of salt and pepper, and a tad of whole cream. She kept stirring until the kernels became opaque. Spooning some up, she took a little taste. "Good 'n sweet," she said, more to herself than to Dalia. She stirred the corn some more. "Back when we was slaves, my grandmama whistled while she toted food from the outside kitchen into the big house. It was called the whistler's walk. Know why they made her do it?"

"No, ma'am."

"It was a way to protect the white man from dark lips tasting," she said, dipping up another bite, sliding it between her lips, chewing. Without warning, a sad look drifted over her features. "I'm worried about that sweet child of mine," she said, shaking her head as she thinly sliced a tomato. "Last I checked, she be upstairs in her bedroom. 'Resting,' she said, but she be resting a lot lately. Been different for two weeks now, ever since that recital." She thought for a second, a tomato slice dripping juice as she held it between her fingers. "Like a turtle duckin' its head inside its shell, choosing silence over chatter."

"She's just mad at Papa, same as you," Dalia said, sauntering over to the warming oven and peeking in. "I thought I smelled fried chicken," she said as she tore the skin off a breast, popped it into her mouth, and crunched.

"Don't you go pickin' at my chicken."

Dalia whistled the chorus of "The Battle Hymn of the Republic" and said, "I'm just protecting the black woman from white lips tasting."

"Ya just being a bother," she said, batting at Dalia's hand. Then, returning to the topic, she said, "Since he be gone, my child's anger has turned to something else. Sad, she is. Black circles beneath her eyes. Her skin a deep yellow. That poor sweet girl." Katie Mae shook her head. "Do ya think one of my burnt sugar cakes would make her feel better?"

"Would make me feel better," Dalia said, but Katie Mae wasn't listening to her. Her mind was on Nellie Ann. Right then, Katie Mae smiled. Rolling her small, wide-set eyes, she dumped some sugar into a clean skillet—never needing to measure—and plunked the cast-iron pan on the stove. With her forefinger, she traced the ridge of her high cheekbone. Like melted wax, the skin was pulled tight over it. Inherited from some strong tribe of African women, Dalia thought, the scorched odor of sugar filling her nose. Immediately Katie Mae poured some cold water into the skillet, stirred the mixture with a wooden spoon until the sugar had melted, then removed the pan from the burner. They waited for the sugar water to cool. For as long as Dalia could remember, Katie Mae had been as forceful and steady as the undercurrent in Snake River. Kept Miller's Mansion running smoothly. Told the housemaid what to clean, the gardener what to plant and trim, the footman what to do when he wasn't busy. The field hands came to her before they went to Papa with a problem. Their mama had no friends, but Katie Mae had plenty. More friends, Dalia figured, than the number of purple-tinged bottles her mother had hidden, over the years, in her bedroom.

Katie Mae was cutting shortening into sugar with the tines of a fork. No sooner had she creamed them together in a large clay bowl the color of daisies than she blurted out, "I won't let her go."

"You won't let who go, where?" Dalia asked, confused.

Katie Mae blinked her eyes, said nothing. Seizing a fresh egg from the basket on the worktable, she deftly cracked it against a small blue bowl, separating the yolk, letting the white slide into the bottom. "Just like that, I'll break his will," she said, plopping the yellow center into a bright red container. Then, taking another egg from the basket, she repeated the process.

"Oh, we're back to Papa, aren't we?" Dalia said.

"Mind ya own business," Katie Mae snapped, whipping the yolks into a daffodil-colored froth. Her lips pressed firmly together, she slid the yolks into the creamed mixture and tossed in a spit of vanilla.

"If this is about Papa, it is my business," Dalia pressed on. "I've been furious with him, too, since the recital."

"Well," Katie Mae said, sifting several cups of flour along with baking powder and soda into a white mixing bowl, "if ya must know, I has been worried about something."

"What is it, then? You can tell me. Aren't we friends?"

She sifted the flour six more times before she answered. "Just as he was leaving for his pines, I overheard him talkin' to my baby. *Ya is growing up. Soon ya be a young woman,* he told her. *Come this fall, I'm gonna send ya off to school. Want ya to become strong and independent.* Then he wheeled around, scuffing my clean floor with his nasty boots, leaving her—by herself—to deal with his mischief, tears big as mothballs running down her cheeks."

"He's gonna send her off to school. Where?"

"Off to that blind girl's school in Taylorsville, I reckon."

"That's too far away," Dalia said, trying to restrain the worry in her voice. "He can't do that."

Katie Mae added the sifted flour to the creamed mixture, then splashed in a bit of sweet milk and mixed it up. More flour, more creamed mixture, more milk. One right after the other. Stirring, stirring, and stirring—the stirring becoming angrier and angrier, her eyes growing smaller and darker, like two pellets of buckshot, until everything was all blended together. Then, seizing the skillet of burnt sugar water, she dumped it in. "Naw, I won't let him do it," she spat.

"But how?"

"Right now I don't know, but I'll be figurin' on it." She pinched up a thumbful of snuff, tucked away in her apron pocket, and packed it between her gum and bottom lip, nursing the flavor for a minute before attacking the egg whites with a wire beater, rapidly rotating her strong wrist until their translucence turned into white peaks, rising so high they grazed her dark skin. With meticulous strokes, she folded them into the batter. Next, she poured the batter into two pans, slick as ice with butter, dotted with snowflakes of flour, and slid the pans into the oven. "In twenty minutes, they be ready," she said. Inhaling deeply, she retied her apron and spit brown saliva into an old tin can on a stool next to the stove.

"What are we gonna do?" asked Dalia, her hands trembling.

"I promise ya, I'll think of something," Katie Mae told her. "I got my own ways of fighting back. Trust me. Now get out of my kitchen. I need to finish my cookin'. Need some quiet time so I can think and scheme."

"Please, help me," Nellie Ann whimpered as she struggled to raise herself up. She was propped on a stack of pillows, looking weak and wispy, when Dalia closed the bedroom door behind her. Katie Mae was right. Nellie Ann looked sad, sicker than usual. "There's blood coming out of me," her sister said.

"Show me where," Dalia said, hastening over, quickly folding back the bedcovers.

Nellie Ann spread apart her twiggy legs. "There," she whispered, pulling up her smock and plucking at the red smear on her bloomers. She wove her fingers together and tried to cover the stain with her hands. "I'm not old enough for this," she said, questioning Dalia with her eyes.

"I don't understand," Dalia said, clearly puzzled. "Ya don't even have hair down there." She went over to the washstand to dampen a rag. "Have you told anyone about this?"

"No, just you."

Dalia had removed the soiled underpants and bloomers and was cleaning her sister off with tepid water when she heard Katie Mae's knock down the hallway. "Dinner's served," came Katie Mae's voice, followed by their mother's faint *I'll be down in a second.*

Dalia made a beeline for the door and slit it open. "Psssss. Pssssss," she buzzed, flicking her head to call Katie Mae over.

"What is it?" Katie Mae asked, pattering toward Dalia, rushing into the room.

"She's having her period," Dalia said.

"Aw, no . . . no . . . no," Katie Mae said, hurrying to Nellie Ann. "Ya is way too weak for this. Much too puny."

"Then why?" asked Nellie Ann.

"Nature, child," Katie Mae said. She went over to the dresser, where she retrieved a handful of fresh undergarments from the second drawer and some safety pins from a dish on top. Snatching a clean rag off the washstand, she folded it over, placed it inside the underwear, and pinned it. "Now listen up, child," Katie Mae said. "Don't go tellin' nobody about this, not even your mama. Lift up your legs so I can slip these things on. Not a word, do ya understand me?"

"Yes, ma'am," Nellie Ann mumbled.

" 'Cause if your papa gets wind of this, he'll be sending ya off to that school he be talking of. Bleeding means old enough, child." She slid Nellie Ann over to the edge of the bed. "Now raise them arms," she told the girl, pulling her soiled smock off. "Ya is too sick to be leaving us." She tossed the smock on the floor and put a clean one on her. "Your bleedin' is our little secret. Are ya listening?" Nellie Ann nodded. "And remember to drink all the warm milk I give ya today at dinner. Now, don't ya worry none. Katie Mae is gonna do her magic, make it so no one can send ya away from us."

The crusty smell of the biscuits signaled they were done, so Katie Mae headed back to the kitchen. Dalia rose from her seat and followed, leaving her mother and sister eating at the table. After pulling the biscuits from the oven, Katie Mae poured a cup of milk into a saucepan and placed it on the stove. "Your sister ain't going nowhere," she said to Dalia. Whereupon, she brought a handkerchief, its tip ends tied, from her apron pocket. Unknotting the hankie, she pinched up some yellow powder inside it and rubbed the powder between her thumb and forefinger. "Stanch the flow," she said as she sprinkled it into the milk. "Womanhood go away. Childhood here to stay."

"What are you doing?" Dalia asked nervously.

"Performing my magic," Katie Mae told her. "Queenie Villiers, a Creole woman down by Snake River, taught me how to do it. This potion will protect my baby, keep her from having monthlies for a while." She snatched a spoon and stirred the milk slowly until the yellow was blended in. Untwisting the top off a bottle of vanilla extract, she poured in a tad, stirred the milk again, then emptied the contents into Nellie Ann's favorite cup, the one with the upraised roses around the rim.

"What else are you going to do?" Dalia wanted to know.

"You'll find out in good time," Katie Mae said. "All in good time. Now bring the biscuits for me."

"Yes, ma'am," Dalia said, trailing Katie Mae into the dining room.

"Katie Mae, the chicken is delicious," her mother said from where she sat at the end of the table.

Dalia eyed her mother's plate. As usual, she'd taken no more than two bites of anything on it. After setting the platter of biscuits down, Dalia returned to her chair. Nodding at Katie Mae, she brought her eyes to rest on her sister, directly across from her.

"Drink this down," Katie Mae said, putting the cup of milk on the table beside Nellie Ann's hand. "It'll make ya feel better."

"Who's sick?" said their mother, glancing around.

"Your daughter," Dalia snipped, her face sour. "If you ever left your room, you'd know it."

"You shouldn't judge me so harshly," their mother said. "I'm trying to be better."

Dalia forked up a sliver of tomato and sucked it angrily into her mouth. "Nellie Ann," she said, fixing her eyes on her sister, "remember you must drink your milk."

"Yes, darling, your sister's right. You need to put something in your stomach." Reaching for a biscuit, their mother held it beneath her nose, sniffed, and nipped off a tiny bite, scattering crumbs upon the white linen. "Here," she said, placing it on the edge of Nellie Ann's plate. "Have one of Katie Mae's good biscuits."

"I don't want it," Nellie Ann told her. "I have to drink my milk," she said, raising her cup to her mouth.

Their mother frowned. "Since when do you turn down Katie Mae's biscuits?" she said, worry flitting over her features. "You must not be feeling well." Leaning over, she placed her hand on top of Nellie Ann's and let it rest there for a second. "You do feel a little warm, my dear."

"We all feel a little warm," Dalia retorted. "It's hot out."

"No, my daughter is warm," their mother insisted. "I know when I feel a fever." Blotting her lips with her napkin, she announced, "We'll fetch Doc Green tomorrow."

Immediately tears sprang to Nellie Ann's eyes. "Please don't," she blurted. "If he comes, he'll see I'm growing up, and I'll be sent off to school. Come this fall, he said he'd do it."

"Doc Green won't send you away, my darling," their mother said.

Katie Mae went over to Nellie Ann, eased the cup from her fingers, and deposited it beside her plate. "Miz Violet, just look at that child. See them black circles beneath her eyes," she said forcefully. "All that girl needs is rest. She's plumb tuckered out 'cause of that recital. Let me nurse her for a while. Get her a little stronger 'fore Doc Green comes pokin' around."

"Yes, Mama, all she needs is rest," said Dalia.

"Mama, please, don't make me leave," Nellie Ann whimpered.

"What do you mean, darling?" their mother said, abruptly rising. "I don't know what she means," she said to Dalia. "Tell me what this is about."

"Papa said he's gonna send me off to school," Nellie Ann said, sobbing. "To that school for blind girls in Taylorsville."

"That will never happen," their mother vowed, stepping away from her chair. "Never. Never. Never," she asserted, her dark eyes darting from Katie Mae to Dalia as she began to pace the length of the table. "Don't you worry about that, sweetheart," she said, halting behind Nellie Ann's chair, placing her hands on her shoulders. "I'll fight him tooth and nail. Tooth and nail," she repeated, bending over, brushing her lips against Nellie Ann's forehead. "Now I must go upstairs and rest." She flicked a gray stand of hair off her brow and, with a spin, headed for the doorway. Within seconds, Dalia heard the short, staccato sound of her heels on the stairs.

"Nellie Ann," Katie Mae gasped. Nellie Ann had slumped back in her chair. Her breathing was short and raspy; a furious rash was crawling down her neck. Seizing a napkin, Katie Mae dipped it into a glass of water and dabbed Nellie Ann's forehead. "Let's tote her to the guest bedroom," she said, taking Nellie Ann's right arm, while Dalia took hold of her left.

Together, they lifted her body upward, her matchstick legs resting in the crook of their arms, and carried her to the downstairs guest room, cool because the shutters had been closed to the light. They laid her on the green satin bedcover. "Nellie Ann," Dalia whispered, throwing a blanket over her, pulling the blanket up to her chin, "are you all right?"

Rousing, her sister nodded.

Katie Mae picked up a bell on the night table and inserted it between Nellie Ann's fingers. "Ring this if ya want something," she said. Turning to Dalia, she whispered, "We best leave her be. She needs some rest and quiet."

But instead of accompanying Katie Mae to the door, Dalia motioned for her to leave without her. "No one is gonna send you away," Dalia said, sitting on the side of the bed, clasping her sister's hand. "Remember Hannah's birthday party?"

Nellie Ann inclined her head.

"Remember that loud boy who kept asking to dance with you?"

"Yes," her sister murmured.

"Remember how I wouldn't let him?"

"Uh-huh."

"I protected you, didn't I?"

"You did."

"From now on, I'll always protect you like I did at Hannah's party. Do you believe me?"

"Yes."

Dalia lowered her head, momentarily closing her eyes as she recalled an incident from last winter. She had found a cedar waxwing, its bright yellow feathers quivering on the hard, cold ground, and had rescued the defenseless creature. Cupping its fragility in her palms, she felt needed, and—right then and there—decided to nurse the bird until its wing mended. When spring arrived, she took it to the carriage house. Anxious, she opened her hands, but the little creature amazed her, fluttering upward like a spray of gold in the sunlight. Around and around it flew. As it circled, Dalia came to understand the reason for her life. God had sent this broken creature to her, and she was destined to save it. But then she watched, helpless, as the bird smashed into a pane of glass. She stretched out her arms and tried to grab it with her fingers. "Little bird," she called out, as it soared and struck the comb where the sides of the roof met. Her face lifted, Dalia had cried into the soft rain of feathers, "I should never have let you go."

"I'll never let you go," Dalia told her sister, a troubled expression passing over her features. "Last winter, I made a mistake. One careless mistake and that beautiful little bird was gone. I'll always keep you safe and close, my sister." In the hallway, Katie Mae was pacing impatiently. Dalia followed the broken black lines of her shoes through the space below the door. Then, in an undertone, she spoke, "One mistake can sometimes change your life forever; but, my dear sister, one mistake can't undo all the love that has come before. You're tired," she said when Nellie Ann sighed wearily. "I'll let you rest now." The bedsprings creaked as she rose. "Ring the bell if ya need me."

"Dalia," her sister ventured as she started to go. "The loud boy at the party. His name was Freddy."

"I know. I know," Dalia said, heading for the hallway. Wrapping her fingers around the china knob, she twisted it quietly and peered around the doorjamb, only to see Katie Mae, her lips tight, her head straight and steady, coming toward her.

"He was funny, and I liked him," her sister said as Dalia shut the door.

"Nellie Ann," their father said when he rounded the corner into the parlor. Dalia noticed his eyes falling on her sister, stretched out on the settee, her ankles thick and swollen beyond the blanket. Tentatively, his gaze moved up to her rash-covered neck, her puffy face, her sunken eyes. He made a face—unreadable to Dalia. Pressing his hand against his chest, he wobbled, his cheeks blazing from too much drink. "My Darling Doll," he said, licking his lips, aiming his eyes at her.

"Hello, Papa," she said, refusing to meet his gaze. From where she sat, she could smell the liquor on him.

"Violet," he said. Her mother was sitting at the opposite end of the sofa, nibbling her top lip while she sewed.

From his pants pocket, her father pulled out his flask of bourbon, twisted off the cap, and guzzled. "Where's Katie Mae?"

"In the kitchen preparing tea and biscuits," her mother answered, inspecting the satin stitch with her forefinger.

"Tea and biscuits," her father said. "Well, ain't we proper? Katie Mae!" he yelled. "Bring me a cup, too." He glanced down. There were clumps of clay on the carpet next to his boots. He shook his leg, watched the clay fall. Dalia noticed the ripped arm of his shirt, the sticky smears of gum on his dungarees, the sharp bristles on his cheeks. "I don't reckon I look proper enough for tea and biscuits," he said, loping over to a wingback chair, slumping down. "Should I put on my fancy clothes?" He stared quizzically at them, then focused his gaze on Nellie Ann. "Ya don't look too good. What ails ya?"

"Nothing," she told him.

"Nothing?" He tilted his head to the side, merriment in his eyes. "Why, it don't seem like nothing to me. Does it seem like nothing to you, Violet?"

"She's tired," her mother said, sucking a pinpricked finger.

"What do ya think, my Darling Doll?" he asked, shifting his attention to Dalia.

"She's just tired," Dalia said, glowering at him. He was about to speak but, for some reason, didn't. Scanning the room, Dalia saw that her sister and mother were scowling at him, too. The three of them were standing up to him, damming up his speech with their judgment.

At that moment, Katie Mae strutted in carrying a large silver tray. She acknowledged him with a forced smile. Adroitly, he plucked up a lemon slice from off the tray, opened wide his lips, tossed back his head, and dropped it into his mouth. "Sour, like you." He chortled. Katie Mae thumped the tray on the low table in front of the sofa and wheeled around. "But then, I'm used to it," he added, following her departure with his eyes. "Sour and bitter." He upended his silver flask and gulped. "Sour and bitter. The tastes I like best." He downed the last of the bourbon, burped loudly, screwed the cap back on, and slipped the flask back inside his pocket. "Guess what?" he said, his mood swiftly changing. "No need for me to get dressed for tea and biscuits." He smiled broadly, exposing his tobacco-stained teeth. "No need for Nellie Ann to put on a pretty smock."

"And why is that?" Dalia asked, her attitude flippant.

" 'Cause today we're gonna do something different," her father said. "Something we ain't done before. Something a man likes to do with a son if he's fortunate enough to have one. On my ride home, I happened upon the idea."

"So what is it we're gonna do?" asked Dalia.

"Fishin'."

"Fishing?" Dalia echoed, cutting her eyes to her mother, who had picked up the teapot. "Mama, he's not serious?"

"It's out of the question," her mother said, clinking the teapot down. "Nellie Ann's too tired to go out in this heat. Think about your daughter."

"I am thinkin' about her," he said. "Ya'll say she's tired. I say she's sad. Fishin' will fix what ails her."

"But . . ." her mother protested.

"It'll teach her how to be strong, independent. Nothing better than fishin' to teach that."

"But I don't think . . ." her mother said, her head swiveling from side to side, her dark eyes darting frantically.

"Time for ya'll to put on some fishin' clothes, not finery." Her father rose abruptly from his chair. "And you," he warned, twisting around, "quit your infernal spying." The swish of Katie Mae's skirt and the flap of her shoes could be heard outside the door in the hallway. "There will be no more talk about it," he said, his face resolved, shameless, as he faced them again.

"A fine day," her father gloated, his voice rising above the creaking wagon. Her mother, on the seat beside him, drew her shawl tightly around her shoulders. The team of mares clomped slowly. The sunlight beamed through the Spanish moss, splashing doilies over their faces. "Did we bring bait, line, and tackle?"

"You're drunk," her mother said icily.

"Will someone please tell me where I put the gear?" he demanded.

"It's back here with us," Dalia told him.

"Thank you, dear daughter," he said, jangling the reins, quiet for a moment. Then, with boisterous irony, "The breadwinner on an outing with his loving family. Ain't we havin' fun?" Her mother stared straight ahead, saying nothing, while Dalia and Nellie Ann remained silent in the back of the wagon. "Wish Willard Croton could see me now," he said. "All my girls, right here with me. He ain't the only family man around." Dalia heard a noisy gulp and knew he was drinking. She stared at the back of his neck, hating him, wondering if he could feel her contempt. "Snakes'll be out today," he said with a laugh. "Those cottonmouths are mean. Will swim right up to your boat, try to flip themselves in. It ain't called Snake River for nothing." He took another long drink. "Want some?" He offered the flask to her mother. She just sat there—stonily still, sucking air through the slits between her teeth. "Have it your way," he said, gingerly snapping the reins, saying nothing else till they came to their property on the river, his pine-planked fishing shanty like a stump amid a copse of locust trees forty feet from the bank.

"It's peaceful here, ain't it?" her father said, jumping off the wagon.

Dalia thought the quiet was as deadly as a hiss. Like a snake shedding its skin, mist levitated above the water in the lagoon. No sooner had her father called it peaceful than a coot's cry, loud and shrill, interrupted the silence. Bracing the edge of his hand against his brow, her father scanned the river, then gruffly ordered her mother out of the wagon.

Her mother grabbed a blue woolen blanket from off the seat plank, and with a huge sigh, much too big for her fragile body, climbed down.

Dutifully, she walked to the water's edge and spread the blanket on the ground. "Dalia, go keep your mama company," her father said.

"No," Dalia said defiantly, taking firm hold of her sister's hand.

"Today is about a father and his loving daughter," her father said, his mouth set and determined. "Your sister's comin' with me."

"No," Dalia repeated. "She's gonna stay right here."

"It's all right," Nellie Ann said, her white eyes on Dalia. "I'm not scared. Papa will watch over me."

"Thank you, child," their father said proudly, leaning over and seizing her sister's hand. Helping her down, he reached for the gear in the back of the wagon. "Wait here while I get the boat ready," he told Nellie Ann. He staggered toward the bank, the cane pole in one hand, the tackle box in the other. "I'm taking Nellie Ann out first," he said as he lurched by their mother. "I'm gonna save her from your pity."

"No, you won't," she said, lifting up on her calves, her shoulders rising, but with a shove he forced her back down.

Dalia caught sight of a rowboat and dinghy, nestled behind a stand of cattails near the water. She watched as he turned the spine of the rowboat over, retrieved the fishing gear from off the ground, and put it inside the boat. He gave the rowboat a shove and tossed out the anchor. He returned to the dinghy. Gripping the rope at its bow, he pulled the dinghy over the wet, sandy bank and pushed it into the water. Then, tying the dinghy to the stern of the rowboat, he trudged back to the wagon where her sister waited.

Impassive as her mother, Dalia squatted on the blue blanket, following the two boats, which skated over the glassy surface to the opposite side of the lagoon. The heavy air bore down on her like an anchor. Dalia strained her ears to hear her father's voice. If she squinted her eyes against the light, she could make out their forms through the sun-speckled haze. Although they were no farther out than a stone's throw, it seemed like he had taken Nellie Ann to another world. Leaning forward, her hands on her knees, Dalia feared what might happen. She looked over at her mother, but she had lain down and closed her eyes.

"I've baited the hook with a minnow," their father said loudly, his voice skimming over the placid water. They sat facing each other—Nellie Ann on one seat, he on the other. Leaning over, he placed the baited hook into her sister's outstretched palm. "What does it feel like?"

Her sister said something, but Dalia couldn't hear her.

"Maybe we'll get lucky," their father said, laughing. "Maybe some big bass will swim by and gobble that minnow up."

A bullfrog near the shoreline bellowed. The heat was so intense that the two boats appeared to be floating on a mirror. Dalia could see her father and sister clearly now.

"Is he scared?" she heard her sister ask.

"No," their father replied with conviction.

"But what if he is?"

Her father's voice boomeranged back, "I told you, fish don't have feelings." He began casting out the line, whisking the cane pole to and fro. With a bright splash, the bait hit the water. "Did ya hear that? The minnow is deep below the surface, swimming in the dark with the big fish."

"It must be scary down there," her sister said, her voice rising. "I'm cold," she whined, wrapping her arms around her narrow shoulders.

"It's hot out here," their father snapped, his voice bristling with annoyance. "But if you're cold, drink some whiskey." He removed the flask from his shirt pocket and thrust it into her sister's hand. "Come on. Try it."

Her sister pressed the silver rim against her lips and tilted back her head. Vehemently, she fanned her mouth with her fingers.

"Ah, to burn in the cold," their father said.

For a full minute, there was silence, broken only by a fish, its silver scales breaking through the smooth surface of the water near the bank, the soft, muddy silt at the river bottom eddying upward. Then again Dalia overheard their father's voice. "Take another swallow," he said. "It'll put hair on your chest, make you strong."

"No," her sister said defiantly, lurching forward. Dalia saw the flask plummeting from her hand, saw it banging against an oar and sinking beneath the water.

"Goddammit!" their father was yelling. He stood up and began drunkenly rocking the boat. "If I can't drink," he said petulantly, "I'm gonna smoke. Hold out your hand." He placed the fishing line across her sister's palm. "Close your fingers around it. When ya feel this," he said, pulling on the filament, "it means a fish is nibblin'. The minute you feel that tug, take hold of the line and snatch it back. Ya understand?" Her sister nodded. "I'm gonna set this pole down for a minute," he said, sitting, inserting the pipe stem into his mouth, digging his hands into his pants pocket. "You're in charge till I finish my smoke." He struck a match against the side of the boat and cupped his hands over the bowl of his pipe. Snakes of smoke wafted upward, dispersing into the sunlight.

Dalia listened to a fish splashing loudly amid a fleet of lily pads, followed by the low and throaty garrumping of a frog. A mayfly whirred above the water.

"Are you pouting?" their father asked.

"No, I'm thinking about Katie Mae," her sister said.

"Better if ya think about what you're doing."

"Papa!" her sister called out.

Dalia could see the fishing line growing tight in the water.

"It's a big one!" their father shouted. "Hook it! Do what I told ya."

"It's cutting my skin. Take it." Nellie Ann jumped up from the seat, her knees bumping against the pole. It toppled over the side of the boat and disappeared in the murky water. "Please, Papa, take me back now."

"Sit back down," their father said, the rowboat creaking and swaying when he rose. He put his hands on her sister's shoulders and pushed. "First my flask, now my goddamn pole. Ya won't even try. This fishing lesson is over." He stepped past her, over the plank seat, latching on to her arms, pulling her toward him. The boat tossed wildly from one side to the other. "I won't let pity ruin you." Dalia saw the dinghy banging into the stern of the boat, her sister putting her arms around their father's neck, their father dragging her from one boat to the other. "Listen to me," their father said.

A strange calm had entered his voice, and this calmness frightened her. "Mama, Mama, wake up," Dalia said, tugging at her mother's skirt. "Papa is acting crazy." Her mother opened her eyes and raised up on her elbows.

"Today you'll learn about self-reliance." The dinghy swayed like a thimble on the water. "Make more of your life than your illness." His voice was detached, devoid of pity. Crawling back into the rowboat, he unknotted the rope that tied the two boats together and, positioning himself on the plank seat, began to row. Dalia listened to the oars squeaking in their sockets, to the paddles sloshing through the water, watching the boat as her father brought it to shore.

Her mother cried, "You devil, you can't have left her!" She yanked out a piece of blue wool from the blanket upon which she was sitting. "I'm going to get her," she threatened.

"You better not," he warned, standing over her, his tone hard and dark as the flint-colored river. "I'd rather drown you both than have her drown in all your pity."

As soon as he spoke, Dalia sensed the resolve draining from her mother's body, leaking out like air from a balloon. "I hate you," her mother mumbled, slumping over, her shoulders heaving.

"She must learn how to be independent," her father said. "She must make her life useful."

Locked in wordless fury, Dalia stayed fixed on the blue blanket beside her mother. She saw his lips moving but turned a deaf ear to him. Even his boots were noiseless as they headed toward the wagon. She chose, instead, to hear a coon dog's distant howl. Nearby, whippoorwills were crying. Above her, there was shrieking. She looked up to see a hawk floating upward—a small creature in its talons. Dalia wrapped her anger around her like a blanket, then turned back to the river, her gaze ripping through the stifling heat, seeking out the dinghy, feeling as her sister felt—out there all alone:

Nellie Ann—willing her mind and her body to be still. Telling herself not to think about the darkness at the bottom of the river, the silent tomb of water that lay below. Closing her ears to the buzz of mosquitoes, deadening her skin to their bites. Warding off thoughts of moccasins flinging themselves into the boat. Trying to ignore her heartbeat, growing louder and louder, as her father rowed back to shore. Nellie Ann—turning her thoughts to Katie Mae, trying to do as she had been told. Feeling the beauty around her, replacing her fears with sounds and colors, remembering how Katie Mae had picked cotton years ago—imagining that the cotton bolls were spits of foam, that the foam was Snake River, that the river was song. "Yes, we'll gather at the river, the beautiful, the beautiful river." But now Nellie Ann's mind was coming back to the river—the waves lapping against the hull, seeping through a crack, filling up the dinghy, drawing her under, into the darkness at the silty bottom where there was no sound at all. Drawing up her legs, wrapping her arms around them, she would be trying to resurrect Katie Mae's song, Dalia's promise, Papa's protective arms, but only the shrill cry of a swamp bird, slicing through the haze like a sharp warning, would find its way to her heart.

Her arm around her sister's chest like a harness, Dalia helped Nellie Ann down from the wagon while their father hitched the teams of mares to the horsehead post out front. Drunk and slobbering, he stumbled toward the veranda, singing, *The time has come when the darkies have to part,* making Dalia shudder with shame when she spotted Katie Mae's face pressed against the glass panel of the door.

"Miss Nellie Ann," Katie Mae cried, flinging the door open. Hurrying over the porch, she took the steps quickly and came rushing toward them, but their father held out his arm and blocked her path.

"Get back inside," he warned her. "You're what's wrong with my daughter." When she tried to get around him, he clamped a hand on her shoulder and shoved her back. "I'm going to the goldfish pond where the fishing's better," he slurred, loping over the grass, clutching a jar of moonshine bought off Wilson Trambley, who lived in a shack by the river.

"Dalia. Nellie Ann," Katie Mae called out as soon as their father had clanged the garden gate behind him.

"Please, help my baby," her mother said from her seat in the wagon, her eyes already dull from the vial of laudanum she'd taken at the river. "I must rest now."

"Here, let me help ya," Katie Mae said, running over. With strong arms, she and Dalia bore Nellie Ann over the flagstone drive and up the porch steps. After carrying her through the front entrance, they headed down the hallway toward the guest bedroom, where an oil lamp glowed on the mantel. Breathing heavily, they took her over to the bed and laid her down. "Let her rest here for now before we take her upstairs," Katie Mae said.

Her sister's face was pale against the dark green coverlet; her eyelids closed; her breathing thin and strained. Dalia stared at the raw cuts between Nellie Ann's fingers, at the dozens of mosquito bites on her neck and arms.

"They done eat my baby up," Katie Mae said as a mosquito buzzed around her frizzled head. Reaching out, she crushed it in her palm.

Popping and sizzling, a beetle flew down the neck of the oil lamp, emitting a nasty, scorched odor. The air felt clammy and cool. Going over to the wardrobe, Dalia pulled out a blanket and brought it to Katie Mae.

"Now fetch me a rag, some ointment, and warm water," Katie Mae said, while she tucked the blanket around Nellie Ann's legs. "If I had me a gun, I'd kill him," she muttered, just as Dalia stepped into the hallway.

Her arms straining from the heavy tray, Dalia returned several minutes later.

"Put it on the night table. Quiet, now, 'cause she be sleepin'," Katie Mae cautioned. "Evil," she said, snatching a rag off the tray, angrily dunking it into the pan of warm water, yet the instant the rag touched Nellie Ann's skin, Katie Mae's manner became soft and tender. "Do ya see what he done to your sister?" she asked. After draping the rag over the edge of the pan, she snapped the cap off a jar of turpentine ointment, dipped her finger into the purple-black gel, and rubbed it on the cuts between Nellie Ann's fingers. "Did ya try to stop him?" Dalia didn't answer. "Talk to me, girl," Katie Mae demanded.

"I was too scared," she said.

"Do ya think she weren't scared?"

Dalia shook her head.

With a sharp thump, Katie Mae set down the jar of ointment. "So why didn't ya help her?"

"I didn't know how. He left her there for hours, all alone, in the dinghy."

"All by herself in that boat?"

"Yessam."

"Shameless," Katie Mae said, drawing her lips up in disgust, her nostrils flaring with fury. "Child, you is a coward for doing nothing." Quickly, she stood up. "All of this"–she waved her arm excitedly around the room—"is his doing. All of this misery. This sickness. Your sister's and your mama's. He done it all—in his lust and vainglory."

"I don't understand," Dalia said.

Katie Mae's eyes were hard and narrow. "Ya is not a child anymore. It's about time ya understand the sickness he brung to his family."

"You're talking about his drinking?" Dalia said.

"His being a drunk is jist another one of his 'cures' for what's rottin' inside him, for the sickness he be carryin' around."

"But Papa doesn't act sick," Dalia said. "He's out working all the time."

"Ya can't see it now 'cause it be in hiding, waxing and waning, toying with him, jist waiting to come back out. But when he first turned sick, my eyes seen the rash on his palms, the sores on his fingers and mouth. Later, I seen the chancres on his cheeks. His eyes turned dull, not the cold blue they was before. The fork trembled in his hand as he tried to eat his dinner. My ears heard him complainin' about his aching head, his ailing body. More 'an once, I listened as he retched in the backyard. In the summer heat, he'd be shaking all over. 'Influenza, bad food, bile,' he lied. Tried to heal himself, gulpin' down mercury. His teeth turnin' dark from the cure. My herbs done taught me about woes and remedies. I warned your mama, but she be blind to the sickness in front of her, deaf to the words I said, and I knew what would happen. He'd give the scourge to her, and she'd give that affliction to our sweet baby."

"What scourge? What affliction?" said Dalia. "If you're going to tell me, then tell me."

"Syphilis, child. The devil's mark. Satan's poison."

"I don't know what that is," Dalia muttered. At that moment, her sister moaned.

"Shush," Katie Mae said, casting a worried glance at Nellie Ann. Taking hold of Dalia's hand, she led her to the door. "I said ya was old enough, and I reckon ya is. Let me tell ya the family secret, that's no secret around these parts, not to white folk and not to black folk, neither. This is what your papa done. Took the riverboat to Savannah, made a beeline through the door of the first cathouse he saw, right into the arms of some honey-blond hussy, and peeled off her skin of satin. Done it 'cause your mama, her belly big with you, wouldn't. It was then the snake man bit him." Dalia gasped, imagining a snake man with a diamond-shaped head and a jaw that unlocked to clamp down with fangs of poison. "Your papa caught the curse from that back-alley whore and gave it to your mama, who passed it on to Nellie Ann, deep inside her womb. Your sister was burdened with his sin before she even came into this world. And now she be payin' for the guilt he carries."

"Oh, God," Dalia groaned, slumping to her knees upon the floor.

Katie Mae knelt down beside her. "Everyone has suffered," she went on. "Your papa has grown mean with drink. Your mama's medicine has killed her spirit, and in your fear, ya lose your fight. Come here, baby," she said when Dalia started weeping. She opened wide her arms and hugged Dalia close, letting her sob against her shoulder until her tears grew raw and cold. "It's up to you to protect your sister. Ya gotta be strong now." Dalia's chin trembled. "Don't be scared," Katie Mae reassured her. "If ya love Nellie Ann the way I know ya do, the courage will come."

In these early morning hours, Dalia couldn't sleep. She stood over Nellie Ann, watching her toss fitfully on the featherbed. A tremor passed over her as she recalled the sight of their father, up front in the rowboat, cruelly sweeping his paddle through the water, Nellie Ann behind in the dinghy, crying softly as he rowed them to shore. Why did he do it? To be the great teacher. His face coiled up from righteousness and liquor. Obsessed with his property—his Darling Doll, his horses, his bird dogs, his pine trees, his woodsmen, his liquor. *A family is a man's own thing.* That was his motto.

Was she her sister's defender? Two years ago, she had tried to be the kind of girl Katie Mae wanted. Strong and full of spirit. She was thirteen, with a mass of dark curls, full of herself and pretty, and had curled Nellie Ann's hair to make her feel pretty also. Straight and fine, it took only seven strips of muslin, the soft hair rolled around them, the tip ends tied together. The following day, corkscrews of hair hid her sister's eyes from their father's bold stare. "You look pretty," he told her, and for a fleeting moment, it seemed that her sister had felt so. "Pretty," she had parroted, touching her face gently.

Yet before Dalia could savor this memory, another long-forgotten image rushed in to take its place. It was her eighth birthday, and she was cuddling a beagle pup, named Fawna because of her tan color. *For my Darling Doll. From Papa,* the card had read. At first she had been unable to win the pup over. Bit by bit, she gained her trust by feeding her tiny squares of ham cut up after Sunday dinners, by caressing her ears during the summer storms that frightened her. Her father dubbed her a "no 'count, spoiled beagle, too soft and cowardly to love," but Dalia had loved her anyway.

As she stood there in the milky light, staring down at Nellie Ann, at the cuts on her hands, pusing yellow, she remembered her father's passion for procreation. "Evil," she whispered. Time and again, she had seen his prize hunting dogs mate—the narrow hips of dogs, drool streaming from their mouths as they bred with bitches, panting with pleasure. He demanded puppies every spring. She was ambushed by the memory of the time Papa had forced Fawna to mate, her fearful eyes, her arched top lip, her bared teeth. In the end she had succumbed, the way Dalia's mother always did with her father. Whenever the jewelry box on her dressing table quivered, she knew what her parents were doing. In the bedroom down the hallway, thin hips were slamming together, leading Dalia to believe that the desire to procreate, to endure violent pain, to put forth an image of oneself was meant only for those too overwhelmed by fear to run, too driven by instinct to revolt.

Afterward, she had found Fawna whining in the barn, fiercely licking her matted, crimson fur; but blood had staying power. Racing to the house, she had put the kettle on the stove, then pulled old socks and frayed petticoats from the third shelf of the pantry. When Dalia approached, the dog rolled over on her back. Seeing her tender stomach, the red-smeared sex between her legs, Dalia had cried out. The bucket slipped from her fingers, falling into the hay, spilling water over the animal's brown belly. Looking away, she slid the wet petticoat over this aftermath of sex—violent wounds in the flesh, a tumor of a fetus implanted. No mirror likeness was worth the pain of this birth, she had thought, washing away the blood with warm water.

Dalia had listened to her father's insistence and her mother's mournful sighs, and had only one explanation for it. Procreation was the price of man's vanity, his hallway of mirrors, reproducing himself over and over. "No," her mother had said; so he'd run off to Savannah, satisfying his lust, burdening his family with illness forever.

Going over to the night table, she lit the stub of candle and pulled the nightdress over her head. She was buttoning up her shirtwaist when Nellie Ann groaned. Motionless, she waited for her sister to become quiet. Putting on her skirt, she picked up the candle holder and crept down the stairs. In the kitchen, beside the cast-iron stove, was Katie Mae's pewter lantern. With trembling hands, she removed the glass cover and set the wick aflame.

Quickly, she stepped out the back door into the starlit night. She didn't know what she was going to do, but knew she had to do something. For once in her life, she had to protect her sister. She rushed through the flowering shrubs, avoiding the twigs, the lantern swinging from its handle. The night air was rife with the sweet smell of honeysuckle. She ran on. "Be brave," she told herself, her slippers sliding on the pebbles along the pathway, the lantern heavy in her hand. Her father's hunting dogs, penned up, began howling; but when they picked up her scent, they grew silent. She raced past the carriage house, the barn and cribs blurred outlines in the distance.

She ran some more. Suddenly she was at a standstill, catching her breath in front of the stable. She listened to the horses moving around inside. Nervously, she unlatched the door and entered, inhaling the musky odor of hay. Tarkel snorted. The lantern light flickered against the knotty pine stalls. A bat shrieked and swooped down at her from one of the rafters. Startled, she ducked, the lantern almost slipping from her fingers as the bat whirred through the open door into the darkness where the barn swallows cried. She heard the fat bay gelding grazing his flanks against the planks of the stall. The two mares that pulled the wagon whinnied. She looked up and saw Tarkel, staring at her with his dark, ravenous eyes. The lantern rattled in her hands, light danced over the stable walls. She threw back her head, and the grief spewed out in one long cry—"Nellie Ann!"—as she resurrected the cuts on her sister's hands, the red mosquito bites on her body. She saw her mother bowing down to her father on the bank of the lagoon, herself quietly kneeling when he came back to the weed-choked shore, alone, without her sister. She imagined him entwined in the arms of that harlot, and her hands began to shake. Like a bird of the night, the lantern flew unexpectedly from her fingers, the kerosene spilling into two fiery wings. In the straw lay the glass cover, cleaved in half as though cut clean through. At once the straw ignited, glowing red, then yellow, then blue. Dalia flapped her long skirt against the heat, pounding at the edges of the flames with her slippers until her skin grew hot. The horses kicked at their stalls and neighed. Gasping for breath, she ran through the smoke to the nearest stall. The gelding looked fearfully at her. Fiercely, she flung the door open. Nickering loudly, he galloped through. The hay crackled. Her lungs ached. She heard the horses calling, throwing themselves against the wooden planks, as flames shot up through the roof. The mares shoved against their stalls. Running over, she unlatched the gates and watched them swing open, both mares tearing through. "Tarkel!" she screamed when she heard his shrill whinny. She spun around. In the pitch of his coat, the firelight flickered. He was throwing his body from side to side, hell-bent on living. She stared into his frightened eyes, his nostrils splayed with terror, and listened to his heavy breathing as he swilled the smoke-drenched air. She winced at the barbed odor of pine burning. The black stallion heaved up on his hind legs and came crashing down. She heard the gate splintering, his frightened bellowing. His pitiable fear was as palpable as the hate she was feeling. She took an uncertain step toward him, her heart torn between saving him and fleeing, when he rolled his startled eyes, black as pitch, at her. She began to move quickly through the smoldering straw toward him, but then the beam above her head groaned loudly, sending sparks like streaks of lightning flying, and she feared the roof would collapse. She heard the pop of wood and the hiss of flames as the straw inside his stall ignited, and wheeling around, she ran as fast as she could toward the stable door and the creeping morning light. Wheezing, she slumped to the ground, tormented by his frantic shrieks, but then she remembered Fawna, the red-smeared hurt between her legs, her sister torn and bleeding, and knowing that Tarkel was her father's favorite, a stallion driven by instinct and procreation, she felt glad.

CHAPTER 7

Nellie Ann and Violet were upstairs while Dalia sat at the kitchen table, watching her father through the window. Like a madman, he raced around the backyard, barking out orders to the field hands. Lined up from the well to the stable, they were passing each other buckets of water, trying to put out the flames. But in less than thirty minutes, it was over. The stable had turned to smoke and ash.

Now he pressed his face against the glass top of the door, his ash-stained hands bracketing his eyes like parentheses, his irises skittering back and forth. "Tarkel is dead," he said, his lips smashed against the glass. He jerked the door open and staggered into the kitchen. "My beautiful horse is dead," he said, collapsing into a chair. He braced his elbows on the table, cupped his forehead in his hands.

Dalia coolly bit into a biscuit with honey.

Her father lifted his head and, in a confused voice, said, "Why don't ya say something?"

"Would you like a biscuit?" she asked, offering the plate to him.

"Tarkel's dead," her father said, holding her gaze until she broke it. "Don't ya understand?" He held up his black palms. "I've got soot all over me. Why would I want to eat?"

"Because it's morning," she said flatly, setting the plate of biscuits down.

"Morning?" A baffled grin made a mockery of his features. "Who cares if it's morning? My horse is dead."

"Go wash up," Dalia told him.

"Tarkel's dead," he whimpered, once more burying his forehead in his palms. "Burned alive, and I don't know how it happened."

"God willed it."

"God willed it?" he said, his voice climbing. Dalia took another bite of biscuit, chewed it mechanically. "You know something, don't you?" Monroe accused, coming quickly to his feet. He kicked the table leg in front of him. A glass of milk toppled over. "What happened, Dalia?"

"Calm down, Papa," Dalia said, her eyes following the spilled milk as it soaked into the cloth and dribbled over the edge of the table.

"How can I be calm when ya won't tell me what happened?"

"But I don't know," Dalia said, shrugging casually.

Monroe strode over to the basin and ferociously pumped the handle. "You were there when I got to the stable," he said, taking his hand off the handle, keeping his back to her. "You must've seen or heard something. You know how they really feel."

"How who feels, Papa?" Dalia picked up her cup of coffee and began walking toward the soapstone basin. Her father wheeled around. "Would you like a taste?" she asked, pushing the cup at him.

With a jerk of his wrist, Monroe sent the coffee flying, shattering porcelain on the floor. "Why are ya doing this?" His neck was thick with tension. "I don't like the way you're acting."

"You don't like anything, Papa."

"You act like you don't love me. You act like you don't care about my horse."

"I'm not grieving." Dalia bit her bottom lip and met her father's stare.

Her father started to inch away from her, as though afraid of what he might hear. "I know ya wouldn't hurt me," he was saying. "All I want to know is—"

"Ham and biscuits," came Katie Mae's voice through the window.

"If ya heard your mother—"

"Papa."

"Or your sister talkin' to—"

"No."

"Come and git 'em," Katie Mae shouted.

"That witch," Monroe hissed, turning toward the window, pointing at Katie Mae. "Just listen to her. Givin' away my food like it's hers. Pumped up with pride and self-importance, thinkin' I don't know what she says about me, thinkin' I don't know how much she hates me. I know you're protecting her, Dalia, but I found her lantern in the ashes, proof that she did it." He crossed over to the door and kicked it hard, his jaw fixed as it flew open. "Katie Mae!" he yelled.

"No, Papa," Dalia protested.

Spinning back around, Monroe confronted her. "If ya won't tell me the truth, I'll have to trust myself, believe what I feel, see, and hear."

Dalia tried to find the courage to speak out as he strode through the door, but couldn't—her heartbeat suspended between fearlessness and fear.

After he had sent Katie Mae away, he had begun singing, *"Yes, we'll gather at the river, the beautiful, the beautiful river,"* stealing the hymn from Katie Mae, making it his own. Spying on him now through the landing window, Dalia loathed him so much she would have killed his horse again, but there was no need to. Given enough time, the syphilis would return, come out of hiding, and hurt him for her. Wasn't that what Katie Mae said? Then, once again, he would be a witness to his own debauchery as he shaved himself in the mirror. He'd see the signs of illness returning—his hair coming out in bunches, his fingers trembling as he tried to hold the blade steady, his features twisting in confusion as the scourge infiltrated his brain. The symptoms would tease him, coming and going, before waging their last deadly battle. Her mother, passive as always, would follow in his footsteps. But then, Dalia was no different from her mother. When her father had blamed Katie Mae this morning, Dalia's own final act of silence had been one of collusion. Ultimately, she had settled for vengeance without ownership. Same as her mother, she'd surrendered to cowardice, choosing fear and avoidance over truth and honor. Closing the curtains, Dalia fled up the stairs to her bedroom.

"There ain't no death," Nellie Ann said, as soon as Dalia had clicked the lock against him.

"Nellie Ann? I thought you were sleeping," Dalia said.

"Clouds are beds of cotton," her sister said, pulling the sheet up to her chin. "*That's what heaven is.* Katie Mae told me so, but I'll never hear her say it again." She was quiet for several seconds as Dalia sipped down air, anxiously breathing. "I heard you last night," Nellie Ann said, her face stiffening. "I heard you dressing, creeping down the stairs. *There ain't no death,*" she said again, pressing her hands against her ears, lowering her eyelids, as though she longed to shutter Dalia out.

When Dalia removed the roll of bills from her jewelry box, her hands shivered in the room's chill. She clutched the money tightly. It was enough, she hoped, to tide Katie Mae over—through the fall and winter seasons—until the spring planting came. Enough to assuage her guilty conscience and put an end to the nightmares that woke her often, drenched in perspiration, during these cool October days. The dream never varied. In it, cataracts grew over Katie Mae's clear eyes to bless them with blindness, to erase Dalia from her sight.

Her father was in his study, gulping down liquor, finding peace in forgetting. Her mother was in the small, warm sickroom down the hallway, nursing Nellie Ann, whose wheezing pulsed in Dalia's ears like a recrimination, bullying her down the staircase and out the front door.

Wrapping herself in a black shawl, with the money bundled in her skirt pocket, she leaned forward, buffeted by the wind—her skirt blowing behind her, her hair flying out from her head. The gusts whooshed through the trees, ripping off the crimson leaves, which were hurled against her body. The earth, upon which she trod, seemed as though it were about to crack in two, like a severed iceberg on the ocean, leaving her stranded on one piece, her sister on the other.

Still, though, she pushed on, arriving finally at the river, fizzing with whitecaps. The cypress trees swayed and howled ghoulishly along the shoreline. She drew the shawl tightly around her and started across the narrow footbridge, her mind going back to the day they'd gone fishing. With shame, she remembered sitting on the blanket, watching and waiting. She had sealed her courage behind closed lips and let her sister suffer in the dinghy alone for hours. Then she had become silent again, too soft and cowardly to confess to her father that she, not Katie Mae, was responsible for the stable fire. She heard the waves slapping against the bridge pilings. *Jump in. Jump in,* they were saying. *Let us baptize you in brave waters. Let us wash you free of sin.* Staggering over to the side of the trestle, she peered down at the river. *Jump in. Jump in.* The water swirled below her—the whitecaps breaking apart, spinning into the flinty dark. Above her, black clouds were moving in. Dalia shoved away from the railing, tumbling upon the weathered wood. Struggling up, she lurched back over the bridge and, as fast as she could, ran home.

A few days later, Dalia met Zara, her father's field hand and Katie Mae's friend, behind the carriage house. The smell of wood smoke filled the air. A strong breeze whistled through the pines in the distance and whisked over the cotton field, dried up and barren, toward them. "Did you give it to Katie Mae?" Dalia asked, pulling her shawl tightly around her shoulders as the gust hit.

"Yessam, Miss Dalia," he said, his voice soft as a whisper. "I took it to Miss Chestnut."

"And how do you think she is?" Dalia said, staring at him.

"So much sadness on her face, I could cut it off with a knife."

Dalia groaned, recalling everything that had happened. "Is she eating?" she wanted to know, leaning in toward him.

"Yessam," he replied, "but she be thin."

"How is her shanty?"

"Two clean rooms," he said. "Paper mush in the cracks to keep the wind from blowin' in."

"Sad, you said?"

"*Low,* she calls it."

"Did you say what I told you about the money?"

"Yessam," Zara said, nodding. "Said that Miss Sallie, the new cook, give it to me, told her it come from Nellie Ann. She be happy. Put her fingers to her lips, smiling. *Well, come on in,* she says, *and visit for a while.* Asks if I want a cup of her cold well water. *Ain't no sulfur in it,* she tells me. *Yessam,* I say, *'cause it be a long walk over.*"

"And did you tell her how sick my sister is?"

Zara fixed his light brown eyes on her. "Don't gotta say 'cause from my face Miss Chestnut knows it, but she don't shed a tear, jist sits there, those sad eyes of hers staring hard at me. Finally takes that hankie with the money in it out of her apron pocket. *My child loves me,* she says, plunking it on the table. *Ain't this proof enough?*"

CHAPTER 8

Scattered hardwoods gave off bonfires of color as Monroe rode out to his camp on Friday. The woodsmen were elsewhere, raking up pine needles and underbrush around the longleafs, leaving clean rings at the bottoms of the trees. Monroe breathed in the crisp air but got no joy from it, for the smoky smell of the brush fires made him sad. Like all farming, turpentining followed the seasons, and the blazes, deliberately set toward the end of autumn, signaled that the hard physical labor was over for the year. Where would he find refuge from his sorrow if he didn't have his trees to work?

All morning he had been drinking steadily, trying to rid himself of memory. At Miller's Mansion, one daughter was suffering from a disease of his doing; another from her disappointment in him; both from his heavy drinking. His wife's demise already showed in her empty eyes. The field hands looked at him with misgiving because he'd sent Katie Mae away. Johnny Cake, who'd always accepted him, now didn't. Monroe gulped down more bourbon, his eyes traveling over the sand-filled boxes, his melancholia growing. The piney woods in the fall were a lonely, despondent place.

Recapping the bottle, he leaned forward and slid it back into his saddlebag. If nothing else worked, the liquor would deaden his pain. This sadness was just a brief fit of sorrow, he reasoned.

In the near distance, he heard a woodsman shouting, "Bainbridge!" It was a call to let Tick know that the worker's task had been completed.

"Snake River!" yelled another.

"Bourbon," Monroe slurred, maneuvering his horse around the piles of underbrush.

As a child, he had walked to school through this same country, through these same woods, in bare feet and on an empty stomach, only to suffer the taunts of his classmates. He'd witnessed the deaths of three siblings from poverty and hunger and swore an early death wouldn't be his fate. As a young man, he had dreamed of making money because he thought money made a man happy, kept him and his family safe, but now he knew that sadness and death knew no boundaries.

Dismounting, Monroe tethered the gelding to a spruce, seized the bourbon from his saddlebag, then staggered over to an old dying pine, its trunk scarred by deep boxes and white blazes. The ground around the roots was spongy. It had given its life to progress, to naval stores, to ships on the sea. From a sapling, it had grown to be old and grand, only to be killed by slashes inflicted by a woodsman's hand. Slumping to the ground, he drank, recalling his transgressions, and in less than ten minutes, his back against the pine, the bottle on the ground beside him, he was fast asleep.

Voices came to him during his slumber, the voices of people in his past. A strange dream with only sounds. Mary Lou's soft slur was unmistakable. She spoke his name so sweetly, as though she were still his wife, even unto death. He heard the weak cry of his newborn, the son who died before he could know him. Then came the garrulous Irish voice of his mother, followed by the booming laughter of his father, which grew louder, but never mean, when he was drinking. Both had been born poor, with little breeding. Yet these were the voices of sturdy country people, the voices of those who had loved him. Acceptance and endurance were in the sound of each word they spoke, but Monroe knew that acceptance could be dangerous. Too often, his mother had been resigned to her fate, rolling her grief into a ball and tossing it away after each of her three children died. The dream shifted from sounds to images, and now Monroe was seeing Violet. She was slipping out of her clothes, draping them over the low bushes that edged the bank of Snake River. She tiptoed toward the water and walked along the shoreline until the sandy bottom glimmered white through the flint-colored water. Lifting her arms upward—her breasts small and plump, her body more like a girl's than a woman's—she parted her lips, swallowed, and—with her dark eyes wide open—dove in, only to slice through the still surface into the bright sun a moment later. That was the Violet he had fallen in love with, that was the Violet who had fallen in love with him.

"Violet, Violet," he was mumbling, when the loud talk of his foreman broke through his dream. Startled, he jerked himself upright. Disoriented, he blinked wild-eyed into the sunlight, but then Tick's full-tongued drawl resounded from the piney woods, and—like a splash of cold water in his face—brought him back again. Rising, he went over to unhitch the gelding. The scent of fire filled his nostrils. His eyes watered from the smoke that moved along the ground like a living, breathing thing as the flames destroyed the undergrowth, as the heat unfurled the pine cone, setting the seeds inside it free. It was the woodsmen's job to set the blaze, if lightning failed to do so. Beautiful and dangerous, Monroe thought, lowering himself onto his saddle, laughing out loud when the gelding began to toss its reddish brown mane.

He was two miles from Millertown when Tick came riding up beside him. "We've already burned off two crops this morning," his foreman said, "and the day's just started."

"Two crops, huh?" Monroe said. "That's a fair amount of work, I'd say."

Tick nodded, and they rode on in silence. At last, Monroe asked him, "Where's Johnny Cake? I ain't seen much of the boy lately."

"Busy with schoolwork, Mr. Miller."

"And Mary?"

"Gettin' bigger every day."

"Your son's avoiding me," Monroe said flatly, directing his gaze on the road in front of him. The horses clopped on. Monroe cleared his throat, flicked the reins, and added, "Ya know how much I like the boy." He shifted his eyes to Tick and waited for his foreman to speak.

"Mr. Miller," Tick began, hesitating a few seconds before saying, "ya shot that pinto, and Johnny Cake ain't got over it yet."

"I know. I know," Monroe said. "I didn't mean to."

"But he seen ya. Overheard me and the missus talkin' about that ruckus at the jook. Snuck out and took the shortcut to the creek."

"I didn't know he was there," Monroe said. "It just happened. Before I knew it, my finger was pullin' the trigger."

"Ya killed a horse, Mr. Miller, and the boy loves horses." Monroe lowered his head. "He can't understand why ya done it. And now he seen ya riding this gelding. Thinks ya must've shot Tarkel, too."

"Ya know that ain't what happened," Monroe said, looking up, his blue eyes urgent. "My stable burned down. Poor Tarkel was trapped inside it. Didn't ya tell the boy the truth?"

"I done told him over and over how it happened, but he don't believe me."

"What can I do?"

"Jist give him time."

"What if I bought him a pony?"

"Time is all he needs."

"Time," Monroe said, nodding. "Later," he mumbled, resigned, as he touched the brim of his hat, dug his heels into the gelding's side, and galloped off.

Dalia was sitting in the sickroom, gazing out the window at the pecan trees and live oaks. Called live oaks because they never looked dreary, never shed their dark green leaves in winter. Whereas the pecan trees, with their skinny, naked limbs, put Dalia in mind of sad, orphaned children. She shivered with repulsion, thinking of the cockroaches rustling through their fallen brown leaves.

Downstairs, Sallie, the new cook, was banging pots and pans as she prepared another inedible meal while her mother rested in her bedchamber, coming out less and less. Dalia shifted in her chair and returned her attention to Nellie Ann, who was mumbling something, her breathing shallow, her arms crisscrossed over her chest. Her lips were cracked from a running fever; her cheeks were flushed. "Nellie Ann, would you like a glass of water?" she whispered, pouring from the pitcher on the night table. As Dalia held the cool glass, her mind resurrected the brook behind their house. She had taken her sister there for the first time last summer, led her over to the soft murmur of water, then knelt down on the moist ground beside her. "Feel the moss," she told her sister, placing her hand against the velvet softness. "Now the water," she urged, dipping her sister's fingers into the chilly brook.

"Take my hand deeper," Nellie Ann had pleaded, and Dalia obliged her, sliding her sister's fingers down deeper, over the cool, slick surface of pebbles being gently rocked by the moving stream.

"Doesn't it feel soothing?" Dalia asked her.

Smiling, Nellie Ann brought her fingertips to her lips and dribbled droplets of water on her tongue. "It's all green, isn't it?" she said.

"Yes, darling. You always amaze me," Dalia told her.

"I'm not so amazing. I can't see the trees, but I can smell them, and from their smell, I know their color. It's green. Green is soothing and cool. Green gurgles. It hums in your ears and makes you feel safe. Green is the color of this stream. Let go of my hand, Dalia. I need to go deeper. I need to follow the water."

"Be careful," Dalia said.

"Don't worry about me, sister," Nellie Ann had reassured her. "Look. My hand is green, too. I'm the water flowing free."

Nellie Ann moaned again. "Please, sweetheart . . . some cool water will help," Dalia said, confused by the memory of that day. *I'm the water flowing free,* her sister had said, but what had those words meant? What if Nellie Ann was tired of being different? What if she longed to be with other sightless girls, if she wanted to feel their fingers exploring her face?

"Come on, Sugar Cane, darling, bring that load to your daddy," Columbus baby-talked the mule.

Woodsmen were reputed to be a tough, rough breed, but Columbus's love for that mule made Monroe wonder if all the fights he had broken up through the years, if all the cutter tools he had snatched away from drunk, crazed workers before they could inflict damage on each other, were no more than figments of his imagination, created to reinforce the image of the woodsman as a volatile, dangerous man. Still, though, he had witnessed too much in his lifetime of turpentining to think otherwise. Five years ago, he had looked on, impotent, as a woodsman, wild on buck and ego, threw hot water with lye into another man's face. They were a tough, rough breed, all right.

The wagon rumbled by, its stack of lightwood and heartwood jiggling. The heartwood, heavy with deposits of resin, bit at the air, and Monroe fanned his hands in front of his face, the residue stinging his eyes.

"Web wants to burn off the last of the wood before winter sets in," Tick told him.

"Web's a hard worker," Monroe said. "If he sets his mind to it, he'll get it done." Then, in a voice low and apologetic, he added, "I'm gonna make it up to Johnny Cake. Gonna change my ways."

Tick's mouth twisted as he worked his tongue, pushing a plug of tobacco against the inside of his cheek. Gathering up a glob of brown saliva, he pockmarked the sand with his spit. "Like I told ya, Mr. Miller, all that boy of mine needs is time."

"Do ya know if he's around?"

"Only kid in town to come here," Tick replied, his eyes gleeful. "The others are eating birthday cake at Jody Austen's house."

Monroe saw Jude Taylor, his hank of blond hair swept back off his forehead, loping toward them. "How's that baby girl of yours?" he asked, acknowledging Jude with a nod.

"Leg's mendin' jist fine. Gettin' so big, she's chewin' on rosin balls."

"They'll make her teeth strong," Monroe said, nibbling his mustache. "Before too long, she'll be chewin' fatback, sliced off that mean ole sow's hide."

"Yessir," Jude said, grinning.

"And the boys?"

"Wild."

"Not so deep!" Web shouted from the edge of a sixty-foot circle.

Monroe wheeled around and waved his hat at the woodsmen digging a slight incline from the edge of the circle to its center.

"Puts me in mind of a big washbasin," Tick said as the three of them moseyed closer to where the men were working.

"Daddy," Johnny Cake called out, racing over. "Look at Mr. Web. Ain't he something, buildin' that tar kiln?"

Monroe reached out to touch the boy's shoulder, but with a duck of his head, Johnny Cake sidestepped him.

"Pound it down," Web said. "Smooth as a baby's behind."

"Daddy, I done changed my mind," Johnny Cake bubbled, rocking restlessly on his heels. "I wanna be a tarkel burner like Mr. Web." Wrenching up the left side of his face, he flashed a toothy smile at his father.

"A boss has gotta know it all," Monroe said, but Johnny Cake wasn't listening to him.

"I might be mistaken, Mr. Miller, but I don't believe I ever seen ya poundin' out metal in my shop," Jude joked, ruffling Johnny Cake's hair, causing it to spike out from his head.

"Since when ya been markin' trees with palmetto leaves?" Tick asked, raising his eyebrows, ejecting a stream of tobacco juice at a hoed-up clump of clay.

"Well, I guess I ain't smart enough to be a blacksmith," Monroe countered. "But I been stuck by plenty of palmetto leaves." He moved toward a wooden trough, which the black men were burying in the ground. One end of it was near the circle's center; the other, eight feet beyond the perimeter, dangled over a deep pit.

"Ain't no better way to do it," Tick said as he and Jude walked over to where Monroe was standing.

"Mr. Web!" Johnny Cake waved his arms to get the black man's attention. Web waved back, and Johnny Cake took off in his direction.

"Been doin' it like this since the beginning of time," Jude mused.

Monroe watched while the men stacked billets, small thick pieces of lightwood, into an inverted, truncated nine-foot-high cone. As soon as they were finished, they began inserting green pine boughs between the ends of the billets to keep the dirt from getting in. This way, the tar would cook out clean. Next, they'd erect the embankment, packing the tiny space between the billets and the wall with dirt. Finally, the whole thing would be covered with pine branches and sod, except for a hole at the top where the fire would be set.

"I could do with a cold drink of water," Tick said.

"I'll walk over to the springhouse with you," Monroe told him.

"Ya'll go on," Jude said. "I'll stay here and keep an eye on the boy."

As they started down the pathway to the springhouse, Monroe could hear Web telling Johnny Cake about the embankment, talking loud so that everyone could hear. Monroe kicked at a rock. A clump of wiregrass parted, and he stopped dead in his tracks. Tick came to a halt beside him, but it was only an indigo snake, as benign as it was resplendent, glowing dark blue in the autumn sun. There was a tapping noise, and Monroe glanced up to catch a red-cockaded woodpecker, vigorously digging its beak into the trunk of an old longleaf. Monroe studied the woods around him. He had let too many of his young trees be worked. From now on, he'd spare those less than twelve inches around. Next spring he'd put up metal cups to collect the gum. This way, his pines would live longer. In the future, he'd have to be more cautious with the burning. Wait till January when the ground was really wet. If the fires got too hot, the mature pines, bearing cones, also went up. No cones meant no seeds. No seeds meant no pine saplings. A man had to act responsibly when it came to his trees.

And even more so when it came to his family, he decided, but maybe families were harder to save. In the woods, a slip of the axe caused no real problems. If the box at the base of the tree wasn't cut smoothly, if a silver coin refused to roll down the outer edge of the box and back up the other side, it wasn't a mistake with consequences lasting forever. The woodsman just moved on to another tree. But a slipup with a painted woman was another thing altogether. Just yesterday, Zara had brought him news from home. It was sickness and sadness, same as always. A year ago, Monroe could have outworked any woodsman, but lately he felt his own strength waning. Bouts of nausea made him listless. His hair came out when he combed it, and then it hit him. Maybe the pox was returning, but just as quickly he rationalized the notion away. Nerves and worry, he decided. Made worse by his heavy drinking.

He paused to pick a weed. Holding it up to the sunlight, he stared at it for several seconds, examining its network of veins. "Yes, I'm gonna make it up to Johnny Cake, gonna change my ways," he said, a thoughtful expression passing over his features as he let the weed drop from his fingers.

Tick nodded gravely, and the two men walked on, not talking. Somewhere a bobwhite quail called. High up in a slash pine, a fox squirrel, donning a black mask and white nose and ears, chattered. A chipmunk scurried through the underbrush. Monroe spotted the delicate web of a wood spider woven between clumps of grass. Next to the springhouse, the weeds were beginning to fade and shrivel. The dogwood behind it was changing from green to red. The springhouse door had been left ajar, making it easy to slip inside.

Monroe ran his fingers over the moist, cool wall. He grabbed a metal cup hanging from a nail on the doorjamb and, leaning over the low stone ledge, dipped it into the pool of water. Bringing the rim to his lips, he gulped long and deep. The next mouthful he let linger, swishing it from side to side before swallowing. "Work and liquor," he said thoughtfully. "Always been a big part of my life. But the work came first. Kept my mind from playin' tricks on me, kept me from hurtin' people. It was the liquor that done the other," he said, breathing in the dusky air. Tick was scooping up water with a long-handled ladle, sipping. From a dark corner of the springhouse a cricket chirruped, precipitating a chorus from others, filling up the dark silence.

As soon as they returned to the tar kiln, Tick rode back to the side camp, while Monroe stayed on to watch the burning. "Johnny Cake," he said, going over to the boy, "ya daddy says for ya to get on home."

"But I wanna learn it all," Johnny Cake said, inching closer to the embankment.

"Let it burn some more," Web told his men. "It needs to get real hot before we make 'em other holes."

"Another time," Monroe said firmly. "Go on home now. That's what your daddy wants."

"Mr. Web, can I stay?" Johnny Cake asked, pressing the black man. "Please, let me."

Webster shrugged his wide shoulders.

Monroe moved toward a long wooden rectangular box lying on the ground a few feet from the kiln. "Ya see that?" he asked, aware that the boy's curiosity would spur him over. "It's where the tarkel burner stays. He stays in there for days and days. Two days before the tar starts flowin'. Then ten more while it's runnin'. Twelve days altogether." Johnny Cake stared at the box, ridges forming between his eyebrows. "It's his job to look out for any open flames. To keep enough air flowin' or else the whole damn thing'll explode." Monroe clapped his hands loudly. Startled, Johnny Cake let out a little gasp. "Yessir," Monroe said solemnly. "Burning a tar kiln is dangerous business. Now, ya need to head home, where it's safe."

"Fire!"

Monroe spun around to see a dark rope of smoke twining up the base of the embankment.

"Smother it!" Web yelled.

"I'll do it," Johnny Cake said, running past Monroe.

"Come back here," Monroe demanded, chasing after him.

"I'm a tarkel burner," the boy declared, picking up a pine bough and holding it up high for everyone to see. "And I'm gonna put that fire out," he boasted, sprinting toward the blaze. Excitedly, he waved the branch over the embankment. With a sizzle and a pop, the pine bough ignited.

"Don't," Monroe warned, falling as he hurled himself at the boy, but Johnny Cake kept fanning the flames.

"Stop!" Web cried out, running over. With his long arm, he reached out and seized the fiery bough from Johnny Cake's fingers. "This ain't no playground." He threw the branch down. "Now git home. Right now," he fumed, stomping out the fire with his brogans.

"I'm sorry, Mr. Web. Real sorry," the boy said, oblivious of Monroe as he walked by him, turning down the trail that led back to his neat whitewashed house.

Dalia dipped a washrag into a pitcher bowl of cold water and squeezed it out. Sighing, she wiped Nellie Ann's forehead then placed her palm against it. Her sister felt warm, though not as warm as before. Her face was so bloated that it looked like a pin could pop it, her feet and ankles also swollen. Dalia was growing weary of taking care of her sister by herself, with no one to keep her company. She wished Katie Mae were here with her.

Fall had always been Katie Mae's favorite season. She would bake pumpkin pies with thin, flaky crusts for Nellie Ann. In the early afternoons, she'd warm up spiced apple cider and serve it along with her raisin-oatmeal cookies. "Katie Mae. Katie Mae," Nellie Ann would say. "Please describe the fall colors." For Katie Mae's birthday last year, Nellie Ann had given her a delicate Belgium lace handkerchief, with pink flowers embroidered in each corner. Katie Mae had been thrilled. For this reason, Dalia had chosen another beautiful hankie in which to send Katie Mae the money.

"Where's Papa?" Nellie Ann asked, rousing.

"Out with his trees," Dalia told her.

"He hurt me," her sister said, licking her dry lips, blinking back tears.

"I know," Dalia said.

"He hurt me because he loves me."

"He hurt you because he was drinking."

"He drinks because he loves me."

"No," Dalia said adamantly. She closed her eyes so tightly she hoped they'd never open again. "He doesn't drink out of his goodness. He drinks because he's bad."

CHAPTER 9

When Monroe spotted a red scarf around the neck of the statue of the Confederate soldier, he let out a great big laugh. A Christmas wreath, fashioned from the branches of a cedar, hung on the courthouse door, while wooden cutouts of carolers stood on the gallery of the second floor. Close by, an old man who looked to be a hundred was roasting pecans in a shallow pan over a small open fire. "Five cents," he croaked, scooping nuts into a brown paper funnel, adding a sprinkle of salt. Monroe breathed in the strong odor, as pungent as roasting ears of corn, walked over, and bought himself a bagful. Lighthearted, he tossed the man a dime and stepped into the throng of Christmas shoppers. He tipped the funnel into his open mouth and was instantly energized by the salty, meaty flavor of the pecans.

A little girl dressed in green velvet brushed by him, and he winked at her, remembering a time when Dalia's face had been sweet and innocent, though Nellie Ann's face had never looked like this, for her white eyes, blank and unseeing, spoke of his guilt the minute she came into the world. A finger tapped him on the shoulder. "Mary Jones," he said, twisting around, surprised to see her. He tipped his hat, his eyes traveling over her large belly. She was very pregnant, and he suspected the baby would come early, not in the spring, like Tick had thought. "How's Johnny Cake doin'?" he asked anxiously. He wondered if Mary could hear the apprehension in his voice.

"Fine," the woman said. "Excited about this baby." She ran her palm gently over her stomach, as though she were stroking the newborn's head.

"What are ya gettin' him for Christmas?"

"Marbles. All different colors," she said, holding up a burlap bag, jangling it. Monroe could hear the marbles clacking against each other. "A pair of dress shoes." She eyed the gift, tied with a blue ribbon, tucked under her arm. "Peppermint candy canes. A tin of fudge I made for him."

"And Tick?"

"Chewing tobacco, same as always."

Digging his hand in his pants pocket, Monroe pulled out a ten-dollar bill and thrust it at her. "Merry Christmas, Mary. Buy yourself something, too."

Reluctantly, she took the money, uttered a timid, thank-you, before leaving him there, muddle-headed yet cheery, while shoppers, like schools of fish, flowed around him. Pulling himself together, he inhaled deeply and headed straightaway for the bank. To buy his girls something special, he needed more money than he had in his pocket. He spotted a wooden barrel by the gas lamp at the corner of Patterson and Central and tossed in the brown paper funnel. After which he crossed the street, striding beneath the bank's granite entrance before lingering mindfully in the quiet of the foyer. He had to remind Stuart Benson to get the paperwork ready for the loan he needed so that he could switch over to metal cups. Also, he had to talk to him about investing in a new plant under construction in Brunswick. If he intended to stay in the turpentine business, he needed to invest in its future.

He took off his hat, greeting his favorite teller as he stepped through the glass doors and into the lobby. Whatever Violet thought of him, he wasn't without manners. In the center of the bank stood a cedar tree decorated in red, while bunches of holly dotted the counters.

"What can I do for you today, Mr. Miller?" Dudley Simmons asked in his most official manner.

"I'll be needin' some money," Monroe told him. "Women's finery is expensive."

Mr. Simmons slid a form over the marble-topped counter and waited while Monroe carefully filled it out. "A hundred and fifty dollars," the teller stated, counting out the sum in tens and twenties. "Anything else, sir?"

Monroe was about to wish the man a Merry Christmas and get on with his shopping when, out of nowhere, an idea jolted him. "My safe deposit box," he said suddenly. "Would you please get me the key?"

"Right away, Mr. Miller," he said, leaving his station, returning several minutes later with a small golden key dangling from his fingers. "Just bring it back here when you're finished."

Key in hand, Monroe walked through the lobby toward a long, narrow room at the back of the bank where a portrait of Mr. Horace Jenkins, the bank's president, a thin-faced man with an underslung chin, smiled down at him. To Monroe's left was his box, number one hundred and ninety-four. He thumped his hat on a long wooden table, inserted the key, and opened the door. Rolling up his sleeve, he stuck his arm inside. He felt sadly nostalgic, as he always did when he touched the cold metal edge of the box. Sliding the container out, he set it next to his hat and untwisted the wire that kept the lid fastened. With the promise of hope, the habit of despair, he lifted off the top and beheld the pearl necklace. He had bought it for his first wife that special Christmas long ago when his hard work had paid off at last. After her death, he locked it away, for it belonged to another time. All these years, he meant to give it to Dalia—his Darling Doll, his firstborn, his raven-haired beauty. Time and again, he had imagined the flawless white pearl against her perfect alabaster skin, but now he knew differently. He would give it to Nellie Ann, for she was the one who deserved it. He would put it in her palm with the hope that her heart would soften toward him and Dalia's would open up to him again. Looping the chain between his fingers, he held up the pearl. Sunlight flitted across the gem's milky surface as he swung it. Maybe it had the power to bring him forgiveness. If not, he had made other plans. Again he swung the necklace, contemplating all the wonderful possibilities it presented, when the clasp gave way and the pearl cascaded onto the table. Cupping the gem in his palm, he examined the broken clasp. The jeweler would have to fix it. He felt his hopes faltering. A sour taste filled his mouth. But then he came up with another plan. For Christmas, he'd give all three expensive bolts of fabric. Yet Nellie Ann would get something more on New Year's Eve. Right as the clock struck twelve, he would place the pearl necklace in her hand.

He returned the key to Dudley Simmons and, optimistic about the future, headed for Stuart Benson's office down the hallway on the other side of the lobby. His fist was poised to knock when Stuart yelled out, "Come on in." Monroe swung the door open. "Well, Monroe, how are you doing?" Swallowing hard, he quickly added, "The missus says your youngest is ailing. I'm sorry to hear it. It's hard to have a sick child during Christmas."

"Yes, it is," Monroe said, standing by the doorjamb. He thrust his hand into his pants pocket. "But I've got something right here that should lift her spirits," he said, walking over. "A pearl necklace. It belonged to my first wife, but now it's gonna be Nellie Ann's. I reckon such a gift will make her feel better."

"Yes. Yes," Stuart Benson said, a thoughtful expression passing over his features. "Have a seat, why don't ya?" He nodded at a brown leather chair.

"Don't mind if I do," Monroe said, sinking down. He put his hat in his lap and brought his eyes to rest on the dapper man behind the desk, whose thin mustache looked like an ink smear above his mouth.

"My Julie's been beggin' me for a birthstone ring," Stuart said. "As soon as girls turn thirteen, they start wantin' pretty trinkets. So last month, June made a special trip to Savannah, looking for a little sapphire. I can't wait to see the look on that youngin's face when she opens her present." He leaned back in his chair and laughed loudly. "We wrapped it in a great big box to fool her. Told her we couldn't find what she wanted." Suddenly he grew serious. "What business brings ya here, Monroe?"

"Nothing that needs doin' right away," Monroe told him. "Just wanted to mention a few things to ya. Do ya recollect our conversation about those metal cups last summer?"

"Matter of fact, I do," Stuart said, pulling at his earlobe.

"I'm still thinkin' about switchin' over to them. The French swear they'll extend the life of your trees."

"Will cost you a bundle."

"I know. I know. But I hear a plant in Savannah is gettin' ready to make 'em, and I might be able to strike a good deal with the owner. Aston Hughes is an old friend of mine."

"So you want Citizen's to loan ya some money?"

"I reckon so," Monroe said, fingering the brim of his hat. "In late spring, I'll be making a trip to Savannah and will come back with a figure for ya. Just wanted to set the process in motion. Get ya thinkin' on it."

"I'll do that."

"Know anything about that rosin plant goin' up in Brunswick?"

"I've been lookin' into it," Stuart said. "Heard they're interested in research."

"Will ya let me know what ya find out?" Monroe asked him. "If it's solid, I'd like to invest in it."

"I'm thinkin' about putting some money into it myself," Stuart said, rising.

Monroe rose with him. "Give my regards to your family. And Merry Christmas," he said, before slipping out the office door.

Once outside, Monroe tugged on his hat and headed for Gerrell's Jewelry. Eyeglasses on the tip of his nose, old man Gerrell was bending over a worktable polishing a diamond brooch when Monroe entered. "Good to see ya, Mr. Miller," he said, momentarily stilling his hands. "How can I help ya?"

"I've brought ya something special," Monroe said. "I'll need it back New Year's Eve, though. Gonna give it to my youngest daughter who's sick." He slid his hand into his pants pocket and brought up the necklace. The pearl danced in the glow of gaslight coming from a brass fixture hanging from the ceiling. "See where it's broken," he said, pointing to the place where the necklace had snapped. "It also could do with a good polishing."

The jeweler took the necklace from Monroe's hand. "Don't worry," he said, running his wrinkled finger over the gem's satiny surface. "I'll have it ready for ya in no time."

"Merry Christmas," Monroe said, tipping his hat, smiling gratefully as he left.

Monroe shuddered in the raw, wet air. Above, the sky was turning soft gray, the temperature growing colder. Although snow was an aberration in this part of the country, he hoped for it. Maybe snow would imbue his family with the Christmas spirit and lighten their dislike for him. A sharp gust of wind cut through his jacket; and, wrapping his arms around his shoulders, he was tempted to buy himself a drink. Perhaps a little shot of brandy would warm him, but then he recalled his words to Tick that day at the tar kiln—*I'm gonna make it up to Johnny Cake. Gonna change my ways*—and, steeling himself against his craving, he kept on walking, right past Jason's Saloon. As he cut across the street bustling with horses and carriages, he felt the first cold drop on his skin. Glancing up, he saw them—snowflakes swirling soft and airy like bits of cotton. A good sign, he thought, his heart aflutter. Pulling his hat down low, he hurried on until he arrived at the draper's. Madame de Sagan was a pompous, shrill-voiced woman with silver hair, and usually Monroe went out of his way to avoid her, but today his fingers itched with excitement as he sauntered beneath the store's ornate archway.

Monroe could hear Dalia in the kitchen, pouring them glasses of eggnog. No bourbon in his this Christmas. As was their custom on Christmas Eve, they had retired to the parlor after supper. The cone ornaments of silver-plated brass, filled with candies, glimmered on the cedar tree. The candles burned brightly. The tin tinsel, twisted to reflect the light, dangled from the branches like a rich man's candy canes. Ornaments of Santa Claus, his helpers, and his reindeer, as well as little glass angels, had been tucked amid the spiky foliage. The Nativity scene was lined up on the mantel, stockings below it, presents on a bed of cotton beneath the tree. Violet sat on the settee threading a string of popcorn. Beside her, Nellie Ann was reclining in a wicker wheelchair with a thick blanket over her legs. Monroe studied Nellie Ann, the fruit of his loins, the birthmark of his shame. Her skin was deep yellow; her face, puffed up with water; her mouth, pulled to one side in a grimace. He ached to say how much he loved her, to say how sorry he was for everything, but these words had always been hard for him to speak, so he asked what she wanted for Christmas. She shrugged her narrow shoulders. "I've got something special for ya," he said, staring intently at her, "but ya have to wait till New Year's Eve. It's beautiful, and it'll look beautiful on ya." To his delight, her lips curled upward, but then Violet leaned over and, with one quick movement, wiped the red arc of peppermint off his daughter's mouth. "Christmas is my favorite time of year," he quickly added. "And there's snow on the ground, Nellie Ann. A sheet of white, everywhere. This is only the second time I've seen it. The first was long ago in the mountains of north Georgia, years before I married your mother, and I tell ya it was a sight to behold. A whiteness so clean and pure, it scared me. Soft as feathers from an eiderdown pillow and cold as driblets of fresh spring water. A snowflake will melt in your hand before ya know it. It's strong and delicate, like the present I have for you."

"Papa?" she said. He rocked forward in his chair to make sure she'd really spoken. "Papa?" she repeated, her tone fraught with fragility and worry.

"What is it, dear?" he asked her. His voice was tender.

"I didn't get you anything."

"Don't you be worried about that. It doesn't matter." It was then the tears ambushed him, and he blinked against them. When he looked up, Violet was eyeing him suspiciously, fiercely piercing a kernel of popcorn with her needle.

"Papa?"

"What, dear?" His gaze was upon her. Her blind eyes were smiling at him, and, desperate with confusion, he was about to lean over and hug her when Dalia sashayed into the room, her icy glare freezing him. She placed the tray on the pink marble table, then with false servility handed him his tumbler of eggnog.

"Thank you," he told her.

Smiling carnivorously, she said nothing.

He drank some of the eggnog, the sweetness coating the inside of his mouth. Glass in hand, he stood and walked over to the window. The wind was blowing, unsettling the snow, misting the tips of the pine trees white. Sighing, he drew in a deep breath and turned to face his family. "Your presents are in my study. I hope you'll like them." Violet ignored him, stuck to stringing her popcorn. Dalia pressed a glass into Nellie Ann's hand and guided the rim to her lips. "Dalia," Monroe tried again, "you'll love the present I got your sister, but I can't tell ya what it is. It's a secret till New Year's Eve." He downed the rest of his eggnog, licking the white froth off his mustache.

"Why should I care what you got her?" Dalia said coldly, snatching the glass from her sister's fingers, thumping it on the pink marble table. Her heart was beating so fiercely that she feared it would break through her chest and flee, forcing her to stand gutted, like a coward, before her father.

Monroe went over to the mantelpiece, depositing his empty tumbler beside the manger. "It's my way of saying I'm—"

"Why should any of us care?" Dalia said, groping for some courage, which she hoped was where her heart used to be.

Monroe cut his eyes to Nellie Ann, straining forward in her wheelchair, her white eyes staring at him. "The gift I want to give you is something from a more innocent time in my life. It was Mary Lou's," he said somberly. As soon as he said this, Violet jerked her head up, stilled her hands.

"Your dead wife's?" Dalia said, her biting tone victorious. "It belongs in the grave with her, then. My sister doesn't want it."

"Why don't ya ask her if she wants it?" Monroe took a step toward Nellie Ann.

"I don't have to," Dalia declared, blocking his body with her own. "You think you can save your legacy of pain and sorrow by passing out jewelry. Why don't you be more like Lollie Morris and keep your wealth? See if that will get you into heaven."

"I'd rather burn in hell than be like that man," Monroe said, staring into his older daughter's face, hardened by hatred. His eyes fell on Violet, her face stony with resentment, then on Nellie Ann, whose features looked pinched and strained. "But, Dalia, I want your sister to have it," he said, staring into her lavender eyes, devoid of any feeling. Shaken, he looked away and focused on the angel that, for as long as he could remember, had decorated the top of their tree. He regarded the angel's face sadly, now sightless, with loose threads where the eyes used to be. "I'll be going now," he said, turning toward them. "I know where I'm not wanted." They didn't say a word to stop him as he strode toward the door and down the hallway.

He went to his study, where his valise was packed and waiting. Gripping its handle, he scanned the rows of books, his desk, his chair. So silent, so lonely, he told himself. "I'm sorry," he whispered to the bolts of fabric, which he'd propped against the bookshelves. Then, like a thief in the night, he quietly stole away.

Christmas Day, only the three of them sat around the dining room table. The red tallow candles flamed in their silver holders. A sprig of mistletoe dangled from a red ribbon tied to the crystal chandelier. Dalia dug her fork into the mound of dressing and brought it to her lips. It was dry and tasteless, and she missed Katie Mae's.

Over the years, Dalia had watched as Katie Mae threw together her famous dressing every Christmas Eve. She would announce the name of an ingredient and then add it to a bowl of crumbled-up cornbread, biscuits, and week-old bread. *Some onions, celery, garlic, oregano, sage, and a tad of salt and pepper,* she would say. Followed by, *chicken broth, melted butter, eggs, and wild mushrooms,* if she could find them. Whereupon she let the mixture sit. *Soakin' up the juices,* she called it. On Christmas Day, the dressing would be served golden and moist, unlike this hard brick of chaff that Sallie had made.

Dalia cast her gaze on her mother, who, having abandoned the dressing, was chewing the tough, overcooked bird with fervent determination. Nellie Ann was sipping a cup of hot apple cider. Their father's chair was empty. Last night, after he was gone, Dalia had stolen to the study and seen the luscious fabric. Now she tried to harden her heart to the guilt she felt for the cruel way she'd treated him.

"More mashed potatoes?" her mother asked, lifting up the bowl.

Dalia shook her head. Thus far, every morsel had been unappetizing. The potatoes were too salty, with not enough milk in them. The giblet gravy was thin. The Brussels sprouts, soggy. Dalia wondered what Katie Mae was eating. Was she celebrating Christmas with Zara, or had one of the families down the road asked her over? Was she eating her own turkey and dressing, or was it made by someone else's hands?

"If Katie Mae were here, it'd be good," Nellie Ann said finally.

The sound of her sister's voice, silent all morning, startled Dalia—so much so that it triggered a choking jag. "Raise your arms," her mother told her. Dalia stretched her arms up high above her head; and at once the choking stopped.

"Katie Mae's a great cook," Dalia said quickly, wanting to elicit something more from her sister, who had sealed her lips again.

"Girls," their mother said, looking nervously around the room, "watch what you say. Sallie's feelings would be hurt if she heard you."

"It might be white outside," Dalia added, observing the thin film of snow through the window, "but it still doesn't feel like Christmas."

"Did it ever?" her mother sniffed, her tone as bitter as the cranberry sauce on her plate.

"Long ago," replied Dalia. In the distance, a horse whinnied. Footfalls clumped through the kitchen. Dalia put down her fork, the beat of her heart wavering like it always did when her father came home. Gluing her eyes on the doorway, she sucked in a mouthful of air, breathlessly waiting. "Papa," she blurted out, just as Sallie, cocky as ever, pranced into the room.

"Miss Dalia," Sallie said, hastening toward the table, "are ya'll finished?"

"Yes, ma'am," Dalia mumbled with a little bob of her head.

"The meal was lovely," her mother said politely.

"Wait till dessert," Sallie said, winking mischievously at them. "I'll be back directly," she said, after stacking the dirty plates on a tray from the sideboard, the dishes clinking as she left. "Pumpkin pie," she announced minutes later, strutting into the room, the silver tray held high in her hands. She thumped wedges of pie in front of them, poured chicory coffee into their cups, then just stood there, watching and waiting.

Apprehensive, Dalia glanced down at her plate. Katie Mae's pumpkin pie was light and fluffy, topped with walnuts and dollops of whipped cream. Her crust was soft and thin. She had always baked a whole pumpkin pie just for Nellie Ann. Suddenly Dalia spotted the walnut sticking out from the splash of whipped cream. She glanced over at her sister, wondering how on earth Katie Mae had managed to get the pie to them today.

Nellie Ann was touching the plate with one hand, while forking up a bite with the other. She slipped the tines between her lips, the corners of her mouth curling upward. "Light and fluffy," she said softly, "like always."

CHAPTER 10

By New Year's Eve, Nellie Ann had gotten worse. Whenever she mumbled, Dalia leaned over, placed her ear close to her sister's mouth, and listened. She longed to hear words of love, but all she could make out was the single word, *Papa,* the *P* breathily pushed out, as though her sister were encased in a chrysalis of ever-present pain. It was a physical throbbing, a spiritual aching, which took over everything, reduced life to the basics. At the end, a cold stillness would take its place, but right now it was the pain, demanding and constant, that puffed through her sister's lips. "Papa," Nellie Ann murmured, and if Dalia could have, she would have taken this pain from her sister and made it all her own.

At age ten, Dalia had tried to do just this. Tying a blindfold over her eyes, she had wanted to share in her sister's darkness. Unable to dress herself, she asked Katie Mae to help her. During dinner, she spilled food, dribbling gravy on the white linen tablecloth, dropping peas as she blindly guided the fork to her mouth, knocking over a glass of water. She stumbled through the house, bumping into furniture, breaking one of her mother's fine porcelain teacups. All day she had tried to ease her sister's blindness by being a part of it.

"Papa," Nellie Ann mumbled.

"No, it's Dalia."

"Katie Mae?" her sister asked.

"Don't you remember, sweetheart? She came this morning. Brought this rose to you. Said she'd never seen one blooming this time of year." Dalia held the Cherokee rose beneath her sister's nose. "Doesn't it smell sweet?"

Nellie Ann took a raspy breath. "Katie Mae's gone," she said. Dalia could feel the pain, pulsing from her sister's lips. "Papa. Papa," Nellie Ann whimpered.

"Yes, he sent her away," Dalia said. "I know how much that hurt you, but he won't hurt you anymore. I promise."

"Papa's gone," Nellie Ann said.

"But you've got me and Mama. We're here," Dalia told her. "And we'll never let him hurt you again." Dalia breathed in, made her voice sound calm and level. "Here, feel the rose Katie Mae brought you," she said, trailing the velvet petals over Nellie Ann's face. The muscles in her sister's cheek tightened. Snatching the rose away, Dalia spotted a drop of blood where the blossom had been. She pinched the stem tightly between her fingers and dug the thorns in. "Papa. Papa," Dalia said, echoing the name perched on her sister's lips. "Papa. Papa," she kept saying, his name stinging her mouth, the thorns burning her flesh. "See, darling, I spared you," she said, letting the rose fall from her fingers, knowing, at last, what the truth had always been. Regardless of how hard she had tried to share in her sister's blindness, Papa was the only pain they'd ever really shared. Wanting him gone, not wanting him to leave them. Getting him to love them, pushing his love away. Trying to forgive him, hating him for having to forgive him. It was Papa. Papa. Forever Papa. His clothes. His breath. His will. Yes, always and ever, Papa. Their sadness, their joy, their fate—willed by him.

Mended and polished, the necklace was waiting for him as Monroe passed through the doorway of Gerrell's Jewelry. He placed the pearl inside a white satin box and slipped the box into his coat pocket. After paying what he owed, he wished Mr. Gerrell a happy New Year; and, despite the debacle on Christmas Eve, he felt hopeful about the evening and gave the old man a hefty tip.

As he stepped out the door, his boots slipped on the thin coat of ice that covered the walkway; so he made himself be still. Standing there, breathing in the frosty air, he envisioned what the new year promised. His daughter's special moment would come when the clock struck twelve midnight, as she cradled the pearl necklace in her palm. Cautiously, Monroe edged forward. "Mr. Miller," came a voice from behind him. "Mr. Miller." He glanced back over his shoulder and saw Doc Green's wife sliding over the icy walkway toward him.

"Whoa, there, Marjorie," he said, grabbing her by the arm to keep her from falling. "If you're not careful, you're gonna hurt yourself."

"I was at the confectionery when I saw you through the window," she said, panting as she tried to catch her breath. "My husband told me what happened, and I wanted to tell you how sorry I am for your loss."

Monroe kept his clear blue eyes upon her. It was six hours till midnight. Dusk had come, and the streets were mostly silent. Only the whooshing sound of the gas lamps swam through the frigid air. Fingering the box in his coat pocket, he felt the promise of the pearl fading and braced himself to hear about his daughter's death.

Barren and lonely, the cemetery had only six trees. Sandy pathways stole on to burial plots and abducted the sparse grass around which the small group of mourners gathered. Monroe watched the pallbearers move slowly down the narrow, desolate road, surrounded by neglected gravestones, with cracks in their cement casings. Clutching his black woodsman's hat, Monroe squeezed his hurt into its brim. The slight coffin bobbed toward him, and he sensed a wetness on his cheeks. For a moment he thought he might be crying, but what he mistook for tears was only the cold, damp air settling on his skin.

"God works in mysterious ways," Reverend Holloway said, his eyes sad behind small round spectacles. "But for you and your family . . ." He nodded in Monroe's direction. "This is a pain no tongue can speak."

Dalia saw the reverend nodding at her father, and she reluctantly turned toward his broad hands strangling the hat's brim, his face scrunching up, his eyes welling, yet even now she didn't trust his pained expression, the theater of his sorrow. She was the one who was hurting, discreetly mourning so as not to make a mockery of her grief.

Monroe looked on as the pallbearers lowered his daughter into the ground. Refusing to let her be worm food, he had shunned his cherished soft pine wood and chosen the hard wood of mahogany for her coffin. While he wanted to believe that God worked in mysterious ways, he didn't. The Supreme Being gave life, then took it away. There was no mystery to it. Nellie Ann had been flesh and blood, now she wasn't.

Dalia shivered as her sister's coffin disappeared into the black hole. There would be even more darkness, after the dense red clay was shoveled on top. Nellie Ann would leave the world the way she had come into it—cradled by the dark.

The reverend waited until the coffin was roped down, then he opened his Bible. "Psalm Twenty-three," he said. *"The Lord is my shepherd; I shall not want."*

The Supreme Being is my operator, Monroe thought. I shall not want.

"He maketh me to lie down in green pastures; he leadeth me beside the still waters." The reverend paused and glanced at Dalia.

Dalia remembered taking her sister's hand, leading her to the brook behind Miller's Mansion, guiding her fingers over the velvety green moss that carpeted the bank, making her dip them into the chilly water.

"He restoreth my soul," the reverend went on. *"He leadeth me in the paths of righteousness for his name's sake."*

"Beneath the longleaf's needles, He restoreth my soul," Monroe whispered. "He leadeth me in the path of the woodsman for his name's sake."

The psalm fluttered inside Monroe's ears while the reverend continued, *"Yea, though I walk through the valley of the shadow of death, I will fear no evil: for thou art with me; thy rod and thy staff they comfort me."*

For so many years, Monroe had hauled his sins around, waiting for this moment when the townsfolk would see him dissolve under the burden of his own judgment, but here he was, whole and solid, in front of his daughter's grave. There had been no joyful New Year's Eve, no moment of reconciliation. He had been cheated out of it. The worst had happened. The ground wanted the innocence of his daughter, not the guilt that was his.

"Thou preparest a table before me in the presence of mine enemies," Reverend Holloway said. *"Thou anointest my head with oil; my cup runneth over."*

Once, Dalia had been his Darling Doll. Once, Dalia had loved her father. Now she hated him, for he had anointed her head with sorrow, so much sorrow that she doubted she would ever be happy again. The pine needles wailed in the cold breeze. A limb cracked in the distance, echoing her broken sadness. Dust unto dust. The hope of Nellie Ann's life reduced to ashes.

Monroe remembered a day long ago when, if not for his stubbornness, his cup could've *runneth over.* They had been in the music room. Dalia and he on the settee. Violet in the wingback chair. Nellie Ann on the bench in front of the piano. An odd tension had filled the air. Suddenly Dalia wanted to know if he was nervous. Why should he be nervous? he wondered. This recital would be no different from all the others. It was then his daughter began to play—not the classical music he'd expected, but one of his favorite tunes, a melody from his past, played aboard the *Dixie Queen* as he accompanied his barrels of turpentine up the Mississippi. "*The sun shines bright in the old Kentucky home,*" they had begun singing, while he had held back his voice, squandering any hope the day had promised.

Her shoulders shaking, her mother sobbed into a black handkerchief, which she pressed against her face, but try as she might, Dalia couldn't soften her heart toward her, either.

"She'll go blind from all that weeping," Monroe heard one of the mourners say. *Blind from all that weeping,* his mind repeated, but years ago he had made his wife laugh. Violet had loved him, married him against her parents' wishes because he was the one she wanted. Just like Monroe, she had longed to be free and daring. Yet over time, she had relinquished her dreams, living not the life she yearned for but a life she'd never wanted. Groaning, he turned toward her, desiring her sympathy, something born of their shared hot grief. Violet lifted her eyes to him, her naked stare illuminating the source of all her sorrow, and finally he understood they were more alike than she would ever know. If she had been in his shoes in that dark Savannah alley, she would have done as he had—carelessly fallen into the arms of that honey-blond, cat-eyed whore.

Tears of guilt were washing down her father's cheeks now, but Dalia would not be moved. He had brought this on himself. He hated pity, and she would give him none.

"*Surely goodness and mercy shall follow me all the days of my life: and I will dwell in the house of the LORD for ever,*" the reverend finished, gently closing his Bible. "Let us pray."

Abruptly, Dalia averted her eyes from her father. She looked up to see Katie Mae. Not twenty feet away, she was holding on tightly to an angel's marble wings, trying to hide herself in the shadow of its uplifted face. When a mourner behind Dalia coughed loudly, Katie Mae coughed also, as though trying to bridge the space between herself and the mourners. Still, it was Katie Mae's lonely freedom that Dalia most wanted. For after the funeral, Dalia would have to suffer her family again—Papa comforting himself with bourbon, Mama comforting herself with laudanum. But who or what would comfort Dalia now that her sister was dead? "I love you, Nellie Ann," she whispered, her eyes dry and tearless, as the hard stone arms of loss wrapped themselves around her and comforted her like a friend.

They sat quietly in the parlor, the last of the visitors now gone. The funereal smell of flowers and food sullied the air, making Dalia nauseous. Her father was seated in the chair by the mantel, his face ridged from pain and guilt, his eyes red-rimmed from the tears he'd shed at the burial. She saw his boots, planted firmly on the floor, red smears of clay on the rug beside the heels, same as always. He would never change. Dalia shifted toward her mother sitting primly on the settee, her hands folded neatly in her lap, a wan smile on her face, her olive skin sallow. In the past few hours, she'd visited her bedroom twice, fleeing the parlor when it was most crowded so as not to be noticed, but Dalia had seen her. She'd heard her pattering over the floorboards, returning minutes later, her expression duller, her eyes feverish, the pupils smaller, showing the effect of the opium she had taken upstairs, making Dalia hate those purple-tinged bottles. Although her father wasn't drinking now, she knew he would succumb later. When the guilt became too much for him, he would slip away to his study and reach for his bottle.

Dalia's sick feeling began to pass, as anger bullied its way into her stomach and elbowed the nausea out. "What are we going to do now?" she said at last, placing her hands on the armrests, standing. "Are ya'll hungry? There's a luscious chocolate cake on the dining room table and also a pot of coffee. I told Sallie to go to her room and rest, so tell me what you want, and I'll get it for you." She looked at her mother, who hadn't heard a word of what she was saying, then at her father, who had heard her but wasn't speaking. "Well," she said, taking a step forward, "I think I'll go pour myself a cup of coffee. Mama?" she said, glancing over at her. "If not cream, would you prefer a little medicine in your coffee?" Her mother said nothing, just wrung her hands together.

"Let your mother grieve," her father said. "Take your anger out on me, if you must."

"Of course, Papa," Dalia said, "but I didn't know if I'd get a chance to chat with you. So you're staying for supper?"

"No, I won't be staying," he told her. "If your mother needs anything, I'll be at my shanty by the river."

"Stocked well with bottles of bourbon to ease your conscience," Dalia said with a shrill laugh.

"You can't hurt me," her father said, rising slowly. "I know what I've done. I know who I am."

"Too late for that now, Papa," Dalia said, pressing her lips together. "The damage is done. My sister's dead."

"She was my daughter, and I loved her, too," her father muttered, the tears filling his eyes, rolling down his cheeks.

"Yes, Papa, I know about your love," Dalia said, fixing her furious eyes on him. "Mama always said you loved your trees more, but I don't think so. Your love is the same for everything and everybody . . . deadly."

"I may be cursed," her father said, swallowing hard, "but I know I loved her."

"I know I loved her, too, and I curse your soul to damnation for killing the person I loved most in this world."

He opened his mouth, the air whooshing through his lips as though she'd punctured him with a knife. With the flat of his hand, he wiped the tears off his cheeks and in a voice whittled down by his own harsh judgment spoke to her. "I know what I done," he confessed. "It is my cross to carry, and I won't be coming back here until you can forgive me." His black hat in his hands, he strode over to her mother. "I'm sorry, darling," he said, her mother's face revealing nothing as he brushed his lips against her skin. He began walking wearily toward the foyer. Dalia stayed where she was. A minute later, she heard the front door closing shut and his boots crossing the veranda.

CHAPTER 11

The roustabout ran madly over the sandy ground—pushing a barrel, rolling it down the bank—until it seemed as though both would plunge into the river, but at the water's edge he gave the barrel a twirl and abruptly brought it to a halt. It was early May, and the hands were loading the steamer, an eighty-two-ton stern-wheeler, eighty-four feet long, twenty-six feet wide, and six feet deep. Monroe's barrels of pitch and spirits of turpentine were being stacked on the deck until they looked like bunkers rising from the water. Monroe ran his eyes over the *Lily.* A wood-burner, she was capable of carrying two hundred and fifty barrels along with thirteen crew members and twenty-five passengers. He had always liked this journey up the river, the excitement he felt as the captain navigated through the nooks and crannies in the narrow, murky water. After attaching a cable to a strong cypress, the crew would ease the steamer along for a thousand feet, then hook the cable to another tree and repeat the process. "God makes the weather. I make the trip," the captain would say as they embarked.

For the past five months, Monroe had holed himself up in the fishing shanty by the river, not caring about much, not even his liquor. He would sit in a chair on the front porch, brooding and staring out over the lagoon, the gray cylinders of the cattails reminding him of his daughter's blank eyes. Time and again, he would relive her burial—those well-meaning mourners stressing her virtues, making her faultless, as though only the pure deserved love after they died. Night after sleepless night of tremors and hallucinations, he would rise at dawn and swallow a pot of coffee. He had grown himself a beard, become thin and dirty, not bothering to shave, wash, or eat. Afraid of what he might see in the mirror, he had broken it into a thousand pieces and thrown them into the river. Every morning he would check his face with his fingers, fearful that the raw sores of syphilis were hidden in the thickness of his beard.

But when he woke up this morning, everything had changed. For the first time in months, he noticed the salmon sunrise as he flung the shuttered windows open. He wasn't happy, but he wasn't sad, either. After eating a bowl of grits, he washed and dressed, sat in his chair on the front porch as usual, but today he was different. He could almost taste the clean air, enjoy the breeze off the river. Not quite smiling, he stroked his beard, confident that he had, at last, turned a corner, that he was whole and solid, that absolution was possible for someone like him.

Feeling hopeful, he saddled the bay gelding, his thin haunches rubbing against the saddle as he headed upriver toward the landing. Raking his fingers beneath his hat, he felt strands of hair come out. Lack of food, he reckoned; from now on he would eat better. Sober, he saw the landscape clearly—the moss hanging like gauze from the trees, the pampas grass sprouting in clusters along the bank, the cattails rising, somber in their beauty. He breathed in the fishy smell of the water, the musky odor of loam and algae amid the reeds. Close by, he heard a coot crying, then a dove cooing for its mate. He could almost hear the hum of the water. He had forgotten to pack a valise, but, cheered by the warm sun on his body, he didn't care. After three hours of steady riding, he had arrived at the landing and stabled his horse.

Monroe walked over the boarding plank onto the freshly scrubbed deck. Women in white dresses and plumed hats were leaning over the top deck railing, peering down at the barrels still spinning over the bank. Men in dark frock coats stood protectively behind them. These fancy-dressed passengers amused him, for he had traveled down the mighty Mississippi on truly grand steamers, but the *Lily,* he knew, was no more than a backwater boat hauling barrels of turpentine on Snake River. "Almost finished," shouted one of the roustabouts, his shirt wet with perspiration, his tough feet crusted with calluses. Monroe helped him roll the last barrel across the deck. After wrestling it upright, he stepped back to admire the stack. For the first time in a long while, work was doing its magic, curing him of his ills.

The musical chimes of the *Lily*'s whistle resounded, signaling she was ready to begin her journey. "Thank you for your help," Monroe told the men. Digging into his pants pockets, he tipped a little extra into each worker's hand. Then, leaning back against the railing, he looked out over the bow. Sloops, fishing smacks, and other small boats dotted the water. He smelled cigar smoke drifting down from the upper deck, heard the waves lapping against the hull, and felt his nerves unwinding as the *Lily* pulled away.

When he was young, he had constructed rafts out of half-filled barrels and steered them down many a tight, crooked river, his arms strong from handling the long, heavy oars. He had maneuvered Florida's Apalachicola and Georgia's Flint and Chattahoochee. A strong swimmer, he had survived the *Betsy*'s sinking after she slammed into a deadhead in the Yellow River. All his life he had worked hard and been happy for having done it. Yes, work would be the balm for his wounded spirit.

Exhausted, he mounted the stairs to the top deck. A soft breeze was blowing through the window when he stepped inside his stateroom. The whistle chimed again. He lay down, closed his eyes, and slept, the voices of the passengers sweeping over him. Hours later, the smell of fish frying lured him awake. Hungry, he crawled out of his berth. There was nothing like the taste of baby catfish, caught fresh from the river, fried up crisp and tender. Yawning, he poured tepid water from a pitcher into a cracked white bowl, then splashed a handful against his face. He wiped off his skin, scouting for sores with his fingers, his eyes steering clear of the oval mirror. Without warning, the *Lily* listed, and he took hold of the dressing table so as not to lose his footing. Going over to the window, he peered out. Black clouds were massing in the distance. Faint streaks of lightning zigzagged through the sky.

When he entered the dining room, it wasn't crowded. Seated around three oval tables were twelve people, the women cooling themselves off with fans, the men drinking sherry. Monroe spotted a table with an empty chair. "May I join you?" he asked a man with blond whiskers.

"Most certainly," the man said, standing, as the others slid their chairs over to make room for him. "I'm Dallas McCullers," he said, shaking Monroe's hand. "And this is my wife, Emma." He nodded at a tiny squirrellike woman.

"Monroe Miller," he said, lowering himself to his seat.

"So pleased to make your acquaintance," the woman said.

"I'm Earl Baker," said a poker-faced man on the other side of the table.

"Henrietta Baker," the woman next to him stated.

"What a lovely little steamer!" Emma McCullers declared. "This is our first trip on the *Lily*. How about you, Mr. Miller?"

"I've taken her many times before."

"We're going to Savannah to visit with my wife's mother," Dallas McCullers said.

"Mama's been ill," his wife said, frowning. "Rheumatism. The poor thing doesn't get around much anymore."

Dallas McCullers rolled his eyes. "My mother-in-law suffers from many maladies. Sadly, she keeps us going, from Columbus to Savannah and back."

"At least your mother has her health," his wife countered.

"Like mother, like son," her husband replied.

"Darling, may I have a little glass of sherry?" Henrietta Baker asked.

Earl Baker held up an index finger, dipping his head at a white-jacketed waiter by the dining room door. "A glass of sherry," he said as the black man came over.

"Yessir." Then, swiveling toward Monroe, the waiter inquired, "And you, sir?"

"I won't be drinkin'," Monroe told him, placing a clean and creased napkin across his lap. In the center of the room, a brass chandelier, dull from lack of polishing, was flickering. The wainscoting, Monroe noticed, needed another coat of varnish. There were scuff marks all over the red pine floor.

"And where are you from, Mr. Miller?" asked Henrietta Baker, her plump cheeks rising with the question.

"From the piney woods around Valdosta," Monroe said. "I work the trees there."

Her husband ran a manicured finger down the lapel of his coat. "I've drawn up contracts for some operators in that part of the country. For whom do you work?"

"I am my own boss."

"How on earth do you do it, working alongside such rough people?" Henrietta Baker asked.

"I reckon I'm too rough myself to take offense."

"Dear, dear," she added, clicking her tongue.

"Years ago, I rafted barrels of turpentine up this river," Monroe said proudly, " 'cause it was cheaper that way to haul them."

"How quaint!" Emma McCullers cooed with a dainty clap of her hands.

"It's hard work," Monroe said.

"And where is your little raft now?" Henrietta Baker asked him.

Monroe coughed into his hand, didn't answer.

"Is this your cargo on the *Lily*?" questioned Emma McCullers.

"Yes, ma'am," Monroe said, fixing his eyes on her. "I own fifteen thousand acres of longleaf pines, and my turpentine will be traveling all summer up this river. If ya'll excuse me, I seem to have lost my appetite," he said, abruptly standing. "I think I'll go have me a smoke."

He took his time going down the metal steps, stopping every so often to look out over the water. He could hear the rumble of thunder, closer now than before. The wind whistled through the stacked barrels as he walked toward the bow. He could smell the rain that was probably hiding around the next bend in the river.

Lightning slashed through the darkness as Monroe stood on the deck, tamping the bowl of his pipe with tobacco. The cypress trees swayed above the water. Cawing loudly, a flock of crows flew toward a stand of oaks on the other side of the river. Bowing his head against the gusts, Monroe struck a match against his thumbnail and lit up.

All of a sudden the *Lily* tipped violently, waves smacking against her, water sloshing over her bow. Monroe stumbled against the railing, his pipe tumbling from his fingers, falling into the swirling depths of the river. There was another bolt of lightning, another crack of thunder. A sheet of rain began pinging. Monroe lifted his face to the downpour, the droplets stinging his flesh.

"They gonna tumble," he heard someone yell.

Whipping around, Monroe saw the barrels toppling and spinning toward him. The wind and rain lashed against his body. He slipped on the wet surface and slid over the wood with his arms splayed out in front of him, splinters piercing his fingers. Tightly, he shut his eyes to the rain and the wind. When his hands touched the slick side of a barrel, he jerked his eyelids open, threw his arms around it, and rolled it close. Another big wave slammed against the *Lily*, and the vessel rocked savagely. Clutching the barrel to his chest, Monroe pressed his face against the curved wood, holding on to his work, to his life. With the next wave, he plowed through the railing and into the churning water.

The barrel plummeted against him, spiraling him down into the darkness with it, pinning him in the soft silt at the river's bottom. Overhead, the water swirled. With all the strength he could muster, Monroe dug his boot heels into the sand and pushed against the wooden staves, but the barrel lay heavy upon him. Again he tried, but the barrel held him. He could hear the storm raging above. Lunging forward, he bumped the cargo with the full force of his chest. It didn't budge. The river grew silent around him, cocooning him in warm darkness. It was then he heard her cane tapping against the riverbed, saw her white eyes staring at him through the murky water. With a curl of her fingers, she called him over. Wrapping his arms around the barrel, he hugged it to him, and she smiled—her fingers moving upward, touching the pearl, dazzling white against her breast.

Dalia picked up a lily pad of leaves that the wind had ripped off the magnolia tree last night. The storm had done some damage, scattered a carpet of its shiny green leaves, splintered a thin branch in half. All night long she had lain in bed listening to the unhinged shutter outside her bedroom window banging against the brick, but today the sky was clear, not a cloud above her, just a handful of crows, their caws raucous as they wheeled. She noticed a patch of late daffodils bending over, their heads touching the ground. She went over to them, dug up some dirt, and patted it around their stems.

Back inside the house, Sallie was cooking and chattering to herself. It seemed she couldn't do one without the other. Which was why she did neither well, Dalia decided, rising, meandering toward the goldfish pond, wanting to catch a glimpse of Moby Dick. There was a twig of pine needles on the head of the bronze maiden, a flurry of dead leaves on the pond's surface, but no sign of the big orange fish. Dalia sank down on the granite bench and stared at the silent water. Empty and lonely, she thought, the tears streaming down her face before she knew it.

Her mother, drugged, had slept through the storm last night while she had endured it with no one to talk to. No Nellie Ann to take care of, no Papa to cause her worry. But she was glad that he was gone, relieved that he had left them so that she and her mother could deal with their grief alone. She wiped her eyes with the back of her hand, gazing at the sun on the water, the way it skipped over the surface like a stone, recalling what Katie Mae had said that day after their outing at Millertown. *Mr. Monroe was fishin' in the middle of the night,* she'd said. *Did you catch anything, Papa?* her sweet sister had asked. *I was aimin' to catch Moby Dick*, their father had said, *but was so drunk I forgot to bait my hook.* Sitting there fishing dead drunk, Dalia thought, the beginning of a smile on her lips, when she saw a blaze of orange cutting through the water, the black stump of Moby Dick's head. "Papa! Papa!" she called out, looking around frantically. For a moment, she felt foolish. But then the slight smile returned. Yes, he had moved out and was still living in his shanty by the river. Quit his drinking, Zara had said. Her eyes scanned the pond, searching for the fish again, but he'd already disappeared beneath the algae-speckled water.

It was hot. Georgia went from a cool early spring right into a humid, blistering summer. *No dilly-dallying around with daffodils,* her papa always said. Dalia stood up, glanced around. The grape arbor was beginning to fill out. The leaves on the pecan trees were emitting their sour, bitter odor. The longleafs, forever green, stood tall and proud. If Katie Mae were here, she'd be setting out her garden, tucking the little seeds into the ground, saying a prayer over them. Which was what she had always done, every spring for as long as Dalia could remember, until Dalia's sin of omission had let her take the blame for something she hadn't done. Now Katie Mae was lost to her forever. The look of judgment that would be in her eyes was something Dalia never wanted to encounter. Yet, according to Zara last week, Katie Mae was doing better—fixing up her shanty, painting the inside white, sewing dimity curtains, and hanging them from the windows. Too busy to be full of self-pity, he'd said. Trying to be happy in spite of her sorrow. Upon hearing his words, Dalia had felt less guilty, but still she grieved. Lonely, she was, aching for the old familiarity of those strong dark hands.

Dalia was beginning to understand that grief was a hard, slow process. She would be eating her breakfast, listening to the jays building a nest in the pecan tree outside the kitchen window, enjoying the possibilities of spring, when out of nowhere the memory of the cedar waxwing would flood through her and she'd be sad again. She'd be in her bedroom, combing her hair in front of the oval mirror, admiring her thick dark curls, and suddenly Nellie Ann's white eyes would be staring back at her, her thin hair plastered against her skull. *Dalia, do you think I'm pretty?* she'd say. The smallest things triggered the most painful memories, so painful that when they came rushing in Dalia couldn't breathe.

Same as she, her mother was vacillating—talkative one day, taciturn the next. Lately, she'd taken to leaving the house, ordering Zara to drive her into Valdosta, where she'd shop until late evening, coming home with armloads of boxes filled with dresses, hats, and undergarments, forgotten as soon as she put the items away. Then, like a vampire, the melancholia would rise in the darkness and drink down her hope again.

Whereupon she'd lock herself in her bedroom with her purple-tinged bottles, no longer making an effort to hide her craving, leaving the empty vials out for Dalia to find later.

Would this sadness never cease? Dalia thought, her eyes misting over, falling on a chipmunk scurrying from his hole, making her smile. She was blinking back tears when she caught the sound of hooves galloping in the distance, growing louder and louder on the rutted road as they neared Miller's Mansion, then slowing to a stop. Who could it be? she asked herself as she stood there facing the house. A strong breeze rattled through the wet trees, misting her arms with raindrops. "Papa," she whispered, barely breathing, taking a tentative step forward. "Papa," she repeated, her heart skipping a beat, stopping, then beating rapidly as she moved over the grass. All of a sudden the back door flew open, slammed shut. Dalia came to a halt, stared anxiously. "Miss Dalia, Miss Dalia, come here!" Sallie yelled, waving her arms high above her head. There was something in the way Sallie called her, something in her high, shrill voice, in her dark flying hands, that reminded Dalia of birds. Of starlings before a storm, she thought, as she began running. Of young starlings seeking shelter in the canopies of the ancient pines.

Dalia

CHAPTER 12

As Dalia peered out the window, clouds shaped liked circus animals performed tricks in the tented blue sky. There was a rumble and a bellow, the grinding of steel against iron, the rocking motion, taking her forward. The heat was suffocating, a liquid hand pressing down, and she gagged trying to catch her breath. Tucked in the tunnel of her fist was a white lace handkerchief. Pinching the lace between her fingers, she gave the handkerchief a little snap, then brought it to her brow, dabbing the sweat from her high forehead. On the seat opposite, a heavyset woman with slits for eyes fanned her face with a plump hand and sighed. The woman hadn't uttered a word since the train had left the station in Valdosta, but then neither had Dalia. It was hot and humid, requiring too much effort to talk. The train chugged past a cornfield, the stalks vain and erect, their green leaves bleached by the sunlight. At the back of the car, a baby began whining and revving up for a cry, but then came the mother's voice, cooing softly, quieting the infant.

Dalia stretched in her seat and, yawning, closed her eyes. Three thousand dollars, two trunks, and one valise were the only things she had left in this world. Nervously, she felt for her string purse but calmed when her fingers touched the soft, stuffed bulge of velvet nudged against her waist.

Her father's acres and acres of pine trees, his shanty by the river, Miller's Mansion—all of it was lost, and even now, as she headed into her new life, she couldn't quite believe what her mother had done. It had begun with her extravagant spending. Her endless trips to Savannah, where she bought new furniture, carpets, jewelry, and dresses. Days and days of nothing but frenzied buying, the items forgotten as soon as the money was spent. Next, Stuart Benson had persuaded her to purchase metal cups for the pines, and she had sent Tick Jones to Savannah expressly for that purpose, but alas, he had paid too much for them. Then, toward the end of last summer, during the worst drought in the four years since her father's drowning, a brush burning leapt its boundaries and ravaged the longleafs, their rusty pine needles igniting like straw, the mature pines, bearing cones, dying. All this in a year in which the price of tar and pitch fell. The loans came due, and the money wasn't there. A few operators had offered to help out, mostly out of respect for her father, but ultimately Lollie Morris had forced the bank into an auction and paid one-tenth of the actual value for the properties. As always, her mother had turned to her medicine for comfort, swallowing bottle after bottle of the licorice-flavored opiate, too fuzzy-headed to make informed decisions, until one morning her body had simply stopped. Dalia had found her lying in bed, a half-empty vial of laudanum on the floor beside her, leaving this world as she had lived it, passively, without a fight.

The train whistle blew, and Dalia wearily opened her eyes. Though she'd only rested a few minutes, her head ached, and she felt hung over. In the wet heat, her blouse stuck to her skin, and she plucked at the sleeves, the peaks of fabric rising, then falling. Perspiration had formed a string of droplets around the base of her neck. Her fingers were sweaty, their tips tingling with numbness. Glancing down, she saw that they were swollen; so she shook them, her bracelet jingling with each flick of her wrists. The woman across from her was now sleeping, her large breasts heaving with each guttural breath. The train clacketa-clacked along, funnels of steam billowing upward like miniature tornadoes, toward the little town of Samson, her destination. A place, she hoped, where no one knew her, where she could wrap herself in a cloak of anonymity and start her life again.

Upon arriving, she checked her baggage and meandered the town's straight, dusty streets, the sun slicing through the leaves of the pecan trees, casting birthmarks against her skin, until she came to the corner of Rose and Lee, happening upon a nondescript white house as blank as a sheet of paper, with nothing memorable about it except for the veranda—its ceiling painted sky blue to ward off evil spirits, its wide gray floorboards spanning three sides. Framed by flimsy voile curtains in a front window was a sign saying FAIRCHILD'S BOARDINGHOUSE. Dalia strode up the walkway, burnt-orange marigolds on either side, and twisted the door chime. After several minutes, a short, bowl-shaped woman with steel-gray hair peeked through the screen. "May I help you?" she asked, blinking behind clear-rimmed spectacles.

Dalia motioned acknowledgment with her head. "I'm Dalia Miller. I'm new in town and wanted to know if you've a spare room to let."

Muttering, "Yes—yes," as though to no one in particular, the woman eased the screen door open. "Would you like to see the room?" she asked as Dalia, nodding, stepped inside. She led Dalia through a small foyer, bordered by a hall tree, and into a tidy, though faded, parlor. "Have a seat," she said, sinking down on a brown velvet settee, absentmindedly patting the spot beside her. "I'm Miss Frances Fairchild. And you are Miss . . . Miss . . ."

"Miller." Dalia sat down primly. "Miss Dalia Miller."

"Yes. Miss Miller," the woman said, a distracted look on her face.

"Dalia will be just fine."

"Well, Dalia, have you come from far away?" Dalia followed the woman's eyes as they veered toward a dark hallway.

"Oh, no," Dalia said. "About sixty miles. East of Valdosta. When my mother died, I decided to leave the area. Too many memories." She let her gaze linger on Miss Fairchild before snatching it away.

"Do you have any other relatives?" Frances Fairchild asked, her eyes returning to Dalia.

"A distant cousin in Atlanta, but no, not really. I'm quite alone, you see." Embarrassed by her frankness, Dalia felt her cheeks flaming.

"Well, then," Miss Fairchild said, her gaze again seeking the hallway, "you've come to the right place. We're one big family here." She listed forward and was on the brink of tumbling over when she mumbled something unintelligible and rocked back.

"What did you say?" said Dalia.

"Oh," said Miss Fairchild, batting her eyelashes in momentary confusion. "Dora, my help, is in the kitchen cookin' dinner, and for the life of me, I can't remember if I told her to fix biscuits or cornbread for the guests."

"If you need a word with her, go ahead," Dalia said, making her voice sound agreeable. "Really, I'm not in the least bit of a hurry."

"I'll only be a minute, Miss . . . Miss . . ."

"Miss Dalia Miller."

"Yes. Just a second, Miss . . ."

"Da-li-a," she said, pronouncing each syllable distinctly. "Just remember the flower, except I don't spell it that way."

Her round arms swinging outward as if to give her legs momentum, Frances Fairchild popped up on her tiny feet, her brown skirt rolling over the floor like one of Monroe's barrels of turpentine. "Back in a jiffy," she said over her shoulder. Dalia heard her shoes pitter-pattering down the hallway, then her laugh, like a short bark, followed by a sputter of words.

A lackluster secretary, flanked by bookshelves, lined the inside wall across from Dalia. Two channel-backed chairs in plush rose fabric faced the settee. A brown leather wingback chair with matching ottoman squatted near the fireplace. Somewhere in the room, a cat meowed. Dalia glanced around. The cat meowed again, not so much a meow as a hysterical squeak, and Dalia followed the sound with her eyes. A watermelon-striped tom, curled up between two large volumes on the bottom bookshelf, glared haughtily at her. "Kitty, kitty," Dalia beckoned, extending her palms, wiggling her fingers. "Kitty, kitty," she was saying when Miss Frances Fairchild came scurrying toward her.

"His name is Claus," she said breathlessly. She spit at a strand of hair annoying her forehead, next wiped her hands on the bottom of an apron, which she'd put on in the kitchen. "She made both," she added. "If I'm not in there telling her what to cook, she does it all. Scared I'll get mad if she leaves anything out. 'Me?' I tell her. 'When have I ever fussed at you, Dora?' And naturally she can't tell me, because I don't. In all the years she's been with me, I've never said a cross word to her. Enjoys making me feel bad, I guess."

"How many boarders are there?" Dalia quickly asked.

Miss Fairchild thought a few seconds. "Six, right now. Mr. Sears has been with me the longest. The others are more recent. The room that's available is on the second floor. Will the staircase be a bother?"

From where Dalia sat, she could see the stairway—broad, plain, and boxy, the steps dark as coffee. "Not at all," she said coolly. "I'm quite accustomed to climbing."

"Three meals a day, fresh linen and towels, for five dollars a week. A little extra and I'll see to your laundry."

"That seems fair," Dalia said. Then, shyly, "Do you permit visitors?"

"Of course, my dear, but I do have rules." Frances Fairchild retrieved a dish towel stuffed into her apron pocket and patted her glistening cheeks. "You can visit with your friends on the veranda and right here in the parlor, but no one is allowed in your room. Usually, if I don't forget, that is" —shaking her head, she emitted another one of her barking laughs—"I lock the front door at ten, but I'll give you a key, if for any reason you need to stay out later."

"Yes, ma'am," Dalia said, already envisioning herself with gentlemen callers courting on the front porch, sipping tea in the parlor. "May I see the room now?" The bottom cushion complained as she rose. Jangling her keys, Frances Fairchild followed Dalia up the stairway, their shoes slick against the threadbare runner. It was a short climb to the second-floor landing, spacious enough for a cream-cushioned love seat with roses and leaves carved into its mahogany legs and arms. A swinging pendulum clock, held aloft by a bronze draped maiden, was wedged into a corner beside it. "Lovely," Dalia said, reaching out to touch the love seat.

"These pieces were my mother's," the landlady told her, nodding at the love seat and clock. "But I've put my favorite things of hers in this bedroom, which is yours, if you want it." Darting ahead, she inserted an arthritic key into the lock and gave it a determined crank. Because the house was so dreary, Dalia was surprised when the open door revealed a cheery green room. She took in the massive oak wardrobe next to the door, then the catercornered white iron bed with an ecru crocheted spread. To the left of the bed was a white enamel fireplace, flanked by a maple dresser with an attached oval mirror. A moss-green rug, splashed with violet and peach flowers, lay on the red pine floor. Tattered silk curtains, their once-deep purple now splotched and faded, hung over wide windows stretching along the front and back walls. Beneath the back window sat a chaise longue in a champagne brocade. Along the front window was a small writing table. A brass gas fixture with eight arms dangled like a spider overhead.

"It's delightful," Dalia said, forgetting her manners, rushing through the doorway. She went straight to the dresser, trailing her fingertips over the lilac bowl and pitcher, then spun around to whip the curtains apart. The backyard was cramped, surrounded by a white picket fence in much need of painting. She headed back to the bed. "Good and firm," she muttered, testing the mattress with her palm before dashing to the wardrobe. Big enough for both her and Nellie Ann's dresses, she thought, when she threw open its double doors. But then, as always, her sister's death hit her. There was no one for Dalia to take care of anymore, and she clutched the sides of the wardrobe as grief, fresh as if Nellie Ann had just died, swept over her. Staring into the darkness of the closet, she waited until her sadness passed, and turned around to welcome the bedroom, bright as a lime awash in sunlight. "Yes. Yes. I'll take it," she said.

CHAPTER 13

Dalia had met Dr. Herman McKee three weeks ago, having gone to his office complaining of a toothache. He was one of the men on her list of prospective husbands, which she had drawn up several months ago. Twenty-seven years old with a thriving practice and no living relatives, he seemed like the best choice from the slate of six names. As soon as she saw him, she had been struck by his frailty. The dimple in his chin was too prissy. His skin was as blanched as peeled almonds; his fingers, long and delicate, like those of a pianist, not a dentist. "What's the problem, Miss Miller?" he had asked in a voice that wasn't exactly effeminate, yet bleached of virility, as though it had crept into the soul of a male fetus by mistake.

"Up here, in back," she complained, grimacing through the dull throb.

"Yes," he said meekly, running his slender fingers over her puffy cheek, "you're a little swollen there."

Pumping back the cane-woven chair, he had inspected her mouth, his fingertips trembling as they parted her lips, suggesting to her that his sperm were passive. Good, she thought, relieved at the idea of no children. With a long-handled silver tool, he scraped and prodded her aching tooth. Smiling wanly, he walked away, leaving her tilted back. Several minutes later, he had reappeared with a bottle of dark green medicine.

"Aren't you going to pull it?" she asked.

"Oh, no, Miss Miller, you're much too young to lose a tooth. I intend to do everything I can to save it. Let's not give up so soon." His tone was concerned, his eyes straining through thick lenses. "After you brush, you need to gargle with this solution. Twice a day for a full minute." His fingers lingered against her skin when he handed her the bottle. His soft touch was appealing. "Then mix a little salt with warm water and gargle some more. I removed a particle of food from beneath your gum, the cause of your discomfort, but I want you to come back next week, to be certain." Awkwardly rising, she headed for the waiting room. "There'll be no charge," he told the blue-haired woman ensconced behind a tidy compact desk. With not a single word of protest, Dalia had flung him a smile of gratitude and left. The next week, she had returned as scheduled. With her mouth pried open, drool humiliating her lips, she was taken aback when he asked if he could call upon her. Before thinking, she had nervously batted her eyelids and gurgled, "Yes."

Dr. McKee will be here soon, Dalia thought, glancing over her shoulder at the clock on the mantel. It was time for her to get dressed. It wouldn't do to keep her first gentleman caller waiting in the parlor. She tapped the chignon pinned snugly to the back of her head, breathing in the lilac-scented fragrance of bath oil on her skin. Going over to the wardrobe, she opened the doors, her eyes flitting over the dresses. Immediately the lavender lace dinner gown with silk gauze above the bodice caught her attention. She hadn't worn it for a long while and wondered if it still fit. Removing it from the hanger, she went directly to the large oval mirror above the maple dresser and held it up. She had learned through the years not to acknowledge her beauty, for to do so would have disrupted her relationship with her sister. Now, as she studied her reflection in the mirror, she saw her nineteen-year-old self more clearly. Like the white wings of a moth fluttering in the glow of a lamplight, her skin was translucent, pale, and pearly, save for the rosettes of pink on her cheeks. It was her eyes that most conveyed her beauty. Large and almond-shaped, they were deep violet, sometimes blue, depending on the color she was wearing, with thick dark eyebrows arching over. Her nose was strong, classic Roman, her lips satisfied but not greedy, her black hair wispy around her oval face. Over the past four years, a half-expectant look had crept into her features, making her seem both warm and distant, as though she were frightened by the tenderness she craved.

After draping the gown across the foot of the bed, she removed her satin wrapper, returned to the dresser, retrieved her undergarments, and put them on. Next she slipped the dress over her head and went back to the mirror for a second look. All over, she was bigger—her stomach, rounder; her thighs, plumper; her breasts, fuller. She winced at the plunging bodice. Around her armpits, the fabric was creasing. Troubled, she touched the cushion of her breasts. *Maybe I'll bind them,* she'd once told her sister. Fascinated, she watched her chest rising as oxygen swished into her lungs. The mole on her left breast heaved, enticing as a blackberry in a bowl of cream. Suddenly her flesh seemed separate from her, an entity with a will of its own. She took a step back, marveling at what she saw. It was power. Pure power. Camouflaged as a gift. Then, like a bolt from the blue, she remembered the necklace.

Sallie had happened upon it while cleaning the shanty after her father's death. Spotting a flash of metal, she had lifted the straw-filled tick and pulled out a tin container wedged between two slats. Prying open the rusty lid, she found a white satin box and the pearl necklace inside. *Glowin' like a frozen teardrop,* Sallie had said when she gave the necklace to Dalia, who had known instantly that it was the New Year's Eve gift her father had wanted to give Nellie Ann.

So it was with some misgiving that Dalia slid out the dresser drawer in which she'd hidden the satin box beneath a pair of her long blue gloves. She laid it on the dresser top and lifted off the lid. Plucking up the silver chain, she twirled the pearl in the sunlight. As soon as it came to rest, she reached slowly behind her neck and snapped the clasp into place—staring mesmerized as the gem slipped between her breasts, feeding now upon the movement of her bosom, the way it had, as a grain of sand inside an oyster, once fed upon the movement of the shell, swelling and transmuting into a pearl of uncommon beauty.

While Dalia waited for her suitor, Claus purred on the settee beside her. The other boarders were resting in their rooms. In the kitchen, Dora was preparing a pot roast for supper. Dalia hadn't eaten since breakfast, and the sweet odor of simmering onions made her hungry. The moment the door chime sounded, her stomach complained noisily. Couching her belly in her hands, she stalled until the hunger pangs subsided. Breathing in deeply, she stroked the cat's back—once—for good luck, and, with her stomach aflutter, answered the door. Dr. McKee was beaming at her when she unlatched it—his eyes like mashed green peas behind cloudy lenses. "Your timing is perfect," she told him. Her gaze traveled upward, toward the reddish rivulets of hair raked off his forehead, the lines of white scalp that showed through.

"That's a lovely necklace" was the first thing he said, staring at the pearl between her breasts.

She brought a protective hand to her chest. "Let's sit in the parlor," she suggested, abruptly turning. As they approached the brown, fringed archway, the cat thumped down from the settee and scampered over to his spot on the bookshelf. "Claus is my furry friend," she said, easing onto the sofa, shifting her legs so as to make room for him.

"How's your tooth?" he asked, sliding too close to her. She felt her cheeks flushing, her face aching from holding a smile. Hadn't she told him she was fine, just last week in his office? "A foolish question," he said, nibbling his top lip. "Your loveliness, I think, is making me nervous."

His compliment unsettled her, and she felt her smile breaking. "D-Dr. McKee," she stuttered, placing a cool palm against her cheek.

"Truly, Miss Miller, I'm quite taken with your beauty." The lenses magnified his eyes as he listed toward her.

She responded by tilting back. "You're much too kind," she said modestly.

"I wish kindness were my only problem," he said, laughing. "Are you hungry?"

"Famished," she replied. "The smell of Dora's pot roast is making my stomach grumble." She tossed him a charming smile.

He took a deep breath—his long, thin nostrils like gills flaring. "Onions cooking," he said, his tone nostalgic as he fluttered his eyelids. "The smell reminds me of my mother. She was from New Orleans, where every Creole dish begins with a sauté of onions, celery, and garlic."

"I'm afraid I've no predilection for the culinary arts."

"Then we complement each other," he said, holding up his feminine hands and wriggling his long fingers. "These are the tools of a talented chef."

"I would've never guessed."

"Yes, cooking is one of my hobbies."

He was looking hard at her, breathing with his mouth open. Dalia could feel the seconds dragging, the silence unnerving as a fingernail breaking. "I'm quite dull, really," she finally said.

"No one as lovely as you could be dull, Miss Miller." Pulling down the corners of his waistcoat, he came to his feet. "I think we should be going. The Suwannee Inn is holding a table for us at seven. It's the best restaurant in town," he added. "I know the chef there, and I promise you won't be disappointed."

He extended his hand and helped her rise. Standing thus side by side, she noticed for the first time that her frame was sturdier than his. Long-limbed and gawky, he had legs like a heron's. A giggle threatened her throat as he tripped toward the foyer but dissolved as he struggled with the door. His weak, watery presence made her feel safe.

"This is delightful," Dalia said as they entered the dining room at the inn. Her eyes took in the pink hibiscus blossoms woven into the pale green pile of the rug. In each corner, a fern billowed from a squat Chinese urn. A chandelier glowed like an upside-down Christmas tree from the ornate medallion. With the exception of two other couples, the restaurant was empty. The maître d', a middle-aged man with brown muttonchops, pulled out a green-cushioned chair for her. "I hope you enjoy your meal," he said when she was seated. Bowing slightly, he retreated.

"He's white," Dalia whispered.

"That he is," said Herman, settling into his chair, sliding it beneath the table. She noticed his furrowed forehead, his quirked lips, and wondered if he was being condescending. Unfolding her napkin, she carefully placed it across her lap. "This is an excellent restaurant," he was explaining, slicing off each word for emphasis, when a waiter, erect as a pine plank, interrupted him.

"Good evening, Dr. McKee," the waiter said, handing them each a menu. "It's always so good to see you."

"Good evening, Frank."

"A glass of sherry to whet your appetite?" The waiter's speech was refined, with not a whisper of poor breeding.

"Miss Miller?" Herman inquired.

"No, thank you," she said primly. "Hot tea with a thin slice of lemon will do me just fine." Tense, she pinched the napkin between her fingers.

The waiter shot her a starched, nipped smile. All the while, he was nodding—his white hair, like dandelion fluff, wafting upward.

"If it's all right with you, Miss Miller, I'll have a glass of that sherry?" Herman said.

"Please do, Dr. McKee. My father adored a little sherry before dinner," Dalia lied, knowing full well that bourbon was her papa's drink of choice.

The waiter bowed, turned tersely. Diamonds of light from the crystal chandelier cascaded over his black frock coat as he hastened toward a small side entrance.

"The smothered dove here is delicious. A favorite of mine," Herman said, making a steeple of his fingers, fastening his gaze on Dalia. "The beef consommé is also superb, and I believe asparagus is in season."

"I like the taste of dove," Dalia said obligingly. "Still, though, I must confess that quail's my favorite."

"Order whatever you want, my dear."

"When I was a young girl, Papa would go hunting and bring home quail for me, dove for my mama and sister. Katie Mae, our cook, would prepare them for supper, smothering them both in rich creamy gravy, but I always liked the quail gravy best. It was white, with a hint of lemon juice in it. Katie Mae would serve the birds over grits. Hers was the best quail in the county."

"The dark meat of dove is sweeter," he pointed out.

"Perhaps," she gave him. "Still, though, I prefer the white meat of quail."

"I promise you the dove here is top-notch." He wove his fingers together and tilted toward her.

"Fine," Dalia consented, in an effort to please him. "I'll give it a try."

"No, really, my dear, if you'd prefer the quail?"

"Dalia," she said. "You may call me Dalia."

"Dalia," he repeated, smacking his thin lips together. "This meal is for you, my dear. If you want white meat, just go ahead and say so."

"All right," Dalia said, confused. "I'll order the quail."

"But the dove . . ." His voice drifted off. His green eyes became soft and dreamy.

"The dove . . . ?" she echoed, baffled, her tone rising.

"Yes, my dear."

"Let's order the dove, Dr. McKee. I insist on it," she said.

"Are you certain?"

She nodded enthusiastically. "You've utterly convinced me," she declared. "Perhaps Katie Mae didn't know the best way to prepare it."

"So it's settled, then?"

"Yes."

"Dove," he said aloud as the waiter rounded the corner.

"Dove's a wonderful choice," the waiter said, setting a silver tray down on the far end of the table. "Dr. McKee, I think you'll find the sherry satisfying," he said, placing their drinks in front of them, pouring each a glass of water. "Our soup tonight is beef consommé."

"Ah!" Herman said in a voice as smug as a soothsayer's.

"Our salad—fresh beets and tomatoes."

"No asparagus?" Herman questioned, priggishly shaking his head.

"No, I'm sorry, Dr. McKee, but I can assure you the beets are small and sweet."

"Will grits be served with the dove?"

"No, wild rice, sir, but I can order grits if you prefer."

"Dalia?" asked Herman with an arch of his eyebrows.

"Don't bother," she said. "Rice will suit me just fine."

"But you had grits with your quail, didn't you?"

"Quail?" the waiter parroted. "I thought you wanted dove, Dr. McKee."

"We want the dove with grits," Herman said, his tone precise, as he flipped his hands over and gave his knuckles an emphatic pop. "Dove with grits," he repeated, unleashing his fingers and thumping them on the tabletop.

"Sir, may I suggest the saffron grits? It's new on the menu and quite delicious."

"Is this acceptable to you, Dalia?"

"Oh, yes," she said, anxiously biting her bottom lip. Inhaling deeply, her nostrils narrowing, she quickly added, "Dr. McKee, truly, whatever I have tonight will be a real treat for me." No sooner had she spoken than she noticed his fingers growing lax upon the tablecloth, the nervous blush in his cheeks vanishing.

"Fine, sir," the waiter hastily said. Then, snapping up the tray, he strutted like a king's footman toward the doorway.

His table manners were meticulous, totally unlike her father's. His posture upright and straight, his elbows a jot above the table, he closed his mouth while he ate, and sipped, never guzzled, the red wine he'd ordered. With the edge of his knife, he pushed dark slivers of meat over his plate toward the tines of his fork. After three or four bites, he would daintily dab his lips with the tip of his napkin, then sit absolutely still for several seconds, breathing through his mouth, his green eyes glassing over as though the taste of dove drugged him the way laudanum had drugged her mother. Pressing his hand against his chest, he would gulp down air, tick his head as though he couldn't possibly manage another morsel, but in the next instant tear off a thumb of biscuit, smear it through a dollop of gravy, pinch it up with some dove, and pop it into his mouth. Puckering his lips, he'd nurse his fingers, as greedy as a baby at the nipple. Over and over again he did this, mumbling he was too full while obsessively cleaning his plate, his manners vacillating, deteriorating as he ate. "I hope you liked your dove," he said as soon as he was finished. He frowned at the little heap of bird she'd left on her plate. "You could've ordered something else if you'd wanted."

"But why?" she bubbled. "It was heavenly, just too much for me to eat."

"You don't look like a picky eater," he said, his voice skeptical as his eyes settled on her bosom. She held her hand to her mouth and produced a little cough. Immediately he withdrew his gaze and picked up a rib cage. With his pinkies aloft, his thumbs and forefingers mincing like claws, he broke it in two, the little breast bones crackling. "Hmmmmm. Scrumptious," he crooned, as he nibbled on ribbons of meat and slurped the sauce off the bones. When done, he dropped the halves on his plate, drank the last of his wine, then licked it off his lips.

"What I mean is, I don't eat a lot at meals," she explained. "Just nibble a little bit all day long."

"That's how I eat, too," he said, meticulously wiping each finger with his napkin. She scanned his empty plate. "My health is delicate," he went on. "A little heart murmur. Nothing too serious. Stress and too much food make it worse, so I have to watch what I eat." Sighing, he fanned his face with his long, feminine fingers. "When it's this hot out, all I want to do is drink something cold," he said. The night calls swam sluggishly toward her through the open window. "Some ice tea or lemonade, maybe, with a sprig of mint. I like fruit juices, too." His fingers were crawling toward the bread basket, folding back the cloth, dipping in, coming up empty. Disappointment clouded his features, but he bounced back. "There's nothing more invigorating than freshly squeezed orange juice," he continued, his fingers mesmerizing her as they crept back over the table. He brought them to his mouth and sucked. "Ah, here's dessert!" he exclaimed as the waiter came toward them.

"I don't remembering ordering it," she said.

"You didn't, my dear," he confessed. The waiter set a bowl of peach cobbler in front of her, a glass of port in front of him. "I whispered cobbler into Frank's ear while you were eating. A little sugar, I felt, would lift your spirits."

"But Dr. McKee, there's nothing wrong with my spirits."

"To our health. To your spirits, Dalia." He lifted the port and took a stingy sip. "I don't remember when I've had a more delightful evening. The food. The company. Your darling self." She spooned up some cobbler and slipped it between her lips. "You're a jewel," he prattled on. She swallowed the mouthful of whipped cream, then savored the smoky sweetness of the peaches, wondering if the chef had added a splash of brandy to them, her spirits rising as she turned a deaf ear to him, banishing his voice from the room.

At the front door, he leaned in toward her. Immediately she turned away. "Would you like to go on a picnic with me this Sunday?" he asked. Not in the least bit embarrassed by her rebuff, it seemed. "I know the perfect spot, down by the Altamaha River. Everyone goes there on Sunday. It'll be fun. Clarice'll pack us some picnic lunches. She's a very good cook."

"I've not been there yet," she admitted.

"Then it's decided," he said, brandishing a smile. "I'll pick you up after church. Around twelve-thirty."

"I look forward to it, Dr. McKee," she said, smiling back.

"Please, dear, call me Herman," he said, quickly grabbing her hand, but before he could kiss it, she was breaking her hand free, twisting the doorknob, and swiftly stepping through the open space.

"Thank you, Herman, for a lovely evening," she said, clicking the door into place.

CHAPTER 14

The morning after her dinner with Dr. McKee, Dalia pulled out her list of marriage prospects. "R. C. Winton," she mumbled, stopping at his name, remembering she'd spotted it just last week in the obituary column of the *Samson Register.* Consumption, it seemed, had taken the president of First Farmers Bank before she had the chance to meet him. She took a sip of her coffee from the silver breakfast tray, which she had discovered fifteen minutes earlier outside her bedroom door in the hallway, along with a plate of biscuits and a tidy note saying, *You got in late last night, so I thought you might want to sleep in late this morning. Can't wait to hear about your meal at the Suwannee. Believe it or not, I've never dined there.* Busybody, thought Dalia, clattering the saucer as she snapped her cup down. She took several anxious breaths before tearing off a piece of jam-smeared biscuit and popping it into her mouth. As she chewed, the strawberry preserves consoled her, and she found herself appreciating Miss Fairchild's thoughtfulness, after all. She looked at her list again, her eyes alighting on number three—Nolan D. Durbin, the proprietor of one of the largest textile mills in Georgia, but rumor was he'd sailed to Europe for an indefinite stay. Sighing, she mentally struck him off her list. Pinching off more biscuit, she slipped it between her lips and moved on to Bubby Porterfield. According to Miss Fairchild, who knew everything there was to know about everyone, he was certain to ask Minerva Atkinson for her hand in marriage by the end of the summer. And nobody could tell Dalia, not even her landlady, what Hamilton Bright, number five, was up to. That he was the wealthiest landowner in the county was a given; that he was peculiar, another. "Why would anyone set her cap on a man whose relatives sweep the gamut from eccentric to mad?" Frances Fairchild had said one day while they were discussing the pros and cons of the men on Dalia's list. The only name left, apart from Dr. Herman McKee, was Dinky Bridges. The first time Dalia had set eyes on him, he was unhitching his horse in front of the pharmacy. He was undersized and squat, with the shortest legs Dalia had even seen on a full-grown man, and the idea of kissing him made her feel faint. Minutes later, she had procured a bottle of calamine lotion inside the drugstore, thereafter linking him unfairly to the splotches of poison ivy on her hands. Her mind was on Dinky Bridges when a dark line of X's at the bottom of the page captured her attention, but though she tried to decipher the crossed-out name, she couldn't. Just as she was about to tuck the list away, the letters seemed to rise above the page. "Walter Larkin," she read aloud, the name levitating before her. "Walter Larkin. Walter Larkin," she repeated, trying to recall why she'd marked through him. Then, out of the blue, it came to her. It was his age. He was at least forty, much likely older.

Rapidly, she ran her fingertip back up through the column, letting it come to rest on Dr. Herman McKee. Though plain, he was certainly more kissable than Dinky Bridges, and definitely not as old as Walter Larkin. "Dr. Herman McKee," she whispered, tracing each letter in his name. "Mrs. Dalia McKee." She liked the way it sounded. "Mrs. Dalia McKee," she repeated, her thoughts sailing back to their dinner last night at the Suwannee Inn. No one was perfect, she reasoned. Everyone was afflicted with those annoying little habits that only others could see, and at least he wasn't cheap, she thought, reassured by the memory of the fancy restaurant, the refined waiters, the expensive menu. Her uneasy feelings about him began to fade. A picnic on the bank of the Altamaha with Dr. Herman McKee was exactly what she needed. It would be refreshing, a cold compress on this dagger-edged heat, she decided, but then she remembered his long fingers snapping the dove's rib cage in half, his tongue lapping up the gravy, and she grew uneasy again. Pressing her fingers against the base of her throat, she took a deep breath and analyzed herself instead. She was being too critical, judging too harshly, just as she always did, not giving him a chance. After all, he had treated her to a high-priced evening out. Yes, a picnic at the river would be lovely, her inner voice convinced her. There was a knock on her bedroom door. "I'm coming," she said, quickly standing, pattering over the rug and the red pine floorboards.

"You must tell me everything that happened. I want to know every little detail," Frances Fairchild began as soon as Dalia opened the door. Whisking into the room, her landlady rushed over to the chaise longue. "I'm an impatient person," she said, sitting, patting the space beside her. "Now, quick. Tell me. How was your dinner?" she asked after Dalia sank down. "Celestine Potter says it's the best restaurant in town."

"It was wonderful," Dalia enthused, crossing one leg over the other. "Though, in all honesty, dove's not one of my favorites."

"Then why did you order it?" her landlady asked. "Surely there were other dishes on the menu."

"Because he insisted," said Dalia. "At first I said no. Told him I preferred the taste of quail, but he convinced me. As you know, he's very persuasive."

"Did you like it?"

"Not especially," Dalia replied. "I guess I've been spoiled by Katie Mae's quail."

"Whose quail?"

"Katie Mae's. She was our cook, back when I was a girl."

"Did you tell him?"

"Of course not. I said the dove was delicious."

"Because you wanted to please him?"

"Let's say I wanted to be agreeable."

"Wise," her landlady said. "Bullheaded never got a beau."

"Nor a husband," Dalia added. "And I must've been on my best behavior, since he's invited me to a picnic at the river this Sunday."

"Marvelous," Miss Fairchild said, clapping her pudgy hands. "Margie Stuart at church says Sunday at the river is such fun. Lots of families. Oodles of children, laughing and playing. Fun. Fun. Fun."

"His cook is going to pack us a lunch basket."

"Well, avoid anything with mayonnaise in it," her landlady cautioned. "Last summer, Edwina Carpenter ate deviled eggs on a church picnic at the Altamaha and got an awful case of food poisoning. She said a team of mules couldn't drag her back there."

"But you said it would be fun," Dalia reminded her.

Frances Fairchild wrinkled her brow and thought for a moment. "I don't always believe what Edwina tells me," she amended. "She's a whiner, not at all pleasant. Such a negative person. Thinks Christmas is gloomy, Easter hopelessly tragic. I listen to her with half an ear, but Dr. McKee is pleasant," she asserted, smiling as she changed the topic. "Is he as considerate as he appears?"

"Very solicitous," Dalia told her. "Perhaps a little too much so."

"One can never be too solicitous, my dear. Especially these days, with the turn of the century upon us. All the frightening changes we're facing."

"Regardless," Dalia said, pausing, "a woman has a mind and a will of her own. She's not some helpless creature who needs to be told what to order."

"If the most eligible bachelor in town were pursuing me, I wouldn't be complaining," Frances Fairchild contended.

"I just don't know," Dalia murmured, gazing distractedly out the window. The leaves of the pecan trees were curling up in the heat. The lilac bushes were drooping, the deep-red rose wilting. She, too, was limp upon the seat. She looked anxiously at her landlady. "Please be truthful with me," she said, her tone earnest. "Tell me exactly what you think of the good dentist."

"That's easy," Miss Fairchild said in a voice that was confident and reassuring. "First, his features are pleasant."

"Effeminate," qualified Dalia.

"He's stronger than you think he is."

"How's that?"

"Pulling teeth requires some strength, my dear." Dalia nodded. "Second, he's highly educated. And third, he's a gentleman with money."

"Financial security is a must," Dalia agreed.

"Now, here's the icing on the cake—he's sensitive."

"Really?" said Dalia, amused.

"He likes to cook, doesn't he? Likes to help out with those things that a woman usually does."

"My, my," said Dalia, "you must have learned the art of persuasion from him."

"Then you're feeling more positive?"

"Most definitely," Dalia said, smiling. "I'm delighted we had this little conversation. By the way, would you help me with something else?" Frances Fairchild uplifted her palms and shrugged her round shoulders. "Would you wash a dress of mine for the outing this Sunday?"

"Bring it to me when you come down," Frances Fairchild said, groaning as she got up to go. "I'll wash it right after lunch. Guess what we're having tonight for supper."

"I haven't a clue," Dalia said, rising.

"Country ham, redeye gravy, and a pan of Dora's buttermilk biscuits."

"Miss Fairchild, I believe you're plotting against me," Dalia said, laughing. "You want to stay trim and look good for Dr. McKee, while trying to make me fat."

"If only I were younger, Miss Miller"—with a toss of her head, her landlady strutted toward the doorway—"I'd give you a run for his money."

CHAPTER 15

"Why is every river in Georgia wide, flat, and muddy?" Dalia asked as he spread the star-patterned quilt over the parched ground near the pink-feathered mimosa.

"We're a plain people," he told her. His nails were manicured, his white linen suit creaseless, his tan shoes brightly polished. "No prissy rivers for us," he stated crisply. He gingerly patted a red and blue star with a rip running through it. "Now give me your hand and sit right here."

Her skirt crumpled beneath her as he guided her down. "It's terribly hot, isn't it?" she said, crooking her legs to one side, pulling her straw bonnet low over her brow.

"I've seen hotter."

Thrusting her fingers inside her collar, she scratched her itchy neck. The collar was high, hot, and constricting, but she wore it because of the way he had stared at her breasts over dinner.

He peered down his nose at her. "That blouse you're wearing looks hot," he said, eyeing her critically. "Why didn't you wear something more . . . more comfortable? Something like what you wore the other night at the Suwannee Inn?"

"Dr. McKee," she said coyly. Her gesturing hands froze in midair. "The gown I wore that evening is far too formal for an outing by the river."

"Not the exact gown." He peevishly whisked around and took several quick steps toward the mimosa, where he snatched up the picnic basket.

"What goodies do you have in there?" she asked as he lowered the basket upon the ground. "Any deviled eggs?"

"They're standard fare for picnics, but none today, my dear."

"It's probably for the best," she said, blowing at a mob of gnats that swarmed around her eyes. "Mayonnaise won't hold up in this kind of weather."

He leaned over, plucked up a red-checked tablecloth tucked over the top of the basket, and spread it deftly over the quilt. Reaching into the basket, he raised high a quart jar. "Lemonade," he announced after setting the jar down, the lemon slices inside it rocking like jellyfish in seawater. He returned to the basket and retrieved two tall pewter tumblers, lining them up next to the lemonade. His hands dipped down again, brought forth a large, deep pan. "Fried chicken," he said, whipping off the lid. "Biscuits. Sweet pickles. Spiced peaches," he said, ticking off the dishes, clustering them around the pan of chicken. "Shall I present my contributions to our little picnic this afternoon?" For a full minute, he held aloft a large blue bowl. "German potato salad," he declared, resting the bowl next to the jar of spiced peaches. "Don't worry about the mayonnaise," he told her. "There's none in it. And for dessert"—he struggled to unlatch the top of a pie pan—"I made these beautiful strawberry tarts. See?" He dropped the top on the quilt and angled the pie pan in her direction. Sprinkled lightly with powdered sugar, each tart looked like a large ruby. "Don't they look scrumptious?" She smiled and nodded at him. He set the tarts down and poured them both glassfuls of lemonade. "Are you hungry?" he asked, taking out two pewter plates, some silverware, and several bright red cotton napkins from the bottom of the basket.

"I'm starving," she replied, though, in truth, she wasn't.

To their left, a group of children was playing Drop the Handkerchief. A tiny flaxen-haired girl skipped around the circle of interlaced hands, forgetting to drop the blue handkerchief clutched tightly between her fingers. Dalia heard the whiz of a jump rope slicing through the air behind her, then girlish voices chanting, *"I like coffee. I like tea."* Just beyond the mimosa, a baseball game was ongoing, the ball and bat making contact, cracking sharply. "Home run!" she heard a boy yelling.

"The river is the place to be on Sunday," he said, spooning a smidgen of each dish onto her plate, giving her a drumstick. She watched enviously as he bit into a breast.

"Yes, everyone in Samson is out here today," she agreed. She picked up the drumstick, peeled off the crisp fried skin with her teeth, took a bite of the dark meat, and chewed with irritation.

"Dalia," he began as soon as he'd swallowed, "I think you're a lovely woman with impeccable manners."

She reached for a sweet pickle. "This is tasty," she said as she crunched the crisp flesh.

"Did you hear me, Dalia?" He rocked forward on his haunches, a flake of chicken skin sticking to his upper lip, a dollop of grease shining from the dimple on his chin. "I said, I think you're lovely." He flicked out his tongue, rosy pink and pointed as though he sharpened it every night before going to bed, snared the crusty flake, and swallowed, his Adam's apple bobbing conspicuously.

She wavered for a second, strategizing. "I've a distant relative in Atlanta, wants me to come live with her since I'm all alone here."

He slumped back on his buttocks, his shoulders slouched and deflated. "Dalia, would you like this other breast?" he asked, the oil glistening on his fingers as he offered it to her.

She bobbed her head, took the breast, and added, "But Atlanta is so far away."

"Then you're not leaving?" His mouth moved with hers as she ate. She swallowed and dabbed her lips with a napkin, grabbed her glass of lemonade, and drank. "Well, are you?" he asked, slanting toward her.

"There's nothing holding me here," she replied coolly.

He frowned with his forehead, was speechless. "But Dalia," he said seconds later, "I'd like for you to stay. I'd like to get to know you better."

She gnawed at the chicken breast as though she hadn't heard him. From above, there came a shrieking noise. "What was that?" she asked, looking up to see a green-backed heron, its feathers like emeralds in the sunlight as it glided toward the river. "Oh, how lovely," she said softly, returning the breast to her plate.

"No, you're what's lovely. The loveliest creature out here today."

She looked hard at him. This time, she was the one who didn't know what to say. "You flatter me," she said finally.

"I'm only stating what everyone can't help but notice." Reaching out, he touched the hem of her skirt, his manner pleading. "I hope I can persuade you not to leave."

"I'm beginning to appreciate Samson," she said, picking up her piece of chicken and taking another bite.

"I'm quite alone, too," he said, tears welling behind the thick lenses.

"My family died from influenza." For an instant he struck her as tragic, like one of her helpless, broken creatures. "Father went first. Next, my kid sister. Then Mama. I was only twenty at the time. A few years later, my grandparents on both sides passed away. Though of old age," he clarified. "The only one left was my father's brother, but he died of a stroke last May. No wife, no children. I don't want his lonely legacy to be my fate."

"My sister, papa, and mama died within a few years of each other," Dalia confided. "I moved here to start over. To heal, so to speak."

"Loss and longing. Loss and longing," he said sadly.

"Do you believe in spirits, Herman?"

He shook his head. "I'm a man of medicine. Of science, Dalia."

"After my sister passed away, I wanted to believe in them," she said. "I longed for a visitation from her, but it didn't happen." He appeased her with a smile. "It was difficult living in our home with all the memories, with no ghostly apparitions to comfort me. Same as you, Herman, I don't want loneliness to follow me to my grave."

"So we have this in common," he said, gazing into her eyes. Embarrassed, she lowered her head. "Why don't we sample one of my strawberry tarts?" he suggested.

"Only one?" she teased.

He brought the strawberries to her. Red velvet through white lace. With her thumb and forefinger, she picked one up. The delicate crust crumbled between her fingers as the pastry floated toward her. In anticipation, she parted her lips. Right then, she felt the sting.

"Get away!" Herman said, angrily clapping. The bee whirred off toward the pink mimosa blossoms. "Let me see, dear." She rocked toward him, her lip burning, her eyes brimming. "It's swelling. Are those tears?" he asked, cupping her face between his palms, drawing her close to him. "Please don't cry. Don't ruin that lovely face of yours," he said, his voice caring. "I'll go get my pipe tobacco. I left it in the carriage. A little on your lip is sure to draw out the sting."

At the day's end, she lay on the chaise longue in her bedroom, thinking. The instant she'd returned from the picnic, she hurried to her room and inspected her puffy lip in the large oval mirror. A strand of tobacco was clinging stubbornly to the sting. A pink heat rash dotted her cheeks, and she'd felt a rush of humiliation, a hot flash of shame, knowing he'd seen her like this at the river. But now she recalled his kindness, the way he'd held the tobacco against her lip until the pain had subsided, the tender way he had spoken to her, telling her again she was lovely, even though her lip was bruised and swelling. He'd even offered to come back later with some medicine. Yes, his gentleness had been touching, she thought, closing her eyes, finally resting. "Dalia, Dalia," a voice called out, just as she was drifting off. Her eyes flicked open. "Dr. McKee is here to see you," her landlady said from behind the closed door. Wincing, Dalia raised up on her elbows, swinging her carpet slippers to the floor. She ran her tongue over her lip. Which had grown even larger. The late afternoon light shone a soft, deep purple through the parted draperies. Dark enough, she hoped, to cloak her swollen features. Groggy and sluggish, she rose and went over to the washstand. She poured water into the basin, splashed it over her face, and patted the residue off with a towel. Gathering up her courage, she headed for the staircase. At the landing, she halted, fingering the top button of the blouse she still wore. On the bank of the Altamaha, he had said she was lovely. "Lovely," she whispered, fumbling with the tiny pearl-shaped buttons, releasing them, one right after another, until her long, soft neck was exposed.

CHAPTER 16

Dalia rested in the drawing room on the brown velvet settee with Claus curled up in her lap. Across from her was Miss Pinbroke, primly sitting in one of the channel-backed chairs, while Mr. Sears was lounging in the leather wingback, his feet propped up on the ottoman. All three were sipping glasses of vermouth, conversing before the evening meal. From the kitchen came the sound of something shattering upon the floor. "There goes my bowl of batter," Dalia heard Dora say.

"I didn't drop it on purpose," snapped Miss Fairchild. "It's your big feet, getting in the way."

Dalia nodded knowingly at Miss Pinbroke.

"They behave like little schoolchildren," Miss Pinbroke commented in a precise, boxy voice.

Apparently she was not from this part of the country. "Where are you from?" Dalia asked.

"A little town north of Cincinnati," Hester Pinbroke answered, "but I've been in Georgia for several years now."

"What drove you south?"

"The cold weather," she said, laughing. "I get sick easily, wanted to live in a warmer climate."

"And your family?" inquired Dalia.

"I've a brother and sister-in-law here, but everyone else is back in Ohio." Miss Pinbroke's eyes lit on Mr. Sears, who in turn was staring at Dalia. "My brother invited me to live with them, but I've an income of my own and enjoy my independence, so I declined."

"Miss Miller," Mr. Sears began. Careful so as not to disturb Claus, Dalia shifted in her seat toward the short, slight man, whose deep voice was disconcerting. "That pearl necklace of yours is exquisite." According to Miss Fairchild, he'd worked as a clerk in Copeland's Jewelry for over twenty years. "How did you come by it?"

"It was meant to be my sister's," Dalia explained, "but she died before she got the chance to wear it."

"Well, it's splendid, absolutely gorgeous." He eased his legs off the ottoman and walked over to where she sat. "Simply beautiful," he murmured, his breath hot against her neck.

The bitter scent of dill rose off his skin and assaulted her nostrils. She could see the bald patch of scalp beneath the light brown strands of hair that he combed over it. "You're the second person to say that." Her skirt crinkled against the brown velvet sofa as she leaned back. "Dr. McKee thought it was beautiful also."

"Mr. Sears," Miss Pinbroke rushed in.

"Lawrence," he said politely.

"Lawrence," she corrected with a stiff little nod, "you must see my diamond necklace. I wear it to church sometimes." She released a tinkle of laughter. "Dr. McKee says I look lovely whenever I wear it."

Dalia blanched, tried to speak, but the words jammed in her throat. So he made a habit of complimenting all his female patients. Told this emaciated old spinster that she was lovely. Dalia raked her fingernails over her skirt, inadvertently grazing the cat's belly. Meowing shrilly, he rose up on his back legs, his rump high, his tail upright, and indignantly jumped off her lap. "Dr. McKee is very generous," she said, trying to disguise her frayed feelings. "It's one of his most endearing qualities."

"If either of you decide to sell your lavalieres, please let me know," Lawrence Sears said, stepping backward, his calves bumping against the ottoman.

"I could never part with my sister's necklace," Dalia said firmly. From the hallway drifted the obese scent of chicken and dumplings. "Doesn't that smell good?" she said. "The aromas coming out of that kitchen always make me hungry."

"You do eat well, Miss Miller," observed Miss Pinbroke. "I don't seem to be able to put on a pound." She extended one of her skinny arms and displayed it proudly.

"Eating is one of life's great pleasures," Dalia countered. "I pity the person who can't enjoy a good meal." Hester Pinbroke bristled, pressing her lips so tightly together they all but disappeared. Whereupon Dalia drew forth a beige cotton handkerchief from the pocket of her skirt and casually blotted the skin below one eye, then the other. "Dr. McKee—I mean, Herman—" she said, "has been blessed with a healthy appetite, just like me."

"I'm very familiar with Herman's love of food," Miss Pinbroke rejoined, her gaze shifting from Dalia to Mr. Sears. "He's a gourmet cook, you know. I've sampled some of his dishes."

"Last Sunday on a picnic at the river, I had some of Herman's German potato salad and one of his delicious strawberry tarts."

"Yes, I heard about your unfortunate incident."

"It was nothing, really," Dalia told her. "We had a lovely time."

Hester Pinbroke crossed her legs and uncrossed them. She pushed a lock of her bird's-nest hair behind her ear. In a voice more square-edged than ususal, she said, "He has also asked me to go on picnics with him, but I couldn't. Being out in this wet Georgia heat is detrimental to my health."

Mr. Sears quickly finished off the last of his vermouth. "Pardon me, ladies," he said, coming to his feet, glancing meaningfully at Dalia, "but I need to wash up before supper." On his way out the door, he halted behind the settee where Dalia sat. "Miss Miller," he said, tapping her gently on the shoulder, "it was such a pleasure visiting with you this evening."

"Likewise," Dalia said, her eyes shifting to Hester Pinbroke, who was turning a deep shade of red.

Pleading a headache, Hester Pinbroke excused herself from supper, which suited Dalia just fine, for she found the woman tiresome. Beazy Turner, a newcomer at the boardinghouse, was seated to the left of Dalia, Lawrence Sears to the right. The only other boarder joining them for supper was Theodore Bushell, a middle-aged engineer for the Georgia Pacific Railroad. From the beginning, he'd struck Dalia as coarse and vulgar, always plunking himself down at the head of the table as though he were the proprietor of the house.

"Whatcha got there?" he asked Dora as she came into the dining room.

"A mess of greens," she told him. "The turnips is coming in strong this summer."

"I thought only pigs ate turnips," he said, stomping his foot against the floor, guffawing, shaking the loose skin around his neck.

Dora thumped the steaming bowl on top of the table. "Must be true, 'cause I seen ya eating bowls of 'em," she said, looking at him sideways. Opening her mouth wide, she let out a laugh, her dark eyes gleeful.

"Dora!" Miss Fairchild hollered from the kitchen. "Don't forget the onions and the hot pepper vinegar."

"I ain't forgettin' nothin'," Dora said crossly under her breath. "Here I come."

"Poor ole Dora," Beazy Turner commiserated. Her white hair was stacked like a snowball on top of her head. "In Miss Fairchild's eyes, she can't do anything right."

"Don't let them fool you," Dalia told her. "They thrive on bickering."

No sooner had Dalia spoken these words than Miss Frances Fairchild, clutching the bottle of hot pepper vinegar like a hunting dog retrieving a bird, plunked the bottle down. "Dora, quit dawdling around!" she yelled. "I brought the vinegar for you. Now hurry up and fetch me that bowl of onions."

"Onions," Dora announced seconds later. The two women brushed shoulders as they passed. "Where's the butter?" the black woman asked, ambling toward the table. "I done churned it fresh this morning, but it ain't here." She set the onions in front of Dalia, then with a grunt headed back to the kitchen.

Again the two women crossed paths. "Chicken and dumplings," Miss Fairchild sputtered. She lowered a heavy iron kettle onto a trivet.

"Sliced tomatoes, cukes, and sweet onions," Dora said.

"Did you dribble a little dressing over them?"

"Ya know I didn't," Dora said, tenting her eyebrows.

"She always serves them plain, but me, well, I like a sprinkling of vinegar and peanut oil on my salad. Along with a smidgen of thyme, some garlic, and plenty of salt and black pepper."

"Red's better," Dora said.

"If you want your mouth on fire."

The black woman shrugged and, pivoting slowly, moseyed toward the doorway. For a brief few seconds, the dining room was calm and quiet, before Dora announced triumphantly from the kitchen, "Miss Fairchild, Miss Fairchild! Ya done messed up now. Set my butter on that hot damn stove and ruined it."

A sheen of perspiration on her forehead, her cheeks pink, Miss Fairchild finally joined them for supper, bringing with her the dish of melted butter. "God is great. God is good. Let us thank Him for this food," she said, steam fogging her glasses as she lifted the iron lid off the dumplings.

It was hot, much too hot outside for such a dish, and they ate slowly, blowing on the steaming dumplings before slipping them into their mouths. Theodore Bushell was the only one who gobbled down his plate of dumplings, before devouring his turnip greens, doused in hot pepper vinegar and buried beneath onions. As Dalia watched him eat, she wondered if all men could be sorted into one of two categories—those like Mr. Bushell who were coarse and vulgar, their egos, like their stomachs, gorging on everything in sight, or those who posed as refined, well-mannered gentlemen but, ultimately, were just as voracious in their appetites. A woman was caught between a rock and a hard place, Dalia thought, but if she wanted to survive, she had to make a choice. She could live in a boardinghouse among strange men or live in a big, comfortable house with just one.

CHAPTER 17

An annoying drop of perspiration wormed down the inside of her thigh as Dalia rounded the corner of First Farmers Bank, a two-story painted brick building with blisters of white peeling off like sunburned skin. An old man seated on the wrought-iron bench in front of the bank tipped his hat. Dalia mouthed hello and kept on walking, as she wanted to get her shopping done before the noonday heat set in. Only midmorning and her undergarments were sticking like a mustard plaster to her skin. Yet when she passed the door of Dickson's Bakery, the sweet smell of cinnamon rolls seduced her, and she lingered on the sidewalk, taking in the heady fragrance.

"How are you doing, Miss Miller?" asked a young, brassy-haired woman who was leaving with a box of doughnuts under her arm.

"Fine, thank you," Dalia replied, having no idea to whom she was speaking. "And you?"

"I'll be fine if I can survive this heat," the woman answered. "Frances told me you've been sick. A bee sting, wasn't it?"

Dalia's index finger rose to her top lip. "Oh, yes," she muttered, "but that was weeks ago. I'm afraid it's old news by now."

"Frances said Dr. McKee was very solicitous."

"Dr. McKee, why, yes . . . he . . ." Dalia scrunched up her forehead, totally baffled. "News of my little incident has certainly spread, and you are . . . ?"

"Edwina Carpenter," the woman said. "I must apologize for not introducing myself. From my conversations with Frances, I feel I already know you, but naturally you don't know who I am."

Ah, the whiner, recalled Dalia. "Yes, you ate deviled eggs at the river and got sick."

The woman inclined her tiny head, her straw hat tilting forward. "A team of mules couldn't drag me back there, but thank the good Lord you didn't come down with food poisoning, though you were poisoned by that bee. That's what the Altamaha does. Lures people to it. Promises happiness but delivers sorrow." Her gray eyes narrowing, she straightened her hat and slanted toward Dalia. "A strawberry tart, wasn't it?"

"A bee," stated Dalia.

"Wanted a taste of strawberry?"

"Bit me instead."

"Dreadful," Edwina Carpenter cried. "Simply dreadful. You go on a picnic, expecting romance, and what do you get? The kiss of death."

"It was just a bee sting."

"That's true," the woman said, "though you must admit it hurt, didn't it?"

"Yes, for a while it was unpleasant," Dalia said blandly. The conversation was becoming increasingly boring. Then a curious thought popped into her head. "How did you recognize me, Miss Carpenter? Until now, we've never met."

"Your eyes," the woman said fervently. "Frances is right. They're violet."

The bells of Christ Church on Main Street began chiming. Eleven chimes altogether. "It was so nice meeting you, Miss Carpenter," Dalia said promptly, "but I should be going." Spinning around, she hastened down the sidewalk, waving good-bye over her shoulder, skirting the iron lampposts, which sizzled from the heat. Crepe myrtle bloomed pink pom-poms along the street. There were two boxes of white petunias on either side of the barbershop door, a basket of red ones hanging from the peppermint-swirled pole. Dalia's eyes were drawn through the large window to the sharp glint of a blade as it plowed through lather. Blinking, she hurried on, nodding to the statue of the Confederate soldier across the street in the center of the square, smiling when she saw the sculpture of Cleopatra, the three-legged cat who had served for years as the mascot of the Samson Volunteer Fire Department.

Beneath the green-and-tan-striped awning of the tobacconist's shop, she came to a standstill—drinking down air thick as water, pondering the questions that swam in her head. Hadn't Herman called her a lovely woman with impeccable manners? Hadn't he pursued her from the start?

Why, then, hadn't he called on her for weeks? *Don't you fret,* her landlady had consoled her. *There are other fish in the sea.* She was right, thought Dalia as she stood in the shade of the awning. Dr. Herman McKee was not the only bachelor in Samson. Why, just yesterday morning she'd spotted Walter Larkin slowly mounting the front steps to his office, his salt-and-pepper hair gleaming. Now he didn't seem as old as she'd first thought him to be. Most certainly he was a possibility. "Other fish in the sea," she mumbled.

"Morning," greeted a freckle-faced boy in a green-billed cap. "*Samson Register*?" he asked, thrusting a stack of newspapers at her. Smiling, she shook her head, her stride determined as she headed toward the druggist's, where she needed to buy a bottle of witch hazel for her eyes, puffy lately when she awoke in the morning; lotion for the heat rash that pricked her skin; baking powder for her teeth; Epsom salts for her tired, aching feet. As soon as she was finished with her shopping, she intended to treat herself to an ice-cream sundae at the black marble counter. She would imagine Nellie Ann beside her, their kneecaps brushing through light cotton dresses, their spoons dipping into dish boats of ice cream. She needed a little treat. Deserved a reprieve from her nagging insecurity about money.

Dalia darted through the drugstore's double doors, propped open to let out the heat. In front of her, a blue-haired woman was holding up a bottle of bubble bath, shaking it so vigorously that Dalia thought it might pop its stopper and spew its contents all over the place. As she headed down the center aisle, her long white skirt brushed against a tin of bath powder, toppling it over. She bent down to retrieve it and was replacing it on the shelf when a familiar voice froze her. "Why, Hester, you've not touched your float! Is that tooth of yours still hurting?" Immediately she ducked down, her breath lodging in her throat. "Oh, no, I'm fine," Hester Pinbroke replied. "But it's so kind of you to ask."

Squatting, Dalia swiveled around and began to waddle back up the aisle until she came to the front. Her calves strained as she tiptoed upward and peeked around a display of turpentine ointments. At a small round table to her left, she saw them—sipping on sarsaparilla floats.

"Hester, you're such a lovely woman," he was saying.

"Hypocrite," Dalia blurted, her lips puckering with reproach.

Herman jerked his head up, his green eyes veering in her direction, but Dalia quickly crouched, goose-waddling toward the rear of the store, unable to ignore their silly fawning. At the end of the aisle, Dalia leapt to her feet and dashed out the door.

At once the delicate, lacy fragrance of French toast from the Blue Café on the other side of the alley hit her, and she closed her eyes, her mouth watering with thoughts of maple syrup, butter, and cinnamon. Her stomach grumbled, and suddenly she felt very hungry. How could he trust someone who didn't like food? she asked herself. At least she could enjoy a sarsaparilla float, she thought bitterly, the stinging odor of chicory bringing tears to her eyes.

When Dalia heard their voices coming from the backyard, she went straightaway to the garden. She needed to vent the anger that bubbled inside her like gum in a tar kiln. "Frances! Frances!" she cried out as she threw the gate wide open.

"Why, child!" said Frances, dropping her clippers, stretching out her arms.

Dalia ran to her, fell against her shoulder, sobbing. "I saw him." She wept. "Downtown. At the druggist's with that . . . that . . ."

"Who?"

"Dr. McKee," Dalia groaned, heaving loudly. "With that . . . that . . ."

"That pencil-neck," Frances snarled. "I don't like that woman."

"Drinking sarsaparilla," Dalia blubbered, her nose running, her eyes reddening. "Like they were sweethearts, and I thought he liked me."

"He does, darling," Frances said, taking Dalia by the shoulders. "You're the loveliest thing he ever did see."

"Much prettier than that ole scrawny-necked chicken." Dora clamped the blades of her shears together and flung them on the ground.

"A hankie," Frances said, snapping her fingers at Dora, who drew a frayed square of cloth from her apron pocket and plopped it into the woman's hand. "Let's sit on the porch," Frances said, dabbing at Dalia's nose with the handkerchief. "Have us a glass of lemonade and a slice of Dora's gingerbread. You can tell us all about it."

"Yes, ma'am," Dalia mumbled, sniffling as they walked to the porch. "I don't understand why I let him upset me. I don't even like him." The purple clematis, twining around the railing, brushed against her fingers as she topped the last step.

"He led you on," said Frances Fairchild, following her. "No lady likes to be toyed with."

"He acts shameful," Dora snorted.

"Sit right here," Frances said, touching the arm of a rocker. "We'll be right back with some refreshments."

Slumping down, Dalia stared out over the porch at the weed-choked garden, her eyes falling on a cluster of hollyhocks in full bloom, their colorful blossoms round as saucers. Katie Mae had grown them every summer in their garden at Miller's Mansion, arranging them in tall crystal vases, which she scattered on mantels throughout the house. Dalia smiled as she remembered Nellie Ann following their fragrance from room to room. She shook her head, recalling how she'd told Nellie Ann she'd never marry, back when she was young and naive, when she hadn't understood the value of a dollar, hadn't appreciated her papa for giving her the gifts of time and money. From inside the kitchen came the hushed voices of Dora and Miss Fairchild. For once, Dalia found their gossip consoling. It was good to know they cared.

"Here we are," said Frances Fairchild, wedging the screen door open with her foot as she plowed through. "Pink lemonade and Dora's gingerbread." She set the tray on top of a round wicker table, before sinking onto a old pew from Samson Baptist Church, which extended the length of the railing. Dalia picked up the lemonade and took a big swallow. "Not so fast," her landlady cautioned. "Slow down or you'll get one of those cold aches in your head."

Dalia pressed the chilled glass against her temple and let her mind wander. *Feel,* she'd said, guiding her sister's hand into the cold creek that ran behind Miller's Mansion. *Feel the little pebbles.* Caressed smooth by the flowing water, thought Dalia, sliding the glass downward, rocking it against her cheek, sighing. She was tired of growing older.

"Now tell me what happened," Frances said, leaning so far over that the hem of her skirt touched Dalia's.

"I caught him," Dalia murmured, gazing abstractedly at the garden. "In the drugstore with that woman." She cradled the glass in her palms. "They were drinking sarsaparilla floats. He told her she was lovely."

"Nonsense," her landlady said. "The woman's older than he is and looks every bit of it. Did they see you?"

"No," Dalia said, biting her lower lip to keep it from trembling. "I crouched behind a display. It was all so humiliating."

"Why don't you take a bite of Dora's gingerbread?" Frances whispered. "She's waiting just inside the door."

Dalia set her glass of lemonade on the wide porch railing. She retrieved her plate from the round wicker table, forked up a mouthful of gingerbread, and chewed. "The best gingerbread I've ever had," she declared loudly.

At once the screen door whipped open. "I done seen her, Miss Dalia," Dora said as she stormed onto the porch. "Just last week, sneaking into the ice box. *I need a little chip of ice for my tooth. Dr. McKee says it'll make it feel better.* Smacks that bony hand of hers against her jaw, moaning and groaning. I looked hard at her, couldn't see no swellin'. That hussy's been after him for weeks," she grumbled, her eyes tight with anger. "Asked me to iron a dress for her. *Where ya goin' in this frilly thing?* I want to know. Tells me she is visitin' the dentist. Her tooth been hurtin' her so."

"Malingerer," growled her landlady. "An old maid like that will do anything to catch a man."

"I thought he liked me," Dalia muttered.

"Take another bite of my gingerbread," Dora said with sympathy. "It'll make ya feel better."

"Dora, come over here and join me," Frances Fairchild demanded. "I can't see Dalia for your big, broad fanny."

Dora moseyed over to the bench and sat, her leg inches from Miss Fairchild's.

"I think he's forgotten all about me," Dalia murmured.

"Naw, he ain't. Miss Chicken Lips," Dora said, pressing her lips together, making them disappear like Hester Pinbroke's, "wouldn't be scramblin' so hard if he had."

"Dora's right," her landlady said, abruptly standing. "The woman's working too hard to snare your dentist." While she spoke, she paced back and forth in front of Dalia's rocker. "No tellin' what else she's up to, but you . . . you gotta do something, too. Go to town more often. Pay a visit to Copeland's Jewelry. Waltz in and flirt some with Mr. Sears and that other man who works with him."

"But—"

"No buts about it," Frances said, coming to a stop, fixing her eyes on Dalia. "Mr. Sears won't court you," she said. "He's a confirmed bachelor, but word'll get out you're available."

"How?" asked Dalia.

"I'll make sure of it," her landlady promised. "Dora'll gladly help, won't you?"

"I know other housekeepers," Dora said, vigorously nodding. "I'll tell 'em what they need to hear, beg 'em not to flap their lips about it, and first thing ya know they'll be whispering it into their bosses' ears."

"Meanwhile," instructed Frances, "make yourself some plans. Go for a daily stroll. The good dentist eats lunch every day at the Blue Café. By one-thirty, he's back at his office. Bump into him while you're out walking."

"But it seems so scheming," objected Dalia.

"The game of love must be played shrewdly," her landlady argued.

"There must be another—"

"Ain't no other way," declared Dora. She adamantly fanned her face with the hem of her apron. "Ya fight fire with fire. Miss Chicken Lips is secure and comfy with all her money, but ya ain't got nothing. Ya be needin' that man more than she do."

"I understand what you're saying," Dalia conceded. She offered Dora her empty plate.

"You best eat like a bird for supper," Dora added, eyeing Dalia from top to bottom.

"Right now you look just fine," said Frances, "but your corset's getting a little snug. Ya don't need another ounce on your figure."

At five in the morning, Dalia rose and went downstairs to wait for her landlady in the kitchen. Exhausted, she leaned her head against the chair back, peering at the dawn through the window above the soapstone basin. A dull blade of light sliced through the leaves of the pear tree. Beyond it, the hydrangeas shone like paper lanterns in the fading darkness. Yesterday she was childish and weepy, but after a long night of thinking, she'd come to her senses. She was not above scheming. She'd manipulated and plotted her whole life, but the scheming, she decided, must be of her own making. A code of honor was imperative, even when it came to plotting.

A door closed. Footsteps sounded in the hallway. "Frances," Dalia whispered when her landlady set foot inside the kitchen.

Frances yelped, spasmodically jerked her shoulders. "Lord have mercy," she said, squinting through the dim light at Dalia. "Girl, you scared the life out of me."

"I couldn't sleep."

" 'Cause you're still worried about that woman." Frances didn't wait for Dalia to speak. "Don't you worry another second about her. Mark my words. My plan will work. By Christmas you'll be engaged to Dr. McKee." She ran her fingers along the shelf above the stove. "Aha!" she said, shaking a box of matches. "Let's shed some light on the subject." The match flared blue. "There," she said, lighting a candle on the table, which illuminated the kerchief on her head, her puffy face, her eyes bleary without her glasses.

"I'm not going to flirt with Larry Sears or with anyone else in Copeland's," Dalia said bluntly.

"Oh?" Frances said, pulling out a chair, sitting across from her. "Have you got another plan?"

"Was up all night thinking," Dalia told her. "Have decided to follow through on what I first threatened. Buy myself a train ticket to Atlanta. Let him know I'm going to leave Samson and move in with my cousin."

"Uh-huh," Frances said, scratching the side of her nose.

"I'll have the ticket in my hand. Wave it right in front of him."

"What if he doesn't believe you?"

"He will," Dalia said.

"But sweetheart, if he doesn't try to stop you, you might have to go, and Dora and I don't want that."

"Don't worry," Dalia said. "That won't happen."

"Well, then," said Frances, her tone serious, "my offer still stands. What can I do to help?"

"Tell all of your friends I'm leaving for Atlanta."

"In a week's time, half the town will know what color dress you'll be wearing for your trip," her landlady stated proudly.

"Red," Dalia said, her voice strong and confident. "Tell them I'll be wearing red."

CHAPTER 18

Keep your dignity, Dalia thought as she strode down the street, a haze syruping the air, gray clouds squatting in the sky. She fingered the train ticket to Atlanta, which she'd shoved deep into her dress pocket, and maintained her pace, her shoes *tsk*ing against the street. Keep your dignity, her mind kept repeating. This morning she'd selected a raspberry taffeta walking suit, long-sleeved with white lace at the cuffs and a scooped lace bodice. Not exactly red, but near enough, she decided. She'd also attached a matching raspberry ribbon around the crown of her close-fitting straw bonnet, the brim like blinders around her face. She wore lace gloves and, in case of rain, carried a small white umbrella over her wrist.

The clock chimed one. His office was only a block away. There was no need to hurry. Leisurely swinging her umbrella, she strolled in front of the milliner's salon beside the picket fence, where an array of sweet peas bloomed. She snapped off a stem of purple blossoms, using this moment to steal a glance up the sidewalk, but saw no one, only heat waves shimmering over the dirty brick street like lava. She let the sweet peas drop from her fingers. She was dawdling on the sidewalk when shoes scuffling came from the alley behind her, and she shifted toward the noise.

"Why, Dalia!" Herman gushed as he rounded a thick evergreen hedge that bordered the alley, "it's so nice to see you. What brings you out in this heat?"

"Dr. McKee," she said, solemnly nodding.

"I haven't seen you in ages." She said nothing, sucked the hot air through her teeth. "I've been busy," he said, his manner somber as he made excuses. He took a step toward her. She ignored him by popping a toadstool with the tip end of her umbrella. "Sadly, summertime plays havoc with the teeth."

"Must be all those cold sarsaparillas your patients are drinking." Her tone was chilly.

He drew back his narrow shoulders, stood speechless in the hedge's shadow. "I see you brought your umbrella," he said seconds later. "Ah, the delicious smell of rain," he said, lifting his head up, sniffing.

"Shame it can't be eaten."

A worried grin crawled over his face. "D-Dalia," he stammered, his voice shaky and uncertain. She pivoted slightly, as though to walk away. "Please stay." She turned back toward him. His reedy body inclined toward her. "You must believe me," he said earnestly, his eyes traveling over her dress. "Hester said you were leaving, moving to Atlanta. Said you found Samson boring."

"You shouldn't believe everything you hear, Dr. McKee." She judged him harshly with her eyes.

"She overheard you at the boardinghouse talking to Lawrence Sears. She said you didn't like me."

"If you want to believe her, it's your choice," Dalia said. "Really, though, I must depart now."

"But you're wearing red," he whined.

"It's raspberry." Her tone was wooden.

"Why are you wearing red?" he demanded. "Where are you going? Are you leaving here forever?" She brushed his questions aside, stuck her hand deep into her dress pocket, wanting to shock him with the ticket, but brought up her handkerchief instead. "What's that?" he asked, his pale skin coloring.

"A handkerchief," she said, returning her hand to her pocket, her fingers scrambling for the ticket.

He leaned over. His hand swooped down and snatched up the orange ticket where it lay at her feet on the ground. "No, this!" he cried out, wild and frantic, waving the ticket in front of her eyes. "You're going to Atlanta," he scolded, "and you weren't even going to tell me."

Airily, she dabbed her nose with the hankie. "What concern is it of yours?"

"But Dalia," he sputtered, "I didn't think you cared. That's the only reason I paid attention to Miss Pinbroke."

"You flatter yourself, Dr. McKee, if you think your courtship with Miss Pinbroke offends me."

"Then why are you leaving?"

"Because there's nothing holding me here."

"I don't want you to leave," he said, panicked. "You're beautiful," he blurted out. "So very lovely. Please," he begged, "don't go. Don't leave me here alone."

"You have Miss Pinbroke to console you," she said flatly. "Now good-bye, I have to go." As she turned to leave, his hand gripped her shoulder, and she rocked backward.

"No," he said, pulling her toward him with a virility she hadn't seen before. "I won't let you." Holding up the ticket, he vehemently ripped it in half.

"Dr. McKee, I believe you owe me the price of another ticket." She held herself erect, flashed her indignant eyes at him.

"Dalia, please, listen to me," he implored her. "I loved you the minute I set eyes on you. Can't you see that I adore you?"

The air shivered with thunder; flecks of rain dotted the sidewalk. "I see nothing of the sort," she snorted.

He reached out and grasped her gloved fingers. "Don't go."

"What's there to stop me?" She snatched her hand away.

"Me," he said meekly, looking so dejected he aroused in her a stab of pity. "Just me, Dalia. Standing here, asking you to marry me. Please, Dalia. Please, be my wife."

Along the fencerow, the sweet peas dipped their purple heads in the sun of the summer shower. Slowly easing her umbrella open, Dalia nodded: Yes.

CHAPTER 19

As soon as they walked into their suite at the Finmore Hotel, the porter put down their bags and hurried over to open the shuttered windows. "To let in the breeze from off the river," he said, wrapping his fingers around the dime that Herman tipped him, bowing slightly before leaving.

"My darling," Herman said when they were settled in the sitting room, the breeze through the window cooling them, hooves clip-clopping on the brick street below. "Dearest, you must be famished," he said. Reaching across the round table, he grasped her left hand, the gold wedding band and one-carat diamond crowning her finger. Seven hours earlier, they'd been married in a small country church, surrounded by a shriveled-up cornfield, three miles out of Samson, with no one present but Frances Fairchild, Dora, and Clarice, Herman's housekeeper and cook. The ceremony had been brief, the way Dalia had wanted it. The trip to Savannah had been long.

Dalia sat in a white chintz chair; a gold-embroidered white cloth was draped over the table beside her. At each end of the pink marble mantel was an azure vase of camellias, radiating a perfume that made her lightheaded. Directly in front of her through a gold-draped archway was the bridal chamber. A white satin canopy hung from the ceiling over the bed like a lace-capped mushroom. There was a blue-velvet studded bench at the foot of the bed, and lush blue curtains pooled on the cypress floor. A Chinese screen stood to the left of the bed, but Dalia had yet to venture behind it.

"I've ordered us a bottle of champagne and an iced plate of oysters. Doesn't that seem wonderful?" Herman asked. Yet before Dalia could muster enough energy to answer him, he was on his way to the door.

Dalia leaned back and closed her eyelids. A bird was singing beyond the balcony. A Bachman's sparrow, she guessed, then knew it wasn't, for the little gray bird nested only in the ground beneath the needles of the longleaf pine forests. She heard footsteps in the hallway, the click of the door as it opened, another click as it closed, the rattling of dishes, and footsteps coming toward her. She blinked open her eyes just as the waiter placed the tray on the table.

"Thank you," Herman said, dipping his hand in his pants pocket, tipping the waiter a nickle, dismissing him with a nod. "How about a glass of champagne?" he asked Dalia. Picking up the bottle, he upended it, poured the bubbly froth into two fluted long-stemmed glasses. Dalia pressed the rim against her lips and sipped. "Is it good?" he asked. She smiled and took another sip. "Only the best for my darling," he said, his voice as sugary as the scent of the camellias on the mantel. She drained off her glass. Cupping an oyster shell in his palm, he pitched it toward his lips, his eyes glazing over as he swallowed. "They're sweet and juicy," he said. With the tips of his fingers, he took hold of a silvery black-streaked shell. "Open up," he said, expecting her to tilt back her head and part her lips. Giggling, she wouldn't oblige him. "Come on," he cooed, as if he were hand-feeding a baby. "Open up for Daddy." Shaking her head, she tightly pressed her lips together. "Open. Open. Open," he singsonged, changing positions, moving behind her chair. She caved in, made a well of her mouth. The shell rocked forward; the oyster slid down her throat. "Did you like it?" he said after she swallowed.

"Yes, yes, yes," she told him, giddily pointing at her glass. He refilled it, then sank down into the chair across from her. "Savannah is different," she said gaily. "Not at all like Atlanta. It's so mysterious . . . so magical . . . so . . ."

"Romantic," he finished, picking up his glass, punctuating the adjective with a noisy gulp. He ate another oyster, smacked his thin lips. "I think I'll order us something else," he said. She nodded, flashed him an exorbitant smile. "Shrimp cocktail, pickled asparagus, deviled eggs, artichokes in vinaigrette sauce, and, of course, another dozen oysters. How does that sound?"

"Scrumptious," she replied. "What about some stuffed crab?" she suggested as he strode over to the bellpull. "Isn't that what Savannah is famous for?"

He turned to look at her. "Stuffed crab," he said thoughtfully, stroking the dimple on his chin. "Perhaps later," he said, giving the bellpull a sharp tug. "That is, if we're still hungry."

Too tipsy to argue, she shifted back to the window, welcoming the cool breeze off the river. "Papa often came here on business," she said dreamily, as though to no one in particular. "Atlanta wasn't his cup of tea, but he loved Savannah." Herman cleared his throat, tugged the bellpull again. "But like all big cities, it can be wicked."

"I certainly hope so." Unfolding his fingers, he blew her a kiss. After several minutes of waiting, he whipped the door open and stuck his head out into the hallway. "There's no one," he complained. "I'll have to go downstairs and place the order."

"Another bottle of bubbly," she called out as he closed the door behind him. She giggled girlishly. The champagne made her throat tingle, momentarily eased her nerves. She tried to stand, but the room spun around her. Clutching the edge of the table, she wobbled upward. From the silver wine bucket, she grabbed some ice chips and pressed them against her forehead. It was then it hit her. Tonight was their wedding night. Breathing in deeply, she aimed herself toward the bedroom and tottered forward. "My wedding night," she murmured, a shiver of fear running through her as she recalled the sight of her father's bird dogs mating, the violent aftermath of blood on Fawna's belly. She teetered toward the pile of bags stacked beside the wardrobe, seizing the valise on top, the easiest one she could get to, but just as she turned around, her hands gripping the handle, he came rushing through the door.

"That's mine, dearest," he said, gently loosening her fingers before dislodging her valise from the bottom of the pile. "Here you are," he said. "How sweet of you to want to slip into something soft for me." He carried her bag over to the bed and placed it on the mattress. "I feel silk," he said, unlatching the clasp, easing his hand through the aperture. He raised his arm, dangling her nightgown from his fingers. "I can't wait to see you in this."

She watched as he let it go, the wings of silk floating downward. She reached out and tried to catch it. "Whoops," she said, losing her balance.

He caught her beneath the elbow. "Here, let me help you," he said, guiding her over to the Chinese screen. "No monsters." He laughed as he peered behind it. But her nerves had gotten the best of her, and instead of laughing back she was vague and silent. "Why don't you rest a minute, darling?" He helped her lie down on a white chaise longue and positioned a blue heart-shaped pillow beneath her head. Seconds later, she heard the staccato sound of knocking, his voice saying, "Our food's here. I'd better go take care of the waiter."

As soon as he was gone, she rose unsteadily, unbuttoned her shirtwaist, and draped it over the Chinese screen. She went over to the bed, fearful as she stared at the nightgown coiled upon the coverlet. She took a deep breath. She was a married woman now, she told herself. She had a husband, who had certain needs, and as his wife, it was her duty to fulfill them. She removed her collar, blouse, skirt, and undergarments, then lifted the nightgown over her head and let its sheer white silk fall over her. On her way to the sitting room, she passed by the dresser mirror, her eyes catching the womanly roundness of her reflection. Her arms crisscrossed over her chest, she walked shyly to the table.

"You look enticing, my dear," he said, rising from his seat like a gentleman. With a tiny two-pronged fork, he pierced an oyster, eased it between his lips, and swallowed. "I could eat everything on this table," he said, waving his arm over the platter of artichokes, the bowl of vinaigrette sauce, the shrimp, the asparagus, the bottle of champagne, "but I don't have to because you're the dish that's most delicious. I could just eat you," he said, popping another oyster into his mouth, gulping it down. "You're my delicate truffle." The seawater smell of shellfish rose off his fingers. "Are you a fungus or a piece of chocolate?" he asked, coming toward her. "Do you grow underground or are you dipped in sugar?" He presented his hands to her, and she obediently took hold of his fingers. Wrapping his arm around her waist, he led her to the bed. "Sweetheart," he cooed. The silk of her nightgown was moist against her skin. "My darling," he purred, pulling her down beside him. "What a tiny blue vein!" he bleated, exploring her neck with his fingertips, his thin lips flaking like poached fish against her skin. Her heart was racing, panic charging through her breast. "Your little pulse is throbbing." He leaned over, straddling a leg across her body, and began to kiss her lips. She felt her chest caving in, the muscles in her throat constricting. Every bit of oxygen, flowing in her veins, was being slurped up by him. Gasping for air, she threw out her arms and lunged upward, knocking him off her. At first he was startled, his thin lips distorted with confusion, then a soft look overtook his eyes, and he said gently, "Let me teach you the pleasures of love."

It was then she began to laugh. A terrible, hysterical laugh that originated deep in her stomach. She collapsed back upon the pillow and clamped her hand over her mouth, but the laugh escaped through her fingers.

"Stop it," he said. "You're my wife now, and you owe me certain things." The word *wife* struck her as uncommonly funny, and the laughter flew mockingly from her lips. "I told you to stop." His eyes were small and tight, his lips white with anger. But try as she might, she couldn't quit. "Goddamn you!" he fumed, hurling himself on top of her, ripping her nightgown down the middle, sending the little pearl buttons flying. Grabbing her breasts, he squeezed them so tightly she thought she would cry out, pinned her down beneath him, and plunged himself inside her.

CHAPTER 20

Rocking on the veranda, enjoying the cool spring weather, Dalia imagined her stomach swelling beneath her dress and grew frightened. Could it be that she was pregnant? She had been so certain his sperm were too weak and passive to penetrate her womb, but she hadn't bled for two months now, and she was worried. If only the townsfolk of Samson, out for their evening stroll, knew how much she'd suffered at her husband's hands. "If only . . ." she whispered, trying hard to camouflage her resentment toward him, but her anger was headstrong and determined and, despite her effort, revealed itself in the snap of the rocker against the floorboards.

In the six months of their marriage, he had forced sex on her every other night. Because she despised his touch, it seemed he was determined to touch her. "Your eyes are mocking me," he'd say, and although she'd shake her head and deny it, the sex would come, a jabbing pain, harsh and swift, as always. Just last night, he held her down—her spine eating into the tick as he forced himself inside her. Afterward, she sobbed, praying for his death. "Don't cry, my darling," he'd said, mistaking her hatred for his own rhapsodic feeling of oneness.

"Miz Dalia, Miz Dalia, I need some help with supper." It was Clarice, his cook, leaning out the front door, calling.

Yesterday he had driven all the way to Lancaster, returning with a seven-pound leg of lamb, his mouth already salivating with anticipation. "I want it prepared the English way," he had instructed Dalia. He was determined that she learn how to cook, even though cooking was Clarice's job, his hobby. "Rub it with salt, pepper, and rosemary. Also a little melted butter. Wives cook," he'd pronounced, clucking softly.

"What took ya so long?" Clarice asked as Dalia strolled into the kitchen. She pulled the lamb out of the oven and set it on the counter. Her nut-brown eyes harbored contempt. "Dr. Herman will be coming home soon. Here," she said, cutting off a sliver of meat, dangling it in front of Dalia. "Tell me if I cooked it right."

"I've never eaten lamb in my life," Dalia said, snagging the sliver of flesh with her fingers. Just as she was about to slip it between her lips, the gamy smell slapped her in the face, and she dropped it upon the floor. "I can't," she cried, and with her hand over her mouth, she fled from the kitchen, made straightaway for the stairs, and rushed to the bathroom. Throwing back the commode top, she was promptly sick.

"Miz Dalia!"

Dalia listened to Clarice climbing the stairs, the soles of her shoes flapping against the runner. She tore off a sleeve of toilet paper and wiped her mouth.

"Ya sick?" Clarice asked from the other side of the bathroom door.

"I'm all right now," Dalia murmured.

"Ya been sick a lot lately."

Dalia hung her head over the commode, was quiet.

"When ya feel better, come back down. It'll be suppertime soon, and I need your help with the gravy."

"The mint sauce," corrected Dalia.

"Whatever ya say, Miz Dalia," Clarice said, walking away.

"Needs more mint," he griped that evening at supper. "Dalia, didn't you use the cider vinegar like I told you?" He forked up more lamb and ate it. "No. No. No," he sniveled. "This isn't right. It should be crisp on the outside, but pink in the middle. Now that I think about it, a cold Cumberland sauce would've been better."

"Cumberland sauce," she mocked, but he was too busy stabbing English peas, squishing them through his lips, to notice.

"It'll be better next time," he said, blotting his mouth, tucking his napkin beneath the rim of his plate. "Clarice, will you please do the cleaning up?" he said politely. "Dalia and I want to retire early."

She followed him dutifully up the staircase. Before joining her in the bedroom, he would brush his teeth—obsessed as he was with oral hygiene. She could hear him pouring the water from the pitcher, the water splashing against the bowl. She envisioned the coin of baking powder in the center of his palm, his long fingers curled around the toothbrush, the bristles dipping into the mound of chalky white, his arm sawing from side to side, scrubbing his teeth until the gums bled, the spitting afterward, then the gargling. Brushing, spitting, gargling. Brushing, spitting, gargling. Brushing, spitting, gargling. Every night, three times altogether. Those tiny yellow incisors never getting any whiter.

"Darling," he said as he crawled into bed beside her.

Just last week, she'd studied his thin, cadaverous face while he was sleeping. He'd looked like he'd been dead for years. A breeze teased the oak leaves outside their bedroom window and for a blessed moment she forgot about him. He moved his legs against hers, and she flinched, mindful of his awful manhood, but then she remembered there would be no coupling tonight. "Yes," she said, as relief washed over her.

"Clarice told me you're not well."

She clutched the sheet tightly between her fingers. "You forget I'm just a country girl. The meals we eat are too rich." She listened to his glutted breathing. He stuffed himself yet never gained a pound, while she grew bigger and bigger.

He clucked his tongue and added, "She said you're sick to your stomach."

"The food is too rich," she insisted. "Some plain eating for a week or two might help."

"If that would please you, my darling."

"Yes," she muttered, rolling over to face the wall.

The following day, she was halfway through the meatloaf when the nausea tackled her. Jumping up from her chair, she dashed through the dining room, out the kitchen door, and onto the back porch, where she hung her head over the railing and was sick.

"Poor darling." He was cuddling up behind her, skittering his fingers up and down her back. "Why don't you go upstairs and rest?"

"I'm fine," she said, turning toward him.

"But Dalia, you're ashen." He slithered a napkin from his pants pocket, draped it over his index finger, spit, and cleaned the corners of her mouth.

"Don't worry about me," she told him.

"It's not only you who concerns me, my darling," he said in a voice as sugary as the caramel in one of his famous flans. "But also the baby inside you."

After Herman left for his office the next morning, Dalia ordered Wilson, their groom, to bring her the phaeton. The dappled gray mare snorted and tossed her heavy white mane as Dalia settled down on the wooden seat and tucked her skirt beneath her. Gently flicking the reins, she directed the mare toward the center of town. Regardless of the consequences, she needed to be around like-minded people. She needed someone, anyone, to talk to; but, before she'd known what was happening, he'd eliminated her few friends. Frances Fairchild was deemed too nosy; Mr. Sears, improper. She needed to be a proper wife. He had a duty to safeguard his reputation, he'd told her. His livelihood depended on what the townsfolk thought of him. The only person he hadn't banned was Hester Pinbroke.

As Dalia drove the carriage past the Confederate soldier and the three-legged cat beside him, she caught sight of a young couple laughing and drinking coffee at a small wrought-iron table on the balcony of the Suwannee Inn. When she saw them, a sadness swept over her. Three businesses down, she spotted a group of workers scraping First Farmers Bank, preparing the surface for a fresh coat of white paint. They were joking and slapping each other's backs, delighting in their camaraderie, and at that moment Dalia would have given anything to be one of them. Then Dinky Bridges waddled out of Dickson's Bakery looking like a well-fed tick, his little legs just visible below his bloated belly. He was carrying a huge paper bag. Filled up with goodies for his friends, thought Dalia, suddenly ashamed that she'd dismissed him for the way he looked. Folding the reins over, she snapped them against Dollie's back. She didn't care what Herman wanted; she'd drive by the boardinghouse to see if Frances and Dora were deadheading the roses outside. If so, she'd stop. But when she passed the corner of Rose and Lee, they were nowhere in sight.

Desperate, she headed for the town square again. If only Edwina Carpenter were out shopping. If only Lawrence Sears were sitting on the bench in front of Copeland's, smoking his pipe. If only . . . if only . . . she thought, her eyes brimming as she repeated her drive through town. Snapping the reins, she urged Dollie to go faster. To go faster where? she wondered, the tears flowing down her face. She seized the whip and snapped it in the air. The carriage was now whirling around the corner, flying by the draper's. "Whoa!" Dalia shouted when a black woman ran out in front of her. Screaming, the woman held out her hands, palms up. Dalia jerked back on the reins. The mare neighed loudly, rose up on her hind legs, and stopped. The black woman stood motionless, as though her feet were tarred to the spot. She fixed her eyes on Dalia, smiling ironically, then, as quickly as she came, her thin body slipped down a back alley.

It was then Dalia thought of Katie Mae. In her mind's eye, she saw her strong dark hands beckoning her to come to Snake River. *"Yes, we'll gather at the river,"* she was singing, her voice strong and inviting, the way it had always been back home.

CHAPTER 21

As Dalia drew closer to the river, the soil changed from red clay to gray sand. The pine trees became scraggly. Scrubby underbrush took over. Before she saw the water, she smelled its wormy scent. Even the spring rains couldn't rid the river of its murky, contradictory odor, the smell of birth born of decay. When young, Dalia had liked to feel earthworms slithering through her fingers. She would dig them up in Katie Mae's garden, let them skate over her skin, then toss them into the fish pond behind Miller's Mansion, where they swaybacked and squiggled beneath the surface of the water. The sticky slime on her fingers was testimony that all living creatures left traces of themselves behind. No matter how small or seemingly inconsequential, they produced aftershocks, those little ripples spreading through time.

Dalia flicked the reins with one hand, placed the other on her belly, thinking about the life inside her, her own little ripple. The scenery along the road became more and more familiar—the forsythia with its bright yellow blooms, the patches of sweet gum and sumac with its tiny red berries, the scratches of loblolly pines. The bald yards of the shanties gave her a lonely feeling, but then she caught sight of the children napping on the front porches on bright rag rugs, and her spirits rose.

The smell of hoecakes and lima beans brought back memories of Katie Mae's cooking: her iron pots of navy beans with hog jowl; her skillets of crisply fried cornbread. Ingredients spilled from her fingertips, a dash of this, a dab of that, the result a masterpiece. Whereas Herman spent hours on his food—gathering together his cookbooks in the library, picking out the most exotic dishes, describing to Dalia the many steps that went into their preparation. The two of them could have been rehearsing for a play, his opening night adequate but ultimately disappointing, in no way resembling Katie Mae's performances, which were impromptu and inspired.

"Katie Mae," Dalia called out as she climbed down from the carriage. Katie Mae was stooped over, draping wet clothes over a scribble of bushes. Dalia began walking toward her, but the black woman kept hanging the garments. "Katie Mae," Dalia repeated, her voice louder.

"What took ya so long?" Katie Mae said as she turned around slowly. They stood, speechless, staring at each other, like relatives who'd had a quarrel but, over the years, had forgotten what it was all about.

Dalia thought the question over. "I wanted to begin again. The past was too painful."

Her bottom lip tamped with snuff, Katie Mae scrunched up her face and spit tobacco juice on the ground. "Ain't no one able to wipe out who she is."

"I know," Dalia said, her eyes wistful and glassy. "The past is like a shadow, always following you around."

"Why ya come now?" Katie Mae asked her, defiantly thrusting out her chin, her shoes sinking into the soft sand as she leaned forward. "All these years and not a word. Didn't ya think I was grievin', too?"

Dalia ironed her eyelids with her index finger. "Sadness made me selfish. I'm sorry."

"I was at their burials."

Ashamed, Dalia nodded. "I saw you."

"Why didn't ya send word ya was comin'?"

" 'Cause my coming here just happened."

"What is it ya want me to do?"

"Forgive me," Dalia said.

"Ain't that what I always do?" Katie Mae said, opening her arms, moving toward her.

Dalia felt Katie Mae's collarbone, thin and sharp against her chest, and smelled the raw odor of lye rising off her body. Dollie, hitched to a branch of sumac behind them, whinnied softly. "I've missed you," Dalia murmured.

"Well, now, I reckon what ya really missed is my cookin'," Katie Mae said, inching back, giving her the once-over. "Ya don't look well. Are ya hungry?"

"A little."

"I got buttermilk, cornbread, and white beans simmering. Come on in, child, and eat a bit." They sauntered down the pathway, bordered by snowbells. Tiny purple and yellow crocuses poked through the sparse grass. Along the bottom of the porch, daffodils were unfolding. Dalia began to smile. She should've known Katie Mae wouldn't let her yard go bare like the others. "Zara tells me you're married to a rich man," Katie Mae said, clattering up the porch steps.

"Dr. Herman McKee. He's a dentist."

"He doctors people's teeth, then," Katie Mae said, holding the front door open for her. Inside, the walls were whitewashed. Glass panes were inserted into the two front windows, from which dimity curtains hung. A matching coverlet graced the iron bed. ln the middle of the room was an oval red and blue braided rug. On top of it stood a familiar wooden table, in the center of which sat a canning jar of double daffodils. "Take a seat right here," Katie Mae said, sliding out a chair. "I'll go fix ya a plate."

Dalia slumped down. A ray of sunlight glinted off a blue glass bottle on the mantel. Next to the fireplace, a blue and yellow needlepointed stool drew her attention. "I don't see your mama's rocker," she yelled above the ruckus of pots and pans. "I thought you took it with you when you left."

"I did. It's down the road getting fixed."

"Oh, I see," Dalia said. The oven door groaned open, thumped shut. The buttery smell of cornbread filled her nostrils.

"The beans is cooked with ham hock," Katie Mae said, hurrying across the wooden floor, setting a ratty wicker tray on the table. "Throwed in some onion and lots of garlic. A pinch of cayenne for good measure."

"That's how I remember them."

"I brung ya a glass of buttermilk."

"Sounds mighty tasty."

Katie Mae began sprinkling chopped green onions over the beans. "Enough?" she asked. Dalia dipped her head, and Katie Mae shoved the bowl of beans at her, handed her the glass of buttermilk, then two yellow squares of cornbread. "Here's a cold cup of water from my well."

Before consuming a morsel, Dalia picked up the cup and took a long, slow swallow. She set the water beside the cornbread and spooned up some beans, eating them slowly, savoring the flavor. "They're good," she said, suddenly aware of just how much she missed the plain, wholesome taste of Katie Mae's cooking. "The good dentist fancies himself a chef."

"The man cooks?" Katie Mae said with a grin.

"He plans the meals," Dalia explained. "I supervise Clarice's cooking."

Katie Mae snickered, her pink gums riding up, revealing teeth stained yellow from the snuff. "But child, you can't boil water."

"I know," Dalia said, crumbling cornbread into her glass. "His food is what's making me sick." She dipped her spoon into the buttermilk.

"Food's food, ain't it?"

Dalia held up an index finger, popped the mushy cornbread into her mouth, chewed, and swallowed. "His meals are too rich," she stated, licking the moon of buttermilk off her top lip. "Butter. Onion. Garlic. Celery. All kinds of fancy spices. Sautéeing. Braising. Whipping. Creaming. 'Remember to start with a roux,' " she said, her voice as shrill as Herman's.

"What's that?"

"Flour stirred into hot butter."

"Fancy gravy."

"I reckon," Dalia said, "but if I even breathe the word *gravy* he has a conniption fit."

"Peculiar, ain't he?"

"And Clarice, that cook of his, is just like him. Thinks he's a saint."

"What color woman is she?"

"High yellow."

"Mighty strange," Katie Mae said, pulling out a chair, sitting. She was quiet for a second, staring at Dalia while she ate. "Now tell me the truth of why ya came."

Dalia cleared her throat, took another drink of water, and shyly said, "He says he loves me, but he hurts me."

"What do ya mean, he hurts ya?"

"In bed," she said simply.

"Ain't tender?"

Dalia shook her head. "He makes me bleed."

"And says he loves ya?"

"Says he wants me to be happy, but"—Dalia hesitated—"he won't let me have any friends."

"He's bad strange," Katie Mae said solemnly. "But he can't do that if ya don't let him." Shifting the lump of snuff from one side of her mouth to the other, she retrieved a jar from her apron pocket. "You is giving him the power," she said, unscrewing the lid, spitting. "Ya gotta be tough, girl. Remember what I told ya about your papa?"

"Yessam," Dalia said, remembering clearly.

"Ya gotta stand up to the man." Katie Mae plunked the jar on the floor, sloshing the brown spit against the glass. "After I was throwed out of your house, life got hard. Nellie Ann's dying. Your mama's passing. I had me a little money, but it weren't enough to tide me over." She stood up abruptly from the table and began to pace, her shoes clumping against the pine plank floor. "I was lonesome, and there was this man, Buster Mullins, who took a shine to me. He's got this shanty down the road, right on the bank of the river. Come summertime, picks cotton for Mr. Jenkins. Got plenty of money 'cause he all alone." Katie Mae coughed loudly, walked over to her chair, picked up the jar from off the floor, and spit. "Commences to court me. Brung me food. Little bags of sugar and coffee. Cornmeal. Dried beans. One time, a slab of fatback. Asks me to come live with him. He ain't no cook, he says. Needs someone to clean up, wash his clothes. Tired of payin' some gal to do it. *Ya can pick cotton alongside me,* he says. *Together, we can make us a heap of money. Fetch me a cold cup from your well,* he bosses me. *Ladle me up a bowl of 'em soup beans.* He was workin' on makin' his ways my own, and I was lonesome. Wanted myself some company, but better to be alone than be with someone who wants to own ya. Ya gotta make better, Miss Dalia, not marry it." Katie Mae paused and angrily rapped her fingernails against the jar. "Ya gotta be brave, make a good life through your own doin'. When I was young, my mama asked me to fry up some chitlins. 'Afore she asked me, I ain't never cooked a thing, but I seen her cookin' chitlins, and I done what I seen her doin', and I don't mind sayin' them chitlins were mighty tasty. Naw, I ain't scared of nothing. I know how to be brave. *No,* I told him."

"But I'm already married," said Dalia.

"Don't matter. That furniture doctor who's got my rocker, he likes me, too, and we done been together, but I made myself clear from the start. *I got a good life here,* I told him. *Plenty of friends, who don't crowd me. I clean when I want to. Cook when I want to. Do as I please, and I ain't gonna let being with ya change things.* What I'm sayin' is, ya can change how ya be married. He can't control ya, if ya don't let him."

"I hate him," Dalia whispered, her features contorting. "I hate everything about him. His prissy talk. His food. The way he eats. His fingers all over me." The color left her face, and, light-headed, she slumped sideways.

Katie Mae hastened over, propped Dalia up with her body. She plunged a hand deep into her apron pocket. "Open up," she demanded, pushing a fingerful of snuff between Dalia's gum and bottom lip. "Suck on it," she said. "Don't swallow. Spit it all out," she said, holding the jar beneath Dalia's mouth. Dalia did as Katie Mae told her. "That'll revive ya. Now I'm gonna help ya over to the bed. Ya best lie down and rest awhile till ya be feeling better."

Katie Mae was standing over her when she woke. Lassoing her hands over her head, Dalia yawned deeply. For a split second she fancied she was back at Miller's Mansion. But when her fingers grazed the rusted iron headboard and her legs cramped against the hard trench in the cornhusk tick, she was brought back to the present, and the brightness that had begun to show itself in the corners of her eyes vanished. Flinging an arm over her face, she began to sob. "I don't want to go back there," she said, her voice quaking with emotion.

"Then don't," Katie Mae stated, sinking down on the edge of the bed. "Ya can stay here and live with me. Don't be afraid to do what ya need to."

"I can't. It's too late now," Dalia mumbled, sniffling back tears.

"It ain't never too late."

Dalia listened to Katie Mae's breathing, the breeze grumbling through the windows, a bird shrieking, wagon wheels creaking on the rutted dirt road. "I'm going to have a baby," she said.

"Do ya know for sure?" Katie Mae asked in a voice that was as flat as the river.

Dalia took her arm off her face and stared hard at Katie Mae, who was looking not at Dalia but straight ahead. "I haven't bled for two months now," she said. "I'm sick with nausea, always tired."

"Does he know?"

"Yes, ma'am."

"Do ya want to have it?"

"I don't know," Dalia said, the tears returning.

"I could give ya a special medicine," Katie Mae said, "but it could be dangerous." Dalia said nothing. "Pennyroyal," she went on. "What works for some, don't work for others. The baby could be born damaged."

"Like Nellie Ann?"

"Maybe."

"No, I won't risk that," Dalia stated firmly.

"Naw, I didn't think so," Katie Mae said, rising, offering her hand to Dalia. "It don't gotta be one way or the other," she said, pulling hard till Dalia was standing. "There's a middle ground. Ya can have the baby and learn to stand up to the man. Let him know ya is your own person." Katie Mae glanced up, gazed out the window. Concern worried her eyes. "It's late in the day."

It was hard for Dalia to release the black woman's hand, but, looking deep inside herself, she found a bit of courage. "I'd better get back," she said, letting go of those strong, steadfast fingers.

CHAPTER 22

"I thought you were dead," he said shrilly, racing toward her. "Clarice came by the office. Said you left early this morning but hadn't returned. I've been sick to death with worry."

"I went to see an old friend," Dalia said, brushing past him. "There was no need for you to be concerned."

"You should've told me you were going."

"It was a spur-of-the-moment decision," she said, yanking off her gloves, flopping them on top of the secretary. She made a beeline for the staircase; he followed her.

"Going off like that, and in your condition," he admonished, mounting the steps with her.

"What condition might that be?" she said sharply, coming to a standstill on the first landing. Light from the wall sconce shimmered against the gold curtains; her heart banged inside her chest.

"You're carrying my baby." He was now alongside her, hovering too close, stealing her breath.

"I am?" She drank down a mouthful of air and fled toward the second flight of steps.

"I'm not a stupid man, Dalia." He was panting behind her, his shoes nipping the bottom of her skirt. "Suppertime and you still weren't here. Clarice and I were worried."

"Clarice can manage a meal without me," she said insolently over her shoulder.

"We thought you were hurt somewhere."

"Herman, I went to visit an old friend." She paused at the top of the staircase. "She lives near Snake River." She began moving across the landing. "The notion just popped into my head. I'm sorry I made you worry, but truly it was nothing." When she twisted the doorknob, he gripped her forearm and tried to spin her toward him, but she snatched her arm away, booted the door open with her foot, and dashed through it.

He chased after her. "You'll not go gallivanting around." He was reaching again for her arm. She stepped quickly to one side, and he lurched forward. "Dalia," he whined, tottering as he turned to face her. "You're not an inconsiderate woman. You know you should've come by the office and told me where you were going."

"You would've said no." Her fingers were sweaty as they fumbled with the buttons on her dress. "Please, Herman," she gasped, "I'm tired, and I need to rest." She stepped out of her dress. Instinctively, he bent over, picked it up off the floor, and draped it over the chair back.

"You need to listen to me, I . . ."

She closed her mind to him and, in her undergarments, climbed into bed. Her head sank into the feather-down pillow, the fluff like stoppers in her ears, his voice sounding empty, as if he were pulpy and combustible inside, like the hollow core of a fungus-ridden longleaf. He droned on, his words resembling pine cone seeds drifting down, but she planted weeds in the clear ground of her mind to keep them from growing. Stand up to him, she thought, lowering her eyelids, his speech skimming over her while she went to sleep, wishing him dead.

"Good morning," Dalia said, striding into the kitchen in her pink dressing gown. The two of them were huddling beside the wood-burning cookstove, whispering like spies or lovers. Clarice gave her the once-over, air fizzing through her teeth, then elbowed Herman, who proffered Dalia a glance. "What's for breakfast?" Dalia asked, moseying over to the stove, raising the lid off a boiler. "Ah, grits." She sighed and raked her fingers through her hair. "Biscuits and sausage," she said, peeking inside the warming oven.

"I thought I'd cook the eggs this morning," he said, avoiding her eyes. "Make us an omelet."

"A cheese omelet?" she inquired.

"Spanish," he told her.

There was a skidding sound. Clarice was sliding a stool over the floorboards. "Gonna get Dr. Herman his favorite skillet," she said, positioning the stool in front of a tall hutch. "I done chopped the onions, peeled and diced the potatoes." Gingerly, she took a step up.

Herman craned his face over his shoulder and tossed Clarice a smile, his top lip riding up, sticking like plaster to his pale pink gums. "Clarice is my angel."

"And you, her saint," Dalia added. She strolled over to the tiny kitchen table and pulled out a chair. Outside, it was overcast and dreary. The tatting of little green buds on the pecan trees looked forlorn and neglected. "A big breakfast is just what the doctor ordered," Dalia said, rubbing her arms against the chill.

Ignoring her, Herman approached Clarice and held out his hand for the skillet. He circled his finger around the inside edge. "She keeps it nicely greased," he said, showing Dalia the shiny residue on his skin.

"Yes, Clarice is a marvel," Dalia stated. "A better wife than I could ever be." She caught him furrowing his eyebrows, his cheeks flushing with fury. She was parting her lips, preparing to needle him again, when out of nowhere a numbness began to creep through her, as though she'd slept too hard on every limb. Her head started to spin. Her breathing quickened. She tried to rise, her legs suddenly buckling beneath her.

When she opened her eyes, he was murmuring, "Dearest darling, I'm so sorry." Clarice was kneeling on the floor beside him, dunking a dish towel in cold water. "I'm not a bad person," he said, swabbing her forehead. "Just terrified that I might lose you. If I did, I'd die."

His words softened her, and for a moment she forgot that he was her husband, that the woman beside him was his ally, and, smiling faintly, she said, "Don't fret, dear. I'm feeling better."

It was then he started crying, driblets scrambling down his face, his dimpled chin quivering. "I'm nothing without you," he said, sniffling.

"Herman," she said, reaching out to stroke his fingers. "You must permit me to be my own person."

"Yes, I know," he blubbed, blinking back tears, wiping his nose with the dish towel. "I promise, I'll try harder."

In the weeks that followed, he kept his promise. No longer did he insist that Dalia supervise the cooking. He even suggested that she ask Miss Fairchild over for tea and cookies, then days later took her back to the Suwannee Inn for supper. Over plates of smothered quail, he ticked off a list of activities she might find enjoyable: Samson's Needlepointing Club, which met every week; the local D.A.R. meeting, to take place next Monday in the church hall of Samson Baptist; followed by the Christian Women's Auxiliary on Friday, whose charity work, he thought, would inspire her.

On Monday, she attended the D.A.R. meeting, but it proved disappointing with its mostly stuffy, middle-aged patrons; so she wasn't looking forward to the Christian Women's Auxiliary a few days later. Yet, Friday brought a change of plans. Mrs. Tierney, his receptionist, had stayed home with a headache, he told her. Would she please pitch in and help him out at the office? Of course, she'd love to, she gushed, all the while listening as he listed her duties. Greet the patients and make them comfortable. Give them their bills. Accept their payments. Write down all transactions and, at the end of the day, take notes of the treatment plans, which he would dictate to her. "I can do it," she said excitedly, banging her kneecaps against the edge of the table as she leapt up from her chair.

She flung open the wardrobe door and surveyed her shrinking garments. Most of her dresses had become too tight, but there were still a few that fit, one in particular, which hung limply around the middle. It was dark blue, plain, and simple—its only extravagance a wide white lace collar. She put it on, then pinned her chignon to the back of her head, dabbed a little lilac water behind her ears, and rushed down the steps, bumping into him at the bottom of the staircase.

He gripped the newel post. "You must remember the baby, Dalia."

"The baby's fine," she said, dashing past him, darting out the front door. Before she descended the porch steps, she pivoted slowly. "What do you think?" she asked, holding out the wings of her dark skirt. "Do I look like Mrs. Tierney?"

"You're much too beautiful." He laughed.

She gazed at his face—for the first time in a long while appreciating its delicacy, as if it had been blown into existence like a piece of glass. She took hold of his hand, a smile dancing over her lips because her life had changed so quickly. Yes, she could learn to love him, she thought.

"A penny for your thoughts?" he asked, swinging her hand as they headed down the walkway.

"I'm happy," was all she said.

Herman went over to a hard dark chair, swords of sunlight from the palladium windows falling over it. "This is your desk," he said as Dalia wedged her hand above her brow to guard against the glare. "Here is the place for the money," he said, sliding out a drawer when she came over. "And this"—he touched a large black ledger—"is for documenting all transactions. The red one"—he nodded at a notebook on the left—"is only for clinical notes. Be polite and sensitive to the patients," he reminded her. "They're always anxious when they come here."

"Do you honestly think I would be rude to the poor dears?" she asked with a nervous giggle.

"Of course not, darling." He pulled out the desk chair for her, and she sat. "I could talk to you forever, but right now I need to get ready for Mrs. Hunter."

"What time will she be in?"

"Around nine-thirty," he said, glancing at the clock on the bookshelf beside the desk. "And the little Olson girl is at eleven. Then there's lunch at the Blue Café at noon, but we must be back by one-thirty 'cause Sassie Mead will be here at two."

"I could learn to like this," she said gaily.

He brushed his lips against her forehead. "But what would become of poor Mrs. Tierney?" he said, laughing as he pattered off down the hallway.

It was three hours before lunch, and she was already hungry. If only she'd eaten her breakfast, but she'd been in too much of a hurry. "Shush," she scolded her stomach. She picked up the red notebook and thumbed through it. Mrs. Tierney's tidy script reflected her life—narrow and efficient. Discouraged, Dalia laid down the notebook. She wanted her life to be bigger than this. Herman was moving about in the back room. She heard his dental tools clinking as he arranged them in a row on his worktable. She imagined him buttoning his white cotton smock, scrubbing his hands with lye soap and water. She could be a good wife and mother if only he'd compromise a little, let her make use of her assets. She had so many ideas to share with her husband—like repainting this dreary waiting room. Strange, she hadn't noticed how ugly it was before. She reckoned her tooth and nerves had gotten the best of her then, but she realized now what he should do—repaint the jaundiced walls with a calm, cool shade of blue, replace the hard wooden chairs with seats that were softly padded, and set out some knickknacks for warmth and color. With a little shared power, she thought, they could build a solid life together.

"Why, you're not Mrs. Tierney," a shocked voice beside her said. Startled, Dalia twisted around. "Where is Mrs. Tierney?" the woman whined, her swollen jaw cupped in her hand.

"She's at home—sick," Dalia said. "And you must be . . ."

"Mrs. Roberta Hunter," the woman replied, attempting a smile. "I haven't slept for three nights now, so I'm not quite certain."

"Your jaw is terribly swollen," Dalia said sympathetically, staring at the squat, stout woman with skin the color of boiled potatoes.

"I didn't come in sooner because I thought it was getting better," Mrs. Hunter said. "Now I'm afraid he'll have to pull it."

"Here, let me help you," Dalia offered. Rising, she took hold of the woman's arm and helped her over to one of the waiting room chairs.

"I'll be snaggletoothed when I smile."

"Don't worry about that now," Dalia said, tenderly squeezing her shoulder.

"But oh, it hurts so bad," she whimpered.

"I'll tell Dr. McKee you're here," Dalia said, hastening down the corridor. "Herman?" she said, rapidly knocking. When he didn't answer, she eased the door open. His profile was to her, the corners of his mouth in a frown. "Herman?" When he turned to face her, he looked concerned. "Mrs. Hunter just arrived."

"I know, dear," he said, his voice anxious. "I heard her. I need a few more minutes before you bring her in." He stared quietly ahead. Then, almost inaudibly, he said, "I don't like inflicting pain on my patients."

His candor was unsettling. After hastily closing the door behind her, she waited a full five minutes before she went to collect his patient.

"It was food beneath my gum," Mrs. Hunter mumbled a half hour later. Watery blood mottled her teeth. "He gave me this," she said, holding up a bottle of dark green medicine, the same medicine he'd given Dalia the first time she saw him.

Without warning, it struck Dalia that maybe Herman wasn't a real dentist at all, just a self-important man playing dress-up in his white dentist's jacket, exploiting patients with his long-handled tools and his green bottles of medicine. Could it be that the desk at which she sat was a figment of her imagination; her marriage, an illusion; the baby inside her, a stomach cramp?

When she took Mrs. Hunter's payment, she felt guilty, yet as soon as the woman had gone, she shrugged off her qualms. After all, *food beneath the gum* was a reasonable explanation. Her husband was the dentist. She was the one pretending to be his assistant. She was foolishly suspicious, she reasoned, fuzzy-headed from having rushed off this morning without any food.

"So Mrs. Hunter had a piece of food beneath her gum?" Dalia quizzed him over lunch at the Blue Café.

"It's a common problem," her husband said, cutting a slice of meat into a perfect little square. "If the swelling doesn't improve, I'll be forced to take her tooth out."

"You didn't have to pull mine," Dalia said, sipping ice tea.

"Yours wasn't as bad as Mrs. Hunter's," he said, holding his fork upright, nibbling the meat.

"She'll be upset if you pull it."

"I know," Herman said, resting his fork on the edge of his plate. "That's why I decided to wait." He picked up his glass of water and took a drink. "I wanted to give her some time to get used to the idea of losing it."

Dalia propped her wrists on the table and laced her fingers together. "But she doesn't think she's going to lose it."

"She has another appointment on Monday. I'll mention the possibility to her then. Plant the idea in her head, so to speak. Pull the tooth out a few days later." Herman scraped the gravy off his mound of mashed potatoes. "Too lumpy," he complained.

"What about the infection? Maybe you shouldn't wait. I thought the point was to heal, not harm the patient."

"It is, my dear." Herman heaved a sigh of exasperation. "By Wednesday she'll be begging me to extract it. This way she won't feel so anguished about the loss."

"And the little Olson girl?" Her stomach cramped, as though he'd pierced it with one of his silver-handled scrapers.

"What about her?"

"Why did she come in?"

"She had a baby tooth needed pulling. All it took was one little twist."

"I see," she said, staring down at her half-eaten sandwich nestled in the center of her dark blue plate. A blue-checked cloth covered the table. Light blue café curtains trimmed the windows. The wallpaper was dotted with tiny blue cornflowers. Maybe blue wasn't so reassuring, she thought.

A little freckle-faced boy was dawdling by the wrought-iron fence in front of the office, poking at an ant bed with a stick, when they approached. At the crunch of their footsteps, he called out, "Dr. McKee!"

Herman removed his glasses and wiped the thick lenses with the end of his cuff. "Good afternoon, Ernie," he said, returning his spectacles to the bridge of his nose. "Miss Sassie's tooth must be better."

"A heap better," the boy said. "She sent me to tell you she won't be coming."

"Ernie, I'd like you to meet my new bride," Herman said, stepping politely to one side.

"Mrs. Dalia McKee," she said, offering the child her hand.

"Nice to make your acquaintance," he said, timidly shaking her fingers.

"Smile, Ernie. Show Dalia your big white teeth."

Ernie parted his lips and smiled. "Why, your teeth are beautiful," Dalia said. The boy blushed, clamped his mouth shut, and fiddled with the stick.

"I wish all my patients took care of their teeth the way Ernie does," Herman said, sidling over to the boy. "Thank you for coming clear across town to tell me about Miss Mead," he said, imprinting a nickle into his palm. "Now go get yourself a treat."

With a quick thank-you, Ernie threw down the stick and took off running.

"Let's hurry and get the notes written," Herman said, seizing Dalia's hand, pulling her through the gate and down the walkway. Fishing a peg-legged key from his coat pocket, he inserted it into the keyhole and twisted. The door sighed open.

"Herman," Dalia said as they crossed the threshold, "I'm in no rush."

"Give it another hour," he muttered. "You'll be eager for me to take you home." He snatched up the red notebook and plunked it down in front of her.

Inching out the front desk drawer, she shuffled through a folder of papers before happening upon a steel-nibbed pen. "I'm ready," she said, staring into the sunlight.

Lacing his hands behind him, he paced back and forth in front of her, dictating sentences she didn't understand. "Bicuspid?" she echoed.

"A tooth with two cusps," he said curtly.

"Could you spell it?"

He halted in front of the desk. "Bicuspid," he restated, breaking the word into syllables, spelling it slowly. "Did you get it?" he asked with a pinched smile.

She nodded, gouging the steel point of her pen into the paper. "Incisor," she repeated after him. He started to spell it. "I'm not stupid," she said, cutting him off. He moved toward the front of the room, while she flipped the page and kept on writing, the muscles in her fingers cramping, her script deteriorating into an ugly, awkward sprawl. He was right. She was growing tired of this office.

"I didn't expect to see you here," Lawrence Sears sputtered as he bumbled through the doorway. "My dear, you look lovely as always," he said, standing in front of her. "I miss our little chats at the boardinghouse."

"I miss them, too," Dalia said, smiling warmly.

In front of the palladium windows, Herman was clearing his throat, spanking his heels against the floorboards. "Mr. Sears," he blurted, much too loudly.

"Dr. McKee," Lawrence said, wheeling around. "I didn't see you when I came in. Why, you've put your beautiful bride to work."

"Mrs. Tierney's sick," Herman said, striding across the room toward them. "Dalia's here for the day only."

"I know I've come barging in," Lawrence Sears said, tensely clasping his hands. "But I didn't know what else to do. I've a back tooth giving me fits."

Herman was quiet for several seconds, then in a clipped voice added, "I'm sorry, but the end of next week is the earliest I can see you."

Dalia leafed through the appointment book. "But Herman?" she said, placing her finger beside an opening on Monday.

"The end of next week," Herman insisted. "Pardon my rush, Lawrence, but it has been a very long day for Dalia, and we need to get home."

"Yes, yes, of course," Lawrence said, slipping out a watch fob from the inside of his waistcoat. "Almost four. My, my, it is late," he *tsk*ed, with a small click of its lid. "The end of next week, yes, but what time should I be here?" He bent over to steal a glimpse of the appointment book.

At once Dalia closed it. "How about three o'clock next Thursday?" she quickly said.

"I'll be here," he replied, "and you, my dear?"

"She'll be at home," Herman stated in a voice that would not yield.

"Dalia, you're not eating your supper," Herman reminded her.

She stabbed a baby pickled corn. "I had too much for lunch," she said. Wearily, she thunked down her fork.

"You must eat for two now, dearest."

Where was the farmer who grew this tiny ear of corn? Dalia wondered. Living in some Lilliputian country among other itty-bitty things? In a place where there was no pretending, she decided, where people were who they seemed.

"Finish the chicken, at least." His skin was stretched tight over his skull, his mouth lipless and V-shaped like a turtle's.

She clenched her jaw tightly, brusquely wiped her mouth with her napkin, and dropped it on her plate.

"It's protein for the baby."

"I'm going to bed now." She pushed back her chair and came to her feet.

"If Lawrence Sears asked you to eat it, you would." His voice was petulant, his face childish.

"What?" she bridled.

"You'd do anything for dear Lawrence."

"Sir, you insult me." Spinning around, she fled from the room. She walked swiftly down the hallway and bolted up the steps. Veering left at the top of the landing, she slammed the bedroom door.

That night she slept peacefully, calmed by a sense of her own power. Sex had been on his schedule, but she, Dalia Miller McKee, had kept him away.

He followed her around the next day. She would catch his eyes as they veered in her direction, but she pretended not to see him. By late Sunday she had reduced him to sulking. He would sit hunched over in his Windsor chair in front of the cold fireplace, staring blankly at the brass fire screen. She would stand to one side behind him, her reflection rippling in the brass. When he flicked his head, like a horse's tail swishing at a fly, she knew he was about to address her, and before he could utter a word, she would vanish. She slept alone that night again.

When Herman came home from work on Monday, he did not seek her out, and Dalia feared he was trying to regain the upper hand. She heard them whispering in the kitchen. Lurking in the dining room beside the doorjamb, she eavesdropped while they plotted. Although she couldn't make out Clarice's words, she heard the menace in them, detected the prig in his, and knew they were hatching a plan. Stand up to him, Katie Mae had said. All at once, they quit talking. Grabbing her skirt in bunches to keep it from swishing, Dalia dashed into the parlor, fingered a piece of Asian porcelain on a small three-tiered table. She listened to his footsteps, heavy on the runner in the hall. "Good evening," she said, wanting to appear calm when he passed through the doorway.

"Dalia, may I have a word with you?" he asked. She did not respond, sealed her lips into a stubborn dash. "I understand why you're still angry at me. It was unpardonable for me to speak to you in that manner."

"Yes, it was."

"Please forgive me and be assured that my jealousy, hurtful as it is, comes from my love and absolute devotion to you."

She sucked in air. "Herman, I am your wife, not one of your prized skillets. You must let me breathe."

"Please, Dalia, let's stop this infernal bickering," he pleaded, coming over to her. Sighing, he readjusted his glasses on the bridge of his nose. "I promise to be better. You'll see," he said. "But as you stated, *you are my wife,* and we need to put this incident behind us. Please join me for supper before we retire."

Her face expressionless, she followed him into the dining room.

That night she tried to close the bedroom door on him, but this time he wouldn't let her. "I want to be with you," he said, shoving through. Unknotting his tie, he spread it across the bench at the foot of the bed. "Remember our discussion earlier?"

"I don't want to."

He unsnapped his suspenders, flung back one, then the other. "It's been three days now. I need to be with you."

She wandered over to the window, parted the curtains, and peered out. "What about the baby?"

"Being close won't harm it." She looked over her shoulder, saw his trousers pooled around his emaciated ankles. With a shiver, she turned back to the window, her eyes drawn to the wisteria arbor, which reminded her of a giant caterpillar in the moonlight. "I'm your husband, and you're my wife."

"I'm sick to my stomach," she said, her back still to him.

"In sickness and in health, remember?"

She wheeled around. He had taken off his shirt. His chest was smooth as peach skin. His nipples, two hard little knots. His legs, like stems, with not a hair on them. He straddled out of his pants, seized his nightdress from off the bench, and snaked it over his head. "To love and to cherish," she told him. "I should have a say in this."

"I agree, but please let's not be apart tonight. I promise I won't touch you," he said, shifting to another tactic. Crawling into the bed, he pulled the covers up to his chin.

"I don't believe you," she said in a voice that was stony.

"On my word of honor. Please, Dalia."

Darts of moonlight shone in his glasses. Pigeons cooed drowsily beneath the second-story eaves. Closing the draperies, she sewed the light out with her fingers, then slipped her frock over her head. She tossed it on a chair back and unsnapped her corset. She put on a nightgown, took off her undergarments beneath it, and dropped them on the chair. Quietly, she slipped into bed beside him. "Hand me your eyeglasses," she said. She felt the cold metal frames between her fingers. Rolling over, she placed them on the night table, turned her body into a statue, and slept.

She and Nellie are in the front yard at Miller's Mansion. Spring is just beginning, and she is picking a leaf from an oak tree and giving it to her sister. "Feel its waxy smoothness," she says. "Smell it," she urges, inhaling its bitter, newborn odor. One of the fence posts has toppled over, downing a nubby fist of withered cotton. Taking hold of Nellie Ann's hand, Dalia leads her over, pinches off a boll of white, and begins to rip it apart—combing and stripping out the dark, thin seeds until the strands are light and fluffy. "Love is as soft as this," she says, inserting the fluff between her sister's fingers. "As soft as waves lapping against dock pilings, as soft as a spoon stirring inside a cup, toes squishing in mud, smoke wisping from a chimney, my hands massaging your back."

Fingertips dusted her neck, and she woke from the dream with a start. Edging away from him, she buried herself beneath the covers. She heard his shallow, rapid breathing, smelled his sterile breath. His hand grabbed her breast. "No!" she said, suddenly furious. She clamped her large hand over his, but he forced himself on her, digging his elbows into her collarbone, holding her body down. He rose, shifting his weight to his knees. His sex was throbbing purple in the moonlight. With every ounce of strength she had, she wielded her power and caught him by surprise. Rolling him over, she pinned her hands against his chest. "What should be the punishment for such dishonorable conduct?" she whispered, inches from his face. His eyes were weak without his glasses. His breathing was labored beneath her weight. "Sex," she seethed, licking his nipples, sucking them fiercely. She took hold of his penis, her full hips heavy against his narrow body, and lowered herself down until his organ was deep inside her. A guttural noise flew from his lips, and for the first time in their married life together, she felt sexual pleasure—gripped as she was in the narcotic of his pitiable fear.

CHAPTER 23

The word *battle* brought to Dalia's mind images of muskets, sabers, daggers, cannon blasts. Battle, to Dalia, meant a fight to the death. Yet as the weeks scrolled by, she learned otherwise. A battle could be subtler, more like a skirmish, the ruthless interlocking of wills, the merciless struggle of egos. Katie Mae had willed her to stand up to Herman, so she drew on her will for the fight. Just a niggling of it proved powerful. She found power as tempting as a Savannah whore, as alluring as laudanum, as enabling as pity. Her self-determination was winning the war. Like a cut daisy in an empty water glass, Herman was shriveling—his chest and arms growing thinner, his face sinking in, his pate balding. He complained of dizziness, of sharp pains in his chest. In the morning, he left a gauze of reddish brown strands on his pillow. He consumed only enough food to subsist and had less energy for lovemaking. As he became weaker, Clarice grew stronger. "I know what ya is doin'," she said one morning while dusting one of the pink clusters on the mantel in the parlor.

"And what might that be?" Dalia asked, dunking a sugar cookie into a cup of chicory coffee, biting off the half-moon.

"Don't go pretendin'," the black woman warned, pointing the feather duster in her direction. "I been with him longer than ya has. If ya keep pushin' so hard, ya might be sorry."

Dalia clinked her cup into the saucer. "Are you threatening me?"

"I got more sway over him than ya has."

"He's my husband," Dalia stated.

"But I has known him the longest." Smacking her lips like a period, Clarice took a step sideways to the other end of the mantel and dusted the prisms on the matching cluster. Which made a tinkling sound. "Dr. Herman's mother left him these," she said, touching the bottom of a prism. "My mama worked hard for his mama. Used to wash these crystals in warm water when they was dirty, like I do now, like I been doin' for years, ever since his family passed. I know everything they is to know about him."

"I am his wife," Dalia said.

Clarice gently ran the duster over the mantel. "This ain't marble," she huffed, thunking the metal surface with her finger. "It's just pretendin' to be something it ain't, painted black with 'em white streaks in it." She laid down the duster.

Her breathing hard and heavy, Dalia took a step toward her. "I'm the mistress of this house," she said firmly, her eyes on the woman's broad back, her hips slim as a man's, her posterior tight as a walnut. For several minutes, Clarice was as still as a wood carving, then bit by bit, her movements almost imperceptible, she recommenced her dusting, all the while humming a little tune over and over, until it virtually buzzed with menace, her hand flitting over the mantel, stinging the dust with feathers. Trembling, Dalia hurried from the room.

She threw the front door open, dashed over to the porch swing, and eased herself down. Beneath her dress, her body was changing—her belly like a watermelon, the skin tight across it. Her breasts, bigger. As her stomach swelled, so did her emotions. She felt a tenderness welling inside her, as though the fetus were already a living, breathing baby, one of those small, helpless creatures she had always been drawn to. She pushed her feet against the gray-planked floor, tilting the swing back and up. Flinging out her legs, she sailed forward, the white muslin of her dress ballooning outward. Once, Dalia had pushed Nellie Ann like this on the porch swing at Miller's Mansion, her sick body at last unencumbered as she floated through the air.

Dalia pushed off again, gliding easily, no longer heavy with the baby she carried. The sweet odor of jasmine enveloped her. She'd have to detach herself from her feelings, she decided. Envision herself as a character in a play. In this way, she would be able to separate her essence from that of her husband, and, God willing, survive her fate.

Up the street, a familiar-looking man was waving at her. She plowed her shoes against the floorboards and watched as Lawrence Sears approached.

"I spotted this lovely vision and knew it was you," he said from the bottom of the porch steps. The bald spot on his head gleamed like mayonnaise in the sunlight. There was a biscuit of yellow-orange lantana in the buttonhole of his coat.

"So you decided to take a stroll in this lovely weather?"

"You bet," Lawrence told her. "In no time, it'll be too hot to walk." He tugged on his earlobe, paused for a few seconds, then asked, "May I join you?" Dalia could hear Clarice dusting on the other side of the window. "I'd love to chat for a few minutes," he said. "That is, if it's . . ."

Dalia inhaled the pure warm air, threw back her shoulders, and in an act of defiance said, "Please, come and sit with me for a while. I've so missed our little conversations."

"If you insist," Lawrence said, tapping up the steps.

Dalia nodded at a white wicker chair. "That is our most comfortable piece of furniture," she said, as the green-striped cushion engulfed him. "I'd like it in my parlor, but naturally it belongs out here. How's that hurt tooth of yours?"

"Oh, that . . . I had that taken care of weeks ago, but more importantly, how are you feeling?" He placed his forearms on the arms of the chair. "Miss Fairchild told me about your condition."

"I haven't said a word."

"There are no secrets in a small town."

"I guess not," Dalia said, wrinkling her brow. "I've kept away from people lately, but the minute I step out—" She broke off the sentence, rose from the swing, and shifted sideways.

"I don't know what you're talking about. I can barely tell, Dalia."

"The worst is now over. The morning sickness, the tiredness." The porch swing groaned as she sat back down. "I knew an obese woman," she went on, "whose weight brought a porch swing crashing down on her leg, broke the bone in half. By the time this baby comes, I fear I'm gonna be as big as that woman." She made a circle of her arms, held them out in front of her belly, and laughed. "A midwife from Valdosta is coming next month. Herman promises she's the best in south Georgia." Startlingly, her lips began to quiver. Her eyes brimmed with tears.

"Dalia," Lawrence said, leaning over, propping his elbows on his kneecaps. "Tell me what's wrong."

Blinking back tears, she was about to speak when, out of the corner of her eye, she saw the curtains abruptly parting, then closing. She held a finger to her mouth and pointed at the window. "Mr. Sears, I wish you could stay a little longer," she said in a voice loud enough for Clarice to hear. "But I know you have to get back to work. Come again when my husband's home. He'd love to see you."

"Please give my regards to Herman," Lawrence said with a dip of his head. "Tell him I'm delighted about the baby."

All of a sudden the front door flew open and slammed shut, as Clarice stomped over the gray floorboards. "My heavens, Miz Dalia," she said, ignoring Lawrence Sears altogether. "Ya better get back inside now. This heat is bad for the baby. Look at them hands of yours. They is already swelling."

At once Lawrence came to his feet. "I must be on my way," he said, brushing by Clarice as he walked over to the porch swing, stopped, and extended his hands. Yet Dalia held back, kept her own hands in her lap. "It was so nice seeing you again. I'll let Miss Fairchild know how you're doing," he said. He went to the edge of the porch. Before descending, he glanced back at Dalia and, with a touch of bravado, added, "You must pay us a visit at the boardinghouse before the baby comes."

Clarice had moved over to the door, where she was impatiently tapping her foot.

"Give Frances and Dora my love," Dalia said, bolstered by his support. "And drop by again, whenever you're out walking." She tipped the swing forward, planted her feet on the porch, and with a bold thrust of her chin walked leisurely to the door. "Just hook the screen," she asserted. "I want to feel the breeze blowing through." She gained a little strength by picturing herself as the heroine of a play she'd written, then in a forceful voice said, "In case you've forgotten, I'm the mistress of this house, and I'll do what I want and not what you tell me."

"Ya don't love him," sniped Clarice as Dalia headed down the hallway. "Don't love that baby of his."

Dalia confronted her. "How dare you talk to me like this!"

Clarice was not intimidated. "Ya love pretty things," she said, her voice sibilant. "Things that cost money. Ya is a spoiled rich gal. Ain't never worked for a thing, but work is a natural-born part of me. I've worked for Dr. Herman long enough to know he don't like that man. I know what ya is doing. Don't think that ya can fool me."

"You don't know anything," Dalia fumed. "You don't know me, and you surely don't know the good doctor."

"I know more than ya think I do," Clarice said, eyeing her coldly. "I know your daddy was a heavy drinker; your mama, crazy from all that medicine she be takin'; your sister, a blind sick girl. I know how that woman who cooked for you was treated, and I don't intend to let you treat me that way. Ya think I hasn't heard the stories? Us colored folks talk, Miz Dalia." Dalia swallowed hard and took a step back. "If ya keep up this nonsense"—her voice was thick with warning—"I be goin' to my boss, tellin' him what my ears have been hearin'."

"Do what you wish," Dalia said, her chin trembling. "I'm not afraid of anything you might say."

"Ya ain't?" Clarice mocked her.

There was not a trace of fear in the woman's voice, making it brutally clear to Dalia that a great battle was unavoidable in the days ahead.

It was seven o'clock, twilight. Their words hummed in the distance. Dalia rose from the chaise longue, went over to the window, and parted the draperies. They were standing in the aura of the street lamp, beyond the porch roof, through the limbs of the pecan trees, like cartoon characters, words of accusation like balloons beside their heads. Clarice's arm waved an indictment at the upstairs window. Dalia didn't have to hear her voice to know what she was saying. *See her up there. Spyin' on us.* She stilled her arm for a second, pausing, Dalia knew, before the kill. *Mr. Sears come by this morning.* Lawrence *was how she called him.* Herman's face contorted, lamplight glinting off his lenses. Clarice was leaning over, whispering into his ear. *I got something else to tell ya. Been hearin' some troublin' things about the missus.*

Holding her belly, Dalia let out a little yelp and jerked away from the window. Breathing in deeply, she waited for her panic to pass. Minutes later, their footfalls were sounding on the porch steps. Dalia dashed over to the linen press on the wall beside the doorjamb and threw her weight against it, shoving it over the floor until it completely blocked the portal. Spotting the footstool near the window, she raced over, seized its spooled legs, and brought it back, heaving it, upside down, on the linen press, its legs in the air like a dead insect's.

She panted, her hand braced against the small of her back, then heard his shoes clattering up the staircase, followed by Clarice's ponderous step. Together, they thudded over the landing. There was a loud, impatient knocking, then the doorknob creaking. "Dalia, open the door this minute," he demanded. She moved closer to the linen press, said nothing. Next came another round of raps. She stood stock-still, breathing shallowly. "This is my house," he declared. "You'll do as I tell you." The legs of the linen press skittered forward. "Clarice, help me," he said in an overwrought voice, strained like burlap tearing. "Now!" he yelled. She listened to them throwing their weight against the door. As the linen press scraped toward her, she set her shoulder to it and shoved back with all her might. "Push," he said, just as the door rasped open. He stumbled into the bedroom. His face was purple, the veins in his neck bulging. His skin was drenched with sweat. "Are you out of your mind?" he accused her. Dalia squared her shoulders, met his anger with her own. "I'm your husband. You're my wife. What do you think you're doing?" he asked, wheezing, pressing his hand against his chest.

"Protecting myself."

"From whom?"

"From you."

"What have I ever done to you?" he asked.

She murdered him with her eyes, said nothing.

"Tell me."

She clamped her lips together.

"You wouldn't treat Lawrence Sears like this, would you?"

She laughed shrilly.

"Don't you dare mock me," he warned. "Clarice caught you. I forbid you to speak to him again." With his fingers, he motioned Clarice over; she positioned herself beside him, creating a barricade with their bodies.

Fearlessly, Dalia turned around, walked to a chair on the opposite side of the room, and, with eyes black as buckshot, sat down.

She was pacing off her nervous energy when she heard his footsteps ascending and raced back to her chair. All evening he and Clarice had been chatting in the parlor like an old married couple, their voices floating up the stairwell, the woman fawning over him, he accepting each compliment as if it were his due. Dalia had eavesdropped on them until she could bear it no longer. Tiptoeing to the bathroom, she had grabbed two plugs of cotton and stoppered her ears.

"Hello, my dear," he said, stepping over the doorsill. Refusing to speak to him, she quickly took out the wads of cotton and slipped them into her dress pocket. He unbuttoned his shirt, wrinkled from their tug-of-war earlier. Putting it on the bed, he folded the sleeves back, slowly and meticulously, as was his habit, but then in the midst of a movement he stopped and just stood there, his hands shaking. "See," he said, his voice rising. "See what you're doing to me." Averting her eyes, she stared at the mantel. "I know you," he said accusingly. "You don't give a damn about me. Do you?" he asked, prodding her for reassurance. She blinked her eyelids and pretended him away. "At least, Clarice understands me," he told her. She detected the whine in his voice, and it made her shiver. "She knows who I am, and she respects me, but you . . ." he said, his tone indignant. She swiveled around until her back was to him. He made a huffing noise. She heard his footsteps, the wardrobe door creaking open, and the click of wood as he hung up his trousers. "Turn around and look at me," he demanded, stomping his foot on the floor. She did as she was told. He was wearing his nightdress, his spindly legs white and thin, his glasses buggy and bright in the lamplight, his head small. He looked like a praying mantis. "Get undressed," he said, his voice surly. "It is our night to be together." She stood, strode over to the chaise longue, and took off her clothes, tossing each piece on the cushioned seat. "Get in bed," he told her. Her back straight, her head erect, she walked over to the bed steps, climbed up, and lay down, her arms by her sides, her body as rigid as one of the iron slats beneath their mattress.

He circled the room, blowing out the lamps. He got into bed, leaned over, and with a hiss puffed out the stub of candle in the holder on the night table. "I am so tired," he said, rasping in air, his body limp. She stayed still, hoping that he would be too tired to touch her, but then she felt his leg, smelled his sour breath as he crawled on top of her. "So tired of this," he said, entering her, finishing with a sigh.

He's not real, she told herself, her eyes wide open, her body still. He slid off her body and onto his back. Her breath shallow, she waited in the darkness for sleep to take her, but the thumping of her heart kept her awake. Strangling the sheet in her fists, she lay there for hours.

When the clock chimed twelve, she heard him gulp loudly. He gasped, quit snoring. She waited for the snoring to begin again, but it didn't. There was no movement from him, no hiss of his breath, only a wetness against her leg and the vile stench of urine. Rolling away from him, she finally slept. In her dreams, she saw faces from her past—Violet, Nellie Ann, her father. When dawn streamed through the parted curtains, she didn't have to see the pallor of his skin, the wrench of his mouth, or the stiffness of his limbs to know that he was dead.

CHAPTER 24

When Herman McKee died, Dalia wanted to bury her memories with him, so she arranged for a prompt interment. At Doogan's Funeral Home, she left orders to dress him in his wedding suit, comb his fine hair back, and leave his wedding band on his finger. She would attend the graveside service, but she refused to go to the visitation, afraid his long, delicate fingers, arranged upon his chest, would force themselves on her again.

On that Sunday summer morning of 1899 when they lowered him into the ground, she wrung her hands together and thought, Thank God, no more sex.

A week after the burial, she fired Clarice and hired Dora's cousin Ophelia to cook and clean for her, though she did much of the cleaning herself. She hoped hard work would vent the volatile energy inside her. While decorum dictated she stick to mourner's black and refuse all visitors, she willed a bit of her life back by eating plain and simple fare. At the end of the day, she'd dab her temples with a black lace handkerchief and drink lemonade spiked with the juice of pomegranates as she rocked on the back porch, away from the prying eyes of strangers. She'd fan her pale, glistening face, as the perspiration and anger seeped out. Waving off gnats, she'd throw back her head and fortify herself to play the role of the grieving widow.

Yet only three months after Herman's death, she could no longer bear the solitude of her house. She had every right to leave it, she reasoned. God had liberated her from one tyrant. Why should she replace his rules with those of the townsfolk?

"For goodness' sakes, come on in, child!" Frances Fairchild exclaimed. She reached out and touched Dalia's stomach. "My heavens, you're huge, Dalia." As always, the foyer smelled of food. "Dora!" she yelled above the banging of pots in the kitchen. "We have us a visitor."

Dalia hadn't stood there a minute before Dora rounded the corner, hastening toward them down the hallway. "Ain't you sight for sore eyes, though?" she said, wiping her hands on her apron. "Last time we seen ya was at the funeral."

"Come with me, dear," Frances said, darting ahead of them. "Let's talk in the parlor." Her former landlady was patting the back of the brown velvet chair with its matching ottoman when Dalia stepped into the room. "Why don't you sit here and rest your feet awhile?"

"My ankles have all but disappeared," Dalia said, hitching up her skirt to show them how much her legs had swollen. She tottered over, positioned herself in front of the chair, and sank awkwardly into the soft brown cushion. As soon as she lifted her feet, Frances grabbed them and lowered them onto the ottoman.

"Your pretty face is beet-red," Frances said. "I think you could do with a cold glass of ice tea. How does that sound?"

"That would be nice," Dalia murmured.

Frances turned toward Dora. "Dora, why don't you fetch Miss Dalia that tea? And remember to put plenty of ice chips in it. Are you hungry, dear?"

"I'm afraid the heat has killed my appetite," she confessed.

"Mine, too," Dora added. "Ya want a squeeze of lemon?"

"Oh, yes."

"Mint?"

"Please."

"Dora?" Frances said, widening her eyes, arching her eyebrows.

"I'm going. I'm going," Dora huffed, dismissing her with a neat flick of her wrist. "Can't seem to do nothing fast enough for ya," she grumbled, her footfalls padding over the carpet.

Dalia fanned her face with her hands. "I probably shouldn't be out and about," she said, folding them on top of her stomach. "I just got so sick and tired of staying inside the house."

"I could've come to see you," Frances said apologetically, "but Ophelia told Dora that you didn't want visitors."

"I didn't then," Dalia said. "Though lately I've been feeling as lonely as I did when Herman was alive. So I decided it was high time to get out."

They didn't speak for a few minutes, both limp and drained from the heat and the humidity. Dalia noticed the sunlight as it washed through the window, exposing a thin film of dust on the side tables, the corpses of flies along the bottom of the bookshelves, and a fistful of cat hair on the ottoman, next to her shoes. Before, the messiness of the house hadn't bothered her, but now it put her off. In the kitchen, Dora tortured a block of ice, the sharp chipping sound echoing in the parlor. "I don't know if I should tell you this," Frances said, suddenly leaning forward, "but Clarice is saying some very unpleasant things about you."

"Ophelia told me," Dalia said with a sigh.

"No one believes a word of it," her former landlady quickly added.

"The woman threatened me often and has made good on her threat."

Dora sauntered into the room, carrying the cold glass out and away from her body, as if the beads of condensation were a virulent contagion. "Gossipin' is the work of the devil," she said, handing the tea glass to Dalia. "That woman been flappin' her gums to anyone who'll listen. Spreading the meanest evil."

"She says you hated your husband," Frances elaborated. "That you killed him with a voodoo curse."

"To get your hands on his money," Dora said, shaking her head.

"Well, I didn't kill him," said Dalia flatly, "but I'm certainly not sorry he's dead."

Frances held her fingers up to her mouth and gasped. "Oh, Dalia, do be careful. Don't go around saying that," she warned, her eyes growing big behind her glasses. "Lawrence told us how awful the man was, but it'd be wise if—"

"Ya kept your feelings to yourself," Dora finished.

Outside, a squirrel made a racket, scampering along the gutter above the window. A blue jay shrieked. Claus let out a shrill meow.

"Where is that sorry rascal, anyway?" Frances asked, looking around.

"Outside, in the monkey grass, where it's cool," Dora said, collapsing on the settee, whooshing out a great big breath.

Dalia plucked an ice chip from her tea glass. "It sure is hot out," she said, pressing it against the front of her neck.

"Your fingers look like little sausages," Dora said, following the movement of the ice up and down Dalia's skin.

"They're so puffy now they won't fit inside my gloves."

"It'll be over soon, sweetheart," Frances said. "Next time we see you, there'll be a baby in your arms."

"I must apologize," Dalia said, easing her feet off the ottoman and onto the worn rug, "but I can't stay long today. I must visit with Lawrence at Copeland's, then do a little shopping for the baby."

"But Dalia, you shouldn't be seen in town in your condition," Frances said. "It's fodder for the rumor mill."

"Idle gossip doesn't bother me," Dalia declared, groaning as she rose.

"Dora and I worry," her former landlady said, reaching out for the black woman's hand, the two of them standing.

"I care about you, too," Dalia said, meaning it, as she walked toward the foyer.

As soon as she set foot inside Copeland's Jewelry, Lawrence Sears waved a lazy hand at her. "Lawrence," Dalia said, walking over, "how are you doing?"

"Just fine," he said, "but I'm the one who should be asking you that question." He slid his buttocks off the stool and leaned over the counter to clasp her hand. "How are you, my dear?"

"Getting ready to have this baby."

The bell above the store entrance tinkled. "Good day, ladies," Lawrence Sears said to two flaxen-haired girls who came waltzing through the doorway.

"Good day, Mr. Sears," they singsonged.

Smiling, Dalia acknowledged them with a nod, but instead of nodding back, they snubbed her. The younger of the two moseyed to the opposite end of the counter, where she pointed at the display case and said, "If I hint long enough and hard enough, maybe I can talk Daddy into buying me that ring for my birthday."

"I don't think so," the other girl told her. "It's much too showy for someone your age."

"Mr. Sears, Mr. Sears," the young one called out. "Please, come here and convince my sister that this beautiful ruby ring is the perfect gift."

"Why don't I come back another time, when you're not so busy?" Dalia said as Lawrence stepped out from behind the counter. Giving his arm a little squeeze, she glanced up to catch the girls whispering and sneering at her. "Good day, children," she bade them as she headed for the door.

She made a beeline to Maggie's, a new store that carried children's clothing, her anxiety mounting as she passed shoppers on the walkway. What had they heard about her? she wondered. Once there, she purchased two pairs of booties—one blue, the other pink—and three dozen cotton diapers for the baby. She went to the grocer's next, buying a smoked ham and a jar of hot pepper relish for Katie Mae. Spotting a stack of *Woman's Home Companion* at a corner newsstand, she got one because Katie Mae liked to decorate her walls with the colorful illustrations. She didn't give a fig what the townsfolk thought, she told herself, taking the back way home.

The following morning, she put the pint of hot pepper relish, the *Woman's Home Companion*, and a quart jar of cold water into a picnic basket. She set the basket on the seat beside her, then placed the smoked ham on the floor by her feet. Since she was leaving so early, she wouldn't have to push the horse too hard, just insist on a steady pace.

Her stomach bounced over the bumpy road toward Katie Mae's shanty, but the movement didn't faze her, for she was strong and healthy, her wide hips meant to carry babies. She inhaled the sharp bite of resin and listened to the woodsmen singing as they worked the trees. She remembered her father swearing that the gum from the longleaf had saved her life as a toddler. For days, she had been sick. Her fever, high. Her chest, congested. Her breathing, labored. After melting hog lard on the stove, he had poured spirits of turpentine into it, stirred it all together, then rubbed the warm balm down her neck, over her chest and back, around her ears and nose. He had covered her tiny body with flannels, putting all his faith into the glorious elixir that oozed from his pines. If the longleafs were respected, they would give of themselves forever, he had often told her.

Katie Mae was sweeping her front yard with a gallberry bush when Dalia drove up. "Miss Dalia," she cried, letting go of the makeshift broom, rushing over. She clasped Dalia's shoulders, held her at arm's length, and studied her from head to toe. "You still grieving?"

"I'm still dressed in black, if that's what you mean," Dalia told her.

"I knew you'd come when you was ready. Ya big as a horse, gal. Now, when is this baby due?" she asked, chuckling, her bottom lip poked out with snuff.

"Sometime in October," Dalia said, ambling toward the porch. There were flower boxes of pink petunias beneath the shanty's windows and an iron knocker in the shape of a horse's head nailed to the door. "Every time I come here, this little house of yours looks better," she said, cradling her stomach as she waddled up the steps.

"Why don't ya sit out here where it's cooler?" Katie Mae said, sprinting up the steps behind her, dashing over to a cane-bottomed rocker. "Rest some while I brew the tea."

"You look good, Katie Mae," Dalia said, going over, lowering her heavy body into the rocker.

"I feel good," she said with a grin. "When I got your letter, sayin' you was comin', I told the boss I was expectin' company and took the day off."

"I brought you a few things from town," Dalia said, "but I forgot and left them in the carriage."

"I'll fetch them later," Katie Mae said. "Right now I got things to do in the kitchen, 'cause ya came here on a mission." Winking, she hurried to the door, letting it slam shut behind her.

Dalia stretched out her legs, rested her hands on her stomach. Her feet hurt. Her back ached. She was ready to have this child. She closed her eyes and drifted off—the door banging her awake minutes later. Katie Mae came toward her, carrying a battered metal tray. She set the tray on a low, narrow table that had a bench behind it. Hiking her dress up, she straddled the bench as though it were a horse. Then, leaning over, she wrapped her fingers around the teapot handle and began to pour—the tea leaves flowing into a chipped white cup. "Now drink it down quick," she ordered Dalia. "Don't go sloshing the leaves. Ya need to let them settle." While Dalia drank, Katie Mae closed her eyes and chanted, "A boy or a girl, a boy or a girl? Tea leaves, please tell us what Dalia brings into this world." No sooner were these words spoken than her eyes popped open. "Ya done?" she asked. Dalia nodded, and Katie Mae yanked the cup from her fingers, placed the saucer on top of the cup, and, turning the whole thing over, set it back on the table. Removing the cup, she studied the pattern of the tea leaves on the white porcelain surface.

"Well?" Dalia said, becoming impatient. "What is it?"

"That be a tallywhacker," Katie Mae said, pointing to a dark straight line. "It's gonna be a little boy."

"A boy," Dalia echoed, her voice falling. "But I wanted a girl. To make things right by Nellie Ann."

Katie Mae slid off the end of the bench and went over to her. "Next time," she said, gently squeezing Dalia's shoulder.

"There won't be a next time," Dalia stated.

"Oh, yes, there will," Katie Mae told her. "I know ya better than ya know yourself."

"You don't know me at all."

"I don't?" Katie Mae said, arching her eyebrows. "I know how it feels to be blamed for something I didn't do. Ya might think me blind, but I have clear vision, just like Nellie Ann. I know ya started that fire," she said, looking hard at Dalia, "and I know ya didn't mean to. Ya wanted to tell your papa the truth but couldn't." Dalia opened her mouth to speak, but Katie Mae held up her hand like a warning and went on, "I know it was you who sent me that money, and I know why ya done it. You see, I do know you."

"I'm sorry," Dalia said, her eyes brimming. "But I reckon ya know that, too."

"Don't be," Katie Mae said, her voice firm. "It weren't my feet running to that stable, and it weren't my hands toting that lantern. I didn't burn the place down, didn't kill your papa's horse, but my heart, girl, my heart . . ." Katie Mae made a fist of her hand and hit it against her breast. "My heart was right there, doing it all with ya."

"Thinking is one thing. Doing is another," Dalia said.

"Ain't none of us pure of spirit," Katie Mae contended, "but you is lucky. This baby is gonna be your second chance."

CHAPTER 25

Clasping the railing, Dalia climbed the steps. A wind had come up, and thistles of rain stung the windowpane on the landing. Water gushed from the eave spout, splashing a hole in the ground. The trees rocked in the dark morning light. Such downpours usually came with the hurricane season, but strangely this year they had come in November—bruising the sky, bullying the last leaves off the trees, harassing the wildlife till it went into hiding. There was just the pounding rain, Dalia thought as she climbed the second flight. At the top, she veered left down the hallway and dithered in front of the nursery. The door ajar, she could hear Marion crying, barely audible in the storm's fume and bluster.

Seven weeks ago, he had been born. "I'll have no newborns pulling on teats like alcoholics pulling on bottles," she pronounced as soon as she saw those long, dainty fingers and that dimple on his chin, which reminded her of Herman. "Let him suck down a black woman's nourishment, she'd thought. Opossum stew, catfish tails, side-meat, collards—breast milk drenched in a heritage that didn't inflict its will on others, the way her husband had forced his will on her.

She lingered in the doorway, staring at him in the crib. The rain whipped against the roof. The eaves groaned loudly. He was lying on his back, complaining. "Marion," she said softly, walking toward him. He let out a cry and threw out his arm, grabbing at the air with his long fingers. Abruptly, she came to a halt, her features drawn and strained with the conflict inside her. She could see his tiny chest heaving, could hear his wail vibrating in the air. Then he was quiet. Fearing for him, she felt her heartbeat quaver—tick-tocking like it once had for her father—and she rushed to him. Gurgling softly, he was fine; but though she wanted to pick him up, she couldn't. "Here I am, sweetheart," she said, guiding her hand toward the soft curve of his neck, intending to stroke him. He raised his little arms and cooed, and before she knew it, she was pressing her finger against his mouth, staring mesmerized as he suckled it, his thin lips pulsing like a blood vein, his blue-green eyes glazing over. She withdrew her finger; and bending over, she scooped him up, inhaled the sour smell of Bertha's breast milk, and was jealous. Opening her wrapper, she brought forth her breast, but before she could offer it to him, she heard footsteps pounding up the stairs, dishes clattering. Hurriedly, she closed her wrapper. In one fluid movement, she put him back in his crib and covered him with the blanket. Scrunching up his face, he whimpered.

"Miss Dalia," came Ophelia's voice from the landing, "I got some breakfast for ya. I burnt the side-meat," she confessed, as Dalia came toward her with her arms outstretched.

"I'll take it," Dalia told her. At her writing table near the front window, she lowered herself into a chair and set the tray down. The rain rumbled in the gutters. When she peeked through a crack in the draperies, the yard was ankle-deep in water. She removed the silver dish cover. The fried egg yolks were billiard balls of dark yellow. The side-meat, charred around the edges. The biscuits, small and hard. Pinching the rubbery side-meat, she brought the fatty wedge to her mouth. The salt seeped into her taste buds, energizing her like a cup of strong black coffee.

It was then the bells began chiming. At first singly, then a chorus of them. They rang frantically, as if the torrential rain had ripped heaven itself open in its desire to slam against the bells. People were shouting. Panicked horses were neighing as their hooves slushed through the swollen street. Dalia leapt up from her seat. With one fierce yank of the drawstring, she whipped the draperies completely open, saw men wading toward their wagons, spotted wives standing on verandas, watching.

She peeled off her wrapper and nightclothes, left them on the floor, and dressed speedily. "Ophelia!" she called out, bounding down the staircase. "Send Bertha to the nursery. I'm going out." In the pantry, she tugged on a pair of galoshes, found her yellow mackintosh on a hook behind the door, and snapped it on. Then she headed for the front door.

"Mr. Washington," she hollered when she saw her next-door neighbor gazing down at the water rising steadily around his ankles. The rain blinded her as she slogged toward the old man. "Are you all right?" she asked, her lips numb from the cold.

"They're saying water sheared off the little hill below the church. Flooded the cemetery at Clay's Mill." He paused and looked vacantly at her. "Caskets, they say, are floating in the river. I'm worried about my Judith."

"I'm certain her coffin wasn't disturbed," Dalia said calmly, in an effort to reassure him. "Now let's get you back inside before you take a chill." She wrapped her fingers around his forearm, but he broke free of her grasp, leaving her there in the muddy water as he sloshed toward his house.

"The bridge at Clay's Mill is down!" a man yelled as Dalia watched her neighbor trudge up his porch steps and go inside. Seized by a sudden image of Herman's coffin, unearthed from the cemetery, rafting down the river, she felt her body shaking like a reed in furious water. Right then and there, she made up her mind to drive out to Clay's Mill and see the flooding for herself.

The rain had slackened to a dull drizzle. Fish lay dying in shallow pockets of water. A white heron, lifeless as a fan, was flattened in a puddle. Squirrels cried in the pine trees rising up from the high water. Dalia maneuvered her carriage along a dirt road that was still passable. Every so often, the horses hitched to a wagon ahead of her stumbled, looking like prehistoric beasts as they struggled upward through the sludge.

When Dalia got there, all that was left of the bridge at Clay's Mill was the pilings, sticking up from the Altamaha like amputated legs, bits of wood coursing around them, dirty white foam spilling against the shoreline. On the other side of the river, a waterbird was shrieking, as though it alone had witnessed the flood. Dalia tied her horse to a windblown bush and watched the men scramble down the hill, their boots sliding and slipping in the muck. She plowed through the mud to the embankment and stared into the distance, hunting for coffins in the water, but could see little in the misty haze. Inching closer to the crest, she leaned forward—straining her eyes—and spotted something bobbing in the current. She took another cautious step, felt the earth beneath her boots give, but shoved her fear deep down into her stomach. Amid the rushes near the bank ten feet below, there was nothing. Then, six feet out, she spied it again, wood and metal seesawing in the current—two people clinging to the axletree of a wagon wheel. "Out there!" Dalia waved her arms at the men. "Out there, out there in the water," she cried, pointing.

"A coffin?" one of the men shouted back.

"No, people!"

For a full minute, the man was quiet, as he turned to face the water. "Out there!" he yelled, running. "Two people!"

It was then Dalia realized why she had truly left the safety of her home to come here. For when the Altamaha flooded, so did Snake River. Her fear was less about Herman's coffin making its way back to town than about her family's coffins floating out to sea.

CHAPTER 26

As Dalia started out, she noticed that the blanket had slipped off Marion's body. She was pulling it back over him when he grinned oddly at her, startling her so much that her arms froze above him. If spirits existed, then Herman's was emanating through Marion's body, like the penciled sketch beneath an oil painting. Dismayed, Dalia began to walk briskly, then run, the black-hooded baby carriage bumping along in front of her, its tiny wheels snagging in the cement cracks as she rounded the corner and bumped down two more blocks till she came to the familiar walkway. Panting, she stopped to catch her breath, her eyes falling on the front door where Frances Fairchild had hung a Christmas wreath with a string of cranberries woven through it. She wheeled the carriage forward—pressing her shoe against the axle, hiking the front wheels up at the bottom of the porch.

Fingers parted the limp voile curtains. "It's Miss Dalia!" Dora yelled, flinging the door open. Bustling down the steps, she seized the front end of the carriage, Dalia the handles, and together they ascended, hoisting the wheels upon the gray floorboards of the veranda. "Miss Dalia, ya look good. A tad thin, though," she said, looping her thumb and forefinger around Dalia's wrist. Right then, Marion cooed. "Ah, the baby," Dora gushed, letting go of her wrist, peering into the carriage.

"His name is Marion," Dalia reminded her.

"Yessam, Ma-ri-on," Dora said, enunciating the name slowly.

"We were planning to visit," Frances said, whisking the door open, "but you got here first. My goodness, how old is this little one now?"

"A little over two months," Dalia said.

Scurrying over to the carriage, Frances edged Dora aside and whisked up the baby. She moved the blanket away, quietly studied his face. "When he was first born, you kept insisting he looked like . . ." She stopped talking, looked askance at Dalia. "I didn't see it then, but he does bear an uncanny resemblance to . . ."

"His father," Dalia finished.

"Same little dimple," she said. "Same reddish hair, pale skin."

Dalia extended her arms. "Why don't you hand him over? For a little tyke, he sure can get heavy." After Frances gave Marion to her, Dalia rocked him upward, cupping his soft spot in the palms of her hands. "Aren't you your mama's little fella?" she cooed, his booties nudging against her stomach. Gurgling, he flashed her another one of his odd grins, which sent a shiver right through her.

"My goodness, where are my manners?" Frances said. "It's getting chilly out, and I haven't even asked you in."

"There's a batch of divinity back in the kitchen," Dora said as she held the door open for them.

"Divinity?" Dalia said, her tone curious.

"Vanilla."

"You aim to fatten me up, don't you, Dora?" Dalia said, hefting Marion all the way up to her shoulder, steadying his head with her hand. "Claus, you sweet old tom," she said, coming to a halt in the entry. The cat stopped grooming himself beside the hall tree and, looking up at her, meowed loudly. Then, arching his spine, he rubbed his head against her leg as he straightened himself.

"He's worthless," Frances said. "Why, just last night, I came down for a glass of milk and saw this mouse, still as death in a corner of the kitchen. Thank God we have Claus, I told myself, then spotted the sorry rascal, crouching beside his bowl, gorging on leftover ham, unaware of that mouse just a few feet from him."

"I been tellin' ya to get a female. A lady cat hunts better," scolded Dora, wagging her finger at Claus as she sped by them.

Dalia peeked through the archway into the parlor. A scraggly cedar tree with slapdash, homemade ornaments had been decorated near the bookshelves. It was nothing like their splendid Christmas pine back at Miller's Mansion, Dalia thought nostalgically.

"I keep it inside this breadbox on account of that mouse," Dora said, just as Dalia stepped through the doorway. She pulled out a bowl of divinity and offered Dalia a piece. The pecans looked like freckles in the lumps of vanilla candy. Dalia took a piece and tentatively brought it to her mouth. Divinity had always been too sweet for her, but manners dictated. Dalia smiled and bit down. "Here, have a seat," Dora said, sliding a chair out from beneath the table.

The minute Dalia sank down, Marion began to grumble. Patting his back, she rocked him from side to side, felt baby spit warming her shoulder. "He's spit up on me again," she said.

"Don't worry. I'll fetch something," offered Frances, who stood beside the doorjamb holding a gift box topped with a red ribbon. Box under her arm, she dashed over to the corner hutch, yanked open a drawer, and whipped out a dish towel. "I reckon this little fella keeps you busy," she said, thumping the box on the table before draping the towel over Dalia's shoulder.

"Yes, motherhood is exhausting. What's that?" Dalia asked, eyeing the present.

"A Christmas gift for Marion. We can't wait for you to see it."

"Well, then, will you open it for me?" Dalia said.

"I'd be much obliged," Frances said, carefully preserving the bow while ripping off the white tissue.

"Please show me what it is," Dalia said.

Frances eased the top off, stuck her hands inside, and brought up a green-gloved fist. "We knitted it ourselves," she stated proudly.

"Sure did," Dora said.

"It's a bonnet for his little head," Frances explained. "This yellow ball of yarn is the baseball. And this"—she traced a puckered line of brown—"is the bat. These four black thingamajigs are the bases." She touched each thingamajig with her pinkie. "The green is the baseball field."

"It's wonderful," Dalia lied.

"Poor dear, he has no father," Frances said with a frown.

"There ain't no reason Miss Dalia can't get married again," Dora reasoned.

"Time has a way of passing, and before a woman knows it, she's an old spinster," Frances said, thoughtfully fingering her chin. "If I hadn't gotten stuck with Mama when Daddy died, I might have found a beau, but she was difficult, managed to scare off my suitors."

"Meanest woman east of the Mississippi," Dora piped up.

"Difficult," corrected Frances. "Once called me poor white trash. Imagine that. Me, her own daughter. Daddy, letting her say it."

"He was too sweet for spit," Dora said fondly.

"Remember how he'd bring us those bags of candy?" Grinning, Dora nodded. "The two of us would be outside playing, and Daddy would come home from work, hollering, 'It's Christmastime for my two best girls.' "

"He be giving us them bags of cinnamon candy, and we be eating 'em till our lips was bright red, our bellies aching," Dora said.

"All the while, my mama would be so jealous, watching us through the back window, while Dora's mama would be in the kitchen cooking, shaking her head in disbelief at the awful things my mama was saying." All of a sudden, the muscles stiffened beneath Frances's skin as the smile on her face vanished. "Soon after Mama passed, I tried to turn her into someone sweet and kind like Daddy, but Dora, here, set me straight. *What's the point in loving a lie?* she told me. I loved my mama the way she was, and she was no saint."

"Crotchety, she was, and—"

"That's enough," Frances said firmly. "There's a limit to the truth I can take."

"My papa was sweet, too," Dora said.

"Yes, Mr. Browning always let us ride that old white mule of his," Frances said. "Baby's Breath, wasn't that what your papa called him?"

"Yessam, Baby's Breath," Dora mused, her eyes glazing over with memory.

Frances drew in a long breath. With a gaze holding wonder, she said, "Dora and I have been friends now it seems forever."

"Been together so long we look like twins," Dora said, beaming.

Dalia's eyes veered from one of them to the other, taking them in, until their features were warping, meshing together, their skin blending, making it seem to her that they were twins. "Yes, I see it," she said sincerely. Marion made a burbling sound, and she was suddenly aware of his head, heavy as a cantaloupe on her shoulder. Twisting around, she saw the bubbles of spit between his lips, and out of nowhere a fierce protectiveness flushed through her. "Before it gets too cold out, I should get him home," she declared, rising. "Now is the perfect time to try that baseball bonnet on him."

"Folk are talking about how you saved that couple in the river," Frances said as she knotted the bonnet strings beneath Marion's chin.

"Don't know what to make of a woman leaving the safety of her home to see a flood."

"Thinkin' ya is strange," Dora said. "Don't know if ya is brave or foolish."

"I'm more foolish than brave," Dalia confessed, "but Katie Mae was sure proud of what I did that day at the river, told me so when she moved in."

"Tragic she lost her shanty," Frances said, shaking her head.

"Yes, ma'am, it is," Dalia agreed. "That river just washed her place away."

"Still, something good has come out of it," Frances said.

Smiling, Dalia nodded. "You're right about that. Katie Mae is just wonderful with the baby, so loving and sweet, and that gives Bertha a rest from all the nursing."

Frances took a step back and regarded the bonnet. "That bonnet makes him look like a spunky little fella," she said.

"Mark my word, he's gonna grow up to be a pitcher," Dora stated.

"That's sweet news to my ears," Dalia said, patting Marion's back on her way to the foyer. "It would mortify me if he turned out to be like his father."

Dalia wrapped the shawl tightly around her shoulders as she headed down the street, eager to get her Christmas shopping finished. She had to buy gifts for Ophelia and Bertha and, of course, something nice for Katie Mae. And, after the baseball bonnet yesterday, she wanted to go to the confectionery and purchase Dora and Frances a tin of sweets. The large cedar in the center of the town square was strung with silver tinsel. Red metallic balls and wooden candy canes dangled from its branches. A big gold star teetered at the top in the slight breeze. Dalia noticed the many banners strung along storefronts, heralding the New Year and the turn of the century. She took a yellow flyer from a brown basket tacked to the doorjamb of Copeland's Jewelry. *The New Century, a play by our own Tyler Wellington,* it read.

"Hello, Dalia," Lawrence Sears said.

"Why, hello, Mr. Sears," Dalia said, startled. She hadn't seen him sitting on the bench in front of the store.

"Are you thinking of going to the play?" he asked. "You should. Maude Johnston is a wonderful actress."

"Who's Maude Johnston?"

He pointed to the flyer in her hand. "She's the leading lady. Could've studied acting in New York City if she'd wanted to, but her family wouldn't hear of it. So she lives out her dream in our local productions, though you'll see they aren't so bad."

"No, I don't think I'll be going."

"Opening night is on New Year's Eve."

"A woman by herself, newly widowed," she said, looking skeptically at him. "It's not been that long since Herman died. What will people think?"

"Altamaha River Reception Hall. Admission only a quarter. You'll enjoy yourself."

Dalia shook her head, gave the flyer to him. "No, I don't think so. It wouldn't be proper."

After straightening the red carnation in his lapel, he looked up at her and asked, "Have you heard the big news?"

"No," she said with a shake of her head.

"Mayor Winterson's getting a telephone," he announced. "The very first one here in Samson."

"And will he be talking to everyone he knows in New York City?" she asked, her eyes sparkling with mischief.

"Make light of it if you will," Lawrence said, "but fifteen families in Samson have already signed up, along with a million others across our great country. Welcome to the twentieth century, my dear."

"If that bit of news is supposed to make me happy, it doesn't," Dalia rejoined. "I don't like the thought of all these newfangled inventions." She paused, scowling. "It all scares the daylights out of me," she said at last.

"But progress is a positive thing, Dalia."

Progress, Dalia thought disdainfully. "Why do you say that?"

"Because progress, my dear, pushes us forward. It is going to bring us a thousand little miracles that will make our lives better."

"I couldn't disagree with you more, Lawrence."

He stared into her eyes and laughed. "Why is that? Don't you have your own little miracle at home?"

"Yes, but . . ." Dalia stumbled, embarrassed.

"When are you going to let me see him?"

"I planned on it today," she said, her tone low and apologetic, "but really it's too cold out for a baby."

"Dalia," Lawrence began, his tone serious, and she wondered what he was about to say, but he asked only if she was happy.

She thought for a moment before replying, "I try to be."

"Give yourself some happiness, Dalia. Go to the play." With a glint in his eyes, he caroled, "Merry Christmas, Dalia, and give that baby of yours a happy New Century hug from me."

"A happy New Century to you, too, Lawrence," she said, smiling as he went back inside.

Dalia bought a bag of roasted peanuts from a black woman down from Copeland's and crunched them as she shopped for gifts. Inside the pharmacy, she bought a bottle of toilet water for Ophelia and a box of sweet-smelling powder for Bertha because they'd hinted about these things. When she entered the confectionery, Christmas music from a gramophone filled the air. She spotted a stack of Belgian chocolates on a table near the entrance, the perfect gift for Frances and Dora, but still she had not a clue as to what to get Katie Mae. In the flood, she'd lost all of her possessions, making the possibilities endless, but Katie Mae wasn't interested in clothes or jewelry, didn't care for fancy soaps or perfumes, liked her own baking more than anything Dalia could have gotten for her at the confectionery. So what would that one special gift be? Dalia asked herself as she meandered down Main Street, window-shopping along the way. A large crimson hat with a white ostrich plume grabbed her attention.

"It is lovely, isn't it?" a voice said to Dalia, who was lingering in front of the display window.

"Quite," Dalia agreed, turning toward an older, handsome woman with the most vibrant gray eyes Dalia had ever seen. "It's very different, a real head-turner."

"And that one, way in the back, in green satin. Well, it's delightfully sophisticated, something you should be wearing in Atlanta, dining on Peachtree Street."

"But where on earth could you wear it in Samson?"

"Where?" the woman repeated, her eyebrows vaulting as though the question amused her. "If it were mine, I know exactly where. To the play on New Year's Eve. Thank you, young lady," she said warmly. "You've helped me make up my mind. I might be old, but I've still got spirit. I'm going inside to try that big, beautiful green hat on. Thank you again, dear. And good-bye."

As the woman clicked toward the doorway, Dalia noticed from the

S curve of her body that she was wearing one of those new health corsets. Apparently she didn't give a fig about what the townsfolk thought. The hourglass shape of the 1890s, more suited to Dalia's figure, was no longer the fashion, but what should a widow wear or do if she wanted to discourage gossip? Dalia felt a stab of shame. So many pulls and tugs, she decided. Plucking up another peanut, Dalia put it in her mouth and was about to crack it open when she inadvertently brushed against a woman, who then huffed and cut Dalia with her eyes. A proper lady didn't crack peanuts between her teeth on Main Street. A proper lady wouldn't take them home and eat them with the help. So many rules for women, for ladies, for widows. Yet the old woman at the hat shop seemed not to care. Defiantly, Dalia placed the peanut between her teeth and bit down. Tossing the hulls into the street, she chewed the meaty flesh flamboyantly. She would do as she pleased and make her own decisions. Like an epiphany, the perfect gift for Katie Mae popped into her head. Two dozen tins of Beechnut snuff. She would march right to the tobacconist's shop and buy them. If the clerk snickered, it didn't matter. If he assumed she was getting it for herself, she didn't care. Relief washed over her as she made her decision. When she stepped off the curb, heading for the other side of the square, a cold gust of wind slammed a yellow patch of paper against the bottom of her dress. She bent down to retrieve it. It was another one of those annoying flyers about the play. Methodically, she folded it over and tore it in half.

CHAPTER 27

"I'm worried," Dalia confided to Katie Mae. With woolen shawls tossed over their shoulders, they were rocking on the screened-in back porch drinking chamomile tea, as they had done every spring for the past three years. A strong breeze hit Mr. Washington's small patch of garden and sent the withered cornstalks swaying.

"What did ya say?" Katie Mae asked. "I was looking at Marion, picking my flowers when he knows he shouldn't. Marion, you quit that," she yelled, wagging her finger at him when he broke off another stem.

"I'm worried," Dalia repeated.

"Worried," Katie Mae said, shifting in the rocker toward her. "Worried about what?"

"About money. It takes so much of it to keep this house running."

Bewildered, Katie Mae cocked her head. "Bertha's long gone. Ophelia's wages is low, and ya know ya don't gotta pay me nothing."

"Herman didn't leave me the estate he promised. The bills never stop," Dalia explained, setting her teacup on the table. "Bills for dental equipment and supplies, the carriage, and cases and cases of expensive wine. He owes on the Persian rug in the library, the settee in the parlor, the sideboard in the dining room, my chiffonier upstairs. And to make matters worse, he left Clarice a portion of what should have been Marion's inheritance. According to my lawyer, there's even a second mortgage on this house." Dalia paused. With brusque little jabs of her fingers, she tucked the shawl into place around her. "What with all the other costs—food, firewood, kerosene, Marion's clothes—it gets expensive."

"If ya bought him some overalls for a change and not those silly outfits he's been wearing, ya could save yourself some pennies."

As though he sensed they were taking about him, Marion abruptly quit picking flowers and turned in their direction. His resemblance to Herman was becoming more and more evident as the years passed. He had his father's long legs and arms, those same fingers that seemed fragile but turned strong as soon as he wanted something. Dalia had dressed him in a long white tunic—a bright red sash around his waist—with knickers above his knees, short white socks, and strap shoes. Regardless of what Katie Mae said, the money she spent on his outfits was worth it. "But I want him to look presentable," Dalia said. She lifted her hand and waved her son over. "And not another word about those flowers," she warned Katie Mae.

"Colored boys don't dress like that," Katie Mae persisted, "and I don't see many white ones around here that do."

"So?" Dalia sighed and fluttered her eyelashes.

"He looks like a girl in 'em shiny velvet breeches." Katie Mae picked up her cup of tea and laughed. "Ya wanted a girl, so ya be dressin' him like one."

"Please," Dalia said, her tone weary. "It's a Little Lord Fauntleroy suit and it's the rage in Europe." Marion was running toward them, the little yellow bouquet of daffodils clutched greedily in his hand. He tapped up the back porch steps, proffered the flowers to her. This was the moment Dalia always dreaded—when she feared she'd be unable to hide from him the confusion that came with her love. Leaning over, she took the flowers from his fingers. "Thank you, darling," she said. He pursed his thin lips, molded them into a perfect oval, and tilted toward her, closing his eyes as he waited for the kiss she couldn't bring herself to give. Instead, she ruffled his hair with her fingertips. "Now take these inside," she said, returning the bouquet to him. "Tell Ophelia to put them into a vase of water so they'll last."

As soon as the door shut behind him, Katie Mae was fussing at her again. "I seen ya. The child puckered up his mouth for a kiss, but ya wouldn't give it to him. Why is your heart so stingy with the boy?"

"Oh, hush, you don't know everything," Dalia said. Katie Mae clenched her jaw, said nothing. There was a little silver bell on the wicker table. Dalia reached out and picked it up. "You think I don't love him, but you're wrong. I love him like I love this sound." She gave the bell a tinkle. "I listen to it, and it comforts me, but when I put it down"—she replaced it on the table—"the silence brings me happiness also, and I don't want to ring it again. That's the way it is with Marion."

"I can tell he feels your coldness to him. Listen up," Katie Mae said, gulping down the last of her tea, wiping her mouth off with the back of her hand. "Lovin' Nellie Ann wasn't always easy. Many a time, I seen your papa in her, but I loved her more than I hated him."

"Hate's stronger," Dalia said with a contemptuous glance at Katie Mae. "Love just is, but hate—it grows inside a person."

"Hush. I don't wanna hear another foolish word from ya," Katie Mae said, thunking her cup on the floor, angrily pushing herself up.

"Please don't go," Dalia said, also standing. She gave Katie Mae's sleeve a little tug. "I'm talking nonsense, I know. It's just there's something I want to ask you and it's making me nervous."

"Spit it out," Katie Mae said, slumping into her rocker. She drew in a long breath, held it, and released it with an exasperated sigh.

Dalia looked down at her, pinching her top lip with her fingers, thinking. "As I said," she began moments later, "my savings are dwindling. Soon there'll be no money left."

"I got a little saved if ya need it."

"It's not your money I need," Dalia told her.

"What, then?" Katie Mae asked.

"I've given this problem a lot of thought," Dalia said, pacing in front of Katie Mae's rocker. "What I need from you is your knowledge."

"My learning?" Katie Mae said, her eyes smiling.

"I want you to teach me everything there is to know about herbs," Dalia said, coming to a standstill, facing Katie Mae. "I want us to go into the herbal business together."

Wide-eyed, Katie Mae looked as if Dalia had slapped her in the face. Dalia could almost see the full weight of the idea squatting on her shoulders, sinking her down into her seat. "Go into business together?" she said finally.

"Exactly," Dalia said emphatically. "We could grow our herbs in the backyard. It's big enough, almost an acre. Make our own remedies and sell them to the townsfolk when they come to us with ailments. This way we could make ourselves some extra money."

"Herbs," Katie Mae repeated thoughtfully. "You and me in business together?" she said with a great big laugh. "Why, I never thought—"

"We'd be equal partners," Dalia interrupted. "Split the work and the earnings right in half."

"Equal," Katie Mae said, nodding, tapping her shoes against the porch. "I like the sound of that," she asserted, the rocker flying backward as she rose. "I always knew I was born for bigger things."

"Let's shake on it, then," Dalia said, walking over to her, their hands uniting in midair.

By August the backyard was overflowing with aloe, bay, cayenne, ginger, rosemary, scented geranium, thyme, lemon verbena, myrtle, garlic, cilantro, dill, and more. Upon gathering the herbs, Dalia and Katie Mae would dry them—hanging them upside down in small bunches, tying bags as seed-catchers around the plant heads. Later they'd pack them in dark glass jars, which were dated, labeled, and arranged alphabetically in rows in the pantry, its only window shuttered to keep out the light.

Dalia learned roses could do much more than look pretty, smell luscious. For example, rose hip tea alleviated the symptoms of colds and influenzas. Rosemary leaves aided digestion, stimulated circulation, and when added to bathwater conditioned dark hair. A bit of aloe soothed a burn. Cayenne was a tincture for arthritis, but crushed in lemon juice, hot water, and honey, it could also be gargled to ease a sore throat. And sprinkled over food, it relieved indigestion. Dalia learned that the oils in herbal leaves peaked just before flowering, that the best time for harvesting them was in the morning after the dew was gone.

"Herbs, herbs, herbs," Katie Mae chanted as she crushed a handful of dried lemongrass with a rolling pin.

"Edwina Carpenter is covered with chigger bites," Dalia said, poking her head through the kitchen door. "Says the itching is driving her crazy."

Katie Mae scraped the pulverized leaves into her palm. "Have ya laid eyes on them bites?" she asked, looking at Dalia sideways.

Dalia sucked the inside of her cheek and shook her head. "She's wearing long sleeves."

"In this heat?" Katie Mae said, her tone suspicious.

Dalia left her spot by the door and went over to the table where Katie Mae was working. "She says they're red and ugly."

"How many times has she been here this week?" Katie Mae asked, siphoning the crushed herbs into a bottle.

"Three."

"Each time a different complaint?"

"That's right. Headache. Upset stomach. And now today, chiggers."

Katie Mae plugged the bottle with a small round of cork. "Well, then, I'll tell ya what I be thinking. As I see it, the woman's lonely. Comes over here 'cause ya listen to her, give her tea, feed her cookies. She's needing company, not curing."

"She pays us well."

"And I feel like a thief taking her money." Katie Mae sighed. "Give her some aloe to rub on them so-called bites, but don't ask her for another red cent."

"We won't get rich like that," Dalia said as she walked toward the pantry.

"Just give her the aloe," Katie Mae snapped. "Then brew up a cure for your miserliness."

Marion was standing by the fire screen when Dalia led Edwina into the dining room for tea and cookies. "This is my precious gift," Dalia said, motioning him over. As usual, she had dressed him in one of those outfits Katie Mae hated, with a dark blue sash around his waist, a sailor's cap on his head.

"We've met before," Edwina said. "Haven't we, Marion?"

"Yes, ma'am," her son replied, bowing.

"What a perfect little gentleman," Edwina brayed, shaking her head in wonder.

"Oh, yes, he's such a dear," agreed Dalia, pulling Marion to her with a yank on his sash. "Please, have a seat, Miss Carpenter," she said as the woman sat down across from her. As soon as Dalia was settled, Marion tried to steal his way onto her lap. Nudging him off, she pointed to the chair beside her. "Sit there," she said, annoyed when he inched his chair closer. These days, he was always doing little things that upset her—following her wherever she went in the house, posing with plaintive eyes and clasped hands so as to be noticed, crying at the most inappropriate times. Only two weeks ago, she had been embroidering a scene of fawns in a meadow when he came swooping into the sunroom, his cheeks red and tear-stained. Begrudgingly, she offered a smile to him, knowing it was a hug he craved. Her stinginess made her ashamed, and she had relented, hesitating as she spread her arms, but as he drew near, she whiffed the scent of onion on his cheeks and below his eyes and spotted a ribbon of it trapped inside his collar. Irritated by his deception, she had drawn her arms away. "Marion, I told you to stay put," she scolded when she caught him once more curling his fingers beneath the chair seat, scuttling his chair sideways, leaving ridges in the rug. He let the chair drop and looked up at her with teary eyes. "You're ruining this carpet," she said, her voice more severe than she'd intended.

"Boys will be boys," Edwina Carpenter said brightly. "They're supposed to be a little naughty. When I get married," she said, dipping her head at Marion, "I want to have a little boy just like you." Sitting back down, Marion smiled weakly at her. "Look at that precious smile," she went on. "See, Dalia, he's not so bad."

CHAPTER 28

Katie Mae was concocting a cure in the kitchen, brewing a sweet-smelling infusion of sage, thyme, and ginger root along with a little bit of honey and lemon juice for Marion's cough. Meanwhile, Dalia worked on the books, every so often looking up to keep track of what Katie Mae was doing. Sometimes it took just minutes for her to work her magic; other times, hours, while she sifted the herbs into small packets of folded brown paper or boiled them in water, stirring in other mysterious ingredients, before pouring the mixtures into little dark blue bottles. They had made some money over the summer and into the early fall, but then word had gotten out that Dalia's cook, a black woman, was also in business with her, and the number of customers had fallen off.

"Clarice is the one to blame for the townsfolk not coming," Dalia said, snapping her pencil next to the pad on the table.

"I know," Katie Mae said, stirring the cough syrup, bringing the spoon to her mouth, licking it off. "Ophelia done told me." She removed the pot from the burner and set it on an iron trivet. "I don't give a hoot what that conniving woman has to say," she said, dribbling in more honey. "I gave up voodoo years ago. Queenie Villiers down at Snake River taught me the good and the bad of it 'cause I needed something more to take care of your sister, something strong to fend off your papa. I used the white spells, mostly potions to make me and Nellie Ann safer, but after that fishing trip, all I could feel was fury, so late that night I turned to the other. Built me a strong fire, lined up a handful of cuttings on the rickety arm of my mama's rocker, threw in jack-in-the-pulpit, horse chestnut, thorn apple, poison hemlock. *Monroe Miller, fall victim to Lucifer's sleep. Twitch in your madness. Thirst in your pain,* I be chanting, staring into that blaze, wishing the worst on your papa—pine worm to eat away his body, a brush fire to burn his soul. No amount of corn liquor could've doused the hate inside me."

"That was the night I burned down the stable," Dalia said. She could hear Ophelia moving around upstairs, cleaning; Marion laughing and playing in the fallen leaves; a murder of crows bickering near the kitchen window, descending like a dark cloud.

"But I ain't dabbled in black magic since," Katie Mae said. "Thank the Lord, my good self took over. I learnt ya gotta make your own strength, not count on voodoo to do it for ya."

Leaning back in her chair, Dalia became quiet—deep in thought about Clarice's gossip, about the toll it had taken on their business, the stack of bills she still had to pay, the house that needed fixing—roof, gutters, cracked windows—all of this requiring money, the money mounting up, depleting her savings until the herbal business was the only hope of income they had, and now Clarice was taking that hope away. As Dalia sat there, she envisioned an endless existence of penny-pinching, panic, and drudgery—her single life not one iota better than marriage. "Not a bit better," she said out loud, whipping up her pencil, scratching out each column of numbers on the page.

"Don't fret," Katie Mae told her. "We can fight back. Start our own stories about folk getting well from our cures. Get help from Ophelia, Bertha, Dora. Before long, everyone in Samson will forget what that witch has said." Dalia rubbed the corners of her eyes where the tension had gathered, said nothing. "Lord help us," Katie Mae muttered, sliding out a chair at the table, sinking down. "More I think on it, more I believe the black woodsman blends into the forests till he ain't seen. His wife is the dark bark scraped off the trees. The wife of the white woodsman, the tender raw flesh beneath. But ain't no man, black or white, got it as bad as us. Us women is less than pine gum, no matter what color we be." She propped her elbows on the table, pillowed her chin in her palms, and was silent for a moment. Then, sitting up straight, she did a little shimmy with her shoulders and said, "But I'm gonna follow my mama's advice and look on the bright side of things. Business ain't really that bad, now, is it? There is Edwina Carpenter and some others still coming to us. The rest will come back in time. And I got some money saved I could give ya, enough to tide us over for a while."

"If you'd ever lived differently, you'd understand it's not so easy," Dalia said, her voice rising.

Katie Mae strummed her fingernails against the tabletop. "I has lived different," she shot back, anger sparking beneath her brown skin. "I has lived in a place called Miller's Mansion, in a shanty by Snake River, and in this city house. I has had men and not had them. I has lived this way and another. I has lived as a servant, my own woman, and a business-person. I has lived every which way."

"But you haven't paid the bills I have to pay," Dalia argued. "This is a big house, Katie Mae, not some falling-down shanty by the river. It costs money." She began ticking the expenses off on her fingers. "The list is endless," she said, pushing back at Katie Mae's stony silence, at that harsh look of judgment on her face. "And then there are the spring taxes. Please tell me, Miss Cup Half-Full, how does one get blood from a turnip?"

"Ya don't fool me, girl. I know where all this is leading."

"Where?" Dalia demanded.

"To another stinkin' man," Katie Mae said, slamming her palms against the table, standing. "I might have lived in a fallin'-down shanty by the river, but one way I ain't never lived is weak."

"If things keep on going like this, we'll soon be living in a teepee," Dalia said, her violet eyes flashing fury.

"Then we go to Snake River. Make us a life in a teepee by the water. Turn that boy of yours into a man and not the sissy ya want him to be."

"I want him to be cultured," Dalia countered. "I want him to act like he owns the land, not be owned by the trees."

"Ya want him to be a white dandy, no better than that man who made fun of your sister. No better than that man who stole your Papa's land after he died. Lollie Morris, that's who ya want him to be, but I want him to be more than that scoundrel. I want us to be happy, strong, and free." Katie Mae turned on one heel, stomped toward the back door, and threw it open.

"You need a wrap," Dalia cautioned, feeling guilty for the way she'd acted.

"I wanna be with Marion," Katie Mae declared. "It's colder in this kitchen than the outside could ever be."

The next day, Katie Mae was still mad, her voice loud and snippy, traveling all the way to the parlor to Dalia's ears. "My kitchen's a mess," she was fussing at Ophelia. "Ya jist movin' dirt around. See these crumbs?

Gonna bring in more vermin. What do ya do all day?" Dalia heard the pump handle grinding, water splattering against metal. "Now pour some vinegar into this pail," Katie Mae ordered, "and scrub this kitchen clean."

"Ya ain't the boss of me," Ophelia sassed, her tone as angry as Katie Mae's.

They began to shout, pummeling each other with words, their bickering prodding into Dalia's skull like one of Herman's dental tools, exacerbating her headache. Quickly rising, she made a beeline for the staircase, halting on the landing to catch her breath. When she got to her bedroom, she felt dizzy and stood in the doorway, one hand on either side to steady herself. It was then she heard Marion, singing above in the attic. She went to the end of the hallway, creaked open the attic door, and tiptoed quietly up the steps, listening to him in the darkness. Without warning, an arc of sunlight trickled through the half-moon window, and there he was, standing beside an open trunk, dressed in one of Nellie Ann's white gowns. Lifting his fragile arms up, he sang into the empty space. Too baffled to scold him, she left quickly, embarrassed by what she had seen.

The three of them were sitting in the privacy of the boardinghouse kitchen, drinking coffee at the table. Dalia explained to Frances and Dora that she'd wait to see if selling the silver was necessary. If so, she had made quiet arrangements to stay in Atlanta with her cousin Juliet, who knew a buyer. "Still, though, I hope I won't have to sell it," she said. "What do you know about Walter Larkin?" she asked Frances suddenly.

"A fine, upstanding gentleman," Frances replied, a puzzled look passing over her features, "but then, didn't I say the same thing about Dr. McKee?"

"The woman who cooks for his mama," Dora cut in, "says the old lady is pushin' him to get married. *He'll do it, if he loves me,* his mama says."

"And from what we've been hearing, Gladys—that's his mother—has taken the matter into her own hands." Placing her short plump arms on the table, Frances leaned toward Dalia. "She's a force to be reckoned with. Been the only force in his life, I can assure you."

"Oh?" Dalia said. She grabbed the silver tongs, plucked up another lump of sugar, and plopped it into her coffee. "How's that?"

"Walter's . . . Walter's . . ." Frances began, hesitating. "Is meek and mild. That's a nice way of saying it."

"Took him three days to come into this world," Dora said, nodding her head three times for emphasis. "When the midwife popped his behind, he didn't cry. *Didn't want to be born,* Miz Larkin says. Didn't take the titty, just clamped his lips shut and closed his eyes." She tilted forward, her fingers slipping over the table beside Frances's arm. "She had to pry his mouth open and poke her nipple in. Mash that tit of hers till the milk come out. *Drink or drown,* she says."

"Otherwise, the air would've had to nourish him." Frances pushed her tongue against her teeth and made a *tsk*ing sound. "He was just a baby when his daddy died, and Gladys has been both mother and father to him. Pushed him out the door and into college. Then pushed him on to law school 'cause her mind was set on it. Made him study hard. Made him finish. Could have gotten that law degree herself, if they'd taken women."

"Daughters is raised, but sons is another story." Dora sighed. "He's over forty, but she still calls him her little boy. Marry the son, marry the mama," she said, smacking her lips like a period.

"A mama's boy at forty," Dalia murmured.

"Naw, that ain't exactly true," Dora said. "She might call him her baby, but she makes him act like a man."

"That's why she's pushing him so hard to marry," Frances said. "He's spoiled, but he's a good son, a fine lawyer, and not bad-looking for his age."

"Stout," Dora added.

"Got some gray in his hair now."

"And that new beard on his cheeks is nasty."

"Well, actually, we don't know what he looks like these days," Frances corrected. "We never see him, but Gladys comes by after her meetings with the Historical Society and tells us how he is."

"So his mama is a member of the Samson Historical Society?" asked Dalia.

"For years," Frances said. "Saved the Mansfield Mansion. The society uses it now for their meetings."

"How did that happen?" Dalia said.

"Talked Nolan Durbin into buying it and giving it to them," Frances explained. "Like I said, she's a force to be reckoned with."

"Sounds like someone worth knowing," Dalia told them. "Exactly when does the society meet next?"

"Not this Thursday, but the following," Frances said.

"I'll mark it on my calendar," Dalia said, clamping her hands on the edge of the table, coming to her feet. "Preservation." She paused, swallowing. "Now, that's an issue worth pursuing."

CHAPTER 29

"I'm Dalia Miller McKee," she said, introducing herself. She wore a black cloak over a heavy upholstered dress of pale green satin and a large emerald hat with a mass of peacock feathers trailing down its back. Her middle was cinched in by the newly purchased health corset she was wearing—her hips, buttocks, and bosom padded to accentuate her waist.

"I'm Gladys Larkin," the woman replied, greeting her in the foyer of the Mansfield Mansion.

The woman was tall and slim, with luminous gray eyes—Dalia knew those eyes from somewhere. Then it came to her. "The hat," she bubbled. "We spoke on the sidewalk in front of the milliner's shop a few years ago. You liked the green hat, I the crimson. Did you wear it to that play on New Year's Eve?"

"Oh, yes, I remember," Gladys Larkin replied. "Of course I wore it, and it created quite a stir. I loved every minute of it. Anyway, it's so nice to have you here, Mrs. McKee. We're always on the prowl for new members." She held out her arms, upon which Dalia draped her cloak.

The style of the house was Greek Revival, the ceilings high with crown moldings, the entryway as spacious as a bedroom. "What a magnificent place," Dalia said as she looked around and saw it was considerably more impressive than Miller's Mansion. "And so fortunate you were able to save it."

"Not me alone," Gladys Larkin said humbly. "I've been the president for just two years. We all saved it. All of us working together," she insisted, her husky voice rising like a singer's from deep inside her diaphragm. "The next home we want to save is the Fitzgerald dwelling.

Federal style, it is. On the outside it appears so plain, so simple, but the inside . . . well, you'll just have to see it for yourself."

"I imagine the business community isn't pleased with what you're doing," Dalia said.

Gladys Larkin handed Dalia's cloak to a plump carrot-haired girl with a face full of freckles. "Posh on them," she said. "They'd tear down everything, given the opportunity. Men have no appreciation of heritage or beauty, but now come with me, my dear. Today we decided to meet in the music room. Bunny," she addressed the girl, "take that to the blue bedroom and hang it up, please."

For an older woman, Gladys Larkin moved swiftly. "Without our heritage, what are we?" Dalia said, following quickly behind her.

"My sentiments exactly," Gladys Larkin responded, her stride strong and determined, her back straight as a pin, no widow's hump between her shoulders. *A force to be reckoned with,* Dalia remembered. Then, swinging left, the old woman swept into the music room, its only instrument a standing harp in the far right corner. "Ladies," she said, raising her deep voice above the clamor. Her manner was calm, Dalia noticed, no shyness or hesitation there. At once the room grew quiet. "This is Mrs. Dalia McKee," she announced, perching her fingers on Dalia's shoulder. "Several days ago, she wrote to me expressing her interest in joining our little group. So I invited her here to see us in action."

"The more the merrier," said a short woman with a double chin who stood directly in front of them. There were silver streaks in her dark hair but no lines in her pie-shaped face, making it difficult for Dalia to discern her age.

"Get back to your visiting," Gladys Larkin said, dismissing the group with a flick of her hand. "We have a few more minutes before our meeting convenes." She went over to a silver tea service set up on a sideboard near the doorway. "Tea?" she asked in a no-nonsense, courteous voice.

"Why, yes," Dalia replied.

The old woman poured the tea elegantly, rainbowing her arm above the cup, not spilling a drop on the white linen. "We have cream and sugar," she said, nodding at the containers.

"Dark will do," Dalia said, taking the cup from her long, knobby fingers. Arthritic, Dalia guessed. Next to the tea service were plates of lemon drop and sugar cookies. A blaze flickered in a marble fireplace at the opposite end of the room.

"The Mansfield place was built around 1850," Gladys Larkin pointed out. "A fire destroyed parts of it a decade later, but when the Mansfields restored the rooms, they remained true to the original hardwood. Can you imagine it, my dear?" Dalia took a sip of her tea, widened her eyes in amazement. "Here, we are in pine country—cheap and abundant softwood for the taking—but the owners brought in oak and mahogany. This alone made the place worth saving."

"It must have cost a fortune."

"The family was from Delaware. Merchants, I believe. Money posed no problem," she explained. "Came south for their health, but the move, I'm afraid, didn't save them. They all died from consumption anyway."

"If the owners had been from the South," said the double-chinned woman, taking a step closer to them, "the town council would've been dead set against tearing it down. I'm Ulva O'Rear," she introduced herself. "We're so fortunate to have you here, Mrs. McKee. Edwina Carpenter says your herbal remedies have done wonders for her health."

"I hope I do some good," Dalia said, wondering what else the woman might have heard—maybe that she'd murdered her husband with a voodoo curse.

"I believe the natural way is best," said someone on the other side of Dalia. Dalia twisted around to see a young woman with sallow, pock-mocked skin. "Lallie Cooper," she said, tilting her head, her brown hairline slipping forward. "This stupid wig," she complained, pushing it back with the flat of her hand.

Embarrassed for her, Dalia grinned foolishly. "So pleased to meet you," she said.

"Now that we've become acquainted," Ulva O'Rear interrupted, "let's get back to the point I was making. Like I said, the town council wouldn't have been so eager to demolish this place if it had been built by Southerners," she persisted. "But the Mansfields were Yankees, so they didn't care. Thank heavens the Historical Society of Samson puts beauty above regional politics, and thank heavens for Mr. Durbin, our generous benefactor."

"Speaking of beauty," Gladys Larkin said, tapping Dalia's shoulder, "notice the egg and dart molding along the walls and around the chandelier. There's bull's-eye upstairs, on the doors and windows, and crown on the ceilings. We think of ourselves as progressive," the old woman stressed. "Determined to preserve beauty by changing old, outmoded ways of thinking." With these words, she seized a porcelain bell from off the sideboard and tinkled it loudly. When no one paid attention, she gave it another jangle. "Ladies," she said in her deep, clear voice. "Shall we begin now?"

The women, clustered around the sideboard, rushed to ladder-backed chairs, placed in a semicircle near the front of the room. A very old dowager, with eyelids so puffy they hid her eyes, motioned Dalia over with a bent forefinger. "I'm Mrs. Dulcie Jennings," she croaked as Dalia, introducing herself in a whisper, sank down on the red love seat beside her.

"Will someone please bring this meeting to order?" Gladys Larkin asked, standing tall and proud like the Statue of Liberty. Dalia decided that all she needed was a torch to complete the picture. Ulva O'Rear volunteered immediately. Whereupon Gladys Larkin said, "Who seconds the motion?"

"I do," said Lallie Cooper, her wig slipping a little when she bobbed her head.

As soon as the minutes of the last meeting were read, the president of the Historical Society of Samson began to speak: "As you know, ladies, we've another huge fight on our hands." Around the room, voices grumbled, heads nodded. "The city council wants to knock down all the fine old houses on Jefferson Street to make room for storefronts. They've zeroed in on the Fitzgerald place because it's in far worse shape than the others. They think the rest will topple like dominoes after they tear it down."

"Not if we have anything to say about it," came a voice from the back of the room. Dalia shifted toward it. It belonged to a handsome middle-aged woman seated next to the harp. Clenching her square jaw, she raised an angry fist. "We have not yet begun to fight."

"That's Maude Johnston," Dulcie Jennings whispered into Dalia's ear. "She's very theatrical. I'm afraid our local productions go straight to her head."

Maude Johnston, Dalia thought, suddenly remembering what Lawrence Sears had said. "The actress?"

"Yes, that's the one. Can't you feel her intensity?"

Before Dalia could incline her head, Gladys Larkin was tinkling the bell again. "Thank you, Maude," she said graciously. "As usual, your enthusiasm inspires us to forge ahead. We can proceed like we did the last time. Purchase a page in the *Samson Register* and sign our names in protest. Our own little Emancipation Proclamation, so to speak. Any suggestions, ladies, on how we can raise the money?"

"I have one," Lallie Cooper said with a vigorous wave of her hand. Dalia noticed that her eyebrows weren't real but were crookedly drawn in.

"Yes, Lallie?"

"We could have another cake sale."

"Which would include three of your wonderful Japanese fruitcakes," Gladys Larkin said.

Lallie Cooper smiled and nodded.

"What about my jam cakes?" Ulva O'Rear asked.

"A must," Gladys said, "but a cake sale won't begin to cover our expenses. We need to raise a lot more money than we did last year. Any ideas out there?" Wedging her hand over her eyebrows, she scanned the room. "We need money to hire that lawyer from Savannah to come down and help Walter and have enough left over for Mr. Wade Phillips, the architect from Valdosta. He demands one hundred dollars for a retainer, but his reputation on these old structures is beyond reproach."

"Remember the Daughters of the Republic of Texas," Maude Johnston declared. "Remember Adina De Zavala and Clara Driscoll in their brave fight to save the Alamo."

"There she goes," Dulcie Jennings sniped.

"We could write a play about those brave women," Maude Johnston went on. "About the women of San Antonio. I will play Adina. If everyone volunteered their time, it would cost us hardly anything. We'd charge a hefty admission and raise a substantial amount for our cause. With lots of hard work we could be ready by next spring."

"That's certainly an intriguing idea," Gladys Larkin gave her. "But too long in the making. Right now we need to move with haste. Remember, the bank doesn't need to rehearse its part." A woman in the back of the room popped her knuckles. Another began coughing. Dulcie Jennings sighed and lowered her heavy-lidded eyes, drifting off for a second. The grandfather clock near the sideboard ticked away valuable time. Again Gladys Larkin checked out the room, her gaze veering from left to right, hunting for signs of a possible solution. "Ladies, please put your thinking caps on. Be creative. I know you can come up with something." At last Gladys came to Dalia, on the love seat to the left of the sideboard. The old woman locked eyes with her, as if expecting a brilliant answer.

Dalia began to squirm, her underarms damp with perspiration. But just as she began to panic, the solution came to her. She swallowed a mouthful of confidence and stated boldly, "I was imagining earlier how beautiful this house must look all decorated for the holidays. How privileged I would be to get to see it. I think most people would agree. We could have a Christmas tour of historic homes, right here in Samson."

"That's splendid!" Gladys Larkin cried.

"A wonderful idea," said Lallie Cooper.

"It's just now October. I think we can do it," added Ulva O'Rear.

"Bravo," stated Maude Johnston.

"We'll need a plan," Gladys Larkin interjected. "We can advertise by word of mouth and in the paper. Make the cost of the tickets reasonable. Publish and sell our own little pamphlet describing the homes on the tour."

"We can appeal to the monied families of Samson," Ulva O'Rear suggested. "Ask them to open their homes to the public."

"Prey on their vanity," Lallie Cooper said.

"Ladies, shall we take a vote on Mrs. McKee's delightful proposal?" Gladys Larkin said. As everyone raised her hand, she pronounced, "It's unanimous. We have made our decision."

Dalia looked at all the smiling faces and felt accepted. Perhaps there was a chance for her, for Marion. Such a magnificent opportunity, she told herself, no longer thinking about historic preservation but about her life as the future wife of Mr. Walter Larkin, the daughter-in-law of the powerful presence before her, and the owner of a grand house, already bought and paid for.

CHAPTER 30

"My cook is under the weather," Dalia McKee said, setting the silver tray on a low marble-topped table, sitting down in the space on the love seat beside Walter Larkin. He was wearing a pin-striped shirt, one she'd seen on display in the window of Jacob's Haberdashery, a white tubular collar, and the latest sack suit jacket, perhaps becoming on a younger man but silly on someone older. Because of his girth, he looked like a burlap bag of sweet potatoes. The beard, which Dora had said she hated, was now gone. In its place was an absurd mustache, its tip ends curled into parentheses, his fat chin like a doughy lump beneath it. "I hope the tea's not too weak," she said, inserting the cup's handle into his fingers when he didn't take it. Passive, Frances had called him, and at this moment he did seem half empty, like someone blended into the world, not a person within it. At last he took a sip, appreciatively dipping his head, but not speaking. "Your mama is a lovely woman," she said. He nodded. "Such energy for her age." He batted his eyelids nervously, muttered a few pleasantries, as though he were decidedly uncomfortable being near her. "I'm so happy your mother planned this meeting. It's important we discuss the Christmas tour and wonderful you might volunteer your house."

"Well, I truly haven't given it much thought, but my mother keeps insisting."

"Oh, you don't like my idea?"

"No, no, I think it's splendid," he said, his voice deep and husky, same as his mother's, "but that old place of mine is not—"

"Your mother is thrilled with the tour," she said, nervously fingering the locket around her neck, looking directly at him. "Said your house is fine, so why wouldn't you want to share it with the community?" His eyes veered to the left or right of her, focused just above her head or below her chin. "According to her, you're a very successful attorney. Lawyers amaze me with their intellect. Are you brilliant, Mr. Larkin?" He responded with a shake of his head. "Oh, but you must be," she said coyly.

"I'm more studious than smart," he said, the alliteration of the *s*'s deepening his voice, making it even more musical. "Mama pushed me hard to earn my law degree."

"You're lucky to have her," Dalia said. "My mother passed away several years ago, as did my sister and father."

"I'm sorry," he said.

"Thank heavens I've got a wonderful little boy," she added. "His name is Marion."

"Marion." His gaze lingered on the locket around her neck.

"He's quite precocious," she said. "Much smarter than most children his age."

"How old is he?"

She watched as he caught a glimpse of himself in the mirror above the fireplace and quickly, as though embarrassed, looked down. "He just turned five. Five going on fifty," she said with a laugh. From above came the sound of childlike chatter. "Right now Ophelia, my housekeeper, is giving him a bath," she explained, glancing up at the ceiling. "Next time you come over, I'll make sure to introduce him to you." She noticed that his hands were trembling—the cup shaking in his fingers, tea sloshing over the rim, staining his sack suit jacket.

"I'm so sorry," he said, trying to stand, tipping the cup over, spilling tea on her deep purple taffeta gown. "My heavens, look what I've done."

"It's nothing. Nothing at all," she said, dabbing at the dress stains with the tip of her napkin. Taking hold of his arm, she wiped at his coat sleeve. For the first time that evening, he smiled, finally relaxing. Not even that silly suit he had on could diminish the genuine sweetness he radiated. She straightened his rumpled sleeve, erased lingering memories of Herman from her mind, and planned for Walter's next visit.

"Walter, do come in," Dalia said. She had decided to wear a burnt orange dress to fit the season, along with quail feathers ringing the chignon on the back of her head.

Thrusting out his chin, he greeted her in a cordial, forthright manner, which seemed to become easier for him each time they met. "I do enjoy children," he'd said last week. "I really want to meet your son." She led him into the parlor, where Marion, dressed in a white smock, his fine straight hair coerced into ringlets, was waiting for them.

Minutes before, she'd set out a pot of hot tea, a saucer of lemon slices, and cream and sugar on top of a folding serving table. Next to the sugar were three white cups and saucers and three dark blue linen napkins. "So you must be Marion?" Walter said, tugging on his jacket, walking over. "Your mama has told me so much about you."

Marion extended his delicate, blue-veined hand, and Walter shook it. "Nice to meet you, sir," her son said, his voice grown-up and prissy. Molded by too many women, Dalia thought, sinking down on the settee beside him, while Walter chose the narrow gold-legged chair across from them, his broad derriere hanging over its cushioned seat.

"Marion's tired of hearing about this Christmas tour, aren't you, dear?" Dalia asked. Marion bit his bottom lip and nodded. "That seems to be all I ever think about," she said, laughing. "This past week, I've been knocking on the doors of prominent families, begging them to loan us their homes for the tour."

"Any success?"

"Five since last I saw you," Dalia said, holding her hand upright, fluttering her fingers. "Let's see. There's Bubby and Minerva Porterfield's Greek Revival. Dinky Bridges's Colonial. We're still waiting to hear from Nolan Durbin. He's in Europe, but your mama is certain he'll go along with the idea. Oh, yes, Dr. Warfeld and his lovely wife have consented. Also, we've enlisted the help of the editor of the *Samson Register.* Ed Safire is quite a coup, I think. Of course, the mayor vehemently declined our invitation."

"Doesn't he always?" Walter said, amused, running his fingers through his pomaded hair, slick and parted down the center.

"Several members of the Historical Society have also volunteered their homes, so we should be fine . . . but I was still hoping you'd relent."

"You're very persistent, Mrs. McKee."

"I try to be," she said, shrugging matter-of-factly.

"Well, Marion," he said, shifting the conversation, "tell me a little something about yourself. Do you like sports?"

"I like to run," Marion said eagerly. "Mama says I'm fast as the wind."

"Right before you arrived, he was dashing up and down the stairs," Dalia said, shaking her head.

"Mama thinks the staircase is dangerous."

"It is a long and winding one," Walter said.

"Yesterday I was running on the sidewalk and fell down. See where I scabbed my knee?" Marion pulled up his black velvet breeches. "That's a poultice Katie Mae put on it."

"He's mostly a good little boy," Dalia said, brushing her fingertips over Marion's shoulder. "Doesn't muss his clothes too much." She ran her eyes over him. "How did you do that?" she asked, spotting a rip in his white stocking.

"What?" Marion said, glancing down.

"The stocking on your left leg. It's torn."

"I don't know how it happened," he said, his voice tremulous.

"Your clothes are expensive," she said sternly. "You'd better watch yourself when you're outside playing."

"Yes, ma'am," he said. "I'll try to be more careful, but it's hard."

"Especially hard when you're playing baseball. Isn't that so, Marion?" Walter said, smiling warmly at her son.

"I guess," Marion replied.

"You guess?" Walter said, arching his eyebrows. "Don't you play baseball with the boys?"

"The neighborhood boys are much too rough," Dalia cut in. "I don't want my son playing with them."

Marion parted his lips as if to speak, but then Katie Mae beckoned him from the kitchen.

"Go see what she wants," Dalia said.

"Marion!" Katie Mae's voice was thistle-sharp and irritated.

"Go on now," Dalia told him when he lingered on the settee beside her.

"But Mama," he whined.

"Please, don't embarrass me, and do as you're told," she said, keeping her eyes on him until he came to his feet and began moving toward the doorway. "How stupid of me, Walter. I forgot your tea." Reaching for the teapot, she began pouring, the citrus vapor floating upward. "It's spiced with cinnamon and orange zest," she explained. "Would you like a little milk and sugar?"

"Lemon only," Walter told her. She passed him the saucer of lemon slices. Pinching the tough rind between his thumb and forefinger, he squeezed the juice out slowly, popped the sour wedge into his mouth, and sucked. Dalia puckered her lips and *tsk*ed at him. "I know. I know. I shouldn't," he said, holding up a finger as he chewed and swallowed, "but I'm beginning to feel relaxed around you."

"I feel I can be myself around you, too," Dalia said, gazing at him. "Now drink up before your tea gets cold."

He took a long, deep swallow, the tea dribbling down the corners of his mustache. After setting his cup on the table, he balled up a linen napkin and patted his thick, full lips. "The tea's good and hot. Takes the edge off this autumn chill."

"I can't wait for winter," she said. "I love it when it's cold. Would move to New England in a heartbeat. To Maine, I think. I've always wanted to go ice-skating."

"I can see you gliding over the ice like a beautiful ballerina."

"I've never tried it," she confessed. She thought for a moment, tapping her top lip with her finger. "Remember when it snowed here years ago?"

"Yes, I do," he said, "but it didn't amount to much, was only a scattering."

"Our sand is our snow," she said. "They both gleam white in the sunshine, pure and clean."

"Pretend the sand is snow," he suggested. "That way you can feel you're in New England without ever leaving here."

"Ice-skating on sand? Why, Mr. Larkin, I'm afraid I'd be a terrible ballerina." She clapped her hands and laughed. He was laughing with her, his plump face crinkling, the creases deepening around his nose, and looking at him now, at the way he seemed to enjoy her company, she felt pleased with who she was, maybe even happy. She heard shoes tapping down the hallway and smiled as Marion came prancing into the room, carrying a plate of cookies on his palm like a waiter. Katie Mae was trekking behind him, her bottom lip in a pout.

"They're gingersnaps," she said, unfriendly, coming to a halt beside Marion. "Will put the weight on ya, if ya don't watch out."

"Mr. Larkin, this is Katie Mae Chestnut, my cook, my business partner, and my friend."

"Nice to make your acquaintance, Mr. Larkin," Katie Mae said.

"Thank you for the spiced tea," Walter told her. "It's delicious."

Katie Mae nodded. "Marion . . ." She twisted toward him. "Give Mr. Larkin one of those cookies, and don't be stingy with them, 'cause I can tell he likes his sweets." Her eyes were critical as they traveled over Walter's body.

Marion offered the plate to him. "No, you first," Walter said. "Try one and tell me if you like it."

Marion thunked the plate on the table, plucked up a cookie, and nibbled. "Good," he said thoughtfully. "But I like Katie Mae's shortbread cookies best."

"Next time, boy, you be doing your own baking," Katie Mae said, snorting. Then, squaring her shoulders, she turned her back on them and walked brusquely toward the archway.

"I think you hurt her feelings," Walter said, winking at Marion as he snapped off a piece of cookie and inserted it between his lips.

"I'm the man of the house," Marion abruptly asserted.

"I was the man of my house, too," Walter said.

"Really?"

"It's true," Dalia said. "Same as you, Walter's daddy died when he was little."

"Who played baseball with you?" asked Marion.

"No one," Walter said. Dalia noticed a stillness in his face, like a cup being emptied, then with a quick grin he added, "But I'll play catch with you, if you want me to, Marion."

Marion looked at her, and she inclined her head, giving him her permission. "Oh, yes," he chirped. "When can we do it?"

"How about next week? That is, if it's all right with you, Dalia?"

"I can't imagine anything better," she said with a smile.

"Now maybe I'll be able to work off these extra pounds," Walter said, patting his belly.

"Ain't likely if you keep on eating those cookies," Katie Mae said, marching back into the parlor.

"Katie Mae," Dalia said with a hint of warning.

Katie Mae seized the plate of cookies and like a dignitary from a foreign country pranced out again.

"I'm sorry for her behavior," Dalia said, turning to Walter. "I think she might be a little jealous of you."

"But why?" he asked, genuinely flummoxed.

" 'Cause she wants to be the papa of this family," Marion said, and as soon as he did, Dalia knew it was true.

CHAPTER 31

Dalia whirled through Walter's home on Pecan Street like a tornado, rearranging furniture, wreaking so many changes that he confessed he no longer recognized it. "Your house will be absolutely charming on the day of the tour," she said, stepping back to admire the recently hung gilt-framed mirror over the dining room fireplace.

"It surely looks different," he muttered.

His words jolted her with guilt, for in the past few weeks she and his mother had, indeed, run roughshod over him. More than once he'd tried to put his foot down, only to have his protestations reduced to a whisper as Dalia had his house plastered, painted, and redecorated. "Don't worry, my dear. He might complain some, but he's beginning to discover how liberating it feels to care about someone other than this old woman," Gladys Larkin said yesterday. "Before too much longer, he won't be able to imagine his life without you in it."

"The deep red in here is a little shocking," Dalia said now, unable to contain a mischievous little giggle.

"This is where I eat my meals," he pouted.

"Which is why it's perfect for a bold color," she said. "You don't spend that much time in here."

"What about the orange in my bedroom?" he asked.

"Dark peach," she corrected him.

"And the cabinets in the kitchen?"

"Williamsburg blue. Why, don't you think they look lovely?"

"I've always been rather partial to white," he said gloomily.

"I like white, too," she said, "but this is a big house, and it calls for color."

"There's not one white room left."

"Now, Walter, you know that's not true?" she said, her tone patronizing as she danced over to him. "The third floor hasn't been touched. It's still white."

"But I never go up there," he said, the annoyance on his face obvious.

She placed a finger against the base of her neck and studied the mantel. "How do you feel about putting a Nativity scene above the fireplace in here and decorating a yellow pine up front in the parlor?"

He rocked back on his heels. "Sounds reasonable," he said, his scowl vanishing.

"Am I ever unreasonable with you?" she asked, her eyes playing coy with his. He shook his head and grinned. "What else?" she said, thinking. "Maybe a Santa and reindeer on the piano top, and naturally some evergreen roping for the staircase, mistletoe for the archways, and gold candles for all the tables. Walter, can you think of anything I've missed?" She paused, biting her thumbnail. "Holly," she blurted out. "I can't believe I forgot the holly. It'll be festive on the dining room and kitchen tables. Any suggestions as to refreshments?"

"Some . . . pecans . . . would . . . be . . . nice," Walter ventured, each word teetering before sliding out of his mouth.

"That's a fine idea," she gave him.

"We could honey-glaze them."

"Hmmmmm—tasty," she hummed. "And Katie Mae could make one of her famous three-tiered jam cakes."

"With blackberry jam between the layers?"

"If you like," she told him. "Punch in the kitchen. Hot tea, coffee, eggnog in here."

"We could have little baskets of candy for the children," he suggested.

"Oh, yes," she agreed, giddily. "And bourbon balls for the grown-ups. I think Le Carre's in Savannah carries them."

"The Baptists won't like that."

She tossed back her head and laughed. "What does it matter? They never like anything anyway." She saw his eyes on her, could almost hear his heart flutter. She toyed with a curl on her forehead, then flicked it off. At first she'd thought him too old, his middle-aged heart too brittle to love her, but now she understood his heart was only stiff from lack of use. "The tour's going to be a great success, isn't it?" she said, taking hold of his hand, girlishly bouncing on her toes.

Dalia peered out one of the long panes of glass that decorated the front entrance. Several more families were just now arriving, lining up their carriages along Pecan Street. They'd tour the Hendrickson house first, because it stood on the corner, next Walter's, which was located midway down the block. There had been a steady trickle of people since noon when the tour started, and it was only one-thirty when Dalia last looked at the grandfather clock in the hallway.

"You should be proud of yourself, Dalia," Lawrence Sears had said earlier. He had been the first person to take the tour. "You must do this every year, my dear," he'd said, touching the brim of his hat, bidding her Merry Christmas as he'd clicked down the veranda steps.

Dalia was still thinking about him when the bell jangled. She opened the door to the two flaxen-haired sisters who had been so rude to her that day in Copeland's Jewelry. Though older, they hadn't grown out of their smugness. With a self-satisfied hello, they waltzed into the foyer.

"May I help you with your coats?" Dalia offered.

"Aren't you the widow McKee?" the tall one asked, as the other one tittered.

Peeved, Dalia bit the inside of her cheek, holding back her irritation. Waving Gladys over, she immediately relinquished them to her and breathed a sigh of relief.

"Charlotte, Mary, so nice of you to come," Gladys said warmly. "How's your mother?"

"Just fine," the girls replied as Gladys led them to the double parlor.

Dalia tiptoed over to the doorjamb and eavesdropped. As always, the old lady was charming, talking to the girls as if they were the only two people in Samson who mattered. "This house was built in 1800," she was saying in her deep, strong voice. "It was the Blackburn residence before my son bought it. Did you notice the windows as you came in?" Dalia saw the backs of their yellow heads bobbing. "They're called jib windows, and the ample doors," she went on, pointing a gnarled finger at the portals, "provide cross-ventilation during the hot summers. The chandelier directly above you is from France. It's not original, though. My son is the one responsible for it." This was only partially true, for Dalia knew Gladys had bought the fixture at an estate auction in Savannah, then persuaded Walter to hang it. "The floors are cypress," she said. "Probably cut from trees on the Altamaha River."

I'd like to throw those silly girls in the river, Dalia thought as footsteps pattered behind her. "Marion?" she said, surprised. "I was wondering what happened to you. Didn't I tell you to stay with Mrs. Larkin at all times? Didn't I say that I wanted you to take over when she got tired?"

Three days ago she had mapped out his work for him. He was to show the visitors the pocket doors dividing the double parlor, point out their china knobs, their intricate carving. He was to explain that the floors in the front of the house were cypress, those in the back red pine. The porcelain chandelier above the dining room table was a must-show, as was the brass and mahogany ladder in the library. Finally, he was to end his tour in the kitchen, where she wanted him to mount the footstool in front of the sink and twist on the faucet with *Voilà!*—amazing the guests with Walter's newly installed running water.

"Mrs. Larkin said I could have a slice of jam cake before it's all gone," he told her, "but Katie Mae wanted me to ask you first."

He tried too hard to be perfect, too much to please her. Such an irritating little boy, she thought, perturbed as she listened to him. "Come with me to the kitchen," she said, taking hold of his hand, pulling him briskly down the hallway, his shoes scuffing the floorboards as he tried to keep up. She heard giggling from the library. The sisters again, she thought. Then Gladys's voice, "It hails from a manor house in England."

When they passed beneath the kitchen doorway, Katie Mae was spilling toasted pecans into a silver bowl, the scorched, sweet odor trailing behind her. "I been keeping my ears open," she said, glancing over her shoulder at Dalia. "Marion's been turning on that spigot, speaking that fancy word the way ya taught him."

"Is Ophelia keeping enough food on the dining room table?"

"Soon as I get it ready, she takes it in," Katie Mae said, dipping her shoulder in the dining room's direction.

"Would you get Marion a piece of jam cake?" Dalia asked.

"Big?" Katie Mae said in a gruff voice, opening her mouth wide. "Or small?" she peeped, winking at him.

"Big," he replied loudly.

Dalia pressed an index finger against her lips and made a shushing sound. "Remember our guests," she told him, then made a beeline for the foyer when she heard the doorbell ring. "Not too big," she tossed back at Katie Mae. "The cake's for our paying guests, not for Marion."

"In Natchez, they have a proverb," Gladys was saying in the sunroom. "The higher the house, the older the house." But Dalia knew those smug, spoiled girls were no longer paying attention.

As she passed by the staircase, she could hear Walter discussing the metal mantel above the fireplace in his bedroom, his manner so sweet and unassuming she couldn't help but be smitten with him. She rushed by the gold soffits on the wall next to the pocket doors, then by the marble-topped table, with the stern portrait of an elderly uncle, long dead, above it. When she came to the foyer, she took a deep breath, let it out through her nose, and drew the door open. It was Maude Johnston, a green satin cape draped over her shoulders, vibrating like a giant dragonfly on the brush mat. "Good day, Maude," Dalia greeted her.

"This idea of yours was a godsend," Maude said, whirring into the vestibule, her silver-streaked hair shining in the sunlight that washed through the glass panes on both sides of the door.

"Why, thank you," Dalia said. Whipping off her cape, Maude folded it once over. "You can put it on the bench over there," Dalia said, nodding at the wall opposite the hall tree. "Have many people passed through the Porterfield place?"

"A dozen families the first hour," Maude said, setting her cape down. "Minerva has decorated the house beautifully, and of course no one knows its history like Bubby, but this past hour has been a little slow."

"Shall I show you around?" Dalia asked.

"Oh, please do," Maude bubbled, her eyes lighting on the Christmas tree in the double parlor. "No matter what some people say, this was the best idea ever."

"Some people?" Dalia said, taken aback. "I thought all the members liked it."

"In life, Dalia, as in the theater, there are always critics, but you've done something very special here. So just close your eyes now," she said sincerely, "and listen to that loud applause."

CHAPTER 32

When Walter proposed on Valentine's Day, it did not surprise Dalia. After all, they had spent almost every evening together since the Christmas tour, becoming so comfortable with each other that they came to believe their lives were united before they ever met. They married in the spring. To Dalia, the wedding was anticlimactic, though Gladys, Marion, and Katie Mae didn't feel this way, throwing themselves into the event with abandon, eating and drinking too much at the reception afterward—even Marion, with his miniature silver goblet filled to the top with watered-down champagne. Now, three months later, their lives together in the house on Pecan Street had become wonderfully routine. Often, in the evening, while Walter was working in his study, she would knock, come in before he could answer, and hand him a cup of tea. She'd climb the ladder, grab and stack his law books on its mahogany top, then carry each over to his desk, where she'd sit beside him, scribbling out notes on pads of long legal paper, doing what he'd taught her. After a while, he'd grow weary and retire to bed, but not Dalia. Tireless, she would work hard until the dawn spilled silhouettes among the trees.

Having stayed up most of the night, she was already drinking coffee when he came down for breakfast. "I do love you," she said, taking hold of his cushiony hand. Like the cool space between the pine trees he existed, and though they'd been married for a few months only, it seemed like fifty years.

"And I, you," he said.

She liked to hear his deep, steady voice so early in the morning, for it made her feel safe. She liked that he let her win at gin rummy. "Dalia, you should have been a lawyer," he'd tell her. "You can bluff with the best of them." But she liked him best when he needed her. She would urge him to play catch with Marion—the two of them making a mockery of baseball—so that she could pamper him later, rub ointment on the strained muscles in his arms or lay hot compresses on his aching shoulders. He was content to glide through his existence and let her dictate the blueprint of their married life together. "Did you hear what Marion called you last night at supper?" she asked. He nodded, a great big smile on his lips. "Daddy," she told him.

"I think it just slipped out."

"You're so different from Herman," she said, lifting up his middle finger, kissing his spongy knuckle. He was staring quizzically at her. "I thought he was gentle, but he wasn't." Embarrassed, she lowered her eyelids.

"Mother went to Dr. McKee a few times," he said, "but she didn't trust him, so she found a dentist in Valdosta, talked me into going with her."

"Do you think Marion favors him?"

"In looks, maybe, but the boy has none of his chill."

Dalia's sigh whooshed the fine hairs on his finger. "You better get dressed for work," she said, replacing his hand on the table. "Ophelia starched and ironed a clean shirt for you yesterday. It's hanging in the dressing room upstairs. Do you have any appointments this morning?"

"I don't know, love, do I?" he said, his smile knowing.

"Mr. Evergreen, at nine-thirty," she replied, standing. "You should hire me to be your assistant."

"You already do more than Mrs. Grayson," he gave her. "Right here at home."

"Wife and partner," stated Dalia, moving behind him, rattling the back of his chair. "Now get upstairs," she said. "Katie Mae will be cooking breakfast before you know it. What should I tell her you want?"

"Just a cup of coffee," he said, rising. "Need to lose this extra weight I have around the middle." His rear end jiggled as he walked by her, and she realized again, as she had on their wedding night and times after, that it was gentle understanding, not strong passion, that brought their bodies together.

When Walter came home from work that evening, he was attentive, constantly reaching out to touch her hand, calling her his beautiful bride. That night after retiring for the evening, just as sleep was taking over, she felt his modest leg against hers, his timid fingers beneath her nightdress. He whispered love into her ear, brushed his lips along her shoulder. Touched by his tender passion, she opened herself up to him, and with a surreal delicateness he entered her, the pleasure over in seconds.

The morning after, she downed four tablespoons of castor oil, then asked Katie Mae to light the boiler. She went upstairs, dropped her nightdress and wrapper into the dirty clothes hamper. With a twist of the bronze knobs, warm water gushed from the faucets. She filled up an enema bag, angled her leg over the porcelain edge, and gave herself a hot-water douche in the claw-foot tub. Whereupon she inserted the stopper, poured in two capfuls of lilac-scented oil, and let the basin fill up with steaming water. She rested her head against the back of the tub, felt her limbs relaxing. Her body had grown thin, her stomach flat, her thighs slim. Yesterday Katie Mae had called her scrawny, but she liked the way she looked. Closing her eyes, she counted her blessings and felt grateful. She loved her husband. Learning to love her son was becoming easier. Katie Mae would always be her friend. Finally, her life was good.

CHAPTER 33

Whenever Dalia tugged on the strings of her new health corset, she felt uncomfortable. Her cheeks were sunken, her breasts tender, her nerves raw and unraveling. She no longer played gin rummy with Walter, no longer felt like researching his cases until the early dawn. Her eyes half closed, her breathing slight, she gave up her corset and took to her bed. The softness of her lips slipped into the corners of her mouth and disappeared. A gray pallor crept into her skin. She drew her nose downward, waving away glasses of buttermilk, plates of baked chicken, stewed okra, and tomato aspic. Clutching her limp hand, Walter sat in a chair beside the bed and placed warm compresses on her forehead. He encouraged her to eat, to do as Doctor Warfeld ordered. She pretended him away, didn't listen.

"What is you doin'?" Katie Mae said, shooing Walter out as she marched into the bedroom. "You gonna die if ya don't eat something. Kill yourself and that baby inside ya."

"I don't care," Dalia muttered.

"You is acting like a crazy woman." Katie Mae spat angrily into her snuff jar, dove down into Walter's vacated chair. "You is worrying your poor husband sick."

Dalia turned her head away, said nothing.

"If you don't eat, I'll tell him to fetch his mother."

There was silence.

The soles of Katie Mae's shoes slapped frustration across the floor. The door irked open. Her angry voice yelled, "Mr. Walter, Mr. Walter, I be needing a word with ya." Dalia heard his muffled footfalls on the thick Turkish runner in the hall, then a frenzied murmuring outside the door. Wrapping her pillow around her ears, she tried to drown out the noise. She didn't want to have this baby.

Last month, with a rag doll in her arms, she had followed her son into the parlor. He was standing in front of the window, pressing his nose against the glass, blowing fog over its surface, frail-looking as always. The wind whistled through the window casing; the twigs of the pecan tree clawed against the glass. "Marion," she said, reluctantly moving toward him. "Will you cradle this rag doll in your arms?" She pushed the doll at him. Dutifully, he took it. "Kiss it for me." Raising the doll upward, he gave its red-button mouth a kiss. "That's a baby doll," she told him, "but I have a real baby growing inside me." She touched her stomach. "Right now the baby is eating what I'm eating. Every day he grows bigger and bigger. Before you know it, he'll be too big to fit inside me and will have to be born. When he comes, we must love and take care of him. Do you understand?" Her son's eyelashes fluttered. His head bobbed on his thin neck. "Let's put the rag doll back on the shelf," she said. He had stepped forward, his arms held out, the rag doll clutched in his fingers, and she had taken it, knowing full well that instead of cradling a rag doll, she should have been cradling him.

"Look at me," Gladys Larkin demanded. Dalia willed her body to roll over. She had lost track of the time that had passed. "You have to eat something," her mother-in-law said, thrusting a bowl of dumplings at her, "if not for yourself, then for my grandbaby." Dalia let out a sigh. "Listen to me," the old woman said, thumping the bowl on the night table. "I've waited for years to be a grandmama, and I won't let you rob me of this chance." Dalia closed her eyes. "Open those eyes of yours this minute," Gladys Larkin said. "You're not behaving like the woman I wanted my son to marry. I never took you for a coward." Dalia made a whimpering sound. "Now look at me," her mother-in-law said, her deep voice climbing. Dalia willed her eyelids open. "Katie Mae has spoken to me, and I know what you're afraid of, but you can put those fears away."

"I'm too scared to," Dalia said, her lips trembling.

"I'm telling you there's no reason for you to be afraid."

"How can you say that?" Dalia muttered, tears rolling down her cheeks and onto the pillow.

"Because of what happened in my bedroom last night," the old woman replied.

"I don't understand," Dalia said.

"Then be quiet," Gladys Larkin told her, "and listen to me." Dalia blinked back tears, breathed in deeply. "The minute my son told me you were pregnant, I got out the divining crystal star my mother gave me and hung it from my bedroom window with some fishing line. Every night since then, I've been waiting for the dream, and last night it finally happened. I dreamt you had a redheaded baby, who cried so loud that it woke me. As soon as my eyelids opened, I knew what I had to do. When I was carrying Walter, my mother did it. When she was carrying me, her mother did it, and my grandmother's mother did it for her, too. I walked right up to that star and twirled it. One, two, three, four spins. An even number. A boy, I thought." Dalia groaned, felt the tears brimming again. "But then, out of nowhere, it spun around again. Five," Gladys Larkin said forcefully.

Confused, Dalia stared at her mother-in-law. "Five?" she repeated.

"An odd number means a girl," she said, smiling.

"A girl?"

"Yes, dearest," she said, leaning over to get the bowl, "the girl Katie Mae said you always wanted." Dalia opened her mouth, and the old woman scooped up a dumpling and slid it between her lips.

CHAPTER 34

"Water will never touch you," Dalia whispered as she rubbed a washcloth dipped in warm milk over Clara Nell's skin. "You'll always be soft, never rough and wrinkled," she promised. "Forever my little girl." Gathering the baby into her arms, Dalia pressed her wet, plump body against her bosom, her breast milk spotting her blouse. She gently put her on the changing table. "Ten little fingers and ten little toes," she said, counting. "All of them perfect. What an extraordinary girl you are."

Every bit as special as Dalia had dreamed she would be. After her mother-in-law's prediction that the baby would be a girl, Dalia had begun to eat robustly—consuming cornbread with freshly churned butter and blackberry jam, fried chicken with mashed potatoes and cream gravy, and black-eyed peas slippery with fat. She drank glasses of buttermilk and quart jars of ice tea, swallowed a tablespoon of iron tonic daily. Craving all things sour and bitter, she had eaten kumquats, green plums, pomegranates, and grapefruit sprinkled with salt. "Miss Dalia, you're carrying this child in your hips," Katie Mae had told her. "The old woman's right. We gonna have us a little girl." Whenever the fetus kicked, the kick was forceful. Placing her hands over the spot, Dalia had blessed the strength of this child.

Whipping Clara Nell up, Dalia gazed into her green eyes, remembering how quickly she had burst upon the world, with her shock of red hair, her loud cry, her ferocious suckling. So ferocious that Dalia's nipples had cracked, but still she had kept on nursing. For this little girl in her arms was special. Her heart beating wildly, her skirt whirling over the floor, Dalia began to spin.

"For landsakes, gal, what are ya doin'?" Katie Mae said from the doorway. A bucket of warm rinsing water dangled from her fingers.

"Dancing for joy," Dalia said, coming to a stop, tossing her a grin.

Katie Mae thunked the bucket on the edge of the changing table and grabbed a big towel that was folded on top. "Give her to me," she said, holding out her arms. "I wanna wash that milk off before it sours."

Reluctantly, Dalia handed Clara Nell to her.

Cradling the baby in the crook of her arm, Katie Mae plucked up a fresh washrag and dunked it into the bucket. After squeezing the water out, she began to wipe the milk off.

"Water will make her wrinkle before her time," Dalia said, frowning.

"Where do you get such notions?" Katie Mae asked, gloving the washrag over the tip of her forefinger, dabbing milk from the tiny belly button. "She's cute, ain't she?" she said, examining the child with her small dark eyes.

"She's more than cute," Dalia asserted. "She's no ordinary girl."

"Special, that what she be," Katie Mae said proudly.

"Yes, special," Dalia agreed.

"All the girls I love is special," Katie Mae added, again dipping the washcloth into the warm water, cleaning the baby's chest, arms, the little rolls of fat on her neck. "All gone," she cooed, wrapping the towel around her body.

"But pray tell, Katie Mae, where on earth did she get that red hair?" Dalia asked, bending over, lifting up one of Clara Nell's curls.

"From my side of the family," proclaimed Gladys, materializing in the hall outside the bathroom. She marched in and took the baby from Katie Mae's arms. "My mother's hair was that same color," she said, holding Clara Nell out in front of her, her eyes drinking her in. "What's in that tub?" she asked, looking up. "Dalia, are you bathing my grandbaby in milk again?"

"I want her skin to stay soft."

"Such foolishness," the old woman said, shaking her head, returning her gaze to Clara Nell. "You don't have to worry about wrinkles, now, do you, sugar?"

"Don't worry, Miz Larkin. I washed her off with warm water," Katie Mae said, nodding at the bucket. "And I best toss that milk out now 'fore she goes baptizing that child again."

"No, I'll do it. A mother's love is stronger than your mockery," Dalia huffed, suddenly irritated with them. Seizing the tin tub, she headed straightaway for the stairs.

Walter and Marion were talking in the kitchen as she strode through the sunroom. "They're all upstairs with the baby, so I reckon I'm the cook today," Walter was saying, while Dalia stood beside the doorway.

"All she does is eat, sleep, and poop," Marion said.

"A baby's a lot more work than you think," Walter told him.

"Ophelia's the only one who'll play with me now," Marion said, "but she isn't here that much anymore."

"We still play catch, don't we?" Walter said, as Dalia loudly cleared her throat and walked into the room.

"Are you two hungry?" she said, putting the tin tub on a long, low wooden table in the middle of the kitchen.

Walter came over and gave her a kiss.

"Mama, will you fix a jelly sandwich for me?" Marion asked in a voice so needy she cringed.

"I'll fix us two jelly sandwiches and two cups of hot chocolate," Walter cut in before she could answer. "Would you like a little butter with your jam?"

"Yessir," Marion said.

"We're two independent men. Aren't we, Marion?"

"Yes, he's a big boy, not a baby," Dalia said, hefting the tin tub up, taking it to the sink, and pouring the milk out. Tea and jelly for the men, milk and honey for Clara Nell, she thought as she watched the white froth swirling down the drain.

That night, Dalia woke with a start, perspiration sheeting down her face, washing her bosom, her eyes brimming with tears, pushing her eyelids up and open. She heard the fretful rattle of her breath, sensed her dread building. "Clara Nell," she whimpered. Walter was grumbling beside her, kicking at the sheet. "It's Clara Nell," she said, pulling anxiously at his waistband.

"Clara Nell," he mumbled, half asleep.

"I can't hear her."

"The baby's fine," he said drowsily.

"But I can't hear her," she whined, rolling toward him.

"Because she's sleeping."

"Walter, please see if she's all right."

Groaning, he flung the covers off and sat up too quickly, knocking his skull against the headboard. "She's in the nursery, dear, just five feet away. Wouldn't we know if something was wrong?"

"But I don't hear her."

"You go to her, then."

"No, no," she said, her body trembling. "I'm scared to. What if . . ." The question flickered inside her until it became a thin, hot line of fear. "What if she's not breathing? Please, Walter, you go." She heard a scurrying noise above her head. "What's that?" she asked.

"Mice," he told her.

"Mice," she said, her voice climbing, her fear flaming. "No, not in this house. No. No. No. Listen. Just listen," she said, suddenly quiet as she twisted the sheets in her fists. She heard the sound again. "Rats," she said, shuddering. "They're gnawing through the ceiling to bite her."

"Dalia," he said, reaching out and pulling her toward him.

"No!" She shoved him away with the flats of her hands. "Get out of this bed, and go save your daughter." She kicked at him until he began sliding over the mattress to the edge of the bed. "They're hurting her!" she yelled, when Clara Nell started crying. She listened to his bare feet smacking against the floor as he hurried toward the nursery.

"She's all right, Dalia," he called out seconds later, but though she heard his words, she didn't believe them, just sat rigid in the bed, her heart beating inside her neck. "First thing in the morning, I'll set out the traps," he said, coming back with her daughter, now fussing softly in his arms.

"My poor sweet angel," Dalia said the next morning as Clara Nell tried to nurse but couldn't. Dalia helped her, guided her nipple into her mouth. Whereupon Clara Nell clamped down and began to suckle, her dimpled palm drawing circles on Dalia's breasts.

"Ya was hollerin' again," Katie Mae said, coming in without knocking. She went directly to the rocker where Dalia sat, pulled over a needlepointed footstool, and lowered herself to the seat. "Sounded like a haint in your body. Why is ya turning into a crazy woman at night?"

"This is my second chance," Dalia said, lifting her head.

"What does that have to do with your screaming?"

"It means I have to pay attention," Dalia said. "What happened to Nellie Ann must not happen to this baby."

"Pay attention," Katie Mae repeated, putting her elbows on her knees, leaning forward. "Nellie Ann was sick, but Clara Nell's hearty."

"Still . . ." Dalia averted her eyes, thought for a second. "It's in my hands this time. I must not fail Clara Nell, like I did my sister."

"Your hands ain't big enough to keep all the bad things out."

"My hands are all she has," Dalia shot back, meeting Katie Mae's stare, holding it, "and I'll protect her to my death with them."

"Oh, no, Miss Dalia," Katie Mae said, quickly rising. "This is your fear talking, not you."

"There will be no more sorrow. No more heartache," Dalia stated, tears scalding her eyes.

Katie Mae took a step toward the rocker. "Don't fret," she said. "We is older, wiser. Able to face life better now." Bending over, she held both Dalia and Clara Nell against her bone-thin shoulder. "It's best to live happy each day," she said, "and leave the past behind."

CHAPTER 35

Her mass of red curls like miniature ribbons all over her head, Clara Nell was seated at the head of a long, narrow table positioned beneath the bald wisteria arbor in the backyard. There was a red velvet layer cake with four white candles, a tub of hot cider, and a wooden bucket of churned vanilla ice cream in front of her. Though it was February, the weather had been unusually warm, and the seven children sitting up and down the table looked overly dressed in their sweaters and jackets. Rosy-faced, her green eyes mischievous, Clara Nell was obviously pleased with the attention she was getting. "You must whoosh really hard if you want to blow them all out," Gladys said, placing her gnarled fingers on Clara Nell's shoulder. "Now blow," she said, giving her shoulder a little squeeze. Clara Nell's cheeks expanded like a bellows, and with one fierce puff, she snuffed the candles out, clapping excitedly, the dimples in her cheeks even deeper because she was smiling. "That was good," Gladys said.

"Very good," said Dalia, waving Marion over when she saw him descending the porch steps, but he sat down when he got to the bottom and stared blankly at her, as though the thread that connected him to his feelings had been clipped.

Next, Katie Mae motioned for him to come, but he obstinately stayed put.

"We forgot to sing 'Happy Birthday,' " Gladys said, humming the first few lines to get the children started. Meanwhile, Walter watched from his spot beneath the mulberry tree near the toolshed. The song finished, Katie Mae seized a large knife and sliced off a wedge of cake.

Gladys spooned on some ice cream and gave the plate to Clara Nell, who stuck her finger in the icing, then licked the icing off.

Just two days before, Dalia had sent Walter and Marion downtown to pick out a gift from just the two of them for Clara Nell. Now Walter was chuckling as his daughter whipped through the mound of gifts, holding each up high for everyone to see. There was a brown teddy bear in a blue-checked vest from Janice Devlin. A red rubber ball from Joey Nichols. A truck from Willis James. A gold hair clasp from Katie Mae. A green velvet dress from Gladys. A doll from Dalia. A dozen hair ribbons. A tin of candy. A box of crayons and a stack of drawing paper. "Walter," Dalia said in a clear loud voice. "Marion," she said, turning toward him. "I think it's time for your present." Marion came to his feet and meandered over the grass toward the toolshed, where Walter waited.

"What is it, Mama?" Clara Nell asked.

"I don't know, angel. It's a surprise. They wouldn't tell me."

"It must be big," Clara Nell said, spreading her arms out wide.

"It must be," Dalia told her. "Otherwise it would be waiting right here beside you."

"I wanna see it now," Clara Nell said, pounding a tiny fist against the table.

"Now!" yelled Joey Nichols.

"Now!" screamed the others, banging the table like Clara Nell with their fists.

"Settle down," Dalia said, clapping loudly, and the rowdy children fell silent. She aimed her finger at the toolshed, into which Walter and Marion had disappeared. "Look over there," she told Clara Nell. Her daughter scooted to the edge of her seat—leaning forward, staring. The toolshed door groaned. Dalia saw a red arch of metal nosing through the open space, followed by a wicker basket, Walter's hand on one handlebar behind it, Marion's on the other. Dalia gasped.

"A tricycle!" shouted Joey Nichols, breaking the silence.

Clara Nell scrambled off her chair and began to run. Dalia went after her. "Walter, how could you?" she said as Clara Nell climbed onto the wide black seat. "It's a dangerous, dangerous toy. Not meant for a little girl."

"But Clara Nell's tough," Marion protested.

"As tough as any boy here," Walter said.

"She's not tough, and truth be told, not every boy here is tough," Dalia said, speaking to Walter but looking hard at her son.

"Dalia, please."

"Marion's not tough. You know what the other boys call him."

"Don't say another word," Walter warned.

Dalia saw the blood draining from her son's face, his eyes scrunching up in a grimace, but before she could say something more, there came the crackling sound of wheels on dead grass. Looking up, she spotted her daughter, her legs pumping furiously, propelling the tricycle toward the brick walkway, which led to the street and a future of broken bones, scraped knees, and gashes, and all she could do was scream, scream, scream.

Clara Nell

CHAPTER 36

"Clara Nell, come here this minute," her mother yelled from the veranda. Minutes earlier, Clara Nell, lured by laughter and the snap of a jump rope against the sidewalk, had unlatched the back gate and crossed the street to the Devlin house, which she knew was forbidden. *Be careful, angel. Don't run. Don't jump. Don't play in this awful heat. It can be dangerous.* These were her mother's constant warnings, but Clara Nell disregarded them because if she didn't she would start crying and never stop. If the days were too cold, she was tucked into bed and ordered to drink one of Katie Mae's nasty medicines; if too hot, she was plopped into a tub filled with ice chips and water. *It is a mother's duty to keep her child safe,* her mother told her, but Marion wasn't protected this way.

"Clara Nell, get yourself home!" she heard her mother call out. Still, she didn't come. Soon it would be her turn to jump rope, and she wanted her turn more than anything.

"Clara Nell!" the group of girls shouted, and she ran toward the twirling rope, skipped into its billowing rhythm as though she were made to do these things—skip, jump, run, and play. *"I like coffee. I like tea,"* they singsonged.

"Clara Nell!" Her mother sounded like a jaybird screeching.

Clara Nell floated above the stinging rope, buoyant and free, while the girls chanted, *"I like coffee. I like tea. Clara Nell's the best jumper on Pecan Street."* The best, she thought, the muscles in her strong legs tightening, propelling her upward. She lifted her dress and leapt even higher. The minute she came down, fingers dug into her arm, pulled her hard, broke her rhythm. The jump rope snaked on the sidewalk next to her feet. The girls backed away, stood looking, mouths open, eyes wide as her mother acted crazy. "Didn't you hear me?" her mother said, running her palm over Clara Nell's forehead. "Why, you're drenched. You could have a stroke in this awful heat." With her crab fingers, she began tugging Clara Nell down the sidewalk, Janice Devlin and the others frozen as they watched.

It was July now. If Clara Nell could just hold on a little bit longer, her life would change. August would fly by, and *with September,* Katie Mae had told her, *comes school.* Like a hand reaching out, school would rescue her.

"Raise your arms," her mother ordered her. Clara Nell did as she was told, and her mother jerked her sweaty dress over her head.

"Why can't I jump rope with them?" Clara Nell asked.

"In this weather?" her mother said, twisting the faucet until the water gushed from the spigot, dumping a bucket of ice into the claw-foot tub, stirring the water with her hand.

"Their mothers let them."

"What their mothers do is none of my business," she said, reaching up and turning off the water. Clara Nell listened to the chanting that rose up from the sidewalk through the open window. "Get in now. I'll call you when it's time to get out," she said, closing the door behind her.

"The birds and the butterflies pecking out her little eyes, and the poor little thing cried Mammy," Clara Nell sang as she sat in the tub of cold water, but the sound of her singing could not drown out the girls' laughter or keep her from listening for her mother's voice. Shivering in the cold water, she imagined the smack of the jump rope against the hot cement, her strong legs pushing her up, the chanting—*I like coffee. I like tea. Clara Nell's the best jumper on Pecan Street.*

Dalia woke up before dawn, filled with dread. All summer long she had pretended this moment away. Now she couldn't. Clara Nell's first day of school had come, and her little girl would be gone. Dalia lay in bed, staring at the peach walls, watching them grow lighter as sunlight slipped through the seam in the draperies. Then she rose—dutifully, mechanically—to get both herself and her daughter ready. It was hard to hear the giddiness in Clara Nell's voice, to know how much she wanted to trade the safety of her home for some strange schoolhouse, with mustard-colored walls, scratchy desktops, and sawdust. It was painful to know that someone else, not she, would be imparting words of wisdom to her child. Painful. Simply painful. As they walked to school together, Dalia held her little hand too tightly. "You don't have to do this if you don't want to," she said, but of course Clara Nell wanted to. She was eager to go to school, her green eyes scouting the sidewalk for her playmates.

"Janice doesn't have her mother walking her to school," her daughter complained.

"Her mother is too busy chasing those six other ruffians of hers to care," Dalia told her, "but your mother will always be there for you, every step of the way."

They walked on in silence, passing Janice Devlin and the group of neighborhood girls. Embarrassed, her daughter put her head down and tried to hide in the broad cloth of Dalia's skirt, until they came to the school, only two blocks down.

Miss Ellison greeted them—"Good morning, students"—in a voice as neat as the starched collar and shirt she wore. Her lips were straight and serious, but sometimes she smiled, especially when she told them about reading, writing, and arithmetic. Which were the cornerstones of a good education, she said. Though Clara Nell didn't know what a cornerstone was, she didn't let it bother her because being a student was fun. She liked the smell of chalk, erasers, and sawdust.

An hour later, the school bell rang. "It's recess," Miss Ellison announced as she lined them up in the hallway and ushered them out to the schoolyard. "Play hard," she told them. "Get rid of all that energy, so that later you'll be quiet and listen."

And play hard Clara Nell did. For her mother wasn't there saying, *Clara Nell, you're too red in the face, too sweaty. Stay out of the sun. Play in the shade. Wear a bonnet. Don't run. Don't jump. Don't eat the mulberries because they have worms. Watch out for ant beds. Be careful of wasps, of bees.* When what she really meant was, *Don't have any fun, please.*

So Clara Nell swung, begging Willis James to push her harder and harder because she wanted to go higher. She went down the big slide, hung from the monkey bars, and skipped rope with the girls. She played tag with the boys until her face turned red and her curls lay plastered against her forehead. She arm-wrestled with Joey Nichols and beat him, her nose bleeding from the exertion, but she wiped the blood off with a hankie, then tossed it into the playground waste bin. She gossiped with

Janice Devlin, joked with Willis James, laughing and playing hard, just like Miss Ellison wanted, until the bell rang for them to come back in.

The rest of the day at her desk, she paid attention, not dozing off like Joey Nichols, not daydreaming like Janice Devlin, because school was where she wanted to be.

When it was time to go home, her mother was waiting for her, waiting there in the schoolyard beside the swings, waiting there with a strange look on her face. "Clara Nell," she called out when she saw her. Her mother was moving too fast, her footfalls urgent and rapid, her arms stretching wider and wider the closer she came, hugging Clara Nell so tight she couldn't breathe. Then, taking her shoulders, she tilted her back, her eyes upset. "What's this?" her mother asked, touching Clara Nell's nose with her finger.

"What?" Clara Nell said, reaching up and pinching the crusty scab.

"This blood," her mother snorted, jerking a lace handkerchief from her dress pocket. She spit on it and wiped hard at Clara Nell's nose. "Look," she demanded, thrusting out her hand, showing her the red stain. She spit on the handkerchief again, wiped Clara Nell's nose even harder, spitting and wiping, spitting and wiping, harder and harder, saying, "And at school, where you're supposed to be safe." Then, grabbing Clara Nell's hand, she pulled her over the playground—past the swing sets, the slide, the monkey bars—where children were still playing hard, even though no one had told them to.

"Mrs. Larkin, we're very worried about Clara Nell," Mr. Lewis said. "School just started a few months ago, and she's missed so much already."

"I know," Dalia said. She and Mr. Lewis, the principal of Clara Nell's school, were sitting in the double parlor near the staircase. "As I've told you before, my little girl's not well."

"For a frail child, she certainly plays hard at recess."

"Too hard, if you ask me," Dalia said, eyeing him coldly.

There was a moment of foot-dragging silence before he spoke again. "The problem is, Mrs. Larkin, if this keeps up, she'll be forced to repeat the school year."

"Repeat the school year," Dalia said evenly.

"That's right, Mrs. Larkin."

Dalia heard a rustling sound on the first-floor landing and glanced up to see Clara Nell trying to hide behind the fern in the porcelain planter. "You don't have to worry about that, Mr. Lewis," she said, lowering her voice a little, "because I'm planning to withdraw her anyway and hire a tutor. I want her to study at home where it's safe."

"But she loves being at school," he protested.

"I think I hear her," Dalia said as the planter skidded over the floorboards.

"I do wish you'd reconsider," Mr. Lewis said. "Public education is—"

Abruptly, she cut him off. "No, I don't think so," she said sternly. "My husband and I have talked it over. Our minds are made up, but"—she stood, looking down, a fixed smile on her lips—"it was so nice of you to come."

"We could—"

"Please, sir, let me show you out," she said, waiting impatiently for him to rise, walking with him to the door, clicking it shut behind him. She made straightaway for the staircase, taking the steps quickly, catching Clara Nell as she stole down the hallway. "Where are you going, little girl?"

Clara Nell turned to face her. Sniffling noisily, she wiped her nose with her hand and glared. There was a brief silence, when the only thing Dalia heard was the grandfather clock tick-tocking on the landing, then without warning her daughter began to yell, "I love school. I want to go! You let Marion go to school. Why not me?"

"When you calm down, we'll speak," Dalia told her. "You'll like it here at home. A very nice woman is going to teach you."

"I don't want a mean ole pencil-necked tutor," Clara Nell complained. "I don't want to study by myself in an empty room."

"You won't be alone," Dalia said. "You can talk to Katie Mae and Ophelia, and I'll be here with you."

"I hate you and everything about you! I'm going back, and you can't stop me!" Clara Nell screamed as she slammed her bedroom door.

The outburst reminded Dalia of Nellie Ann's temper. Fragile creatures must be protected, regardless of the consequences, she thought.

Gladys and Dalia were enjoying the fresh spring breeze, not speaking, as they walked haltingly in the herb garden that Katie Mae had planted. Dalia would point to the herbs—the lavender coming up in each corner of the square, its bottlebrush stems already perfuming the air; the frizzy heads of thyme sprouting along the brick border; the lacy foliage of dill and fennel rising up from the garden's center. "Walter tells me you've had to replace Clara Nell's tutor again," the old woman said at last.

"You know how willful she can be," Dalia said, turning toward her. "The first one was too old. The last one too young. There's always something about them she doesn't like."

"But, my dear," Gladys said, wrinkling her brow, "she may just be missing her school friends. I remember how hard it was for Walter as a child. He was so withdrawn and timid."

"Oh, no . . . not at all," Dalia disagreed, adamantly shaking her head. "She still plays with the neighborhood kids in the late afternoon, after her studies, and I think she was right about those tutors. Mrs. Palmer retired over twenty years ago, and Miss Goodall left teachers college after only one semester. She wasn't even nineteen years old."

"Listen to you, Dalia." Her mother-in-law threw back her head and laughed deeply. "One minute you're saying she's willful, the next she's insightful, when she's only a child."

"A special child. Gifted but fragile," Dalia asserted, her voice earnest, her gaze intense. "Walter agrees that she must be protected."

"She's seven years old and seems quite sturdy to me, and besides, she's growing like a weed." Gladys reached out and took Dalia's hands. "What will you do, dear, when she's ten, when she's fifteen? You'll blink your eyes and see a young woman before you, surrounded by beaus. You can't keep life from happening to her."

"But if we protect her, Gladys," Dalia said, her eyes suddenly misting over, "and keep her safe, then we'll be lucky enough to see our little girl all grown."

CHAPTER 37

"Make it beautiful," Clara Nell said, watching Marion draw lines on parchment-thin paper while they sat in the backyard under an ash tree with thick branches. He was working with a compass, colored pencils, rulers, and other gadgets that she had never seen him use before. Although he was allowed more freedom than she was, he didn't make use of it. All his years of school and not one friend. The only thing he did was draw designs of houses, buildings, and train stations. *Walls are like arms,* he said.

Longing for a feeling of companionship, she had been trying to befriend him all summer. She wanted him to find her as exciting as the neighborhood boys. More than once she'd caught him spying on them. Last summer he'd shared with her what he'd seen. In a field on the outskirts of Samson, he'd watched them carefully cutting hundreds of watermelons, then pressing the two halves back together. He never joined in, and though she resented his lack of courage, she respected him for not tattling on them.

It hadn't rained for weeks, and the grass was dry and prickly beneath her fanny. Her skin was turning pink in the harsh sunlight, while his remained pale. She flexed her arm and was proud of the pumped-up muscle. She pulled up her skirt and admired her strong legs. Marion's legs were skinny. Yesterday she'd overheard their parents talking about the war. The Archduke of Austria had been assassinated last year, and now everyone across the Atlantic Ocean was fighting. If she were a boy, she wouldn't be like Marion. She wouldn't be sitting around all day, drawing. Instead, she would be getting ready to join the army, getting ready to go across the ocean and fight. At age nine, she was already strong enough to tussle with any boy. She would run faster and climb higher than the best of them, if only her mother would allow it. Tough, she wasn't a 'fraidy-cat like her brother. His weakness made her hate him.

"I'll make it like a fortress, but ornate like a castle," he said. With the tips of his fingers, he nudged back his ugly new glasses.

"But I want to help you build it. I want to be your partner."

"It'll have turrets and balconies," Marion said, sketching a turret on the piece of paper, pressing his lips together the way he always did when he concentrated. "Afterwards, I'll carve fleur-de-lis designs into the wood."

"It'll be just ours," Clara Nell said proudly. "Just for us to play in." Her forehead was moist with perspiration, but not one drop of sweat was on his. "Our treehouse will be spectacular," she vowed, bunching up her hair, lifting it off her neck, letting the breeze cool her. "I'm climbing up now." She jerked off her stockings and shoes and tucked her skirt into her bloomers. Then, positioning her feet on the husky lower branches, she zigzagged up. "We'll build the main room here," she yelled, firmly planting her feet on a stout limb, grasping the branch above her. "Throw me some rope, partner." During the last three weeks, Mr. Murphy, the handyman, had brought them discarded wooden planks from the back fence he was repairing, along with nails, two hammers, and a saw. He had also given them some rope, which Marion said they needed to rig a pulley system for lifting up the boards. "Let's try that pulley of yours," she said, smiling exuberantly at him.

Marion perched his hand above his brow and tilted his head back. Daggers of light pierced through the foliage and struck diamonds against his lenses. For several minutes he stood still as a photograph, then just as the clouds shifted he growled, "I'm too old for this."

"But Marion!" she cried.

"It's kids' play," he said, his tone childish. He kicked over the can of nails and, with the sketches tucked under his arm, marched toward the house.

"Four-eyes!" she taunted him. "You big sissy! I'll get the Devlin boys to build it for me." Framed by the branches, she watched as he retreated, his legs blade-thin, his shoulders narrow. In no time, she would weigh as much as he. The two of them could have been allies, she thought bitterly. Together, they would have been stronger than their mother. Together, they could have won the war. Her chest heaving, she glanced down at the pile of fence planks and tools. "Please come back!" she yelled, but he kept on going. When he mounted the first step, one of his sketches slipped through his fingers, and he leaned over to retrieve it, dropping two more, not seeing them. He stomped up the steps and disappeared through the back door.

Scurrying down the tree, she followed him. At the bottom of the porch, she picked up his sketches, climbed the steps, and went inside. She was midway up the staircase when she saw him peeking through the slit in their parents' bedroom door. For several minutes he stood there staring, then dashed off down the hallway, fleeing to the attic, same as always. When she topped the last riser, she tiptoed over the landing and looked curiously through the cracked door. Her mother was gliding like a goddess across the bedroom, her breasts almighty, her thighs forceful beneath her silk wrapper. Shining like the moon, radiating like the sun. It was then Clara Nell understood just how powerful her own body would become. All at once her mother was coming toward her. Clara Nell hid behind the wingback chair on the far side of the landing. Barely breathing, she listened to her mother's footsteps heading down the hallway toward the bathroom. Stealthily, Clara Nell crept out and made a beeline for her parents' bedroom. At the bottom of the floor-length mirror, her mother's chemise lay rumpled upon the rug. Bending down, she picked it up, rubbed the soft cotton against her skin, inhaled the faint scent of talcum powder, but then dropped it when she saw the slip draped over the bedpost. She went over to it and pressed its silky whiteness against her face. Lifting her arms, she let it cascade over her body and felt her mother's strength.

That night after supper, she decided to snub her brother the way he'd snubbed her beneath the ash tree earlier. She had made up her mind: if he wouldn't let her be his ally, she'd be his enemy. She flitted back and forth between her parents, with a cool disregard for him in his seat by the mantel. First she spoke to her father as he lounged in his favorite chair, gnawing on the tip end of an unlit cigar—a new habit her mother hated. Then she went over to the sofa, where her mother was busily embroidering a birthday apron for Dora. "I feel dizzy," Clara Nell said, slumping down beside her.

"It's the heat," her mother said, stilling her hands in the middle of a stitch.

Clara Nell fanned her face with her fingers as her brother rolled his eyes.

"Angel, come closer," her mother said, smoothing Dora's apron over the arm of the sofa, pressing her palm against Clara Nell's forehead. "You do feel a little warm, my dear."

"I'm achy all over," Clara Nell whimpered.

"Walter, did you hear her?"

"Yes, dear," he replied, nursing his cigar.

"Our little girl isn't feeling well."

"The heat is bothersome," her father said.

"Maybe some ice cream would make me feel better," Clara Nell said with a long, drawn-out sigh.

"Hmmmmm, ice cream," her father said. "I was thinking about a cold compress."

"And I was thinking about aspirin," her mother said.

"I don't know about that," Marion said, "but I could do with some ice cream, too."

"So you're dizzy, son?" her mother asked.

Pushing his feet against the floor, her father rose. "That settles it, then," he said, propping his cigar in an ashtray. "One bucket of peach ice cream for our two sick kids."

Her lips slack, her eyelids half closed, Clara Nell was wilting against her mother's shoulder. "Why, Walter, it's a desperate situation. Our daughter's melting," her mother said, standing so abruptly that Clara Nell's head thumped against the sofa.

Inching up on her elbows, Clara Nell followed her parents with her eyes. Hand in hand, they were giggling as they walked toward the hallway, while her brother watched her knowingly from his chair. Perhaps she wasn't such a clever actress, after all.

CHAPTER 38

"Katie Mae, what are the best herbs for warding off evil spirits?" Dalia asked as they weeded in the herb garden.

Katie Mae quit weeding and cocked her head in surprise. "I've told ya many times, I don't visit Queenie Villiers no more," she said, tightening her fingers around the hoe's handle. "Don't dabble in that left-handed magic," she said sternly, "if that be your meaning. The only thing a herb is good for is healing." She swatted at a horsefly on her arm. Squinting, she rocked forward, the hoe dipping with her, and asked, "Why ya be thinking about that again? I thought we done dispensed with it. Mr. Larkin has let me tend this herb garden for five years now, and I reckon he don't expect no voodoo foolishness."

But Dalia knew better. An herb could be much more than a friend of physicians and the praise of cooks. "In Rumania, they hang ropes of garlic around their necks to scare away the vampires," she persisted, snipping off a stem of lemon verbena, holding it up, sniffing.

"How many vampires ya seen lately?"

Dalia ignored the question. "And right here," she argued, "we wear packets of herbs to ward off colds."

"Yessam, I know." Katie Mae chortled. "My mama made me wear one of 'em smelly things when cold season come. Everyone I knowed wore one, but it didn't protect us none 'cause we was used to the stench. Mix and mingled together, same as always. Passed them colds around like pancakes."

"I'm not joking," Dalia barked. "These are serious times—our young men fighting across the ocean, dying. Our woodsmen helping with the war, getting snakebit for their efforts. Danger all around us. Death patiently waiting. We need protection from these things. Something stronger than God to keep us safe."

"Ain't no escaping it. Death's a part of life," Katie Mae told her. She smacked the blade of her hoe against the ground. "So why is you so worried about it all the time?" She released the hoe, and it flopped back like a pronouncement.

"Let's go sit," Dalia said, propping her hoe against the picket fence, heading toward a white wrought-iron bench beneath the mulberry tree. "I told Walter not to put it here," she said, running a finger over the dry purple stains, "but he's turning more willful with age." They lowered themselves down, not speaking, recouping from the heat. At length, Dalia was the one to speak. "Gladys worries me," she confided. "She's not herself these days."

Katie Mae mopped the sweat above her lip with a hankie, tucked into her rolled-up sleeve. "Gladys is old, nearing eighty. Black magic ain't gonna keep her safe, if that be your meaning." Dalia laced her fingers together, cradled them in her lap. Katie Mae pressed her hands against her thighs and with a moan pushed herself up. Out front, a Model-T backfired, and the next-door neighbor's terrier began to bark. "I ain't never gonna get used to that street racket," Katie Mae huffed.

"Nor me that yapping dog."

"Could muzzle him with a rope of garlic," Katie Mae said, chortling, imitating the dog's flapping jaw with her hand.

While Katie Mae and her mama weeded in the garden, Clara Nell was upstairs in her bedroom, sitting in front of the long glass windows, looking out on the morning. The leaves of the pecan trees made palette knife smudges against the sky. The orange daylilies, like wild jungle vegetation, bloomed profusely. Clara Nell puffed on a gold-tipped cigarette, wearing one of her mother's old black dresses, its oversized sleeves rolled up to her elbows. She was only twelve, but her slow, deliberate movements, as she exhaled the wispy smoke, conveyed an air of independence. If she wanted to sleep until noon, she did—refusing to bend to any tutor's will. The poetry of Emerson bored her, so she refused to read it, preferring only those authors whose books seemed exciting and dangerous. Baudelaire's *The Flowers of Evil* was a favorite of hers, as were the novels of Balzac. When Miss Potts, her latest tutor, stumbled over the pronunciation of their names, Clara Nell haughtily corrected her. A tattered copy of Balzac's *Cousin Bette* rested on her knees, but today it held no interest for her. She'd read it too many times. Sighing, she set the book on the floor, unlatched the window, and waved her arms to chase the smoke out. She brought up a bottle of perfume from her skirt pocket and squeezed the rubber ball on its side until a scent of roses misted the smoky air. A branch of oak leaves brushed against her cheek as she straddled the windowsill, one foot on the copper roof. Ophelia was scrubbing the upstairs bathroom; the telephone was ringing downstairs in the parlor. The tantalizing odor of blackberry cobbler wafted up from the kitchen window below her. She inhaled the rich, fruity smell, her stomach grumbling, her budding breasts rising with each breath. Still crouching, she surveyed the endless green lawns and clipped hedges stretching out in the distance. She felt flecks of warm sunlight on her cheeks. A breeze blew, rustling the oak leaves. The air stilled again, the silence suddenly broken by a buzzing cloud. The gold and black specks were oscillating toward her. Glancing nervously over her shoulder, she spotted the hive, wedged in the transom above the window. Shrieking, she whipped up her mother's long dress, pulled her other leg over the windowsill, and began to run—the copper roof beneath her feet crackling. Leaping over the gutter, she grabbed the tree trunk and shinnied down—scratching her arm on a twig as she descended. She was licking the blood off when Katie Mae came rushing toward her.

"Clara Nell, Clara Nell!" she cried.

"I didn't know you could move that fast," Clara Nell said with a giggle.

"Ya gonna be the death of me," Katie Mae fussed. "I was weedin' up front when I heard ya screaming, seen them swarming. Ya ain't supposed to be on that roof."

"Thousands of bees, and not one of them stung me," Clara Nell said proudly, holding out her arms for Katie Mae to see.

" 'Cause ya ain't sweet enough for them," Katie Mae told her.

"Nothing in this great big wide world scares me," Clara Nell said as she wheeled around and sprinted toward a huge magnolia, its blossoms brown-tinged and withered in the heat. Seizing the branch above her, she did five perfect chin-ups. "How about that?" she screamed back at Katie Mae, who was shaking her head but smiling.

The morning had been filled with bees and adventure, but the afternoon was boring. To while away time, Clara Nell watched Katie Mae chop up squash in the kitchen, the yellow crooked-neck squash that Clara Nell loved. She asked Katie Mae what else she was going to put into the dish, but Katie Mae wouldn't say, just grabbed an onion from the basket on the worktable and began to peel it. Still pretending to be angry about the roof and the bees this morning, Clara Nell thought. "Don't talk to me, then," she sassed, "but the next time ya ask me something, I'll remember."

"Uh-huh," she heard Katie Mae mumble as she strode to the back door.

"I guess you're not even going to look at me," Clara Nell said.

"I seen enough of ya to know ya got out of your mama's black dress," Katie Mae said, keeping her eyes down, still peeling.

"I was looking for some polite conversation, but clearly it's not to be found in this house," Clara Nell sniped before drawing open the door and going out.

She checked for her mother, but didn't see her. Coast clear, she hurried down the porch steps and kept going. At the corner of Pecan and Live Oak, she turned right. The day had grown even hotter, but she liked the little worms of sweat beneath her clothes. Liked anything her mother feared. Four blocks down, she turned left onto Grove and walked on until she came to her grandmother's house on the corner. It was big and old, with turrets, balconies, and green shutters on all the windows. She made a beeline for the back door, didn't bother to knock because her grandmother said she didn't have to. "Grandmama!" she yelled. There was no answer. "It's Clara Nell. Where are you?"

"In here," her grandmother shouted. Clara Nell ran to the front of the house and into the parlor. "No, in here."

She crossed into the library, where her grandmother was perched on a ladder, dusting off bookshelves. "You're too old to be up there," Clara Nell said, dashing over, holding on to the ladder legs to stop them from wobbling. "If I tell Mama about this, she'll kill ya."

"Why, Clara Nell," her grandmother said, looking down at her, smiling. "I didn't know my son raised a tattletale. Now grab on real tight 'cause I'm coming down." She descended the ladder carefully, slowly. "I'm not about to fall and break something," she said as soon as her feet touched the floor. "You see, I'm not as reckless as you are, darling."

"I'm not reckless," Clara Nell said. "Just full of mischief. At least, that's what Katie Mae says."

"There's a fine line between the two," her grandmother said, straightening her dress, moving toward the hallway. "I've got a batch of oatmeal cookies in the kitchen, left over from one of my meetings. Would you like one?"

"More than one," Clara Nell said, walking alongside her.

Her grandmother went over to the pie safe, unlatched it, and pulled out a bowl. "Three," she said, counting three cookies onto a plate. "Would you like a glass of cold milk to go with them?"

"Yessam," Clara Nell said, " 'cause it sure is hot out."

"Yes, ma'am," her grandmother corrected, and they sat down at the breakfast table in an alcove to the right, surrounded by ferns in planters, and had themselves a little chat.

"Oh, it's you," her brother said, sniffing the air, looking up to see her brushing the tip of her last gold-tipped cigarette against the blue-white flame. She drew the smoke in and held it until she was standing in front of him. She blew it out. He coughed, spanking the gray haze with his architectural magazine. "I didn't know you smoked," he said, at last. "Mama will kill you if she finds out."

She dallied—puffing away, the smoke leaking from her mouth. "You pitiful creature, don't you know that Mama knows everything? But there are some things she can't do anything about."

"You're too old for your age." He switched his weight to the left, his buttock levitating above the chair bottom, and almost toppled over.

"And you're too young," she said, stifling a giggle as she pressed the red tip of her cigarette against his magazine.

"You're a brat," he spat.

"How do you like my penmanship?" she said, ignoring his anger. "It's a perfect *o,* don't you think?"

"Brat," he said, tracing the pencil-stroke of brown he called a mustache with his pinkie.

"Sissy," she shot back. Insulted, he drew up his chin, his dimple disappearing. "Why do you just sit there reading about architecture when you could go and study it at Georgia Tech? Does Mama have to push you out the door to college?" She took her cigarette from her mouth and regarded it between her fingers. "I've an idea," she said, meeting his gaze with her eyes. "Why don't you take up smoking?" He huffed, opened his magazine, pretended to be reading. "But you wouldn't think of it," she said, thrusting her cigarette between his lips, swiftly pivoting. When she came to the door, she fluttered her fingers over her shoulder at him and was about to zing him again when he coughed noisily, the pages of the magazine rattling in his hands. For a brief second, she experienced a thrust of pity, but then the feeling became too much for her, so she left.

CHAPTER 39

Clara Nell was sprawled out on the settee, playing with the wedge of lemon in her glass, listening to the same old monotonous conversation between her father and brother. "Our stalwart men in uniform are fighting two wars—the Germans and the flu," her father was saying as she bit into the lemon and drifted off.

Yesterday she had sneaked off with the *Atlanta Journal* and read about this illness called the Spanish influenza. According to the article, American troops were waging war overseas, while this imported illness was waging war at home. "Decimating our nation," the newspaper said.

"Thousands of our returning soldiers are dying from it," her father whispered to Marion. "Bodies stacked like cordwood in the mortuaries. Businesses closing their doors. 1918 is turning out to be a terrible year."

Marion, usually all ears in his desire to please their father, was mumbling, not really listening, cupping his hand over his mouth, and interrupting with a cough. It was harsh and hacking. His skin was ashen, his eyes glassy, his cheeks sunken in.

"Dad, if you'll excuse me," he said, setting his glass of ice tea on the end table between them.

"Are you all right, son?" their father asked, shifting in his seat. "You don't look well."

"It's just my allergies," her brother said. He stood shakily and walked slowly through the parlor toward the staircase. Picking up the newspaper on the end table, her father began to read.

Clara Nell slipped off the settee and at a safe distance followed her brother to the second floor. As soon as he closed the bathroom door, he began to cough. Standing by the door in the hallway, she heard mucus spatting noisily into the toilet bowl water, the toilet seat rattling. "Marion, are you all right?" Clara Nell said, throwing the door open.

"Lock it," he mumbled, sitting back on his calves, shivering.

She bolted the door and rushed over, just as another convulsion hit him. "You're hot," she said, placing her hand against his forehead when the hacking stopped. "What's that?" she asked, startled by the red in the toilet bowl water. She took her hand off his forehead, stepped closer to the commode, and looked down. "It's blood," she muttered, a chill running through her.

"No . . . no . . . I'm fine," he spluttered, dragging his shirtsleeve over his mouth.

"You don't look fine, Marion."

"I'll be all right," he said impatiently, lightly touching his chest.

"But the water in there is red," she stated. "I'm going downstairs to tell Daddy."

"Don't," he said, suddenly angry. "Please don't say a word about this now. Because if you do and Mama finds out, she'll go crazy with worry. Send you away to some awful place to keep you from getting sick. Is that what you want, Clara Nell?"

"No," she said, her tone fretful.

"Then give me two more days to get well. Let me be the strong older brother. Let me show you how tough I really am."

For the next two days, Clara Nell was vigilant. Although Marion kept mostly to himself, guarding his symptoms with a vengeance, she watched his every move. She checked for bloodstains in the toilet, caught the shivering beneath his sweater, noted his untouched meals. Still, though, she said nothing to her parents.

"Where is Marion?" her mother asked Katie Mae, who was setting plates of apple pie on the table.

"I been callin' him to supper," Katie Mae said. "He won't come."

"Only he knows if he's hungry," her father said, forking up a mouthful of pie.

"But the boy should eat something," Katie Mae said, frowning with her eyes.

"Clara Nell, go fetch your brother," her mother said, folding her napkin over, putting it beside her plate. No sooner had Clara Nell pushed her chair back than footsteps sounded in the hallway. "Never mind," her mother said. "Here he comes."

"Probably smelled my apple pie, didn't ya, Marion?" Katie Mae said as he walked unsteadily into the room.

Yet before he could pull out his chair, he was coughing uncontrollably, bending over, dotting the white tablecloth with blood.

"Marion," her mother gasped, rising quickly. "It's blood," she said, staring with horrified eyes at the red specks on the table. "Walter, ring Doc Warfeld. Katie Mae, take Clara Nell to the guest room in the carriage house—now."

"Three? Ain't that what the doctor said?" Katie Mae asked Dalia. "Open up," she commanded Marion, dropping first one aspirin, then the other two on his tongue. She filled a glass with water, guided the rim to his lips, and made him take a swallow. Seizing the pillow beside him, she spanked it, raised his head, and slipped it beneath his neck. "Ya is a sick boy," she said softly, depositing the glass on the night table, "and gotta do what the doctor orders."

"Yessam," Marion muttered in a voice so thin it seemed weightless to Dalia's ears.

"Did you give him the salts of quinine?" Dalia said, lowering the covers. Katie Mae nodded. Dalia raised her son's pajama top and smeared a turpentine plaster over his chest. "I think he's feeling better," she said, pulling the top back down. Marion tried to roll onto his side but couldn't. "Poor baby," Dalia said, placing her hand on his shoulder, easing him over. "Katie Mae, go brew him some coneflower tea for his fever." Dalia took his hand and began to stroke his hot fingers, from the thumb to the pinkie and back again. The repetition of the movement seemed to lull him. "I love you," she said, tightly squeezing his hand. "I do, darling. I can't stand to see you this ill." Only she feared he hadn't heard her, for he was asleep now, breathing heavily, his eyelids trembling like the whirring wings of a mayfly standing still.

Over the next four days, Dalia, Katie Mae, and Walter took turns watching over Marion, whose body shook with chills and fever. Dalia would give him spoonfuls of cough syrup, wipe off his forehead, dole out aspirin. She read poetry to him while he slept, checked often to make sure he was breathing. Putting her ear against his chest, she listened, afraid of hearing the gurgling death rattle, and when she didn't, she thanked God for it, but the relief she felt was only momentary because her thoughts always returned to Clara Nell. "Is Clara Nell all right?" she asked Katie Mae, who was coming toward her with a bowl of chicken broth in her hands.

"Last time I checked, she was fine," Katie Mae said, sitting in the chair Dalia had just vacated.

"Darling," Dalia said, gently touching her son's shoulder. Marion opened his watery eyes. "Here, let's prop you up," she said, plumping a pillow, putting it behind his back. "Will you try to eat a little something? Just a taste," she begged. "Please, sweetheart." Dipping up some broth, Katie Mae brought the spoon toward him, and, opening his cracked lips, he had his first taste of nourishment in days.

When Marion was finished, Dalia carried the bowl of soup downstairs and emptied what was left down the drain. She set the bowl in the basin, then washed her hands with lye soap and hot water. Going over to the back door, she peered out the glass top. Dusk was falling. The trees looked smudged and soft. The carriage house was a blur in the distance. Her eyes skittered to the windows. There was no light coming out. Usually Clara Nell lit the lamps at twilight. Panicked, Dalia threw open the door and rushed out, taking the porch steps quickly, once catching the railing, but stumbling on. Her breathing frantic, she ran over the yellow grass toward her daughter, but when she rattled the doorknob, Clara Nell didn't call out. What if God mercifully spared her son, only to take her daughter? she thought, taking a deep breath, pushing the door open. She turned toward the small iron bed. Clara Nell's eyelids were closed, and her face was pale against the white pillowcase. Dalia quickly moved over the cold brick floor, wincing when her fingers brushed against her child's hot forehead. "Walter! Katie Mae!" she yelled, her heart banging against her chest as she raced out the door.

A half hour out of town and already Dalia could see the changes the war had brought—those ominous signs that reinforced her worries about her daughter. The piney woods were being destroyed for the war effort. Faces had been scraped on young trees no thicker than the flue pipe on a wood cookstove, and hundreds of longleafs had been cut down. Rapidly disappearing were those cool, quiet spaces, those sacred spots where the sun shone like God's beacon among the trees. If her father were here, he'd be heartbroken. All this waste to fuel even more waste across the ocean, Dalia thought, her eyes falling on the amputated stumps of the felled trees. Right then, the image of Clara Nell—her parched lips quivering as she burned with fever—hit her. "I must be strong," she said, wiping the image from her mind. Folding the reins over, she flicked them against the horse's flank.

The carriage bumped swiftly over the sandy road. In the distance, Dalia saw a flock of greater sandhill cranes flying like a calibrated machine in the direction of the Okefenokee. She heard the pine needles murmuring as a brisk breeze ruffled through them. Charlie snorted, whinnied, and tossed his thick brown mane. "Faster," Dalia said, with another snap of the reins.

After a while, she whiffed the river's brackish, moldy odor and thanked God that she was drawing near. "Mister," she said, bringing Charlie to a stop when she came upon an old black man walking beside the road. "Could you tell me how to get to Queenie Villiers's place?"

"Ain't far from here," he said. "Turn right at the next little road ya come to. Her place be a half mile down."

Dalia nodded, urging the horse onward until she reached the Snake River.

After hitching Charlie to a gnarly bush, she hurried along a fieldstone path toward a weathered gray shack with a dock, like a mushroom cap hanging over the water. A golden backdrop of cypress trees, soon to loose their needles, rose up from the muddy river. A great blue heron was wading near the shoreline. Waves lapped against the pilings. *Save your daughter. Save your daughter,* they seemed to be saying.

Just as she fisted her hand to knock, a hot breeze whisked the door open and there, in the middle of the large room, stood Dalia's hope—a striking Creole woman in a canary-yellow garment, with a cobalt-blue turban wrapped around her head. "I been expectin' you," she said, not moving. "Do come in." Dalia started to enter, but the woman held up her palm. "Take off your shoes," she said. "This is a house of worship." Dalia unbuttoned her boots quickly and set them on the ground beside the stone step. In her stocking feet, she crossed the threshold, her heartbeat in her throat. "I'm Queenie Villiers," the woman said, pinching her strange robe into little peaks as her bare feet stepped forward. "You're Katie Mae Chestnut's friend, aren't you?"

"Yes, I am," Dalia said, trying to control the anxiety in her voice. "My name is Dalia Larkin."

"In my sleep, my *ti bon ange* flies free from my body, moving as if in a dream, though I'm not dreaming. This is when I have visions. This is how I knew you would be coming." She took hold of Dalia's trembling hands. "Voodoo has always been. It's older than the earth," she said, her long nails digging into Dalia's skin as she turned her hands over. "Those lines on your palms, the seams in the soil, all of it—voodoo. Voodoo is all around. In everything. I am a priestess of Vodun," she said, her voice as full as a wave before it breaks on the shoreline. "Call me *mambo*. And this"—she let go of Dalia's hands and waved her arm around the room—"is my *hounfour,* my temple." She pivoted and pointed at a pole behind her. "That is a *poteau-mitan,* where the spirits talk to believers. And over there"—she twisted her body slightly, aiming her slender finger at an altar cluttered with tiny white candles and statues of Christian saints—"is my sacred place. A while back, ya wanted to come see me, but Katie Mae warned ya not to. Tell me if this be true."

"Yes," Dalia admitted.

"It is white magic and not the other you come for. You come to save your daughter's life." Dalia bit her bottom lip and nodded. "There is black magic, too," Queenie Villiers stated. "But it can be dangerous."

"I only want my daughter well."

"Then close your eyes," Queenie Villiers told her. "I'm gonna blow on ya. Tell me what it is you smell."

Warm air puffed over Dalia's eyelids. "Oranges," she said, breathing in the scent of citrus.

"And this?" asked Queenie Villiers, air pulsing through her lips again.

The smell was vile, but Dalia couldn't place it. She shook her head.

"Once more," Queenie Villiers said, blowing.

Dalia gagged. "Death," she said, her eyes opening wide with fear.

"No, it is that which comes after," the priestess of Vodun said. "It is decay."

"She must not die," Dalia pleaded, pressing her hands against her chest.

For several seconds, Queenie Villiers was silent, calming Dalia with her blue-gray eyes. Then, clearing her throat, she spoke solemnly. "The dead are thought to walk amongst the living when we pray. If your belief is weak, Dalia Larkin, your *ti bon ange* could be captured by an evil spirit. So you must be strong . . . must fortify yourself against the powers of darkness if you want to keep death away."

⁂

They had moved Clara Nell to the downstairs guest room to keep her away from Marion, who was beginning to recover, but Dalia didn't go to her when she returned, for there was no time to waste. She rushed upstairs with Queenie Villiers's bag of magic, blessing Marion's door with her fingers as she passed before hurrying up the second flight. Breathing heavily, her heart racing, she maneuvered the narrow steps to the attic and hid herself behind an old bookcase in the far left corner. Kneeling, she whipped open the burlap bag and began taking out the dried herbs, potion oils, and talismans that she hoped would save her daughter. When she grabbed the brown sack of cremated catfish, it ripped open, dusting the dark floor with white ashes, which she could see in the twilight that came through the attic window. She was frantically using one hand to sweep the ashes up into the other when she heard a furious scratching. Tilting her head to one side, she stilled her hands. There was a scurrying noise. Rats, she thought, terrified, but instead of fleeing she steeled herself against the powers of darkness and mixed the herbs the way Queenie Villiers had said.

That night, while Katie Mae and Walter slept, Dalia set out the white magic. Above the attic doorway, she tacked a luck ball, fashioned from pig blood and hen feathers. She hung luck balls from the arms of the parlor chandelier, from the fireplace mantelpiece in the dining room, and along the top of the kitchen hutch—the blood-splattered feathers spiking out like crazed insects. Above the guest room door, Dalia strung a row of gauzy paper angels. Inside, she slipped tiny silver balls of herbs beneath her daughter's bed and sprinkled a mint-scented oil on the faucets in the bathroom. All the while, she entreated Osun, the Spirit of the Healing Streams, to make her daughter well. She implored Aida Wedo, the Rainbow Spirit, to bring back ordinary, carefree days, and asked the *ti bon ange* to be vigilant whenever it left her child's body. Finally, she lit the wick of a large white candle, unleashing the strong, healing scent of licorice, and lay down beside her daughter on the wide oak bed.

The host of paper angels above the bedroom door began to flutter, and with a start Dalia woke up. She inhaled the bullying sweetness of the licorice, saw the stub of burned-out candle on the night table, and

Walter, rigid with disbelief beneath the doorway. "Darling," he said, stepping toward her. She heard the hesitation in his voice, sensed his uncertainty when he touched her shoulder. "Let's get you upstairs where you can rest."

"But Clara Nell?" she said.

"Don't worry," he reassured her. "I'll be here with her."

Although Katie Mae had been furious about her bringing voodoo into their home, Dalia would not be moved. She intended to play all the odds, cover all the bases. Now that Marion was getting better, she could focus on her daughter. In the days that followed, Dalia gave Clara Nell salts of quinine, aspirin, and plenty of water. She summoned a specialist from Savannah, who had no new remedies to offer. She concocted seed infusions of dill and anise, leaf infusions of angelica, catnip, and hyssop, root decoctions of coneflower and cowslip, and a flower infusion of elder. She prepared a tincture of garlic and brewed a remedy of diced horseradish. She melted hog lard, added turpentine to it, and rubbed the salve on Clara Nell's body. She boiled pine needles, strained them, and thickened the broth with sugar until it was cough syrup. She burned pine tar on the stove, flung open all the doors, welcoming the smoke into the sickroom. Alongside Katie Mae, she prayed to the one great God above. Alongside the spirit of her father, she prayed to the Supreme Being, maker of the piney woods. Alone at night in the attic, she practiced voodoo, promising Ogou Balanjo that she would give him anything he wanted if he would let her daughter live. If he desired her, Dalia would lie with him. If he demanded her life, she would drink hemlock. From a mound of red clay, she sculpted a bust of Ogou Balanjo. He had no eyes, no ears, no nose, only a mouth, stretching from one side of his face to the other. After dipping a crocheting needle into a bowl of ambrosia, Dalia slipped the tip into Ogou Balanjo's mouth and begged him to spare her child.

Yet on the fifth day, as Dalia grew wild with worry, Clara Nell got better. When she stepped into the sickroom, she didn't hear her daughter wheezing, only Walter snoring in the chair beside her bed. Going over, she placed her hand on Clara Nell's cool, clammy forehead. From the kitchen came the ordinary smell of coffee brewing, the familiar sound of a fork clicking against a bowl. Above, the floorboards grumbled as Marion moved about. Drawing open the draperies, Dalia thanked Ogou Balanjo and all the spirits of Vodun, as sunlight flooded into the room.

The Supreme Being always exacted a price for His mercy, so when Gladys Larkin died of influenza, Dalia was not surprised. A sad but fair exchange, she thought, for sparing the lives of her two children, and the old woman must have predicted God's plan. For, just days before she took sick, she wrote her own obituary, planned and payed for her funeral, and updated her will. Her favorite ring she bequeathed to Clara Nell; her father's pocket watch to Marion. All else, she left to Walter—except for the crystal star that had divined the birth of Clara Nell, and a little green booklet detailing Gladys's years of service to the Samson Historical Society. *To Dalia. So that you can continue our important work,* she had written in her strong, upright script on the inside cover.

CHAPTER 40

Clara Nell raised the lid of her jewelry box, removed the bottom panel, and took out Marion's letter to read again. She slid the rumpled pages from the envelope, put them on her dresser, and ironed them out with her hand. Two weeks ago, the first time she'd read it, she had felt conflicting emotions—warmth and pride because she and her brother had grown closer of late, envy and jealousy because his life was so much richer than hers. When she'd read it a few days later, she was no longer confused by his words, only emboldened. As she got ready to read it now, she hoped it would renew her courage for the river trip she would be taking by herself tomorrow.

"*Dear Sister,*" she read aloud, as she paced in front of the dresser with the letter held out in front of her. "*I'm sorry that I'm late getting back to you, but I've been busy. Not with my studies, though they do take up considerable time, but with a girl. Right now, your eyes are probably bugging out of your head. Marion with a girl? you're thinking. My brother who has never dated? Yes, it's true, Clara Nell, my loneliness has been vanquished by a girl. And guess where I met her? Of all places, in the Georgia Tech library. She was sprawled out on the floor, her white-stockinged legs blocking the aisle. Much to my chagrin, I tripped over them, grabbing the shelves on both sides to break my fall. An expletive was perched on my lips, ready to fly free, when I glanced down and saw that she was crying. I held my tongue.*

"*She looked up at me with these big brown eyes and, not in the least bit embarrassed, started talking as though we'd known each other for years. 'Danny Finnegan McPherson,' she began, 'is fickle—fickle as any girl. Arrogant is what he is.' She extended her arm and wiggled her fingers at me. Gentleman that I am, I took hold of her hand and helped her up. 'What an utter gentleman,' she said. 'Why, you're even cuter than Danny Finnegan McPherson, and certainly not as conceited.' She told me her name was Adeline Arlington.*

"At that point, I said something stupid like, 'I've never stumbled over a leg in this library before.'

" 'Well, I've never lost and found my heart at the same time,' she said, in the most earnest voice I've ever heard. It was then she smiled. Clara Nell, it was the sweetest smile, an arrow right through my heart. She asked me if she could please use my shoulder, but I just stood there like a lump on a log, not having a clue as to what she meant. 'Your shoulder, silly? To cry on. You've such a sturdy shoulder,' she said, reaching out, her fingers grazing the length of my arm. The boldness of the gesture shocked me, and I pulled back, but I don't think she noticed because she began to chatter again, nonstop. Told me she came from a small town, Versailles, just south of Atlanta, and that her ex-beau, Mr. Danny Finnegan McPherson, attended school here at Georgia Tech and that I'd probably passed him countless times in these hallowed hallways. Hallowed hallways. Yes, that's exactly what she called them. He's a junior. I told her I was finishing my sophomore year. 'But you look so mature,' she said. When she finds out I'm almost twenty-three, she'll be flabbergasted, I thought. Then she said, 'Your hands are so lovely. Delicate, like a woman's.' Well, I was mortified, felt my face turn red. What on earth did she mean by saying my hands were delicate like a woman's? But apparently she didn't sense my consternation.

"She's not highly educated, only lasted two weeks at finishing school. Yet, she told me the funniest story about her very first day there. Her English teacher asked the class, 'Who can tell me the right verb tense for this sentence? Sir Galahad see, saw, *or* seen *the vision of God through the Holy Grail.' Adeline raised her hand up high for the teacher to call on her. When the teacher did, she answered, 'Sir Gala* had seen.*' Everyone burst out laughing. She didn't know why, just laughed along with them. What could I say to that? She was so absolutely charming.*

"Then, in a flash, she was off again, prattling on a mile a minute. Her father owns a cotton mill. They're very rich, it seems, but she claimed not to care much for money, said Danny Finnegan McPherson was rich, but rich didn't make him a nice man. Not wanting to be outdone, I threw in my two bits, told her about us—about you and Mama and Walter, about how he's a lawyer and does pretty good for himself. Mostly deeds and contracts, I told her. Then I admitted that he wasn't my real father, that my real father died before I was born, but that I love him like my own because he'd been there for

me in all the ways that mattered. She asked if Walter had adopted me, and I was so taken aback I turned purple. Whatever pops into her head comes out of her pretty mouth, and I couldn't decide if she was guileless or stupid. But a moment later, I recovered, explaining that Mama wanted it to be my decision and that long ago I'd decided to keep my own name. 'It's my nature to be direct,' she said, afraid, I think, that she'd offended me. Before we parted, she offered me her hand, and there was nothing for me to do but kiss it. 'You're my Sir Galahad,' she declared, and with those words, I was smitten.

"We've been courting for weeks now. Every weekend, she comes here by train from Versailles and stays with her cousins in Atlanta. 'Ver-sales,' she scolded me, when I tried to correct her pronunciation. 'We pronounce it Southern-style, not the French way.' I share this with you because it is indicative of her spirit. I confess that she is flirtatious, but she is strong also. Doesn't hesitate to stand up to me. We go for excursions in my Model-T and have grown close over long, romantic dinners. I've learned her childhood was one big act—to please her father, who spoils her rotten—but with me, she can be real. Clara Nell, I've never met anyone like her. The girl loves me, and I don't understand why or how, but I don't care because her love makes me whole.

"I must go for now, dear sister. Trig is calling. Please not a word of this to Mama and Dad until I say so.

"A final word of advice from your older brother: If you want to be happy, Clara Nell, you must fight for your independence and find someone who will appreciate the independent spirit in you."

"No need to worry, brother," Clara Nell said, folding the pages over. "I promise you, I will fight for what I want."

"I can't believe I agreed to this," Dalia said as Clara Nell motioned for the deck hand to hurry with her luggage. The heat shimmered hot and white above the river, already sluggish from the drought. Barrels of turpentine and rosin were being rolled onto a barge, attached to the stern of the steamboat. A track of cypress logs, motionless as alligators, trailed behind the barrels.

"It's too late, Mama. You've already given me your permission," her daughter said flippantly over her shoulder. "You let me visit Cousin Juliet in Atlanta, so why all the fuss about my going to Savannah to see her new home?"

"Remember, I went to Atlanta with you," Dalia said.

"You promised," Clara Nell said, "and you can't go back on your word now."

"But you're not old enough to go on this trip without a chaperone."

"Why not? I'll soon be seventeen," Clara Nell said, coming to a halt.

"Dalia," Walter said, his tone abrupt. "You agreed because you alone dissented. Now, enough of this nonsense."

"It was foolish of me to say yes," she persisted.

"You're worrying for nothing," Walter said. "The trip downriver is short, and Clara Nell will be staying with your cousin when she gets there."

"A seventy-year-old woman?" Dalia said with a roll of her eyes.

"Don't you think Cousin Juliet's old enough to be my chaperone?" Clara Nell said, moving rapidly over the wharf.

"That sassy tone of yours won't deter me," Dalia said, following closely at her heels. "I intend to inspect your cabin, and if I find one thing wrong with it, you won't be going."

Her daughter let out a loud, exasperated moan.

"Clara Nell," Walter said, sighing. "There's nothing wrong with your mama checking to see if your quarters are clean."

"Safe and clean," Dalia added.

"I know her. She'll make sure to find something wrong to keep me from going," Clara Nell said, rushing forward.

"Give me your ticket," Dalia demanded as soon as they crossed over the gangplank and onto the deck. Thrusting out her palm, she curtly snapped her fingers.

"Here," Clara Nell said, slapping the ticket into her hand.

"Room fourteen," Dalia said, her voice rising. "It's the top deck, Walter. What if there's a storm?"

"All I want is—to go somewhere on my own," Clara Nell whined.

"Darling, there's not a cloud in the sky," Walter said, pointing upward. "Absolutely no reason for you to be concerned."

"I can't believe I agreed—"

"Not another word, Dalia," Walter snapped, heading for the stairs, mounting them with authority.

The minute they stepped into Clara Nell's quarters, Dalia marched over to the berth, jerked back the spread to inspect the sheets, but they were white and crisp. She looked around, saw a table, and went over to it, trailing her index finger over its surface, checking her skin for dust. "Clean," she said grudgingly, her eyes darting around the cabin.

It was then the *Camilla*'s horn resounded—a deep, short blast.

"Dalia, it's time for us to disembark," Walter said, nodding.

Dalia wanted to voice her disapproval again, but instead she clamped her lips together and in frustrated silence accompanied him to the deck.

When Clara Nell first saw Dayton Morris on the deck of the *Camilla*, he put her in mind of a prancing horse. He drew one long leg upward, halfway to his chest, then brought it down, lifted his chin, opened wide his eyes like a child focusing on a brightly colored toy, and raised the other. He moved with a comical forcefulness, which seemed to be saying, *Believe in me, for I can achieve the impossible.* What a show-off, she thought, but the longer she observed him, the more she realized that prancing was his style, the way acting was hers. His hair, garlanded with silver strands, resembled a crown. His nose was regal. His cheekbones were high. Except for a slight bulging around his waist, his torso was thin, yet his shoulders were large and square.

To set off her pretty face, she positioned the white parasol over her shoulder and meandered in his direction, not daring to meet his eyes. She glided around a large, heavyset woman in an ugly gray garment, all the while flinging out little smiles, like coins being tossed in a fountain. "The weather is lovely," she remarked to another passenger, a slim, angular-faced woman who nodded demurely. She set out toward the bow, where he stood with his elbow on the railing. She could see him watching her. As she drew near, she readjusted her parasol, lifting her shapely arms to show them off. "Excuse me," she said, edging nearer to him, the hem of her white chiffon dress swishing over the tops of his shoes. "Do you know when supper will be served in the dining room?"

He cleared his throat as though a fishbone were caught in it. "Supper is served at six."

She gave him a meaningful look, then asked his name, his profession, the reason for his trip to Savannah. Instead of answering, he yawned in her face.

"I apologize for keeping you from your nap, sir." She snapped her parasol shut, readying herself to go.

"I'm afraid the day is catching up with me," he said quickly. "Please, let's begin again. I'm Dayton Morris." He offered her his hand.

"And I'm Clara Nell Larkin," she said, shaking the tips of his soft, smooth fingers. "This is my first voyage, and I'm terribly excited, as you can probably tell."

"Well, then, you'll love our little trip down the river. I've taken the *Camilla* many times before."

"You're a businessman?"

"That's right. I deal in naval stores products."

"Why, that was my grandfather's business," she said, instantly forgetting her irritation with him. "He owned some piney woods near Valdosta, at least that's what my mama says. I never knew him."

"My family owns land all over, but the bulk of it is in the vicinity of Valdosta."

"And here we are, strangers, but with so much in common," she said, laughing nervously.

"And where does your family live now?"

"Samson."

"That's a friendly little town. I go there on business sometimes."

"You might know my father, then—Walter Larkin?"

"Oh, yes, he's a lawyer." His eyes were fixed on hers. "I've heard his name mentioned, but I don't believe I've ever met him."

"If you had, you'd remember," she said, suddenly and inexplicably giddy. "He's a large, sweet-natured man."

"I would imagine you live at home with your parents?"

"Yes," she admitted, "but being the modern woman I am, it's about time I moved out."

"But you're so young," he protested.

"I'm nineteen," she lied.

"I'm thirty, but an old thirty," he confessed, laughing. "You were probably right about that nap."

"I admire maturity in a man."

"If that's the case, Miss Larkin, would you deign to dine with this mature man tonight?"

"Why, Mr. Morris, I'd love to," she replied.

"You've arrived right on time, my dear," Cousin Juliet said in a voice as brisk as the breeze blowing off the river. She was tall and slender and in spite of her age carried herself well. She gave Clara Nell a quick hug. "It's so nice having you here. You'll love Savannah. Bessie," she said over her shoulder, "have you set out everything on the patio?"

"Yessam," Bessie said with a stingy grin.

"Clara Nell, you remember Bessie?"

"How are you doing, Bessie?" Clara Nell said.

"Bessie has prepared a lovely lunch for us out on the terrace," her cousin broke in. "Shrimp. Fried oysters. Some delicious deviled crab. Come along with me, sweetheart," she said, clasping Clara Nell's hand. "Horace, be a dear and take Miss Larkin's baggage to the downstairs guest room."

"You're too good to me," Clara Nell said as they passed through the double French doors and onto the terrace, which was surrounded by white azaleas and a latticed brick wall. In the center of the round space was a two-tiered fountain—a naked cherub spewing water at the top. "How charming," Clara Nell gushed. "You must be glad to have moved here."

"Oh, yes, Savannah is the perfect city," Cousin Juliet said. "The weather's always pleasant, never cold like it was in Atlanta, and the seafood's a tonic." Clara Nell slid out a chair, gently took hold of her cousin's arm, and guided her down. "You must think me old and decrepit," Cousin Juliet said when Clara Nell looked at the residue of talcum powder on her fingers, "but at my age I'm grateful for every year." Her arm waggling, she pointed to a black wrought-iron chair. "Have a seat, my dear, and sample the many delicacies Savannah has to offer." Leaning over, she picked up the pitcher and filled two tumblers with tea. "Don't be shy, now. Eat up."

Clara Nell chose one of the deviled crabs and several of the fried oysters. Spicy and hot, the crab had cayenne in it; the oysters were lightly battered and fried. She ate rapidly and helped herself to more—this time the shrimp, cold and lemony. She picked up the tumbler and took a long, satisfied swallow. "It's all delicious," she said, dabbing her lips with a white linen napkin while her cousin picked at an oyster. "Aren't you hungry?"

"No, not lately," the old woman said. "These days, I eat with my eyes only, but when I was young . . ." She rolled her gray eyes flamboyantly. "I ate heartily, as much as any man. It embarrassed my poor mama to death. *Don't gorge, Juliet,* she'd say. *If you eat more than the man you're courting, you'll scare him off.* That was the best advice she ever gave me. From that moment on, I made a glutton of myself, and I'm proud to say I sit here before you—a happily unmarried woman. Do I detect a look of pity on your face?" she asked. Clara Nell shook her head. "Good. You mustn't feel an ounce of pity for me," she asserted. "My whole life, I've tried to be strong and independent."

"Did you ever meet Katie Mae Chestnut?"

"No, but I've often heard your mother sing her praises."

"Independent, strong, and free—that's how Katie Mae wants to be."

"And you're wondering how it is that two women, one black and one white, from totally different circumstances, could end up thinking just alike?"

"Yes, ma'am," Clara Nell said with a demonstrative dip of her head.

"Because, as women," Cousin Juliet explained, "we're still fighting for our freedom." She picked up her tumbler and sipped. "Let me try to explain myself better," she said, setting her glass down with a thump. "Your Katie Mae has known slavery. I've known servitude. Two different states, I'll admit, but born of the same dark place. I won't elaborate on what Katie Mae's family had to endure because that would be arrogant and presumptuous of me, but I can tell you that my brothers divided my legacy among them, then resented my ingratitude for their patronage." Clara Nell saw the line of her cousin's jaw tightening, her eyes narrowing with what she was about to say. "Katie Mae's free now," she said, her tone softer than Clara Nell had expected, "and by outliving my siblings, so am I. But until recently, neither of us had the right to vote. And most women still won't vote if their husbands tell them not to. No, my girl, we've not all been created equal," she said with a disgusted moan.

"I agree completely," Clara Nell said, though she had never given the vote much thought. "Cousin Juliet . . ." she began, swallowing hard.

"What is it, dear?"

"Would you grant me a little taste of freedom?"

Curious, Cousin Juliet leaned forward. "What an unexpected, but exciting, proposal. Please, darling, tell me what it is you want."

"I met a charming gentleman on the steamboat. His name is Dayton Morris, and he's staying at the Golden Arms. Tomorrow he would like to call upon me. That is, if you give us your permission."

"Permission granted," Cousin Juliet declared grandly. "Bessie!" she called out. Seconds later, the French doors opened as Bessie hastened through. "Orange juice and champagne," her cousin said, "and remember, Bessie, a third glass for you."

Cousin Juliet was scowling as Clara Nell joined her on the patio the next morning. A gray strand of hair had fallen over the bridge of her glasses, and she blew angrily at it, then slammed the magazine she was reading beside her bowl of peaches. "Oh, hello, dear," she said, looking up. "I didn't see you standing there."

"Good morning," Clara Nell said, kissing her on the cheek.

"It would be good if not for this," she huffed, riffling through the magazine's pages.

"Whatever it is, it can't be that bad," Clara Nell said, taking a seat.

"Do you know who Margaret Sanger is?" Clara Nell shook her head, spooned sugar into her coffee, and stirred. "She's a remarkable woman of vision and courage," Cousin Juliet said. "That's why they still won't leave her alone."

"Who won't leave her alone?" Clara Nell asked, taking a sip of coffee.

"The powers that be," Cousin Juliet said. "She advocates the use of a diaphragm, and for that they want to punish her."

"A diaphragm?" Clara Nell said, setting down her cup of coffee, heaping eggs Benedict onto her plate.

"Your mother has explained lovemaking to you, hasn't she, dear?"

"Mama—never," Clara Nell said incredulously, "but Katie Mae has told me all about it. Baudelaire and Balzac have also been good teachers, but I don't have a clue as to what a diaphragm is."

"It's a device that protects a woman. Keeps her from getting pregnant," Cousin Juliet explained. "Before she lies down with a man, she slips this seashell-shaped rubber into her vagina. The sperm, you see, can't pass through it."

"I see," Clara Nell said, putting her fork, piled high with eggs, back down. Caressing the bottom of her earlobe between her fingers, she thought for several seconds. Then, listing toward her cousin, she said, "I wonder where a person might find one."

"My dear girl," Cousin Juliet said with an impatient shake of her head, "haven't you been listening? You can't get a diaphragm here."

"But it would be so . . . so . . . helpful," Clara Nell said.

Cousin Juliet cleared her throat. "Remember this, Clara Nell. We are born women, coerced into ladies. Always be a woman first, my girl."

"Cousin Juliet, this is Mr. Dayton Morris," Clara Nell said, ushering him into the drawing room that evening where her cousin was ensconced in a Queen Anne chair. Dayton bowed from the waist and held out his hand. As soon as Cousin Juliet placed her wrinkled hand in his, he kissed it.

"Why, Mr. Morris, Clara Nell didn't tell me you were such a perfect gentleman," the old woman said, coquettish as a schoolgirl.

Whatever happened to Margaret Sanger? wondered Clara Nell. "My cousin has just moved here from Atlanta," she explained, walking over to the love seat and sitting. "She simply adores Savannah. Don't you, Cousin Juliet?"

"Yes, I love the heat and humidity."

"Savannah reminds me of Charleston," Dayton said, sinking down on the love seat beside her.

"Don't get me started on Charleston," Cousin Juliet said, tossing out her hand like a bridal bouquet. "When I was young, I fell for a scoundrel from Charleston. Happy to say, the affair ended badly." She laughed throatily. "Would you like a glass of wine, Mr. Morris, or perhaps a mint julep?"

"Please, call me Dayton, Miss . . ."

"Miss Kerry," she said, "but you may call me Cousin Juliet."

"Well, Cousin Juliet, this is a lovely home you have here. You've made it both elegant and comfortable." His tone was magnanimous, with not a hint of insincerity, and this made Clara Nell like him even more. She admired his eyes. They looked right at you, unflinchingly, as though stripping away the skin of manners to see your true self. "A glass of wine would be nice," Dayton said. "Mint juleps are too sweet for me, though I've had a proper one at the races in Louisville." Clara Nell liked the way he talked, fluidly and effortlessly, as if he wrote the words in his mind as he spoke.

"Red or white?" Cousin Juliet asked, gazing with good humor at him. "I don't have much to choose from. Prohibition may have limited my wine list, but it certainly hasn't curtailed my drinking."

"Any white will do."

Cousin Juliet picked up a little bell on the table beside her and gave it a dainty jingle. Within seconds, Bessie, serious as a pallbearer, was in the room. "Bessie, this is Mr. Dayton Morris, Clara Nell's friend." Bessie's lips jerked spasmodically into a stiff grin. "Please bring him a glass of that Sauvignon blanc we have chilling. Would you like a glass, my dear?" she asked, turning to Clara Nell.

"Yes, ma'am," Clara Nell said. "That would be lovely."

"Now that I've had the pleasure of meeting you, Dayton," Cousin Juliet said, cupping the armrests, rising, "I think I'll retire for the evening. You young people deserve some privacy." Dayton came to his feet and waited politely as she crossed the room toward the doorway. "He's absolutely charming, my dear," Cousin Juliet said, her eyes alighting on Clara Nell, before she left.

Later, Clara Nell and Dayton strolled arm-in-arm through the tree-lined streets of the neighborhood, glimpsing spacious drawing rooms through draperies not yet closed, the dark, bold hues of the Victorian years finally gone. Water cascaded in fountains through the upraised arms of maidens in expansive green yards. White roses climbed over trellises and perfumed the humid air. Every so often, a lightning bug would flicker in the encroaching darkness. "I don't want you to take a chill," Dayton said, plucking up the end of her shawl, replacing it over her shoulder.

"In this heat?" Clara Nell said, laughter burbling in her voice. "It must be at least eighty degrees out here."

He stopped and turned toward her, his gaze warm on her face. "But earlier it was even hotter," he said, concerned. "The slight drop could be detrimental."

"Mr. Morris, I might look fragile," she asserted, "but rest assured, I'm stronger than you think."

"Clara Nell . . ." he began shyly.

"Yes?" she said.

"May I call on you in Samson?"

"Oh, yes," she replied, closing her eyes, leaning in toward him, waiting for his kiss.

Hours earlier, Cousin Juliet had asked Bessie to find a box of her old makeup in the attic and bring it down. She had outlined Clara Nell's eyes in brown and thickened her eyelashes with mascara. Then she had brushed rouge along the arch of her cheekbones and blended it into her skin with her pinkie. "Now you look like an individualist, my dear. Intriguing and bewitching. Miss Sarah Bernhardt's double, if I say so myself. If only I were young again," she had said pensively, her liver-splotched hands beginning to tremble, "I'd show you how to be liberated."

Now, as Clara Nell buttoned the silk apricot dress in front of the mirror, she saw not a country girl from Samson but the great French actress herself staring back. She blotted her lipstick on a square of tissue, rearranged the tiara of mock orange blossoms atop her head, and smiled winningly at her reflection. When she heard the knock at the door, it was with the utmost self-confidence that she went to answer it.

He was standing there, smelling of chamomile and oranges. His pomaded hair was slicked back off his forehead, the silver in it glistening like Christmas tinsel. "Do come in," she said as he high-stepped over the doorsill. "There's a light supper set out for us in the dining room. Cousin Juliet sends her regards and regrets. Says she's much too exhausted to join us this evening."

"We will miss her, won't we?" he said, grinning roguishly.

"And what did you do today?" she asked, leading the way to the table.

"Business, as usual."

She detected a note of boredom in his voice. "Is your work really that dull?"

"Compared to spending time with you, it is." She was flattered, sensed a blush coming on, but willed it to stop.

Bowls of potato and fruit salad and a serving dish of tomato aspic had been placed at one end of the table, while at the other sat a tureen of shrimp and grits, large platters of oysters Rockefeller and deviled crab, a basket of biscuits, each one the size of a silver dollar, and a plate of lemon tarts. Sitting across from each other, they dined leisurely. Clara Nell heeded her cousin's words. She ate robustly and freely spoke her mind, trying to be a woman first in his eyes. He gazed tipsily at her. She sipped her champagne, her thoughts becoming as weightless as the candle moth flitting above her head. The blades of the ceiling fan did little to disturb the hot, turgid air. "Let's go outside where there's a breeze," she said, standing.

"We'll drink our next glass of bubbly on the terrace," he told her, refilling their flutes as he rose. Shrugging out of his linen coat, he draped it over the back of his chair. Picking up her glass, she stepped unsteadily toward the open French doors, through which came the night calls of crickets and frogs, the spit of water from the cherub's bronze lips. She walked over the brick terrace, as he followed, downing his champagne, gulping it loudly. She finished off the last of hers and put her flute on the patio table, while he went on to the fountain, setting his glass on its ledge as he sat. He pulled a cigar from his shirt pocket, lit it, and began to smoke, leaning back against the second tier of the fountain, his lanky legs sprawled out in front of him. The smoke, wet and dark, drifted in the air. She inhaled it. Her nerves were jittery, the muscles beneath her skin quivering. She was uncontrollably thirsty. She came toward him, stepped up on the fountain's edge, and bent into the cherub's cool spray. Water misted her lips, her tongue caught the droplets. She leaned over, the bodice of her dress dripping, and ran her hands over her breasts. He dropped his cigar to the terrace and crushed it beneath his heel. Saying nothing, she mounted his knee, unpinning her hair, the orange blossoms tumbling down. A wet curl fell against her face. She slipped it into her mouth and sucked it, while rocking softly against his trousered leg.

CHAPTER 41

"I can't believe you went out behind my back," Dalia said, the color suddenly draining from her face when Clara Nell confessed she'd met someone on her river trip to Savannah. "I thought you would be safe in Cousin Juliet's care, but obviously you weren't."

"Nothing bad happened to me, Mama. He and I just talked. Ate dinner at Cousin Juliet's and strolled through her neighborhood. There was absolutely nothing to it."

"But he has written you, asked for your telephone number. That is *nothing*?"

"Absolutely nothing," Clara Nell rejoined, "except, perhaps, good Southern manners."

"If you're thinking of seeing this man again," Dalia huffed, snapping her coffee cup against the saucer, "good Southern manners would dictate that you introduce him to us."

"That will be difficult," Clara Nell said, pouring herself a glass of orange juice. "He comes here only sporadically—on business."

"So, the next time he's in town on 'business,' as you so conveniently put it, ask him over." Dalia balled up her napkin and tossed it beside her plate.

"That could be months from now," Clara Nell said, sipping at her orange juice.

"I insist on meeting him," Dalia said. "I want to know his name, his age, his occupation. Who is his family?"

"I'll tell you everything you want to know when and if he comes to visit," her daughter said, insulting her with an indulgent laugh. "There's no point in telling you anything now. You'd only find fault with him and make my life miserable." She wrapped one of her red curls around her index finger, pulled her finger free, and let the strand spiral down her neck. "For a little while, at least, I want to be happy," she said in a voice that was strained and tense.

"Happy," Dalia spat out. "To know happiness, my angel, you need to have suffered, but I have spared you that kind of pain."

"You're right, Mama. You've protected me. No beau has ever broken my heart. No girlfriend has ever betrayed me, but I have suffered, Mama—suffered dearly—locked up inside this prison you call a house."

"One day, young lady, you'll thank me," Dalia said, as her daughter bit her lips into silence, stood up abruptly, and left.

"I'll have a banana split," Clara Nell said two days later, sloping forward with her elbows on the drugstore counter, her chin on top of her interlaced hands.

"One banana split coming up," Macy said, peeling a banana, bisecting it down the center. "Would you like pecans and cherries?"

"You know I would," Clara Nell said, her tone scolding. "Why do you ask me that every time?"

"Because it's my job," he told her.

"Today is special," Clara Nell said, gazing up at him.

"How's that?"

"Because the man I told you about is going to meet me at the park later. Our weekly ren-dez-vous," she said, breaking up the word, enunciating each syllable slowly and deliberately, the way she always did when she teased him.

Macy dribbled hot fudge over three scoops of vanilla ice cream. After sprinkling on a tablespoon of chopped pecans, he topped the sundae off with a crown of whipped cream and two bright red cherries, stems intact. "Made especially for you, miss," he said, nudging the ice-cream boat over the counter to her.

She dipped in her spoon and toyed with the whipped cream with her tongue. "Macy, I must introduce him to you," she said at last, plunging the spoon into her mouth. She plucked up a stem, swung the cherry toward her mouth, and bit down, chewing rapturously, dangling the stem from her fingers. Placing it on the counter, she plucked up the other cherry and began the process again, prolonging it for his benefit. "Do you think I look pretty today?" she asked, dabbing her lips with a napkin.

"My dear Miss Larkin," Macy said, picking up the banana peel—Clara Nell heard it *thunk* into the garbage can he kept beside him—"you always look nice."

"Just nice?" She shaped her lips into an astonished oval, which she willed to great effect.

"Sometimes, Miss Larkin, you worry me," he said, seizing a wet rag, leaning over to wipe off the counter's marble top.

"Macy?" she said.

Sighing, he drew himself up. "What now, Miss Larkin?"

"May I please have another cherry?"

He left the rag wadded on the counter as he bent down and brought up a half-empty quart jar of cherries. Curling his fingers over the lid, he gave it a swift wrench. "One or two?" he asked her.

"As many as you'll allow," she said. He treated her to three. "You're very sweet to me, Macy, and I'll be forever grateful," she said, attempting to confuse him further with one of her treacherous smiles.

"I want to taste the ice cream on your mouth," Dayton demanded later that day when they came to a standstill in the park beside an old rail fence, sweet peas vining over it. She pursed her lips and leaned against him. "Ah, sweet!" he said, after they kissed.

"For the first time in my life, I feel real," she confessed.

"*Perfect love casteth out fear,*" he quoted. "Is our love perfect?"

"My perfect poet, my perfect love," she said, throwing her arms around his neck, kissing his face all over.

"We'd better be careful," he said, gently pulling away from her.

"*Perfect love casteth out fear,*" she reminded him. "Anyway, I don't care," she said with an indifferent air. "I'm tired of hiding. Let them say what they will. Mama will find out, anyway, when we go to the dance this Friday." She reached out and pinched off a handful of sweet pea blossoms. "Aren't they beautiful?" she said, studying the flowers as if inspecting jewels for imperfections. "I love how they smell," she said, holding the intense fragrance up to her nose.

"Sweet peas suit you."

"Yes, they're sturdy little flowers. They die from too much care."

"About this dance," he said, returning to the subject. "It may not be quite proper—"

"I love you," she broke in, exuberantly pushing the sweet peas at him, tickling his face with the purple, red, and pink blossoms. Through the spaces between the flowers, she kissed him. "You must throw caution to the wind," she said, taking the blossoms away, kissing his mouth. "I love loving you," she shouted, suddenly sprinting toward the gazebo. "And I want everyone to know it." The thrill of lying was becoming boring. She was tired of secretly meeting him at the library. Weary of stealing off to picnic on the banks of the Altamaha, of eating in the back booth, unseen, at Godfrey's on the river. She was tired of enduring her mother's love, of kissing her father's pomaded head, of envying her brother's freedom. A life of playing games was not a life worth living. What was wrong with having a dashing beau? She craved his embraces, his arms around her shoulders and his lips on her skin, but she had not and would not succumb completely to him.

"You are my Venus," he said, lassoing her from behind. "I adore you." Whipping her around, he pressed her against the gazebo's railing, his tongue tasting the curve of her neck.

Shivering, she reached down deep inside herself and pushed him off her. She loved him, but there were limits to how much she would give. "We'll go to the dance on Friday," she said. "Saturday, you'll come to my house and meet my family. I'm weary of lying and sneaking around."

The evening of the dance, Clara Nell begged an upset stomach and retired early. In her bedroom, she quickly applied her makeup—outlining her eyes in brown, daubing pink on her cheekbones, painting her lips dark red. She slipped into a loose-fitting cobalt-blue shift, which Cousin Juliet had sent her. Inside the gift box was a matching cloche, adorned with a single peacock feather. *Wear this to the dance, my dear, and you'll be Samson's first flapper—unconventional and liberated. Give my best to Dayton,* her cousin had scribbled on a note pinned to the hat. After tugging on the cloche, Clara Nell took one last look at herself in the mirror, and, pleased with the result, she tiptoed to the landing, lingering there until the front rooms were quiet. Then, dashing down the stairs, she slipped out into the dusk.

Dalia had gotten wind of the rumors. When her daughter stole from the house that evening, she was poised to follow, her task made easier by the glaring peacock feather sticking up like a beacon from Clara Nell's cloche. She kept a safe distance, fleet-footed in the shadows, her mind spinning from the gossip.

He was a much older man, Frances Fairchild had said. They'd been seen holding hands beneath the library table, eating lunch at Godfrey's on the river, strolling in the park, smooching in the gazebo. But it was the box from Cousin Juliet that had transformed the gossip into truth. Days ago, she'd almost stumbled over the package propped in front of the door. Not bothering to look at the label, she had opened it, seen the blue flapper outfit, and with dismay read the note. Then, wrapping the package back up as though it had never been touched, she had taken it upstairs and put it on Clara Nell's bed.

The hem of Dalia's dress brushed against a boxwood. Clara Nell glanced furtively over her shoulder and came to a halt. Dalia slipped behind a rose-covered trellis and made a space to peep among the blossoms.

"Who is it? Darling, is it you?" her daughter called out into the moonlit darkness. Out of nowhere, a man appeared, and Clara Nell ran to him. They threw their arms around each other and brought their bodies close.

"I've someone I want you to meet, Mama," Clara Nell said, breezing into the parlor the next morning.

Her face pinched, Dalia refused to look up from her embroidery. Walter had already left for work. Katie Mae was at the butcher's. Ophelia, nursing a sick child at home. "Who?" she asked, focusing her anger on each thrust of her needle.

"That young man I told you about. He's finally come. He's here on business, and I promised to bring him over."

"Oh, yes," Dalia said, obsessively tapping her foot against the floor, stitching with fierce precision. "When will he be coming?"

Clara Nell fingered the antimacassar on the back of her father's chair. "How about this evening?"

"Would supper be in the offing?" Dalia asked, stilling her fingers, glancing up.

"If you think Katie Mae can manage it on such short notice."

"My dear, don't you know by now that Katie Mae can do anything she puts her mind to?" Dalia set her embroidery frame on the end table. "I'd better go and see what we have stocked in the kitchen," she said, her tone brittle, her face rigid as she came to her feet.

Dalia stared straight ahead, her eyes glued to the open pocket doors. Wearing the shift from the night before, Clara Nell sat on the sofa across from her. Walter was settled into his wingback chair. As soon as the doorbell rang, Clara Nell leapt to her feet and without glancing in their direction hastened toward the foyer. Dalia listened to the mumble of their hushed voices, heard the clatter of their heels over the floor. With an agile little sidestep, her daughter let the man enter first.

"Mama, Daddy, I'd like for you to meet a friend of mine," Clara Nell said as he pranced toward them.

Dalia lifted her palm off the armrest and prodded an anxious finger against her throat.

"I'm Walter Larkin," her husband said, extending his hand as he rose.

"Dayton Morris," the man said, shaking it vigorously. "What a pleasure it is to meet you," he said, turning toward Dalia, bowing. "Clara Nell has told me so much about you, Mrs. Larkin."

Dalia tried to say something, but the words lodged in her throat. Pushing the balls of her feet into the carpet, she listed forward, smiling stiffly, her eyes following her daughter to the settee.

"Dayton, why don't you join me?" Clara Nell said, patting the cushioned seat.

Dalia watched as he high-stepped over the rug and sat down on the settee beside her. "Mr. Morris, how long will you be in Samson?" she asked when she finally found her voice.

"Two weeks more," he answered.

"And how do you like our little town?"

"I like it much better now," he said, glancing meaningfully at her daughter.

"What type of work do you do?"

"I took over the family business when Dad died."

"My father was in business," stated Dalia, picking up a porcelain bell on the end table, giving it a brisk jangle. "He was in naval stores products." The icebox door slammed shut in the kitchen.

"Yes, I know. Clara Nell mentioned that to me when we first met," the man said. "Turpentine is my business also, but I don't do the rough work myself. I inherited thousands of drifts from my father."

"And who might your father be?"

"Mr. Lollie Morris," the man replied. "From Valdosta."

Dalia bit the inside of her cheek so hard, she drew blood. She stood at once, swallowed, and, with icy resentment, stated, "Mr. Morris, your father was my father's enemy. He stole my family's land after my papa died. So I respectfully ask you to leave my house and never see my daughter again."

CHAPTER 42

Clara Nell went straightaway to the bathroom at the Valdosta train station and, within its narrow confines, struggled out of her lace dress and put on a heavy cotton skirt and a man's white shirt. She grabbed a hunting knife with a five-inch blade from the small velvet valise she was carrying and eased it through her garter belt, just in case. If Dayton couldn't come to her mother's house, she would come to him. Standing outside the station, she discarded her dainty gestures as easily as she'd shed her dress, and transformed herself into the modern young woman she wanted to be. She spotted a fat middle-aged man in a black sedan, parked and idling. "Howdy, sir," she said, meandering over. He was smoking a cigar, blowing tornadoes of foul-smelling smoke out the window. "I need a ride to the Morris Warehouse in the south part of town. If you're heading that way, could you take me?" He nodded. She went around, flung the car door open, and climbed inside, at once assaulted by the filthy odor. "Looks like your cigar is down to a nub. Why don't you try one of these? They're Turkish," Clara Nell said, offering him a small box. He took one. She inserted another between her lips and waited for the man to light it for her. He struck a match, held up the blue flame, and she tilted toward it—inhaling, exhaling from a corner of her mouth. After which he lit his own, whitewashing the cigar odor with cigarette smoke. "Now, isn't that better?" she asked him.

"I don't know. Ain't nothing better than a good ole fat Havana," the man said, laughing. He released the brake, the gears grinding as he changed into first, and fed gas to the engine. The car rolled forward. "I was waiting for a business partner of mine coming from Augusta, but I reckon he missed the train. Anyway, I got some time to kill. Morris Warehouse, ya said?"

"If it's no trouble," Clara Nell said, taking another little puff. "All I know is it's in the south part of town. My beau insisted I take a taxi, but I spotted you first. Aren't you lucky?"

"Young lady, luck is my middle name," he said, flicking the unfinished cigarette out the window. He pulled another cigar from his coat pocket, nipped off the tip end, and spit it through the open space like he would have the hull of a peanut.

Clara Nell was miffed. Turkish cigarettes were expensive. She leaned back against her seat, didn't speak, blew out huge globs of smoke to camouflage the cigar's stink, concentrated on the scenery: a dead, vine-covered pine in a large, empty lot; some purple-tufted weeds in the cracked sidewalk. They drove by a dilapidated wooden building with white men shouting drunkenly as they followed the car with their eyes. But Clara Nell didn't let their stares bother her. The only look that could was her mother's harsh look of disapproval. She craned her neck to see a black woman vigorously shaking a rug on the porch of her shanty, one among many on both sides of the road. They drove along another ten minutes before the road turned into dust and potholes. Scraggly patches of slash pine dotted the landscape, then came a paper mill and its stench. In the middle of a weedy, overgrown field, an oasis of brown-eyed Susans caught Clara Nell's attention, just as the car slowed down and pulled up in front of a dark brick structure. MORRIS WAREHOUSE, the sign read, but the building seemed more like a prison than a warehouse to Clara Nell.

"Here we are. That door can get tricky," the man said, leaning over, releasing the handle, pushing against the side of the car with the flat of his hand. The door groaned open. "You sure you'll be okay out here by yourself?"

"Yessir," Clara Nell said, sliding out. Her heels clacked against the pavement. "My beau owns this warehouse." She reached in and grabbed her valise on the floorboard. "Thank you so much for the lift," she said, using the full weight of her body to close the heavy door.

"Have a nice afternoon with your fellow," the man said, winking and waving good-bye, driving off in a cloud of dust.

Clara Nell asked two workers, smoking in front of the huge portal doors, to fetch Mr. Morris, while she settled on a bench beneath an ancient magnolia, the undersides of its leaves a toffee-colored brown. The

September sun glinted off the pavement, and she perspired in the heat, moisture beading along her hairline. She liked doing as she pleased, defying the rules, coming here in spite of her mother's shrill warnings. She knew that average people expressed safe, average love, but that her mother's love was different. It reeled through people, splintered them, leaving behind swords of affection, sharp weapons to be proffered later. She didn't want this kind of love; she wanted love that liberated, love that set people free.

She spotted Dayton strutting through the warehouse doors. Leaping up, she waved her arms above her head and called out to him. She couldn't wait to feel his fingers against her skin, couldn't wait to inhale the chamomile, citrus odor of him. Lately, whenever they kissed, all of their energy converged into the emancipation of touch. Touch lured them to forbidden places. Touch led them to shed propriety, baptized them in its liberating waters, then shoved them back into the world—born again. "Dayton," she yelled. Unable to wait another second, she ran toward him. They brought their lips together and kissed passionately under the spotlight of the sun, making the most of their brief time together before she had to catch the afternoon train home.

"I won't have it," Dalia said, turning on Katie Mae in anger. They were in the backyard, spreading mulch over the beds for winter. "As long as she is living in my house, I will not have her slinking around the county like a common whore, doing what I have expressly forbidden. Why don't you talk to her, tell her she can't do this to her mother?"

" 'Cause the louder ya scream, the worse ya gonna make her." Katie Mae puckered her lips and spat snuff-laden saliva onto the ground. "I don't like what she's doing any more than ya do, but tellin' her no won't stop her from doing it. She might be sneakin' around with Lollie Morris's son, but the name Morris don't mean a thing to her. And anyway," she said, slitting her eyes, drawing a bead on Dalia, "just 'cause her beau be that scoundrel's son don't mean he's the same as his papa."

"If you're trying to make me feel bad, you can't." Dalia threw down the shovel and glared back at Katie Mae. "Marion's not like his father because Walter was the one who raised him." Wheeling around, she headed for the back porch.

"That's not what I meant," Katie Mae said, her boots nipping at Dalia's heels. "Ya ain't nothing like your mama, now, are ya?"

Her lips pressed tightly together, Dalia kept on going. When she came to the porch, she took a step up, turned around, and promptly sat down. "Listen," she said as Katie Mae halted in front of her. "I'm going to write Cousin Juliet and demand she put an end to this situation. After all, she has encouraged Clara Nell with all her fancy ideas about women's rights."

"Not too long ago, I heard ya complaining about the vote."

"The big difference is that I complained quietly," Dalia said, drinking down a mouthful of air. "I didn't go around making a spectacle of myself. Anyway, the vote is no longer an issue. We have the vote now. Clara Nell can't use it as an excuse to act any way she pleases. Don't you see it, Katie Mae? Everything she does is *loud*—her manner, her clothes, her behavior. She's always screaming, *Look at me*."

"Ain't nothing wrong with liking a little attention."

"You don't think it's wrong for her to go sashaying into Copeland's with a cigarette holder clenched between her teeth, puffing away like a Broadway actress or . . . or . . ."—she stammered—"like one of those Mother Jones revolutionaries?"

"Leave her be."

"Oh, don't think I don't know what you're after."

"And what might that be?"

"You want her to be sassy, same as you."

"That's right, I like sassy."

"Don't fool yourself," Dalia warned. "She'll aim for much more than that, push too hard, go too far, and something bad will happen."

"She's sowin' her wild oats, that's all."

"But he will kill her," Dalia insisted, her voice now ripe with fear. "Kill her. I've seen it in my dreams. Sassy won't protect her, won't keep her safe. Sassy will be her undoing. It will take her away from me—forever." She stood up, her violet eyes black, glowering at Katie Mae. "If you refuse to act like a friend and help me, I'll go to someone who will."

"Go ahead, do as ya please," Katie Mae shot back. "Ya is acting as contrary as she."

"My point exactly," Dalia contended. "The apple doesn't fall far from the tree." With those words, she mounted the porch steps, marched through the back door, into the kitchen, down the hallway, and out the front door onto the veranda. Her head down, her mind frenzied, she walked until she came to the corner of Rose and Lee. He will kill her, she thought as she stomped up the steps to the boardinghouse. "He will kill her," she hissed, speckling the air with saliva.

"Who got kilt?" asked Dora, skittering to one side as Dalia plunged through the doorway.

"He will kill her."

"Oh, dear, Miz Dalia. You best come with me," Dora said, moving quickly. "Miz Frances is back in the kitchen." Their footsteps echoed down the dark, dank hallway. The strong odor of boiled rutabagas sullied the air.

"Lawrence saw her puffing away in Copeland's. Smoking in public, did you hear me?"

"Yessam."

"Edwina Carpenter saw her at the train station. She's with him everywhere. At Godfrey's on the river, Dickson's Bakery, the Suwannee Inn, the Blue Café. Everyone has seen her. She's fooling no one."

Frances Fairchild was washing dishes and didn't hear them as they passed beneath the archway. "He will kill her!" Dalia shrieked.

Frances jumped, dropped the spoon she was washing into the sink. "Dalia," she said, spinning around. "What on earth are you talking about?"

"She's sneaking around like a cheap hussy," Dalia said, her face clouding. "I bet his manhood is tiny. Not as big as this finger," she said, wiggling her pinkie. "When Clara Nell was a baby, my breasts gave her more pleasure. Where is his warmth?" She shook her head, leaned in, and motioned for Frances to come closer. "I know what he wants," she whispered into her ear. "He wants his sperm swimming inside her, wants to chain her to him, make her a mother, nursing babies—one right after the other—until she shrivels up and dies. I know what he wants. He wants to kill my daughter."

With Dora on one side and Frances on the other, they propped Dalia up, helping her to a chair at the kitchen table. "Pour her a glass of sherry," Frances said as soon as Dalia slumped down.

"*I'm going out,* she said this morning, and I said nothing, just focused on my needlepoint like Katie Mae told me. *Leave her alone,* Katie Mae said. *Leave her be. Don't tell her no. Don't show concern.* And that's exactly what I did when she asked, *Are you sewing me into your canvas, Mama?* Without even raising my eyes to look at her, I said, *It's a still life—a table, some apples, and a knife.*"

CHAPTER 43

"You look handsome in your tux, brother . . . happy," Clara Nell said.

"Thank you," Marion muttered, glancing apprehensively toward the choir room door. "What's taking so long?"

"We're waiting for Adeline. She's running a little late."

"Why? Isn't she all right?" He was nervously tapping his foot on the floor.

"She's fine, silly. You know how far away her parents live."

"She should've gotten dressed at our new place. It's right here in town."

"Yes, your new house," Clara Nell said, the memory ambushing her, sending her back to the day when she'd stood beneath the ash tree, her heart hopeful as Marion drew sketches of their tree house. She remembered how white his skin was, how thin his arms, how delicate his fingers. "You must be so happy," she said. "You have your very own tree house now." No sooner had she spoken these words than she realized the regret they carried.

"Walls are like arms," he responded, his eyes contemplating the sleeves of his black tuxedo.

"You and I . . . we could've been arms for each other," she ventured, her mind still caught in the memory. "We could've been allies." She crisscrossed her arms over the deep red bodice of her dress and gave herself a hug. "We would've been strong together."

He looked up, meeting her gaze. "Back then, I was too afraid. Afraid that if I really loved you, Mama would love me even less."

She took several steps toward him. "Why didn't you tell me how you felt? We could've talked it over, maybe worked it out."

The muscles in his cheeks drew up, as though his own regret had just slapped him. "I was too consumed with jealousy," he confessed. "Tired of you being Mama's joy, me being Mama's burden."

His honesty moved her. "The past is over," she said. "Today is what counts, and today I'm so proud of you. I want to shout out to the world: *This handsome man, standing here beside me, is my brother.*" Tears brimmed in her eyes, and she dammed them back by closing and opening her eyelids. In the aisle outside the choir room, she heard shuffling. She walked over and peeked through the cracked door. "Stragglers. The church is packed," she said over her shoulder.

"Then I better compose myself," he said shakily.

She saw his chin twitching, his glances darting toward her. "Just be happy," she said, going over to him, enveloping his hands in hers. "Remember—strong walls, loving arms, letting go."

"I'm going out," Clara Nell announced when she spotted her mother in the parlor. She wore a lime green smoking jacket over a pair of dark green trousers and had tinted her lips chocolate red. Her hair was woven in a French braid; her eyelashes were thick with mascara.

"Ever since your brother's wedding last month, we seldom see you," her mother said. "You're always gallivanting around town, coming home at all hours of the night. It's just not proper."

"And what would be proper, Mama?" she asked.

"That he call on you like a gentleman," her mother said.

Clara Nell came to a halt. "But you told him not to come here."

"When will you be back?" her mother demanded. Clara Nell made a flat line of her lips, didn't answer. "At least tell Katie Mae if you'll be back for supper. Be considerate," her mother said, spoiling for a fight, but Clara Nell knew her tricks. Before her mother could utter another word, she was out the door.

That night, Dalia slept fitfully—the dream like an omen: *She is cocooning Dayton in the silken web of her arms. Taking hold of his penis, she forces it inside her, the red hourglass on her belly rising and falling above him. He cries out as his sperm swim up her vagina and clamp down.*

"Clara Nell," she cried out, her heart palpitating like a rabbit's.

"What is it?" Walter slurred, his voice soft and sleepy.

"She didn't come home last night."

He snuffled, wiped his nose with the back of his hand. "She does this all the time," he said. "Tiptoes to bed, so you can't hear her."

"I tell you, she didn't come in."

He leaned over and clicked on the lamp. "Katie Mae's right. The more you fight her, the more she fights back."

"I didn't hear her. Didn't hear her creaking up the stairs, closing her bedroom door."

He eased himself upright, his back sliding against the headboard. "If you don't stop this, Dalia, we're going to lose her."

She heard the anger in his voice but didn't care. "You must be firm with her," she said, slinging off the covers. "You must be strong, put your foot down like a man." She saw his face grow stiff with fury.

"I refuse to be her jailer," he said.

"Didn't you hear me? She didn't come home last night," she said as she slid off the bed.

"Dalia," he said, blundering after her.

But she was too fast, already moving down the hallway. "Clara Nell, open your door this minute," she demanded, twisting the china knob, the door squeaking as it swung forward. Dawn crept through the half-drawn curtains and showed her the empty bed. "Clara Nell?" she said, her eyes searching the room. "Where are you? Walter, please prove me wrong," she said, turning toward him. "Find her. Show me she's not gone."

CHAPTER 44

"Most likely she ran away to Savannah," Dalia said. "If she prefers Cousin Juliet as a mother, so be it."

Katie Mae looked at her in disbelief. "If that's what ya really think, why don't ya telephone your cousin to see if she got there safe?"

"No, I will not," Dalia snapped. "I won't give her the satisfaction of knowing I care."

"Ya ain't being honest," Katie Mae said, moving over to the sink. She filled up a kettle with tap water and set it on the counter. "Ya ain't calling your cousin's place 'cause ya know she ain't there. The sooner ya deal with the real reason for Clara Nell's leavin', the better." She made straightaway for the hutch on the other side of the kitchen. When the cupboard drawer stuck, she gave it a hard snatch, then wiggled her fingers inside until they locked upon her favorite tablespoon, the one with the dented handle. Holding it up, she came back, pried the lid off a tin of coffee, and heaped several tablespoons of grounds into the perforated drum. Screwing the top back on, she plunked the kettle on the stove and changed the subject. "Mr. Larkin wants me to switch over to one those modern gas contraptions. A range, he calls it, but I said if it ain't broke, don't fix it."

Dalia was too caught up in her daughter to give a hoot about what Katie Mae thought of stoves. She glanced over at Ophelia, lounging like an African goddess in a rattan chair beneath the back kitchen window, her long legs stretched out, her shoes off.

"I got me a touch of the rheumatism," Ophelia said, grimacing as she flexed her toes.

"That rheumatism of yours is awfully convenient, isn't it?" Dalia said, her tone snide as a blue jay's twitter.

"Before ya go home, I'll fetch ya a jar of salve from the pantry," Katie Mae told her.

"Well, ain't that nice of ya," Ophelia mumbled, nagging at a torn cuticle with her teeth.

"Let that alone." Katie Mae humped an eyebrow at her. "Ain't no different than eating a pile of worms." She cocked her finger at Ophelia, and Dalia readied herself to hear a scolding, but the sound of perking coffee distracted Katie Mae. "How do ya want it?" Katie Mae asked Dalia. "I can't keep up with your changing ways."

"Cream and sugar today," said Dalia.

"Same for me," Ophelia said, moaning as she shifted in her chair.

Cinnamon rolls were cooling on a wire rack beneath the counter window. Katie Mae ran her finger along the edge of the pan. "Ya'll want one?" she asked, giving the pan a hard shake.

"Don't mind if I do," said Ophelia.

"I'm not hungry," Dalia told her.

Katie Mae grabbed a wide knife off the drainboard, cut around a sweet roll until it was loose, and wiggled it down the blade onto a pink-flowered plate. Next she poured the coffee, adding sugar and cream to both cups. She gave Dalia hers first, then handed Ophelia her coffee and cinnamon roll. She was pouring herself a cup when the doorbell rang.

"Who could that be?" asked Dalia, casting an anxious look through the doorway. The doorbell jangled again. "I'll go get it," Dalia said, setting her cup on the table. "I'm coming," she yelled, hastening for the foyer. She took a deep breath and gave the doorknob a sharp twist. "Merciful Lord," she muttered when her eyes fell on the telegram pinched between the young man's fingers.

"Is this the Larkin residence?"

"Yes, it is," she said, her heart pounding in her ears.

"I've a telegram here for Mr. and Mrs. Walter Larkin."

"I'm Mrs. Larkin," she said, her fingers trembling as she tweezed it from him. He pushed a ledger at her and asked if she would sign her name at the bottom. "Wait here," she said, scribbling her name, smiling mechanically. She scrounged up a nickle from a candy plate in the parlor, came back, and tipped him. After he left, she unglued the flap with her thumb and folded it back. *Dearest Mama and Daddy,* she read. *Please don't worry. I'm fine and very happy. We were married on Saturday. Will see you soon. Your loving daughter, Clara Nell Morris.* "Why?" said Dalia. "Why, why, why?" she kept repeating, her hands shaking so hard that the telegram slipped from her fingers and fell to the floor.

When Walter walked through the door that evening, Dalia was waiting for him in the parlor, the telegram in her outstretched palm. "It's from Clara Nell," she said flatly.

Tentatively, he took it from her, lifted the flap, the color draining from his face as he read. "Let's thank God she married him," was all her husband said.

Dalia seized the telegram, her eyes perusing it for the umpteenth time. "Clara Nell Morris. Mrs. Dayton Morris," she said stonily, ripping the paper up, sending the pieces flying.

"What's done is done," Walter said, squatting, picking the shreds up, crumpling them into a ball. "She got married," he said, his voice spent. "That's what young women do."

"She ran off and married him without our blessing." Dalia's voice was harsh and low.

"If we want a relationship with our daughter, we must accept what she has done. We must accept him," Walter said, going to a trash basket, tossing the scraps in.

"He's the son of my father's foe."

"But he is not the man his father was."

"No, he's even more awful," Dalia shrilled. "I've hired someone to look into his life."

"How could you?" Walter said.

"And the more I find out about him, the worse I know he is," Dalia pressed on. "On top of all his other bad qualities, he's a philanderer. *Has women all over,* the man said."

"That was yesterday, Dalia. Today, he's a married man."

Dalia threw back her head, the veins in her long neck throbbing, and let out an indignant laugh. "Do you really think being married will stop him? He wanted a virgin and all the trappings that go with it. He fed on her purity, her innocence. Now that he's had her, he'll start womanizing again, infect her with his vile diseases."

"I will not lose my daughter," Walter said.

She began to sob breathlessly, holding her hands up to her face, but he girded himself against her and for once refused to console her with his embrace.

"If ya think ya is gonna sneak around behind my back while I'm out shopping and turn this house into a mortuary, that bed of yours into a coffin, ya better think twice," Katie Mae snorted, barging into the room. She glared at Dalia, in bed with the covers tucked around her like a shroud. Striding over to the window shade beside the headboard, she retrieved a pair of sewing scissors from her dress pocket and began to snip. "This is pure foolishness," Katie Mae said, her lips pursed in displeasure. She tugged at the black fringe, and off it came. "Is death what ya want?" she asked, dangling the fringe like a woolly worm from her fingers. "Do ya want darkness and misery?" She flapped the fringe in Dalia's face. "All that crepe on the mantels and tables, those ugly black wreaths on the doors. Ain't there been enough sadness in your life already?"

Dalia seized the pillow next to her head and hid her face.

"That's right. Act like a itty-bitty baby," Katie Mae fussed. Dalia heard footsteps, a door squeaking open. "Just black dresses inside this wardrobe." With a huge sigh, Katie Mae snapped the door shut. "Ophelia told me what ya done, but I didn't believe her. Now tell me where your other clothes is."

Dalia embraced the numbness that had crept into her body and refused to answer.

"Don't speak, then," Katie Mae said, her heels thunking over the floorboards. "Ophelia, get back to the kitchen with that tray," she said, her bossy voice coming from the landing. "There ain't a damn thing wrong with the missus. If she be hungry, she can come to the table and eat. I won't let her turn life in this house into a wake."

CHAPTER 45

"It's not manicured like the house I grew up in, but I love it," Clara Nell said, throwing wide the shutters to let out the musty smell. Just yesterday, the white farmhouse on five hundred acres, just south of Samson, had been one of Nolan D. Durbin's many properties, but now it was theirs. "I'd like to paint the outside yellow," she chirped as she bounced through the large empty room, Dayton trailing behind her.

"Yellow?" Dayton said in a dubious voice.

"Pale yellow," she said, "with white trim, but instead of light blue on the porch ceiling, I want to paint it lilac, in honor of my mother's eyes." She stopped and waited for him to catch up. "Thank you for moving here," she said softly. "Living nearby will help me make amends with my mother."

"I'd like to think so," he told her, "but I fear she'll never accept me." He held his arms out to her, and Clara Nell went to him. She began to unbutton his shirt and kiss his smooth chest. He responded by kissing her fiercely—first her neck, then her lips. He was craving her now, like a drunkard craving whiskey, but she knew that over time his passion would diminish, and even as he kissed her, she feared what the future would bring.

"Let's have them over for dinner," Walter said, loosening his tie. "It's clear they want to be a part of our lives, since they've chosen to live nearby." Dalia shut the book with a snap, said nothing. "I think we can find it in our hearts to forgive her," he said, picking up his glass of red wine and finishing it with a noisy gulp.

He lurched from his chair and waddled to the hunt table, where he grabbed the neck of the decanter. The wine poured too freely. Dalia groaned. He made a comma of his body, holding out his arm and sucking in his stomach, as purple driblets spilled onto the gold carpet. "Wipe it up, Walter," she said.

Replacing the decanter on the table, he stuffed his hand into his trousers pocket and rescued a handkerchief. Bending down, he began to peck at the stains, dabbing and sipping. "I love my daughter," he persisted, "and I intend to invite her and her husband over for dinner, whether you like it or not."

"Why even mention it to me, then?" she asked—her tone cold and stilted.

"Because," he said, standing, "I wanted you to know what I had planned."

"Mr. Dayton Morris is not a gentleman."

"That might be so," he conceded, "but he is our daughter's husband, and if he turns out to be the man you think he is, then she will certainly need us."

Dalia held her head to one side, lifted her chin slightly, and stared right through him. Within seconds, the clock chimed. Six times altogether. Soon Katie Mae would be calling them to supper. Walter's face began to soften as he inhaled the lusty odor of crawfish and saffron grits, and Dalia knew that it was now she should fight him, at this moment when he was at his weakest, but she had already begun to change her mind.

After days of agonizing, Clara Nell chose a white lace dress of butterflies; her husband, a white linen suit to complement her dress. Dayton slipped two of his finest Cuban cigars into a custom-made silver cigar case and tucked them into his coat pocket. Minutes before they left, Clara Nell snipped daffodils and lilacs from the backyard, swaddled their stems in a moist cloth, and placed them in the trundle seat of their car. "This should be interesting," she said, the thin tires bumping over the rutted driveway, past the live oaks draped in moss, beyond the pampas grass planted along the front of the property.

"I'm not looking forward to it," Dayton said, turning right.

"Don't fret. Daddy will protect you," Clara Nell said, her voice jiggling as the car rocked along.

"My dear, your father can't protect himself."

"Don't underestimate my father," she rebuked him. "I'm certain it was his idea to invite us over."

"I'm sorry, darling," he said, his voice honestly apologetic. He shifted in his seat to look at her. Out of nowhere a rabbit darted out in front of them. He swerved the car violently, barely missing the ditch. "I should've hit it," he grumbled, straightening the tires. "I could've killed us." He reached for her hand, squeezed it gently.

She squeezed back, didn't speak for several seconds, then in a practical voice said, "It's a first step." Releasing his fingers, she scooted over to the window and cranked it down. They drove along in silence, the light spring air misting their faces. Patches of purple crocuses bloomed by the side of the road. Close by, a copse of dogwoods snowed a cloud of blossoms. In the middle of an empty field, Clara Nell spotted hundreds of butter-colored daffodils, as though God, on a whimsy, had decided to add a shock of color, but then her eyes fell on the collapsed roof and the solid column of bricks, and she understood why the flowers were there. "Please don't be nervous," she told him as he eased onto the main road into town. "Mama blames everyone but herself for her troubles. I don't know anything about her childhood, really—except she had a sister she adored who died too young. And then there's the story about your father stealing their land right out from under them as soon as my grandfather died. But that's her version of the past, and my mother . . ." She paused, not knowing how to go on.

"My father wasn't a thief," he said, his voice low and insulted. "My sisters know nothing about this so-called feud between our families, but we all know our father was an honest man."

"I know, dear. I know," she said.

"All I want is to avoid a scene."

"Me, too," she agreed, sliding back over the seat to him, kissing his hand.

When the knock finally came, the arched smile on Dalia's face cracked and caved inward, as though it had been held in place by papier-mâché and not the solid mortar of conviction. Her stomach heaving, the acid burning up her throat, she stalled with apprehension. "Is there enough food?" she asked Walter, her voice tense as she surveyed the array of dishes on the table—fried chicken, baked ham, biscuits, cornbread, turnip greens, pinto beans, a square of tomato aspic, and on the sideboard a pitcher of sweetened cold tea. "Does everything look all right?"

"It's all looks fine, just fine, Dalia," Walter said, turning toward her. "Thank you, dear, for trying so hard to make this meal successful—this pretty dress you're wearing and not that dreary black, the food, and the flowers—but aren't those place cards a wee bit formal?"

"I only want to show her that we accept her marriage, her new name."

"Uh-huh," he said, nodding, but she could tell he wasn't fully convinced.

"The place cards make the table look nice," she added.

"If you say so," he said. Then, clearing his throat, he tugged at the bottom of his tan jacket as if getting ready to go to the door, but instead he just stood there, his shoes tarred to the floor. "Don't do that," he snapped, when she prodded a sharp nail into his side. "I'm every bit as nervous as you are." She prodded him again, but this time gently, with the palm of her hand, and he lumbered forward, she behind him, as the second knock, more forceful, rattled the glass panes that embellished the entrance. "Sweetheart," he said, his voice jamming, as he threw the door open.

"Daddy," Clara Nell said, stepping into the foyer, avoiding Dalia's eyes.

"I've missed you so much," Walter said, folding his arms around her, hugging her to him. "Mr. Morris?" he said seconds later, as though surprised to see him. "A father never loses a daughter, only gains a son," he added, letting go of Clara Nell, extending his hand. Her stomach spinning, Dalia watched in disbelief as they shook.

"Hello, Mama," her daughter ventured.

Dalia heard the rigidity in her child's voice. "So you're a married woman now?" she said, her tone just as wooden. With a forced smile, Clara Nell nodded. "Mr. Morris," Dalia said, unable to bring herself to look at him. "Please do come in. Katie Mae has already set out the meal for us, and we should eat before it gets cold."

"Yes, it's rude to keep our newlyweds standing in the foyer," her husband said, wedging his hand against the small of Dayton's back, nudging him forward. Dutifully, the four of them filed through the double doors, then down the wide corridor.

When they came to the dining room, Dalia rushed ahead, positioning herself behind two chairs, which had place cards—*Mr. Dayton*

Morris, Mrs. Dayton Morris—on the table in front of them. "This is where I want you two to sit," Dalia said, stepping aside, nodding her daughter over. Clara Nell's cheeks reddened as her eyes fell on the place cards. Her nostrils flared. Her chin quivered, but true to form she quickly recovered. Drawing back her shoulders, she perched her fingers on the top of the chair and playfully played it like a piano. After all, she was the fruit of her mother's loins, Dalia thought, a mixture of pride and anger flashing through her. She watched as Dayton slid out a chair for her daughter, like the gentleman she knew he wasn't, and as Clara Nell, graceful as a ballerina, lowered herself into the chair.

As soon as they were all seated—Dalia and Walter on one side of the table, Clara Nell and Dayton on the other—Clara Nell bent forward, deliberately tracing with her finger the frayed edge of a bedraggled narcissus arranged in a tall vase in the center of the table. "Mama, I picked you the most beautiful bouquet of daffodils and lilacs from my garden, but I'm afraid I left it out in the car. Dayton, would you be a dear and—"

"Later," Dalia said, rudely cutting her off. "We should eat before Katie Mae's hard work turns to naught."

"Why, just look at this meal your mother planned for you," Walter gushed.

"It was Katie Mae who did the planning," Dalia said curtly. "After we've finished eating, I'll call her out from the kitchen and you two can talk. Right now she's busy with dessert. She's eager to know how married life is treating you, Clara Nell." Dalia paused, enjoyed the bitter taste of silence, as tart as the pomegranate seeds in their water glasses. "Mr. Morris," she said after several seconds, "why don't you serve yourself and your lovely wife a piece of Katie Mae's famous fried chicken, then pass the platter around?" As always, her daughter pointed to a drumstick. Dalia glued her eyes on Dayton's hand as he pierced it with his fork and put it on her plate. She followed the silver tines, once more rising upward, gleaming in the sunlight that came through the window, before sinking into a large, fat breast.

"The breast is my favorite part of the bird," he said, smiling.

"Naturally," Dalia responded, her tone acid, the muscles in her face stiff as death.

CHAPTER 46

Clara Nell was puttering around in her backyard garden. The marigolds needed weeding; the zinnias had to be mulched. It was hard being liberated, she decided as she plucked up a dandelion and tossed it into a wire basket along with the disinterred roots of others. Cousin Juliet never hinted that freedom could be so messy. Many of the dandelions had already lost their fluffy balls of seeds, which meant they would be blooming like mad next summer. She should have weeded them out earlier, but wasn't procrastination one of her quirks? She'd always done exactly as she wanted. Yes, she needed to act responsibly. Yet responsibility didn't grow on trees. A person couldn't acquire it by simply picking it like a peach. Even Dayton, who dutifully went to work each day, somehow seemed irresponsible.

Last week, she had smelled bourbon on his breath when he returned from an overnight trip to Valdosta. There was a scent of something else, too—the hint of rose water on his shirt collar. "I miss you, darling," he had said the minute he stepped through the doorway, "and I want to spend more time with you."

But here she was, alone again, digging in her garden, while he was off—traveling. Financing her life of luxury, he said whenever she complained. What luxury? she asked herself, dusting off her dirty dungarees, readjusting the frayed straw bonnet that had slipped too low on her forehead.

From the wire basket she grabbed the weed puller. She squatted and wedged its pointy end beneath the star of dandelion roots, then pressed down. Up it came. Like a surgeon extracting a cancer, she felt successful.

Almost responsible, she thought as she flung the weed into the brimming basket.

She rose slowly, tossed the weed puller back into the basket, and headed for the house. At the kitchen sink, she scrubbed her hands with a bristle brush until her nails were clean, splashed some cool water on her face, and let the warm air dry her skin. In the wide corridor, she cranked the telephone handle until she heard Daisy's voice on the other end of the line. The phone rang four times before Katie Mae answered. "This is the Larkin residence," she said, her voice practiced.

"Katie Mae, it's me, Clara Nell. What are you doing?"

"Now, what do ya think I'm doin'? Working. Bottling up remedies."

"I've been gardening all afternoon." Clara Nell hesitated, waiting for Katie Mae to ask her something. When she didn't, Clara Nell sighed and said, "He's out of town again on business, and I'm lonely. Why don't you come over and keep me company?"

"Because I got work to do. God didn't put me on this earth to do your bidding."

"If you won't come, get Daddy to."

"Didn't he drive out your way last week?"

"Then how about Mama?" Clara Nell proposed.

"She's not here," Katie Mae said. "Left on the train this morning to visit your brother in Versailles."

"Why didn't she ask me to come with her?" Clara Nell said, her tone hurt.

"You best leave your mama alone," Katie Mae warned her. "I know she had you over for dinner, but she's still upset and needs some time to sort this thing out."

"I'm dying of loneliness," Clara Nell whined.

"Don't give up the ghost just yet." Katie Mae chortled. "Now I got work to tend to. Best get going. "

There was a click, and the line went silent. Independence was lonely, Clara Nell thought. Dull and dreary. What happened to all the dances she'd wanted to go to? To all the flapper shifts she'd planned on wearing during her wild nights out?

"Oh, Mother Larkin," Adeline said, fluttering with excitement, as Dalia kissed her on the cheek and stepped inside the door. "We're so glad you came. What we have to tell you is too important. It shouldn't be done—"

"Over the phone," Marion finished, just as Adeline grabbed Dalia's fingers and began pulling her through the foyer in the direction of the staircase.

"Hold on, Adeline," Dalia said, coming to a standstill, jerking her hand free. "At least, let me say hello to my son."

"I'm sorry," her daughter-in-law said, waving her hands in front of her flushed cheeks, her breathing quick and shallow, "it's just that we're so . . . so . . ."

"Thrilled," Marion added.

Smiling, Dalia reached out to touch his arm. "And how are you, sweetheart?"

"Thrilled," her son repeated, grinning awkwardly.

"All we have to do is show you," Adeline said, moving quickly again toward the staircase. "And you'll know." But, of course, Dalia knew already. She'd known it the instant she'd heard Marion's voice last night on the phone. Now Adeline was tapping up the steps, trailing her red polished nails over the railing, with Dalia following her.

"Tell me, Mama, have you ever seen anyone so happy?" Marion asked.

"She's glowing, all right," Dalia said, peering over her shoulder at him.

At the top of the landing, they veered right. Midway down the hall, Adeline paused in front of a door left ajar. Squeezing her eyes shut, she balled up her hands and stood there trembling for a second, then, plinking her eyelids open, she pushed against the door with her palms. "Ooooooooo," she squealed as the door flew open. "Can you guess our good news?" she asked, dashing over to a baby's bed in the center of the room, wrapping her fingers around one of the spooled banisters.

"Adeline, sweetheart," Dalia said, going over, hugging her tightly. "I couldn't be happier for you. When is the baby due?"

"January," Adeline said.

Dalia shifted toward Marion, who was still standing in the doorway. "Marion," she said, walking over to him. "Congratulations, dear, I'm thrilled." Leaning forward, she kissed him lightly on the forehead. "Well, I suppose you're going to make a grandmother out of me. Do I look that old?" she asked, looking sidelong at him.

"You'll be the youngest-looking grandmother in Samson," he told her.

"You're such a liar," Dalia said with a laugh. She took his hand, and they walked across the room to be near Adeline.

"We haven't decorated the nursery yet," her daughter-in-law said, "because we want to wait until the baby comes."

"Yes, I understand," Dalia said, glancing around the room. The dull white walls were much in need of painting. She hoped Adeline would restrain herself, not clutter the nursery with too much furniture, whatnots, and lacy frills, but it was Adeline's nursery, not hers, so she made no suggestions. "I agree with you. It's best to wait until you know the gender." She reached out and touched the crib, beautiful and sturdy like Clara Nell's had been. "I myself always wanted little girls," she said nostalgically. Marion coughed. His face was coloring, his forehead frowning, but it was too late. She had already said it and she feared that he'd known it all along.

Clara Nell had often heard her father say that baiting a field wasn't sporting, but she couldn't tell Dayton this because she'd nagged him endlessly when he got home to take her hunting the following day. She could see the kernels of corn glistening in the sunlight. He retrieved a handkerchief from his shirt pocket and wiped the perspiration off his forehead. His twelve-gauge was on the ground beside him. As they bided their time under a black pine, waiting for the sound of wings whirring, she nurtured the hope that maybe this dove shoot would bring them together again.

He took another swallow from the silver flask, which went everywhere with him lately. "You won't be able to kill anything with that shotgun," he said, eyeing the barrels of the four-ten, "but still we've had fun practicing, haven't we?"

She nodded. For weeks, at her insistence, he had been teaching her how to shoot. After lining up tin cans on the fence rail behind their house, he had shown her how to take aim and brace herself before she pulled the trigger. Most of the time she had missed, but twice she had hit her target, tingling with excitement as the cans toppled to the ground.

He swilled down more liquor, wiped his hand on his mouth. Wings, beating furiously, rumbled in the distance. "Here they come," he said, standing.

They moved in closer to the cornfield, crouching behind a barricade of battered stalks. Squinting, Dayton took aim, hugging the twelve-gauge tight against his shoulder. She did the same with her four-ten. The doves scattered—breaking away, dispersing, and descending. A shot rang out. A dove fell like a piece of granite. Then another. And another. The blasts like billiard balls thumping against each other. The doves nosediving and crashing to the ground. Clara Nell aimed at one flying toward her. She fired, the shotgun whipping against her arm, but she stayed with the bird, following it with the barrel, pivoting as it wobbled through the air, hit the ground not six feet from her.

"I take it all back. You're a goddamn Annie Oakley. Now go finish it off," he said.

She was so close to the dove that she could have reached down, picked it up, and cuddled it in her hands. She was so close that she could see its veiled eyes as death waited.

"Shoot it again," he told her.

She pulled the trigger, shifted backward with the kick.

"Good shot, sweetheart," he said, heartily patting her on the shoulder. "More buckshot on its bones than meat." He belted out a laugh, the liquor on his breath hitting her. "Look," he said, pointing. "There's the feed from its gullet."

Ashamed, she stared at the mass of bloody feathers and the kernels of corn, unblemished as the beads in a necklace.

CHAPTER 47

Outside, the sky was seared white from the relentless heat. Clara Nell pulled the straw hat low over her fair skin and snubbed the sunlight as they crunched over the gravel driveway toward the car. "Am I covered up sufficiently?" she asked, halting, showing Dayton the white long-sleeved shirt rolled up to her elbows, and an old pair of his dungarees, the bottoms cut off. "No snake can bite me through these," she said, moving again, laughter just beneath her voice. "When I was a girl, Mama told me about my grandfather's turpentine camp. He named it after himself. Millertown, he called it, because he was so proud."

"Most camps are nasty places, filled with common folk," Dayton said with a shrug.

"That might be so," Clara Nell conceded. "But Millertown wasn't. My grandfather respected his woodsmen, made sure his camp was clean and neat."

"Probably why he lost everything," Dayton sniffed. "A boss should never cozy up to his workers." He opened the car door and offered her his arm.

"You're such a snob," she said, stepping onto the running board.

"No, I'm a pragmatist," he countered, shutting her in, going to the front of the car, cranking the engine.

"You're dressed like we're going to a wedding," she said as he slipped his white linen trousers beneath the steering wheel.

"I just wanted to look nice for you, my dear." Releasing the brake, he pressed the lever on the steering wheel and fed the engine gas. The Model-T lurched forward.

She stared out the windshield for any sign of life, but the drought had lasted so long that not even the birds were out. The palmetto fronds, usually dark green, were covered in powder. Dust came in through the window, sullied the air, made her cough. Pinching her nostrils, she reached out and rolled the window midway up. The scattering of hardwoods looked sooty. The tips of the pine needles were yellow and dry, the weeds beside the road parched and withered. There was no hint of color as they drove. Like a gigantic piece of unpolished silver, the land seemed tarnished. Inside the car, the air grew even hotter. Sapped by the heat, neither of them spoke. "I'm so hot I'm itchy," she said at last, breaking the silence. She scratched the heat rash blossoming on her cheeks. "Let's stop and get something cold to drink."

"Well, aren't you the little princess?" he said in a voice so smug that if she could have she would have given her heat rash to him. "Ya gonna have to wait until we get to the camp," he told her. "There's no place around here to stop."

For the next half hour, she hugged her side of the car, wondering why she'd ever married him. Last week over the phone, Katie Mae had said something that upset her. "Don't be so hard on your mama," she said. "She has her reasons for not liking your husband. Says she knows certain things about him. *The apple don't fall far from the tree. Dayton is the same as Lollie, spoiled and greedy,* she tells me. She believes he'll hurt you as soon as he gets bored." Wounded then, Clara Nell had defended him, but now she wondered how long it would take for someone so smug and self-satisfied to become bored enough to hurt her.

Through her side window, she saw a chain gang of black men weeding along the road in dusty gray uniforms. She winced at their gritty faces, could almost taste their thirst on her tongue.

"We make good use of them," Dayton commented, pointing at the men as he drove past.

"What?" she asked, her tone perplexed.

"We work prisoners like those at our camp in Florida. Lease them from the state. Have to keep them chained at night, of course."

Speechless, she moved closer to her window, gazed out.

"They help us turn a tidy profit," he said, turning sharply right.

At once the odor of pine gum ambushed her through the top half of her window, stinging her mouth, her eyes, her nose. The gleam of the metal cups beneath the cat-face pines caught her attention. Her gaze followed the brownish gray limb of a longleaf until it came to a spiderweb, spanning two of its needled tufts. Gray squirrels fussed in the coolness beneath the pine branches, and birds twittered.

"My little town in the woods," Dayton said as they bumped down the road toward the camp.

She was hoping to see a replica of Millertown, with its clean, tidy homes painted white, the vegetable gardens out back, the schoolhouse, the commissary, but when he brought the car to a stop, the ugliness of the place hit her. These shanties looked like toolsheds, with their pine-planked walls gray and buckling. There was no glass in their windows. No flowers in the yards, no marigolds or zinnias, no bright coins of color, only gray indentations in the sand. Gray seamed the faces of the brown-skinned children in filthy flour-sack britches. Gray covered the wings of crickets, dirtied a white cat in the weeds, dusted the bench near the pathway in front of the commissary.

"Can I have my drink now?" Clara Nell asked as he opened the car door for her.

A red Coca-Cola sign was tacked on the commissary wall above a bench where two elderly black men were sitting. "Good day," they mumbled, spitting tobacco juice, first one, then the other, into a coffee can on the floor between their legs. Dayton went to the screen door and pulled it back, not greeting them. Embarrassed, Clara Nell smiled at them before she crossed into a large dark room abuzz with flies. She looked at the meagerly stocked shelves lined with cans of pinto beans, stewed tomatoes, baking powder, and coffee, brown paper bags of sugar, flour, and rice, and tin tubs of lard. A few hams, covered with flies, hung from a rafter above the front counter, upon which sat a fly catcher, flies like raisins in the honey at the bottom of the glass. A strong odor of rotting onions dirtied the air.

"What can I do for you, young lady?" asked a middle-aged white man with a stubby beard.

"If it's no trouble, I'd like a Coca-Cola," she said. "A really cold one, with ice in it."

"Oh, hello, there, Mr. Morris," the man said as Dayton came up behind her. She waited for her husband to introduce her, but he didn't.

"I'm Clara Nell Morris," she said with a grin.

"And I'm John Rawlins. I run this commissary for your husband." He came out from behind the counter. "Good to meet you, Mrs. Morris," he said, stepping over to a red ice chest and raising its lid. He dunked his hand inside and rummaged around, the bottles bickering. "Will this do ya?" he said, holding up a frost-covered bottle. She nodded, tossed him another one of her grins. He popped off the bottle cap with a church key hanging by a string from the lid and handed the cold drink to her.

"Thank you," she said, the icy glass burning her fingers as she took a long, slow swallow.

"Another one," Dayton told the man.

"Last time I looked, it was ninety-eight degrees," John Rawlins said, hiking his thumb at a thermometer just inside the doorway, pulling up another Coca-Cola, giving it to her husband. Dayton took it without a word.

"Yes, it's awfully hot out," Clara Nell said, her tone friendly. From the corner of her eye, she caught Dayton, the expression on his face bored. "I'm much obliged for your effort," she said, tipping her bottle appreciatively.

"We'll take our drinks with us," Dayton said, heading for the door. "Come with me, Clara Nell. I need to go to the distillery."

"You go on," she told him as they stepped off the porch. "I'd rather be here beneath the pines, where it's cooler."

"I won't be long," he said as he took off down the trail.

The hedge of honeysuckle to her right was brown, its blossoms withered; the blackberry bushes to her left, fruitless with their barricade of thorns. Lured by children's voices, she started down a rutted, dusty pathway. A black woman, with her head down, her eyes averted, walked by her. In the distance, Clara Nell heard the rattling of a wagon, the tinkling of a donkey's bell. A woodsman called out, "Jerico," his tone bleak and defeated. In the backyards of the shanties, she saw smoke like river snakes twisting up from black iron kettles hanging over flames pitted in the sand, but when she inhaled there was no aroma, no hint of pinto beans simmering in fatback, no smell whatsoever. They could have been cooking air. The path branched off to the right, and she followed it, the tip of her shoe smacking against something hard. Glancing down, she saw the shards of a broken liquor bottle, gleaming in the sunlight next to a filthy rag.

CHAPTER 48

When Adeline patted Morse code on her round belly, Clara Nell felt jealous. She remembered her mother's lectures about the pain and indignities of childbirth, yet Adeline, peachy-cheeked and plump, was ripening into a woman and thriving. "Katie Mae says you're gonna wait to decorate the nursery," Clara Nell said.

"Yes, that's exactly what I said to your mother when she visited," Adeline said, her tone relentlessly perky. "What a waste of time it would be if I painted the nursery pink and this baby turned out to be a boy! I want the color right."

"Why, Adeline, I didn't know you were so conventional," Clara Nell condescended. Adeline looked at her with hurt eyes. "You could choose a neutral color," she added, feeling guilty, wanting to make things right, but stopped short when her sister-in-law's lips vaulted upward.

"That's a splendid idea," Adeline chirped. "I just love lavender." She paused, cocked her head, and asked, "Is it neutral?"

"Lavender's a girl's color."

"What are your thoughts on orange?" Adeline said, moving on to red before Clara Nell could comment. "Red's too audacious for a little girl, I imagine. White, though. How about white, Clara Nell?"

"I don't consider white a color at all," Clara Nell said.

"Then what about black? Everyone wears black," Adeline stated, "so I think it would be fine for boys and girls. Yet black for a baby's room would be so depressing, don't you think?"

"I'm sorry," Clara Nell said, at last catching Adeline's mocking tone. "I'm very sorry," she said, meaning it. "I don't know what got into me. The green-eyed monster, I guess."

"Envy?" Adeline said, widening her eyes.

"You and my brother are so happy, while Dayton and I . . ." Clara Nell let her sentence fade, remembering a time, not so long ago, when sex with Dayton had been powerful enough to blind them to their differences. "I know, we've been married only a short while, but already things are changing." Now their desire was ordinary, unable to lift them to a glory greater than themselves.

"The honeymoon phase is over. Every marriage goes through this," Adeline said with sympathy.

"But he's not the man I married."

Adeline leaned over and touched Clara Nell's forearm. "Believe me, Marion and I have had our little difficulties. When I told him about the baby, he wasn't as happy as I thought he would be."

"Really?" Clara Nell said, surprised. "He told me he was thrilled the other day on the phone."

"Yes, he's happy about it now," Adeline said, leaning back in the overstuffed chair. "But at first he wasn't. Complained a baby would change things."

"He's right."

"Told me he'd always dreamt of being an architect, that his dreaming days were over. He'd have to quit school, give up his drive to Atlanta, work for my father full-time. *Babies will wear us out, make us old,* he insisted, serious as a stroke."

"And what did you say to that?"

"I laughed. Called him silly. Reminded him that he could always return to school when the baby was older. I was prepared to hear him complain some more, but he didn't. Said the news took him by surprise, that's all. Clara Nell," Adeline said, hesitating for a second, looking deep into her eyes, "accept Dayton as he is. If you do this, you'll be able to build a life with him. Anyway," she said, resiliently cheerful, glancing around the drawing room, "just look at the wonderful home you've made here, just perfect for a little family of your own."

CHAPTER 49

Dalia knew the baby would be a boy. That's why she was knitting the baby blanket blue. Her daughter-in-law was meant to have a boy first, for the girl wanted only men in her life. She needed them to follow her around like acolytes. Which was what Marion was doing, worshiping at her feet, elevating her from priestess to goddess. "What do you really think of Adeline?" she asked Walter, who was soaking his swollen feet in a tub of Epsom salts.

"She's a nice girl," he said.

"That's what you say about everyone. That's even what you call that man Clara Nell's married to—nice," she said with irritation.

"There's some good in everyone. I do believe that," he said, drawing himself up. "If that's what you're referring to."

"Don't get me started on that scoundrel," Dalia said acidly. "But it's Adeline I'm trying to discuss. You must admit, the girl is silly."

"Maybe," he conceded, "but she's young."

"She's older than our daughter."

"This feels good," Walter said, wriggling his toes, sloshing water over the edge of the washbasin onto a towel Dalia had spread beneath it.

"She's going to be one of those fawning mothers who start baby-talking to grown-ups," Dalia went on, holding up the half-finished blanket. "What do you think?" she asked him.

"It's very pretty," Walter said. "If my memory serves me"—he lifted his feet up and plopped them down on either side of the basin—"you baby-talked plenty to Clara Nell."

"Really, Walter," Dalia said, stilling her knitting needles, glaring at him.

"Yes, ya did," Katie Mae said, striding into the room with a steaming kettle. "Ya done it. Miz Gladys done it, and me, too." She let out a snuffle of laughter as she poured the hot water into the basin. "We're all guilty of spoiling that child rotten."

"Why, Katie Mae, you read my mind," Walter said, checking the temperature with his big toe. Sighing, he sank his feet back into the water.

"Yessir, I figured your feet was gettin' cold."

"She's going to be using that silly voice with us, and it will drive me crazy," Dalia said.

"Leave that gal alone," Katie Mae barked. "How come ya always pickin' on somebody?"

Dalia huffed and began noisily clicking her needles. "Poor Marion," she said, "managing that store for Adeline's . . ." She stopped knitting long enough to stick her index finger into the side of her mouth. "Pop," she finished, popping her finger against her cheek. She checked their faces to see if the joke amused them. It didn't. "My son was destined to be an architect, not some stock boy. Meant to marry a strong woman, not some silly, insufferable ninny."

"Marion's happy," Katie Mae said. "I don't want to hear another word. You're not fair with that girl, not fair with Mr. Morris. Ya need to give people a chance 'afore ya go judging 'em." Pivoting, she marched toward the pocket doors with the kettle in her hand.

"I do wish everyone would quit defending him," Dalia said, tossing the blanket into a basket by her feet. "Poor Mr. Morris has begun to show his stripes. Clara Nell's finally seeing what kind of a man she married."

"Sweetheart, what are you so upset about?" Walter asked.

Dalia held her head steady and straight and looked right at him. "Katie Mae said he took her to one of his turpentine camps. Clara Nell thought it was ugly and depressing, nothing like the way I'd described Millertown. I think it showed her what an uncaring man he is."

"He's still her husband, Dalia."

"She's unhappy, and I feel it."

"You come on too strong, my dear."

"I don't even think she likes him," Dalia said, not listening. "She won't come right out and say so to Katie Mae, but my gut tells me it's true."

"When she's ready, she'll tell us."

"Katie Mae says he's never there with her. She thinks Clara Nell's lonely."

"Then set aside your pride and go visit her."

"Visit her?" Dalia said, her tone sharp and incredulous. "How can I visit her when we're not even speaking?"

"If what you feel is true, then she needs you."

"I will never set foot in that house."

"Have it your way, then," he told her. "But don't come crying to me when she closes the door on you forever."

"Don't try to scare me," Dalia threatened. "I'm not unreasonable because I choose to see the truth."

"I know, dearest. I know," he said, sighing, easing his wet feet onto the towel. "But if you're not careful, your rigidity will be your undoing."

Her mood changed, her fury spent as quickly as a summer storm, and she glanced timidly at him. "You don't have to tell me that, Walter. I know I've failed," she said, her voice breaking. "But I can't help it. If I don't stand firm, I'm afraid she'll stay with him, and he'll be the death of her."

Walter came to his feet and moved toward her. "Why don't we throw her a little housewarming party? Ask Adeline and Marion over."

She groaned. "We'll have to invite him, too."

"So, let's have it when he's away on one of his business trips."

They were quiet as Dalia fingered her collarbone, thinking. "Yes," she murmured minutes later. "We could do that."

CHAPTER 50

As Clara Nell licked the icing off her finger, Dalia thought she looked tired. Sorrow lay just beneath her smile; a trace of lines spilled from the corners of her eyes. Dalia's intuition had been right. For a newlywed, she seemed unhappy. "Another glass of champagne?" she asked.

Clara Nell did a shimmy with her shoulders. "Oh, yes," she tittered, holding out the silver goblet. Dalia upended the bottle and filled the goblet to the top. "Thank you, Mama, Daddy, and Katie Mae, for this wonderful party," she said, swallowing deeply, driblets of champagne trickling down the corners of her mouth. "And thank you, Marion and Adeline, for coming all this way to celebrate with me." She set the goblet down and wobbled upward. Going around the table, she stopped at Katie Mae's chair and hugged her from behind. "I'm so happy," she said, leaning over, trailing her fingertips over a stack of tea towels that Katie Mae had embroidered. "These are lovely. All the time you must have put into them. And Adeline, Marion, I love the table clock. It'll be perfect in my bedroom."

"Lucky for you I saw that the one you had in there was broken," Adeline said with a giggle.

"My sister has never kept up with the time," Marion threw in, shaking his head, *tsk*ing. "Drove her tutors crazy, forever showing up late for her lessons."

"Old lady Palmer was too senile to notice," Clara Nell said.

"You were awfully tardy, my dear, and a little lazy," Dalia said.

"But you're putting me to work, aren't you, Mama?" Clara Nell nodded at the basket of bulbs in the center of the table. "What's in there, anyway?"

"Mostly irises," Dalia said. "But a variety of colors to surprise you this spring."

"Thank you, Mama," her daughter said, smiling with her eyes. Then, returning to her place at the table, she bunched up a stack of dollars tucked beneath her plate. "This is your doing, Daddy, though you haven't said a word," she said, moving behind him, planting a kiss on the top of his head.

"I want to make a toast," Katie Mae announced suddenly. Sliding back her chair, she swayed as she rose, bumping against the table. "To good times," she slurred, bringing her glass to her lips, but instead of drinking, she blurted, "I miss you, my baby girl." Toppling to one side, she christened the table with champagne.

At once Walter stood. "Let's go sit in the parlor," he said, extricating the silver stem from Katie Mae's fingers. The party followed him as he led Katie Mae out of the kitchen and down the hallway. When they crossed into the parlor, he flicked a switch and the brass chandelier lit up. With his arm around Katie Mae's shoulder, he escorted her to the settee. Adeline and Marion sat down beside her, while Clara Nell lowered herself into a chair near the pocket doors. "Dalia, will you make us some coffee?" Walter asked as he slumped into his favorite wingback.

Back in the kitchen, Dalia filled the pot with water and spooned in seven heaping tablespoons of coffee. She set the pot on a burner and stacked the cups and saucers on a silver serving tray, along with teaspoons and napkins, but no cream or sugar. Muddy black was what they needed. The coffee was kerplopping, on its way to a rumble, when she heard his voice, poisoning the hallway. Her jaw set, she brusquely wiped her hands on a dish towel and hastened to the parlor.

"So you decided to celebrate without me?" Dayton was saying.

Dalia halted in the doorway. "Yes, Mr. Morris, we thought it best." She went over to Clara Nell and protectively placed her hand on her shoulder. "We didn't think you'd be back so soon from Mississippi."

"I realize that, Mrs. Larkin. Imagine my surprise when I came home to find my wife gone, my house empty, but ya'll seem to be having fun without me." He was squeezing his voice into a tight little ball of resentment, holding it under his tongue like a cough drop. A sound Dalia didn't like. "But now that I'm here, I expect my wife to come home with me."

"Dearest," Dalia said, leaning over, trying to snare her daughter's attention, "didn't you want a cup of coffee?"

But Clara Nell kept her head down.

"We need us a cup of coffee. We is a little tipsy," Katie Mae confessed, resting her head against the sofa, closing her eyes.

"Would you like a cup of coffee, Mr. Morris?" Marion asked.

Dayton moved toward his wife, didn't answer. "Clara Nell, we're leaving," he said, fixing his eyes on Dalia.

"Please, Dayton, why don't you join us?" Walter said, cupping his hands over his kneecaps, rocking forward. "This way Clara Nell can show you what we got you for the house."

"Come on, Clara Nell. We're going," Dayton insisted, impatiently thrumming his fingers against his belt buckle.

"Please, let's be civil, Mr. Morris," Walter said.

"My request is reasonable," Dayton shot back. "After all, Clara Nell is my wife."

"A wife, not a child," Dalia rejoined, tightening her hold on Clara Nell's shoulder. "Perhaps when she married you she was a child, but now she's old enough to know her own mind."

"If you're implying I acted dishonorably by marrying her, then you're wrong, Mrs. Larkin. Clara Nell was the one who lied about her age."

"My daughter is not a liar," Dalia said fiercely. Dayton took a step closer, clamped his hand over her fingers. "Sir, take your hand off me and leave my house this instant," she demanded.

"Mr. Morris," Walter said, leaping to his feet, the weight of his indignation flattening his features, "for my daughter's sake, I implore you to reconsider and have a cup of coffee with us."

"For the sake of our marriage, Clara Nell and I are going home together," Dayton said, prying off Dalia's fingers.

"You monster," Dalia seethed as he pulled Clara Nell toward him.

"Mr. Morris," Walter warned, his face a furious red when he took a clumsy step toward him.

Marion jumped up. "Let go of my sister," he said, jerking away from Adeline, who was tugging at his jacket.

"Will all of you please leave me alone!" Clara Nell screamed, breaking free from Dayton. "Each one of you wants me to do your bidding, but I'm my own woman, and I won't have it." Outraged, she threw back her shoulders. With a dismissive flick of her head, she strode through the double doors and out of the parlor. Dalia noticed that she didn't look back to see if Dayton was following.

CHAPTER 51

"I'm off," he said. Dayton had been home for only three days, but he was already leaving. He was taking the car to Mississippi. First to Jackson, then to one of his camps near a little town called Pass Christian, leaving her stuck again on this godforsaken farm in the middle of nowhere. Clara Nell had tried to tell him about her loneliness, about the phone calls during his last time away, but as soon as she opened her mouth, she felt as if cotton bolls were stuffed into it, and she couldn't speak.

"Why don't you let me come with you?" she said. She saw his Adam's apple bobbing in his throat, his eyes, neither brown nor green but some odd in-between color, veering from side to side as he struggled for the right words.

"You'd be bored," he said finally. "I'll call you and let you know where I am." With a kiss on her cheek, he strutted out the door like visiting royalty.

The last time he left, he had been gone for more than two weeks. After a week of being alone, she had been so desperate for company that she had ridden the mare into town. Perched on one of the black stools at the drugstore counter, she ordered an ice-cream sundae with cherries and flirted with Macy, but sadly he had become a stranger to her. Back home, she took a hot bath because it sometimes made her feel better. Soaking in the claw-foot tub, with bubbles up to her nose, she wept quietly, her chin quivering with self-pity. Then, slipping down, she submerged her head, wanting to disappear in the hot, soapy water. It was then the phone had rung, a muffled vibration in her ears. She pushed her feet against the tub, her back skating up the porcelain, as the phone continued to jangle, one ring after another, same as the night before and two days before that. Her feet slippery, she held on to the tub and climbed out, the phone still incessantly ringing. Grabbing a towel, she whipped it over her breasts, knotted it, and headed down the hallway. "Hello. Hello," she had said breathlessly into the mouthpiece, as water puddled by her feet on the floor. "Dayton, is it you? Who is this?" She heard a low, guttural moaning in the background, not present during previous calls. "Say something, or I'm going to hang up," she had threatened, but, like always, the familiar, humiliating click had come.

She watched him descending the porch steps, then closed the door behind him, listening to the engine cough and rumble as he drove off. Wanting to be alone with her misery, she retreated to her bedroom, where she lay down and sobbed quietly into a pillow so that Winifred, the young housekeeper, wouldn't hear her. She wished they could talk, but a barrier, like a thin piece of rubber, stood between herself and the girl.

A second month had just passed without her period. Beneath her robe, her breasts were swelling, the nipples aching whenever she touched them, leading her to think she might be pregnant. Last week, she had almost made up her mind to leave him and admit to her mother that she had been silly, willful, and wrong, but now that she'd missed another period, she was confused. She got up off the bed, walked over to the floor-length mirror, and looked at her still-flat stomach. Her thoughts were constant and contradictory. Was this the cure for their ailing marriage? The one thing that would break the silence between herself and her mother? Or would this baby be the beginning of a lifetime of quiet despair? She stood there, racked with uncertainty, her shoulders heavy with the burden of choice, little moans of doubt springing from her lips. She went to the bathroom, splashed cold water on her face, then dressed rapidly. She would ride the mare into Samson, see Doc Warfeld, and find out if what she feared and hoped for was true.

Though not cold, it was cooler with the approach of winter, and Clara Nell felt a slight chill as she walked by Maggie's, the baby shop down from Doc Warfeld's office. She paused to stare at the delicate christening gowns in the far left corner of the display window, making a cradle of her arms, pretending to be rocking a child. She was pregnant, she thought, both shocked and thrilled with the idea. She liked flower names for girls—Pansy, Lily, Iris, and Rose. She spotted a blue baseball cap with a little matching uniform on the opposite side of the window and thought about a list of boys' names, smiling, but then she remembered Dayton—gone as always, even gone when he was with her, and the enormity of her predicament bowled her over.

She pressed her hands against the glass and leaned forward, unable to catch her breath. She tried to remember what Adeline had said. Hadn't she told Clara Nell to accept Dayton as he was? Acceptance. That's what she had done her whole life—resigned herself to the inevitability of tutors, of no friends, of marriage. She breathed in, closing her eyes for a second, letting the air rejuvenate her. A baby crib on rockers caught her attention. It was sweet and beautiful, she thought, her eyes falling over its turned spooled legs.

Dalia had been pruning on and off all day and was still lopping off globs of rose petals—wounds of dried blood—when she saw Clara Nell rushing around the side of the house toward her. As soon as her feet had hit the chilly floor that morning, the anger, long in hibernation since her estrangement from her daughter, awoke. Whipping off her nightdress, she had tugged on her gardening clothes and dashed down the stairs. Seizing the shears on the back porch, she had hurried toward the rose garden—intent on making her fury work for her. "What's wrong, sweetheart?" she asked now, dropping the shears to the ground. Clara Nell wouldn't speak, just stood there crying, fumbling with her wedding rings, twisting them first one way, then the other. "What's wrong?" Dalia repeated, taking a measured step toward her.

Clara Nell breathed in, her chin twitching, and asked, "Where's Daddy? I knocked and knocked, but no one came to the door."

"He's out of town," Dalia told her. "In Atlanta on business."

"I knocked and knocked," Clara Nell complained, her lips trembling.

"Katie Mae's at the grocer's. Ophelia's at home."

"No one answered, and I thought you were turning me away forever."

"Never," Dalia said, wincing. She took Clara Nell's hands and looked hard at her. Her skin was whiter than usual, her face rounder, her eyes bleary and sad. "Why don't we go sit in the parlor?" she said, leading her by the hand. She held the back porch door open and noticed her daughter's unsteadiness as she passed through the space. "You don't look well, darling," she said, stepping over the doorsill and into the kitchen. "Would you like something warm to drink?"

Clara Nell shook her head, her eyes brimming. "I'm nervous, Mama. I just need to rest awhile."

They walked to the parlor and sat down on the sofa. Neither of them spoke. The tears spiked in her daughter's eyes and trailed down her cheeks. "Sweetheart, I can see you're upset," Dalia said. "Please, tell me what's wrong."

"Mama," Clara Nell began. Her face was strained, her voice tense. She crossed her legs, uncrossed them, crossed them again. "Mama," she faltered, keeping her eyes down, breathing in deeply, swallowing heavily. "I'm going to have a baby," she finally said.

Dalia was speechless. She gripped the edge of the sofa cushion, dug in her nails, ate her strangled cry. Be calm, she told herself. Wait for the right moment. Don't scare her. "You're pregnant, and yet you're weeping. Why do you think that is?"

"I don't know," her daughter said with a snuffle. "All I know is I'm so tired, and I don't want to think about any of it now. I just need to sleep. Could I go to my room and rest awhile, Mama? Would that be too childish of me, to be in my old bed, here in this house?"

"Not at all, my darling," Dalia said. "Come, let's take you upstairs."

Clara Nell's sleep was unsettled by a dream. *"It's your turn . . . your turn, Clara Nell," the girls are shouting. The rope snaps against the sidewalk, and she is eager to jump. As she runs toward the clicking sound, her stomach grows so round and heavy that she can barely shuffle her feet. Her legs, thick as tree trunks, are rooted to the ground. The swirling rope begins changing, swishing like the tail of a cat. The cat yowls, and she fears that it is hiding somewhere—hurt. Her huge belly dragging, she is now crawling beneath the house where she grew up, lured by the cat's mournful cries. In a pendant of sunlight slanting through the latticework, she spots a black mound of fur and draws closer to it. The three black kittens are stillborn. The mother cat looks up, her violet eyes smiling, and eats the lifeless forms.*

"Clara Nell, sweetheart, are you all right?" her mother was saying on the other side of her dream. "Wake up, darling. You're having a nightmare."

Clara Nell bolted up with a start, her breathing rapid, her face moist.

"Oh, Mama, what am I going to do?" She moaned. "I'm pregnant, and he's never home. Even when he's with me, he's a stranger. The only thing he cares about is his business. What if you were right about him all along?"

Her mother sat down on the edge of the bed. "It's not his business that keeps him away so much," she said, clasping Clara Nell's hand. "He has dozens of people who take care of that. You must know this, don't you?"

But Clara Nell didn't know what she was suggesting and shook her head.

"It's the women he sees who keep him busy," her mother said, pausing. "He has many girlfriends, my angel. That, in and of itself, is hurtful and disrespectful to you as his wife . . . but his true betrayal is unforgivable." Clara Nell made a rasping sound. "I just learned he has a mistress in Pass Christian, a Creole woman, who has been with him for years. They have a little boy. I've been told there's something wrong with him."

"I get calls," Clara Nell murmured, "but no one answers."

"That could be her," her mother said dispassionately. "Even women like her can feel betrayed."

"And me?" Clara Nell said, rounding her palms over her flat stomach. "I am his wife, carrying his child."

"A wife's he's already tired of," her mother said, her tone turning hard and cold. "A baby he'll find burdensome."

"But that's so cruel, Mama," Clara Nell said. "Isn't this child mine also?"

Her mother went over to a marble-topped bureau, picked up a brown leather folder, which Clara Nell had never seen before, and began to turn the pages slowly—painstakingly, it seemed to Clara Nell—until she came to the page she wanted. After freeing a photograph with her fingers, she held it up to the light. Then, returning to Clara Nell, she extended her arm, the daguerreotype in her palm. There was an inscription, *my beloved sister,* at the bottom. "This is my sister, Nellie Ann, the one who died so young," her mother said, her voice even. "I don't speak of her often because the memories are upsetting." Clara Nell looked down at the picture of an ugly girl. Her face was bloated, her hair fine, her eyes ghostly white. "Same as your husband, my father had his whore. Along with sin for a season, she gave him syphilis, which he passed on to my mother and the child inside her. My sister came into this world sick and unseeing. The sins of the fathers, my daughter, are visited upon the children."

Clara Nell picked up the daguerreotype, squeezing the edges between her fingers, holding it out in front of her, barely breathing. "What will we do?" she gasped, the air whooshing out of her, the warmth in her face fading, making her feel as insubstantial as fog rising off the Altamaha River, vanishing in the morning light.

"Don't worry, my angel," her mother said. "If you trust me, I'll make everything all right."

By the time Clara Nell rode the mare home, it was late afternoon. The door was locked when she tried to open it. Plunging her fingers into her string bag, she fumbled around until she found the house key. Winifred had left the curtains open, and the golden sunset spread through the windows, highlighting the quiet emptiness of the room.

In the center of the breakfast table was a plate of fried chicken, a bowl of creamed corn, some snap beans, and biscuits, which Winifred had left out for her, but she wasn't hungry. She was putting the food away when the telephone began to jangle. She held her breath and waited anxiously for it to stop. When it didn't, she headed tentatively down the hallway. "Hello," she said, her voice anxious yet timid. "This is Clara Nell Morris, the wife of Dayton Morris, the family that lives here." There was silence, the same silence she'd heard before, broken by the same low, guttural groan. "Why are you mistreating that sick, backwards boy?" Clara Nell said accusingly.

"He's a beautiful child," the voice said, self-composed. "Looks like his father. He can't hear well. That's all."

Next came the click—that familiar, unsettling little noise—that roared through Clara Nell's heart.

While Clara Nell wept in her house alone, Dalia asked Ogun, the Spirit of War, for guidance and strength. "Give me steady hands, a clear mind, and the right proportions," she said, sprinkling the dried leaves of pennyroyal into a bowl, then adding a cup of spirits of turpentine to it. She was stirring the two together when Katie Mae slammed through the back door.

"What are ya doing?" Katie Mae asked, standing in the sunroom in front of the pantry.

"Concocting a remedy," Dalia replied, giving the ingredients another stir.

"Turpentine and pennyroyal," Katie Mae mumbled, her eyes scanning the bottles on the table. "There is only one thing pennyroyal's for."

"You best leave it be," Dalia said, pouring the mixture into a pewter pitcher, trickling it down a funnel into a dark blue bottle, before stoppering the neck with a cork.

"Who's it for?"

"Shouldn't you put away the groceries?"

Katie Mae stepped over the threshold into the long, narrow room. "Tell me. Who's it for?"

Dalia thunked the blue bottle on the table and stared deeply into Katie Mae's eyes. "It's our girl, she's in trouble," she said in a voice that was low and level. Katie Mae opened her mouth to speak, but Dalia cut her off. "That man she married has a son in Mississippi, the sickly, freakish child of his Creole whore. He's no different than my papa, carries life and death in his body, and is determined to pass it on."

"But it might not work," Katie Mae told her. "The child could still come into this world, even more damaged for it."

"Not with the turpentine added to it," Dalia said, her tone stiff and cold. Inside the pantry, the air was stagnant. She inhaled deeply, felt her legs grow weak, and steeled herself .

"I won't let you," Katie Mae said.

"And who are you to stop me?" Dalia asked. "Must you always be meddling in the lives of other people's children?"

Katie Mae drew in a sharp breath and lowered her eyelids, saying not a word for several seconds, clenching and unclenching her fingers. Then, drawing herself up, she said, "I've always told ya the truth of what I see, of what I believe, and I'm tellin' ya now that what you're doin' is wrong, so wrong that I feel it in every part of me—deep in my muscles and in my bones. If you're hell-bent on doing this thing, you'll be doing it alone."

"I've made my decision," Dalia said, her lips tightening.

"I'll be gone before supper," Katie Mae stated, and left the room.

From her bedroom window, Dalia watched as a black taxi pulled into the curved driveway. Her head held high, her eyes straight ahead, Katie Mae stepped up on the running board and with a valise in each hand squeezed herself inside. Dalia averted her eyes from the window. Grabbing the bedpost, she slumped down on the mattress and listened to the taxi groaning over the gravel, speeding off.

She was staring vacantly in front of her when she noticed a rainbow of colors spinning around the room, then vanishing as quickly as they'd come. Curious, she slid off the bed and began moving toward the back window. Right then, there was another burst of sunlight, and the wall was splashed in a spectrum of hues again. Looking up, Dalia was surprised to see Gladys's crystal star, hanging by a piece of fishing line from the edge of the window. Rushing over, she wrapped her fingers around the talisman that had divined the birth of her daughter and ripped it off. Katie Mae will not get away with this, she thought as she hurled it. With a sharp crack, it shattered into dozens of diamond-shaped fragments against the wall.

The telephone rang. Furious, Dalia descended the stairs and veered left into the double parlor. "Hello," she spat into the mouthpiece.

"Mama, that woman of his called again," Clara Nell said, sobbing. "I heard the child, and it was awful."

"I'll pick you up tomorrow morning at seven," Dalia said, reining in her anger, controlling her voice. "I'll leave your father a note, explain that we've reconciled, gone off on a little trip together. I'll take care of everything, like I promised."

"Let me talk to Katie Mae," her daughter said.

"She's resting in her room," Dalia lied. "Was tired when she came back from shopping."

"Did you tell her?"

"Yes."

"What does she think?"

Dalia hesitated and then lied again. "She said you should trust your mother."

The conversation over, Dalia headed for the back porch. Taking the steps quickly, she returned to her roses and picked up the pruning shears from off the ground. So he has impregnated her, she thought, amputating a clump of crimson petals. His sperm has taken seed. She snapped the blades again, decapitating another clot. Damn him, she thought, the clippers seething. Damn him and his lust. She slammed her foot on a low-lying, spindly stem, pressed it against the ground, and severed it. "I'll not let you kill her. You'll not kill her like Papa killed Mama and Nellie Ann," she vowed, the steel blades clicking until the rose garden was a battlefield of red.

CHAPTER 52

White sand, swept clean, surrounded the little gray cabin, amid a semicircle of others on the edge of the Okefenokee Swamp near Waycross, Georgia. A funnel of smoke slithered from the chimney of a cabin, serving as the office, beside the highway. All the others were empty, except for the one that Dalia had rented. The cypress trees, losing their needles, looked like desperate scratches against the sky. It had been three hours, and though the cramps had gotten worse, the fetus refused to come. With each cramp, Clara Nell would moan, grimace, and shiver beneath the covers. "Are you cold, my angel?" Dalia asked. With eyes closed, her daughter nodded, and Dalia went over to put more logs on the blazing fire.

From outside the window came the sounds of the swamp—the gurgle of an alligator sinking beneath the brackish water, the expletives of egrets, the screeches of bald eagles—washing through the room's yellow quiet. A solitary bulb, with a red shade, dangled by a cord from the ceiling; a gray moth performed acrobatics around its dull light.

"How much longer?" Clara Nell asked, air hissing through her teeth.

"Soon," Dalia said, coming back to the iron bed.

Clara Nell shook beneath the covers. She made a face, complained, "It feels like a very bad period."

"It won't be long now," Dalia said, trying to reassure her. "Are you thirsty?"

"No," Clara Nell mumbled, as shadows flickered like bats over the yellow walls.

Dalia slumped into a straight-backed chair beside the bed, kept watch. Nervous, she dunked a washcloth into a bowl of water on the bedstand beside her, wrung it out, and wiped off her daughter's brow. She smiled at Clara Nell; her daughter grimaced back. "Are the cramps getting worse, my darling?"

Clara Nell nodded, let out a weary sigh. "I'm tired."

"Be my strong girl for just a little bit more," Dalia told her. Clara Nell drew in her chin, grabbed the sheets, and squeezed them tightly. She trembled again, then was still. Dalia asked her to roll onto her side. Beneath her body was a mustard-colored blotch—not what Dalia expected. "Rest now," Dalia said, helping her daughter lie back.

Standing, Dalia walked over to the kitchen area on the other side of the room. She filled up a kettle with tap water and put it on the wood-burning cookstove, hot because she had just stoked it. She tucked some chamomile leaves into a tea ball and waited for the water to boil. She wandered through the cabin's two rooms. The grain in knotty pine walls bled through the yellow paint. There was a red-and-gold-braided rug on the floor beside the bed. Red gingham curtains hung from the windows. The cabin was plain but clean—its location near town but far enough out to be private. Dalia went to the bathroom, used the toilet, the seat shaking when she flushed. She washed her hands in cold water, as there was no hot, and returned to the kitchen. The kettle was rumbling. Her tread tired and heavy, she walked back to the bed. Clara Nell's eyes were closed, her face contorting, then falling limp, like clothing being wrung out, then hung upon a line. Finally, the kettle hissed, coughing steam from its spout. Dalia poured in the hot water and waited for the tea to steep. As she reached for the bowl of sugar, she saw two palmetto bugs squeezing between the back of the cabinet and the wall. She shuddered. She had always despised them. They might be called palmetto bugs, but they were big black roaches all the same. Abandoning the sugar, she stirred the tea and blew on the smoking cup. An owl's hoot filled her ears, and she glanced out the window, surprised that it was dark. How many hours had it been now?

Clara Nell whimpered. Picking up her cup, Dalia rushed over. "It hurts," her daughter said.

Dalia thumped the cup on the bedstand, seized the washrag draped over the edge of the bowl, and swabbed Clara Nell's forehead, dotted with beads of sweat. Her cheeks were flushed, and her body shook violently beneath the covers. Dalia pressed her hand against her daughter's cheek, quickly withdrew it. The girl was burning up. Flinging the washrag onto the table, Dalia folded back the covers, slid her fingers beneath her daughter's legs, and felt a slight wetness. She checked her fingers. Blood. At that moment, Clara Nell cried out. Startled, Dalia jumped. Her daughter dug her fingernails into the mattress. "Soon. Soon," Dalia said.

Dawn shone in raucous pinks through the window. Dalia blinked her eyes against the light, lifted up her face, pillowed in her arms on the side of the bed. She looked at Clara Nell, asleep and breathing softly. It's over, she thought with relief, coming to her feet, yawning. She would bring her daughter home, and they would begin again as a family. This time, she would protect her. Like the crow, she would be a good parent—wings keeping her daughter safe.

She came to her feet, hugged herself in the cold. She rekindled the fire before using the toilet. From a metal bucket, she pulled out twigs and newspaper, struck a match from a box on the counter, and started a blaze in the cookstove. She would heat up some water and bathe her daughter. She filled up a kettle and set it on a burner. Afterward, she would brew a pot of coffee, scramble three eggs soft, the way Clara Nell liked them, and butter slices of Katie Mae's sourdough bread, brought from home. The water in the kettle was beginning to boil. She'd keep it on the stove a few more minutes, she decided, her shoulders slumping as the fear that had kept her body rigid began to ease.

"Oh, God, Mama!" Clara Nell yelled.

Dalia wheeled around and saw her daughter's body whiplashing upward. She raced over to the bed. "What's wrong, sweetheart?" she asked, her voice urgent.

"It's . . . it's starting . . . again," her daughter said. "Please, make it stop."

Hours passed, but the pain would not. Dalia slid the soiled bottom sheet out from beneath her daughter's body. She examined the stains but wasn't sure what she was looking for. She shredded the bedding and burned the strips of cloth in the fireplace. Reaching into her dress pocket, she pulled out the name, address, and telephone number of a man in Waycross who could take care of things if her remedy failed. "Mr. Kelley on Third Street," she read aloud as she slipped out the door to use the telephone in the office.

In wire-rimmed glasses, Mr. Kelley reminded Dalia of a bank clerk. He was clean-shaven, dressed immaculately, and was very efficient when he counted the money in the envelope she gave him. His nails were clipped and scrubbed, and he reeked of rubbing alcohol, ammonia, and disinfectant. Which was as it should be, Dalia thought, watching as he unfolded the felt cloth that contained his instruments. "Water is boiling on the stove," she told him, but he shook his head, waved the statement away.

"I keep my tools clean," he said, his tone supercilious. He slipped on a white smock, which hinted of bleach, and buttoned it up over the suit he was wearing. Then, pursing his lips, he pulled back the bedcovers, raised her daughter's nightdress, and began to press on her abdomen with his fingers.

Clara Nell let out a groan.

Mr. Kelley took a clean cloth off the bedstand, sprinkled ether from a bottle onto it, then held it beneath Clara Nell's nose. "She may need more of that once I begin," he said. "If you'll give it to her, the way I just did, it would be quite helpful." Picking up a sharp instrument, he looked at Dalia. "Shall we begin?"

She nodded at him and looked away. "It's over now, my angel," she said, following the path of a cockroach as it scurried beneath the bed.

Mr. Kelley had been gone for only a few hours when Clara Nell touched her stomach and began to moan. Dalia placed another hot water bottle between her legs, fed her spoonfuls of beef broth, and made her sip chamomile tea. Rubbing her forehead with the tips of her fingers, she lullabied her back to sleep. Still, Clara Nell wouldn't get better. On the third day, when the red lines began snaking down her daughter's belly, Dalia ran to the office and made two calls—the first for an ambulance, the second one to Walter. "You must come to the Waycross hospital," she told him. "Hurry. Our daughter is very ill."

The nurses came and went, wearing surgical masks to minimize the foul odor in Clara Nell's room. The walls bred shadows. Dalia understood the ferocity of the battle between the light and the dark. Streaks crawled over her daughter's stomach, as if some monster were digging its way out of her womb. Clara Nell cried out, fingernails eating into the mattress, toes pressing down, her spine bending upward. Then, just as quickly, it seemed the pain subsided, relaxing its claws as the monster swallowed. "Mama, please let me live," she said, lifting her arms, panting.

"Sweet angels don't die," Dalia said soothingly. "Rest now, darling, before Walter comes to take you home. It's such a warm night for late fall," she said, just as a nurse came into the room. The nurse mumbled something, but Dalia wasn't listening. "You know we always took care of you. Remember how I bathed you in milk, put you in a tub of cold water when you got too hot? Walter said I was such a good mother."

Clara Nell's face quivered. She let out a cry, and it rolled toward Dalia. The sound was unbearable, as though coming not from her daughter but from another species with a language of its own. Dalia pressed her hands against her ears and waited for the cry to be over. There was a lull, followed by rapid, short breaths and a silent opened-mouthed scream. Dalia swept the air in front of her, brushing the scream aside. Again the monster swallowed, and silence came.

Clara Nell opened her eyes minutes later. "Mama," she whispered.

"What is it, my angel?" Dalia asked, leaning over, feeling her daughter's breath against her cheeks.

"Can you see them?" Clara Nell said, trying to lift herself up. "Gold and black specks buzzing toward me." Falling back against the pillow, she looked into her mother's eyes. "Not one bee sting," she said, her lips trembling with pride.

"No, darling, not one bee sting," Dalia replied.

CHAPTER 53

The church services had been brief, attended by no more than twenty people. Dayton had come early, leaving after the eulogy. Katie Mae was there, too, discreetly in the background, keeping her distance from Dalia. The air inside the church had been sweet, brimming with lilies and roses, strong enough to camouflage the scent of death, but it wasn't death that filled Dalia's nostrils now. It was that which comes after. It was decay, rising up from the dark red hole as they lowered Clara Nell's coffin into the ground.

Standing there with her hands clasped in front of her, Dalia heard the *thunk, thunk, thunk,* as the clumps of red clay scattered like fists of roses. She breathed in, hoping for the sweet fragrance of the Cherokee, of the Mr. Lincoln, but instead she smelled her daughter's putrid flesh. *Thunk, thunk, thunk.* She took another breath. This time, the air was guiltless. Relieved, she watched through her gauzy veil as the minister spoke to Marion and Adeline. Walter was reaching for her when she suddenly smelled the stench again. "I'm too vile for you to touch me," she said, jerking her hand away, but his fingers, like pincers, kept nipping at her, his mouth kept moving, speaking to her of love, his eyes of forgiveness.

But he could not absolve her of her sins. "She loved you. She knew you adored her," he repeated, wounding her with his kindness.

She walked away from him, moving swiftly down the path toward the church. Feeling a hand on her shoulder, she turned quickly. "Walter, don't—" she started to say, but it was Marion.

"Mama, please stay with us," Marion said. "Let's all walk together."

"You don't smell it, either, do you?" Dalia asked.

"Mama, please."

"I know Walter doesn't. Adeline doesn't. None of you do. All I have left is the smell of death."

"We have our memories," Marion said, his chin quivering. "Our memories will keep her alive."

"Clara Nell," Dalia whispered, closing her eyes, finding her daughter—plump and rosy, nursing greedily at her breast; furiously pedaling her red tricycle over the grass; smelling of cigarettes in Dalia's old black dress; writhing in pain, reeking of death. "No!" Dalia said, opening her eyes. "Memories won't bring her back. My child is gone."

"But I'm still here, Mama," he said, offering her his hands.

"And why . . . why are you here when she's gone?" Dalia heard the accusation in her voice. She saw the deep pain in his eyes, but still she could not bring herself to touch him. "Just leave me alone," she said, drawing the black cape around her shoulders as she fled down the trail. When she came to the wrought-iron gate, she unlatched it. It creaked open, and she went through, following the brick path, slick with dew, toward the unpaved road and the waiting car.

"Miz Dalia," a voice called out. Out of the corner of her eye, Dalia spotted Katie Mae rounding a hedge, coming toward her. "I want to talk to you," Katie Mae said, taking a ragged breath.

"Why would you want to speak to me," Dalia said, "when I never listen to you?"

"This is a day to grieve for our baby," Katie Mae said, shaking her head, "not for judgments or harsh words. All I wanna do is wrap my arms around you, like always."

"If you touch me, you'll be damned, tainted with this horrid smell."

"That's your grief talkin'," Katie Mae said. "I'm still here for you."

"You always have been," Dalia told her, "but there's no comfort you can give me now. I must protect you this time. Let you start over at Snake River. Please, take care of yourself for once." She began walking, her heels clicking rapidly, toward the broad black door that the driver from the mortuary held open for her.

Dalia lay beside her husband, the smell seeping from her skin. It had been weeks since she had buried her daughter, and every day she had washed herself over and over, but the malodor of her sin remained, turning bread into pus and water into blood. Everything she touched—decayed.

"Please try to sleep some, my darling," Walter said. "It's early yet, and you need to rest."

"I cannot sleep, and I cannot cry," she told him.

"I have cried enough for both of us," he said. "I have shed enough tears to fill an ocean."

"You must cry louder, longer, and harder if you want to bring her back."

"All the tears in the world won't do that, my darling."

"Then I'll go to her," Dalia said, "and she'll rise like a winged angel and strike me dead." She felt his fingers grabbing at her nightgown as she slipped from the bed. She rushed over the landing and down the staircase, hurrying through the double parlor, the dining room, and into the kitchen, looking for Clara Nell. But there was no sign of her daughter, no life in the house, no hint of food in the air. No coffee brewing, no biscuits baking. The ashes were cold in the cookstove, the cupboards bare when she drew them open. No whiff of nourishment to feed her grieving soul—only the vile smell oozing from her body.

She went to the sink, picked up a dishrag, and began wiping off the counter, following the grain in the wood, but there were no crumbs on the wooden surface, just the rag in her fingers, soiled by her flesh as it decomposed. She left the filthy thing in the basin, headed for the pantry, and flung open the door, her eyes alighting on the rows of blue bottles, one right after another, shelves upon shelves of them. *Pennyroyal, pennyroyal, pennyroyal,* written on every label in her round murderous script. From a barrel at the back of the room came the sharp, loud odor of turpentine. It brought tears to her eyes, made them sting and water. She choked on the omnipresent smell and felt better.

He was behind her saying, *Dalia, Dalia, Dalia,* like a curse in her ears.

"I smell the turpentine now," she said gratefully, turning toward him, "and not that awful odor."

"There is no awful odor, Dalia. Only the scent of rosin."

She took his arm and pulled him through the kitchen, then out the back door and onto the porch, where the foulness rose off her skin again. She held her hands beneath his nose. "Breathe in," she told him. "Can't you smell it?" He was staring wide-eyed at her, shaking his head. "There is no smell," he insisted. "Nothing, my darling."

"Nothing?" she reproached him. "It's not the nothingness of death you smell, Walter, but that which comes after—the decay of my sins. I wanted to be a crow," she said, confusion in her eyes. "Crows are good parents. They sleep in separate nests, but I crowded out my daughter and pushed her to her death."

He took hold of her hands and clutched them tightly. "We loved her," he said. "We weren't perfect, but we did our best."

"Our best?" she echoed, wanting to believe him.

"Yes, my darling."

"When she got too hot, I bathed her off in cold water, didn't I?"

He nodded, squeezed her hands again.

"And I got tutors for her, so she could be safe?"

"Yes, darling, you protected her."

She tore her hands from his. "Then why is she dead?" she said. Opening his arms, he came toward her. "I wanted to be a crow," she said, stepping back, "but scavenging is all the crow I have inside me. Oh, Walter, where is she?" she asked. Looking up, she began to pivot slowly, her eyes searching for the *ti bon ange* that had escaped her daughter's body, finding only dappled shadows in the weak morning light.

CHAPTER 54

Dalia held her hands to her face and wondered where the smell had gone. For weeks it had been so much a part of her world, breathed in like oxygen flowing through her veins. Yet this morning it was not there, replaced by an emptiness far more unsettling. She wrapped her arms around her body and stared blankly into the darkness of her bedroom, the draperies shut, the shades pulled low, thinking that life was no more than the glistening dew on a spider's web, gone in the hot morning sun.

She could hear Walter downstairs in the kitchen. The faint sounds below made the silence in her room even lonelier. She wanted to go to him. She wanted to tell him that the stench had disappeared, but could not find the strength to move from her bed. Should she reach out for the porcelain bell on the nightstand? Should she call to him? If she did, he would come. Walter always came when she needed him. He would be relieved about the smell. How did it happen? he'd ask her, but Dalia wouldn't know the answer. Had the last bone in her daughter's body crumbled into dust? Had her sweet spirit finally risen? She didn't know. The weight of these thoughts pushed on her chest as she tried to grasp the bell, but her fingers were inert and leaden.

She felt a sadness creeping through her. A sadness heavier than her grief, an unutterable sadness that cut a hole right through her. A sadness more intense than the stench had ever been. She made a final effort to raise herself. Leaning over, she tried again, her fingers brushing against the curved porcelain surface, and watched, paralyzed, as the bell tumbled downward and shattered upon the floor. It was then she began to cry, at first quietly, but then loudly. The cry fed on the last bit of strength inside her, growing bigger and bigger, until it was something anguished and foreign, something from the soul of a woman not human, something from the devil herself.

Walter came rushing through the doorway toward her. He was touching her, speaking to her, but now that the tears had started, they wouldn't stop. "Dalia. Dalia," he was saying, "you're finally crying, my darling." She heard the hope and fear in his voice; and while she wanted to speak, this sadness wouldn't let her. Words were insignificant now that all trace of her daughter, even the smell of her death, was gone.

"Mama," he said, and she looked up. "Mama, please drink some tea. You've not eaten in days, and Dr. Warfeld says you need nourishment."

The face in front of her seemed very far away. The lips were moving, but though she heard the words, they held no meaning.

"Dad is worried," he said. "He doesn't want them to send you away."

She had finished her life, she thought. She was done with it. Let it fly off, like a bit of paper trash in the breeze.

"He says you haven't stopped crying for weeks, that you won't talk to him."

She turned her head and stared at the dark, empty wall.

"Please, Mama, drink some tea. Say something. Anything. If not for me, then for Dad."

We live. We die, she thought. Our lives are loss and longing.

His fingers were beneath her chin, coaxing her face toward him. Pressing the cup against her lips, he urged her again to drink. "I beg you, Mama, take some nourishment. Do it for your family."

At last, she summoned some strength. "My family is dead," she whispered, pushing the cup away, weeping uncontrollably into her hands.

EPILOGUE

The hours inside Milledgeville State Hospital pass slowly. Nothing is left to chance. The atmosphere is safe and repetitive. Only the occasional outburst of a patient breaks the dull routine and disrupts the invading grayness. In the dayroom, the patient with the violet eyes leans forward on the hard bench, perches her elbows on the ledge, and stares out the window. It is what she has done almost every day for seven months now, preferring this solitary bench to the company of others. Except for those times when she goes to the bathroom, the dining room, the room where she sleeps, she is always there.

Nurse Hendricks rolls a medicine cart down the wide corridor toward the woman with the violet eyes. Above her starched white cap, a globe light flickers. The blades of a ceiling fan whine through the hot, heavy air. In an office off the hallway, a phone is ringing. The medicine cart creaks over the black-and-white-tiled floor, but the woman with the violet eyes acts as though she doesn't hear it. Bringing her cart to a stop, the nurse plucks up a thimble-sized paper cup with two yellow pills. She gives the patient the pills and a glass of water. The woman swallows them. "Good girl," Nurse Hendricks says as the violet-eyed woman turns back to the window. The nurse wonders why the view fascinates her when only a wall of stark red brick lies beyond the pane of glass. Shaking her head, Nurse Hendricks leans into the cart and pushes it toward the other side of the dayroom, where a frizzy-haired woman in a cushioned chair is peering out another window.

Above the hospital grounds, a few gray clouds have begun to gather, though the sun is still shining brightly against the dark red brick buildings, making them shimmer in the August heat. Just as the clock strikes three, Nurse Hendricks hands the frizzy-haired woman her medicine. "Good girl, Vita," she says before hurrying off with her cart to tend to other patients.

At four, the visitors come straggling in. There are those patients who never get visitors. The frizzy-haired woman is one of them. This is not the case with the woman with the violet eyes. Every two weeks, Nurse Hendricks greets her husband, a round, sweet-faced man, and the wiry black woman who keeps him company on the long drive over. Once a month, her son pays her a visit. A few times, he has brought his wife and baby boy, but the patient pays no attention to any of them, just sits there focused on the red brick wall beyond her window. The visitors are gone by six when dinner is served.

"Have some cold tea, Dalia. Plenty sweet with sugar," Nurse Hendricks says. She presses the glass like a kiss to the patient's mouth. The patient tilts her head back and sips. "Would you like a spoonful of lime Jell-O?" she asks as the violet-eyed woman swallows. "I don't blame you for not eating that nasty fish." The patient sniffs the air, scrunches up her face. "Still, I'd be happy if you could bring yourself to eat a little something. You need to keep up your strength." After several more mouthfuls of Jell-O, the violet-eyed woman returns to the dayroom and her window.

Black clouds are now stampeding across the sky. Lightning strikes and thunder roars, as sunlight inks to shadow. The violet-eyed patient watches the rain pummeling down, stares at it as if it's the only thing she sees, as if the pinging is the only sound.

In this way, the late afternoon passes into evening, when it is time for Nurse Hendricks to go home. While she is off duty, the patients will do random things. Some will play checkers. Others will work on jigsaw puzzles at the round oak tables. A few will read magazines, but Nurse Hendricks knows without a doubt what two of them will be doing. Dalia Larkin and Vita Morgansen will be staring out their respective windows into the darkness until they are called to bed.

The next day, the sweet-faced man and the black woman come for their visit. As usual, they are punctual, arriving at four o'clock. Nurse Hendricks watches them from the other side of the dayroom, hoping to see some reaction from Dalia—a smile, a frown, a nod—but though her husband is loving, touching her on the cheek, once trying to kiss her, she is as still as a statue. After a while, he gives up and sits back in his chair, but the black woman is relentless. Her lips keep moving excitedly, her hands gesture as she speaks. Once, when the patient turns away, she clamps her fingers on her shoulder and forces her back around. Later on, she picks up a picnic basket, unlatches the top, and brings out a small plate of fried chicken. There is a plate of biscuits, too, but Dalia ignores the food and returns her gaze to the window. "So you're not hungry for my chicken," Nurse Hendricks overhears the black woman say. "I'm gonna have to go to the kitchen and meet that cook who's keeping your belly full."

Nurse Hendricks smiles and shifts to check on Vita, who is staring out her window. The sight of her, sitting alone as always, troubles her. Her soft-soled shoes sucking the tiled floor, Nurse Hendricks heads back down the corridor, veers right, and enters the nurses' station. At the end of her desk is a large clay bowl filled with apples. She grabs it and goes back to the dayroom. "Here you go, Vita," she says, holding out the bowl. Vita grins and takes an apple.

Nurse Hendricks sees the sweet-faced gentleman crying softly as he and the black woman depart down the hall. Embarrassed, she looks the other way, spotting the plate of fried chicken left behind on the bench. That food needs to be put away, she thinks, setting the bowl of apples on the windowsill. Before she can take a step, the frizzy-haired woman leaps to her feet and pushes the bowl off the ledge. It breaks into a dozen pieces, and the apples roll wildly across the wide floor. Nurse Hendricks is half angry at Vita and half angry at herself. It has been over a month since her patient has given in to her breaking and gathering obsession, but here she is on her hands and knees, her fingers fast and efficient as she picks up the clay pieces and frantically slips them into her dress pocket until every single fragment is retrieved.

That night, it is very hot. The end of summer. The season of restless spirits. In white nightdresses, the violet-eyed woman and the frizzy-haired woman look like ghosts as they float up and down the corridor, saying nothing to each other as they pass, yet there is something in their studied avoidance, a slight tilt of the head, a little sidestep here and there, that betrays them.

During the last week of August, Dalia's son comes for his monthly visit. He appears more jittery than in times past. As usual, Nurse Hendricks escorts him down the corridor while he asks about his mother and she answers as best she can. His mother is doing better, she tells him, though she stays by herself too much. She is eating more, she says, but not enough. They come to a standstill a few feet from the bench. Nurse Hendricks waits for the young man to move forward, but instead he clears his throat and fiddles with his glasses. Finally, he looks sheepishly at her and asks if his mother will ever get well. Nurse Hendricks is quiet for several seconds. "Melancholia is unpredictable," she says. "We must keep our spirits up. Be hopeful." Nodding, he smiles at her and begins his journey to his mother's bench. He lowers himself beside her, but same as always she acts as if he's not there.

Although weeks have passed since the incident with the bowl of apples, Nurse Hendricks still sits with Vita for each and every meal. The frizzy-haired woman eats very fast and leaves her bowl so clean it sparkles. The white empty bowl must be tempting, Nurse Hendricks thinks, watching the smile grow on Vita's lips. She glances up to see how Dalia is doing, but she has already left the dining room, her food barely touched, aside from a bit of Jell-O. Nurse Hendricks returns her attention to Vita, but she and her soup bowl are now gone. Within seconds, she hears a crash coming from the dayroom, and, rising, she walks briskly toward the noise.

She sees that the bowl has shattered near Dalia's window. As Vita drops to her hands and knees, two patients nearby hurry off. Crawling across the floor, her fingers scrambling, Vita picks up the pieces and inserts them into her dress pocket, but then she stops, glancing from side to side, as though hunting for a missing piece. She leaps to her feet, her eyes frantic as she searches the floor near the bench. Dalia is leaning forward, her fingers inching over the windowsill toward the porcelain fragment. She grabs it and stands, a strange expression flitting over her features.

Alarmed, Nurse Hendricks begins a slow, cautious walk toward her. "Dalia," she says when she spots the thin trail of blood snaking down her wrist, "why don't you give that to me?"

But Dalia shakes her head and takes a step toward Vita. Extending her arm, she opens her palm. Smiling, Vita plucks up the porcelain fragment and drops it into her pocket. "This is my lifeline," Dalia says, tracing the blood that crisscrosses her palm.

Gently, Vita takes hold of Dalia's hand and leads her across the room. "Sit in my chair," she says, "and look out my window." Dalia does as she is told.

Nurse Hendricks walks up behind them, looks down to see what is going on. Vita is playing with the porcelain pieces in her pocket, while Dalia's lips are curling upward. Confused, Nurse Hendricks glances out the window, then back at Dalia, whose smile continues to grow. She steps up to the glass, pressing her face against it, unable to understand why those few red brick buildings and that old longleaf pine should affect her patient so.

Weeks pass, though less slowly for Dalia now. While Vita naps in the afternoon, Dalia stares out her friend's window at the longleaf pine. Every time, she sees something different. It is so beautiful, she thinks as she sits there, following the ancient limbs, which spread upward and outward, with their tufts of needles swaying in the breeze. Today she hears a tapping sound and to her delight spots a woodpecker, bouncing as it drills its beak into the scaly gray trunk. *Sure to be an old tree, if that bird is around,* she remembers her papa saying. She closes her eyes and imagines drifts upon drifts of longleafs, tall and evenly spaced, the endless piney woods. She feels the thrum of its energy. The gnats dipping and bowing, bestowing pinkeye during the day. The mosquitoes, drawing blood at night. She imagines the cry of gopher frogs, the serenade of Bachman's sparrows, the screech of owls. She opens her eyes to the longleaf, its strong branches piercing the blue vault of sky, and recalls her father's words: *The piney woods can be lonely. The woodsman's life is hard.* She breathes in the sharp, fresh smell of turpentine, remembers barrels brimming with gum, rows of dots on the tallyman's sheet, a chipper yelling, *Millertown.* She recollects the sounds of raking and scraping—the woodsmen hard at work among the trees. *Coarse and common,* her mother had called them. Rough but honest work, Dalia thinks. She envisions Nellie Ann bending over a stream, her eyes white but seeing. She remembers a heron floating upward like a ghost from a stump in the Snake River.

A salmon sunset now bleeds through the window. Dalia spots a pine cone, tight as a baby's fist, hanging from a branch of the longleaf. My

Clara Nell, she thinks, her mind drifting into sadness, and for the first time in many days she returns to her bench, to the window looking out on the redbrick wall, to a view with no pine.

During the last few visits from Walter and Katie Mae, things have changed. Dalia knows this, and so do they. As she acknowledges them with brief looks and shy smiles, their excitement grows. They keep asking Nurse Hendricks for an explanation, but she cannot give them one. Neither can Dalia, who wishes she had an answer for the way she is feeling—a little more aware of her surroundings, a little more awake every day. Katie Mae has lost a tooth up front; the hair around her temples is grayer. Walter has grown rounder through the months. Nurse Hendricks seems to enjoy them whenever they come, and they come more often these days.

Today Katie Mae unlatches the picnic basket, which she always brings with her, and takes out a slice of apple pie. Dalia leans forward, catching a whiff of the cinnamon-sweet fragrance she remembers, and before she knows it, she is forking up a mouthful. "It's still good, ain't it?" Katie Mae asks her.

Dalia nods and swallows.

"It's still my favorite, as you can see," Walter says, patting his stomach, "but I promise to lose some weight when you come home."

Dalia digs her fork in and eats more, chewing slowly, savoring the flavor. "I think it's one of my favorites . . . isn't it?" she says tentatively.

Her dark eyes sparkling, Katie Mae brushes her lips against Dalia's forehead, and Walter trails his fingertips down her cheek, but though Dalia wants to return their caresses, there is a cold spot inside her that won't take the risk. A cold spot she both embraces and pushes away. A cold spot that has stolen into her heart, freezing the muscle—its valves and chambers.

The days pass into autumn. The leaves begin to change colors, and it grows cooler outside. Soon Dalia will be going home, but what will she do with this coldness if it goes with her?

"I'm gonna have to leave my little house at Snake River and help Ophelia get yours in order. Ya know how that woman cleans," Katie Mae says, looking sidelong at Dalia. "If I'm not there to fuss at her, the house won't be ready when . . ."

"I come home," Dalia finishes, her eyes hopeful.

"Marion has been wanting to see you," Walter says, glancing shyly at her, "but he's been busy taking inventory for Adeline's father. He's coming this Friday, though, before we take you home."

"Yes, this Friday," Dalia echoes.

"Such foolishness," Katie Mae snorts. "That boy could've taken off some time. He's married to the boss's daughter. Needs to get him some gumption. Should take a chance and speak his mind."

Take a chance, Dalia thinks, mulling the phrase over as she watches her family go. Marion shies from taking chances. Life has always scared him so.

Early Friday morning, Nurse Hendricks helps Dalia pack. "Dalia," she says, folding the last nightgown over, tucking it inside the front flap. "They need my help on the second floor, and I'll be up there for hours. May I hug you now, in case I miss you at noon?"

"I appreciate all you've done for me, for all of us," Dalia says.

Nurse Hendricks closes the lid of the suitcase, presses it down with one hand, and latches it shut with the other. "I know you'll only get stronger," she says, moving toward Dalia, hugging her close, "because you have a wonderful family to go home to."

"Yes, I know," Dalia says into her starched white collar. "But where's Vita?" she asks, stepping back.

"She says she's tired and needs to rest," Nurse Hendricks tells her, "but she knows you're leaving, and she's sad. She's more fragile than she appears."

Dalia looks out Vita's window one last time. The longleaf is both sturdy and fragile, she thinks—surviving every natural hazard, every insult at man's hands, its roots digging beneath these ugly red buildings, its limbs growing tall enough to reach the light. But it needs company. Other pines nearby. She hears a chattering noise, moves closer to the pane of glass, and looks down upon a yellow-gray fox squirrel, fussing loudly as he tries to tear the husk off a pine cone. With his sharp teeth and claws, he pulls at the outer hull, working hard to get at the seeds inside, but try as he might, he can't. The pine cone resists him. Poor thing, Dalia thinks, just as she spots dozens of pine cones scattered in the grass. Most are fists, balled up tight, yet there is one with its husks unfolding. It is then Dalia remembers her papa's story of how the piney woods were born. *The pine cones have seeds deep inside them, waiting for thunderstorms, lightning strikes, and brush fires. If too hot, the blaze will burn them to ashes, and there will be no seeds, no saplings to sprout up. Most often, the brush fires are gentle—only singeing the pine cones, unfurling their husks, letting the seeds fly free like ashen fireflies shimmering in the heat, before falling to the earth. The risk of fire must be taken for a clan of longleaf pines to grow. Saplings born of chaos and order. A seed within a seed.*

Smiling, her daughter-in-law holds the baby out for Dalia to see how much he has grown. "Miller is a chubby little fella, isn't he, Mother Larkin?" Adeline says.

"He sure is," Dalia agrees.

"And Marion's so good with him," Adeline bubbles. "He gets up during the night if he's crying and talks to him until he drifts off, don't you, darling?" Marion is standing beside his wife, his arms behind his back, smiling. He adjusts his glasses on the bridge of his nose but avoids meeting Dalia's eyes. "It's true, isn't it, Marion?" Adeline nudges him with her elbow.

"I try," he says finally. "But sometimes I'm afraid I might hurt him if I hold him too close. He's so tiny."

"Tiny?" Adeline teases. "Why, he's a butterball! Don't you think he's a butterball, Mother Larkin?"

"He looks healthy to me," Dalia says, smiling. "Hearty," she adds. "Pink cheeks. Bright eyes. If I'm not careful, I could become quite smitten." Her son lowers his head, clears his throat, and rubs the side of his nose with his finger. Dalia comes closer to get a better look at her grandson. "Why, Marion, I didn't see it at first, but he has your hands. Those long, delicate fingers. The first thing I noticed when you were born were your fingers. Yes," she says staunchly, "I'm already falling for this little boy."

Marion coughs and ventures a timid look at her. His red hair, the dimple in his chin, his pale skin touch her, as do the love and sadness that have come to reside in his eyes. "Oh, Mama, you don't know how happy I am that this day has finally come," he blurts out, his pale cheeks coloring.

Like a brush fire, his words burn through her, singeing her heart. "My sweet Marion," she says, taking a sturdy step toward him, fearlessly opening her arms. "Come here and let me hold you."